KT-426-194

ABERDEEN
CITY LIBRARIES
www.aberdeencity.gov.uk/libraries

Kaimhill Library
Tel: 01224 498160

Return to . . . .
or any other Aberdeen City Library
Please return/renew this item by the last day shown. Items may also be renewed
by phone or online

- 3 MAR 2017

THE SECRETS OF ARMSTRONG HOUSE

1888– Arabella Tattinger arrives to attend a glittering ball at Armstrong House as the family's younger son Harrison's fiancée. Her head is turned by the glamorous aristocratic family and most of all by the eldest son and heir, the exciting but dangerous Charles. A chain of events unfolds from that night which casts the family into years of a bitter feud. 1899– When American heiress Victoria Van Hoevan marries into the family she is determined to bring peace at last to the Armstrongs. But everywhere dangers are circling and secrets are ready to emerge from the shadows.

THE SECRETS OF
ARMSTRONG HOUSE

THE SECRETS OF ARMSTRONG HOUSE

by

A. O'Connor

Magna Large Print Books
Long Preston, North Yorkshire,
BD23 4ND, England.

British Library Cataloguing in Publication Data.

O'Connor, A.
    The secrets of Armstrong House.

    A catalogue record of this book is
    available from the British Library

    ISBN   978-0-7505-4206-7

First published in 2013 by Poolbeg Press Ltd.

Cover illustration by arrangement with Arcangel Images

The moral right of the author has been asserted

Published in Large Print 2016 by arrangement with
A. O'Connor, care of Poolbeg Group Services
whose agents are Edwards Fuglewicz.

Magna Large Print is an imprint of Library Magna Books Ltd.

Printed and bound in Great Britain by
T.J. (International) Ltd., Cornwall, PL28 8RW

Acknowledgements

A big thank you to Paula Campbell, Kieran Devlin and the rest of the team at Poolbeg, especially Sarah, David and Ailbhe. Thank you, Gaye Shortland, for your continued guidance and editing skills. My gratitude to the book buyers for their support and to you, the reader.

For Orla

BOOK ONE

1888–1889

PROLOGUE

Present Day

The man came rushing out of the front door of Armstrong House into the winter's night. He was dressed in a black tailored Edwardian suit and his cloak blew in the wind as he quickly made his way down the steps in front of the house and across the forecourt to his awaiting phaeton two-seater carriage. Jumping in, he whipped the horse and took off at high speed.

The carriage raced out of the forecourt and down the long winding driveway that led through parklands. The bare branches of the trees swayed in the wind and stretched out against the clear moonlit sky as he drove past. He continued his journey down the driveway which hugged the lakeshore until the large stone gateway came into view. As he approached it he pulled on the reins and the horse slowed to a walk to go through the gateway.

Suddenly from the shadows of the night a man stepped out in front of the horse, blocking the carriage's journey. The horse drew to a halt. Dressed in shabby clothes and a peaked cap, the man on the road produced a shotgun and aimed it squarely at the carriage driver whose face twisted in panic.

The man in the peaked cap pulled the trigger.

15

The driver screamed in agony and fell back onto the leather seating of the carriage. At the sound of the gunshot the horse plunged forward through the gate and bolted down the road.

'*Cut! Cut! Cut!*' shouted the director in frustration.

Kate Collins quickly made her way to him.

'It's no use, Kate!' he snapped, annoyed. 'This can't be the way the shooting happened!'

'It is, Brian! I've checked and checked it with the inquiry and the newspaper articles at the time,' Kate defended herself. 'Lord Charles Armstrong was just coming out of the main gates of the estate, exactly here, when he was ambushed and shot.'

The film's firearms expert joined them. 'It's as I said – the horse would have bolted with fright when Charles was shot and there was no driver to control it.'

'So then, Charles couldn't have been found here as you insist, Kate!' said Brian. 'The gun we're using is a blank-firing gun which has the same explosive sound and flash as if it was shooting for real. So the horse is reacting as it would to a regular gunshot. The horse would have been terrified by the gunshot and raced down the road to somewhere else, as we've just seen.'

'No! All the reports say Charles was found here at the gateway, shot in his carriage,' Kate insisted. 'Even his mother Lady Margaret testified at the inquiry that she was the first to arrive at the scene and found him at this exact spot.'

Brian shook his head in despair. 'Well, we've retaken this scene three times and each time the

16

horse has bolted, and we've used two different horses!' This was the second night of trying to film the scene, as Kate had insisted the horse be changed.

Kate's husband Nico Collins stepped forward. 'Brian's right, Kate. I've grown up with horses all my life and they don't just hang around stationary after something like this.'

Kate sighed in frustration. 'Well, this *is* how it happened. Maybe Charles' horse was tame and timid?'

Both Brian and Nico looked at her sceptically.

'Okay, I think we'll call it a day, or a night!' said Brian and the film crew all heaved a sigh of relief. 'It's late and everyone's tired and cold and wants to go home. We'll film around this scene for now.'

'Thank goodness for that!' said Nico who had feared they would have to re-shoot the scene when all he wanted to do was get out of this freezing cold and back to the warmth of their home, Armstrong House.

'Are you sure?' questioned Kate, ever the perfectionist. It had taken a long time to get right the exact circumstances of a crime that had taken place over a century beforehand and Kate didn't mind in the least if everyone had to work through the night to get this crucial part of her docu-drama correct.

'Yes, Kate!' insisted Brian.

The film crew was quickly dismantling the equipment and taking away the props.

'What we'll have to do is use a replica prop gun which won't make a noise, as the firearms expert advised,' said Brian, 'and we can dub the gunshot

17

sound to it digitally later. Then we won't frighten the horse.'

'Come on, Brian!' Kate protested. 'I've been on enough movie sets to know those replica guns just don't have the same effect. I know no director who likes to use them and they're only used as a last resort.'

'This is a last resort!'

'But the scene has to be as authentic as possible!' objected Kate.

The actor who was playing Charles was trotting the horse and carriage back up the road after regaining control of the animal. He pulled up at the gateway.

As Kate was talking in depth with Brian about the next stage of filming, Nico walked around the carriage. He had to admit it all looked very authentic to him. The carriage, the long winding driveway behind it and the lights of Armstrong House in the distance. He imagined what he had just witnessed being acted looked very like the real crime back in 1903, the night this shooting actually took place. Nico got an eerie feeling. For the film crew it was just another day's filming. Even though his wife Kate cared passionately about the history of Armstrong House, she was still an actress by profession and had the professional training to be able to look at the filming in purely objective terms. But for Nico it was different. At the end of the day they had just filmed the shooting of his great-grandfather, Lord Charles Armstrong. And he would have to be made of stone not to have somehow been affected by seeing his ancestor being shot down in cold blood, albeit for a docudrama.

It took an hour for all the props and film equipment to be taken away. Then Kate came over to him as he waited patiently for her in their Range Rover.

'Well, I'm at a loss as to why the original horse didn't bolt away after Charles was shot back in 1903!' she said in exasperation as he started the engine.

Nico just shrugged.

They drove back up the driveway to Armstrong House and pulled up in the forecourt.

She saw his unhappy expression. 'Don't you find it all fascinating?' she asked as they stepped out of the car.

'Well, it's fascinating all right ... but just remind me why we're making this programme again?' He looked at her cynically as they walked up the steps to the front door.

'For the money, honey,' she said. 'This house is costing a lot to upkeep, and we need the money.'

Both of them knew that was not strictly true. Ever since he had known Kate she had been fascinated with the history of Armstrong House and Nico's family who had lived there for generations. They had been married only a couple of months when she had come up with the idea of a documentary about life at the Irish 'Big House' during its golden age of the late Victorian and early Edwardian period. She had discussed the idea with film-producer friends of hers and managed to get the project agreed to. Kate had always known it would be harder to convince her husband to agree to it than the film producers.

Nico disliked the idea of their home and his family history being held up to public scrutiny. However, with acting roles thin on the ground for her lately and his architect's practice struggling, she had used the financial rewards offered by the film as the lever to get him to give the go-ahead.

'So are you going to use a prop gun as Brian suggests?' Nico asked as they walked into the drawing room.

'No, not yet anyway. I want to know what the police report has to say first.'

'Police report?' Nico asked, surprised.

'Yes, when the horse bolted last night I decided to send away for the police report on the crime to see if that could shed any more light on it.'

Wearily, Nico sat down on the couch. 'And how long is that going to take?' he asked, frowning.

'I'm assured it won't take long at all. I've a friend in the police press office who said he would help locate it for me in the police archives. A couple of days at most. I haven't told Brian yet because he'd be furious, seeing it as causing a further delay.'

Kate noticed Nico's frown become more pronounced.

'What's the matter?' she asked, pouring two glasses of wine.

'I just didn't realise when we started all this we'd be concentrating so much on the shooting of Charles. I thought it was going to be about the social life at the house.'

'Of course we have to include the crime – that's the hook for the whole film! Audiences love to hear about a glorious crime!' She handed him a glass and sat down beside him, leaning her head on his shoulder.

'It's easy for you to be so clinical about it – it's not your great-grandfather being shown in such a bad light.'

'No, my great-grandfather was probably one of the peasant farmers who cheered when he was shot!' she laughed. Although Kate had mostly been brought up in New York, her family origi-nally came from the area.

'It's not funny, Kate. I feel I'm betraying my heritage with all this. I mean, I'm not saying Charles was a saint–'

'Far from it!'

'But I'm just saying we shouldn't be concen-trating on all his bad points.'

'Oh come on, Nico! Everyone would love an aristocratic cad in their family's past. You should be proud!'

'Well, it's too late to back out now, I suppose,' he said.

'Yes, it is! And I've put too much work and time into this for you even to say such a thing, Nico. I need your support on this!' She looked hurt.

He had to admit she had been working round the clock on it. He knew his wife and when she decided to do something she gave it everything. She had dug up a copy of the inquiry into Charles' shooting and meticulously studied it so she could get the filming of it perfect. She had pored over all the newspaper reports of not only the crime but the terrible land war he had engaged in with his tenant farmers.

He smiled at her. 'I'm sorry. Of course I support

you, and if I'm proud of anyone it's you, for working so tirelessly on what you believe in.'

'Thanks, Nico.' She smiled at him. 'Let's go to bed – we've an early start with more filming tomorrow.'

Kate walked through the ballroom at Armstrong House, speaking as the camera filmed her.

'The ballroom here at Armstrong House witnessed many extravagant receptions. The Armstrongs were known as being generous and hospitable hosts and as one of the great 'gentry' families in Ireland residing in what was known as a 'Big House' would have considerable wealth to fund their lifestyle. The source of their wealth was the several thousand acres in the vicinity rented to tenant farmers whose own lifestyle was in stark contrast to the one led here at the house.

'It was the relationship between these tenant farmers and Lord Charles that erupted into a land war that ultimately led to the attack on Charles. At the inquiry, there were numerous accounts of the increasing animosity and aggression displayed on both sides. Chief witness at that inquiry was Charles' mother, Lady Margaret Armstrong. Lady Margaret at the time lived at Hunter's Farm, a dowager house down the road from the main entrance to Armstrong House. Lady Margaret testified that on the night of December 8th 1903 she heard a gunshot. Concerned, she went to her front door and said she saw what she described as a peasant man race past her house from the scene of the crime, holding a shotgun.

'Suspicion then fell on a tenant farmer called

Joe McGrath. McGrath had recently been evicted from the estate. With a history of violence and known to the police, McGrath had threatened to kill Charles in retaliation for his ruthless eviction. Lady Margaret later identified the man she saw running with the gun as McGrath, from a police photograph. Police made extensive searches for McGrath, but he had fled from Ireland to America before he could be apprehended and interviewed, where it is presumed he disappeared into one of the teeming ghettos of New York or Boston, never to be found.'

'*Cut!*' said the director. 'Great, Kate!'

Kate was glad when the filming was done for the day. Her friend in the police press office had come up trumps and located the file on Charles' shooting. Kate had been handed the file by her researcher that morning and she was looking forward to spending the evening reading through it, to try to get to the bottom of the mystery of why Charles' horse hadn't bolted, as everyone was suggesting must have happened.

She waved off Brian and the rest of the film crew for the day, then walked through the hall and down the stairs to the kitchen where Nico had made them dinner.

They sat up at the island in the kitchen, eating spaghetti carbonara, as they discussed the day's filming.

'Well, I haven't managed to do a jot of work all day with all those strangers in the house filming,' complained Nico as they finished eating. 'So I'll try to catch up now while I have some peace!'

'I'll leave you to your architect's board then,' she said as she stacked the dishwasher.

'And I'll leave you to your police report!'

Nico went into the library and Kate went into the drawing room where she poured herself a glass of wine and put on some music. She took the police folder from the sideboard and settled back on the couch to read through it. She started to decipher all the handwritten reports and then stopped when she found a black-and-white photograph. She picked up the photo. Along the top was written: *Morning of 19th of December 1903– Crime scene, shooting of Lord Charles Armstrong.*

Wonderful! She had found an actual visual of the crime scene! Now they could compare it to how they had filmed the event. She studied the photo and her face creased in bewilderment.

The photograph plainly showed the entrance gateway to the estate. In the centre of the photograph was a vintage car with what looked like a bullet-hole through the passenger's side of the windscreen.

Kate couldn't believe her eyes.

'There was no horse and carriage!' she exclaimed.

She stood, picking up the file and photo, and raced from the room and down the hall into the library.

Nico looked up, startled.

'We got the filming wrong!' she exclaimed. 'We've filmed the whole thing incorrectly!'

'Sorry?'

'The horse didn't bolt ... because there was no

horse! Charles was driving a car that night.' She slammed the photo down on the desk in front of him. 'I can't believe it! We filmed Charles being shot in a carriage and he was shot in a car!'

Nico examined the photograph carefully.

'Brian is going to go mad!' she wailed. 'We'll have to find a replica car and re-film the whole thing! That footage we shot is useless. I can't believe I made such a mistake! Why didn't I research it better?'

Nico looked at his stressed wife. He knew the amount of preparation and research she had put in, which she had shared with him as she went along.

'But why were you so sure it was a horse and carriage, other than the fact that automobiles were extremely rare and a novelty at the time?' he asked.

'Because it's in the official inquiry report!' she said, racing to a shelf in the library and retrieving it. She sat down beside him as she opened the report and went through it. 'See, it plainly describes that Lord Charles was in a phaeton two-seater black carriage when he was shot.'

'Well, he obviously wasn't! This photograph says otherwise!' Nico said.

Kate looked through the inquiry file.

'But look at this! It's the testimony from Lady Margaret, Charles' mother... She states she was the first to arrive at the crime scene and found her son shot, slumped back in the phaeton carriage. She makes no mention of a motor car either!'

Nico was still looking at the police photograph.

'I'm afraid you've got another detail wrong, my dear.'

'What?'

'A shotgun couldn't have been used in the attack. When a shotgun fires the pellets spread and would have completely shattered the windscreen, as opposed to this one single bullet-hole, as can be seen from the photo.'

'Great! I can see my documentary falling apart around me!' Kate pointed to the inquiry report. 'But the inquest distinctly says that the shot was fired from a shotgun, the type – and I quote – "generally used by farmers for hunting".'

'Well, this bullet-hole was made by a hand-held revolver, I would say.'

Nico found another photograph buried in the police file. It was again of the crime scene and showed a side view of the car with the door open. Inside the car was a woman's high-heeled shoe and a fur coat. He showed it to Kate.

'There must have been someone else in the car with him,' said Kate. 'A woman.'

'Those items might have been left in the car previously, by his wife presumably?'

'Not a single high-heeled shoe! No woman is going to leave that behind, or an expensive-looking fur like that. They must have been abandoned in a hurry.' She pointed to the photo. 'And look what side of the car windscreen the bullet-hole is on. It's through the passenger side. Charles must have been sitting on the passenger side of the car, and so somebody else must have been driving.'

'Presumably the woman who owned this shoe and coat... There's no mention in the inquiry or

26

papers of anyone else being with him?'

'Of course not!' said Kate, looking expectantly at the police report. 'Do you think I'd miss something crucial like that? So who was she? And why is there no report of her at the time?'

CHAPTER 1

1888

The ball was due to commence at nine that night as the shadows of the evening began to descend on Armstrong House. A continual procession of carriages delivered guests to the front door. Inside, the house was a flurry of activity as the finishing touches for Gwyneth's debutante ball were being administered by the staff and overseen by Gwyneth's mother, Lady Margaret.

Charles Armstrong had made the journey from London to Dublin the previous day to attend his sister's ball. He had then got the train from Dublin down to Castlewest, from where a carriage brought him the several miles to his family home. As the carriage pulled up outside the house, he stepped out and looked up at the magnificent manor house where all the windows were lit up that evening. He walked up the steps and was met at the door by the butler, Barton.

'Good evening, Barton,' said Charles, stepping into the hall and removing his coat.

'Ah, Master Charles, welcome home. We were

27

beginning to worry you had been held up and wouldn't make it.'

'And miss my sister's debutante ball? I don't think the family would ever forgive me, do you?' Charles handed his coat over to Barton and saw that there were staff rushing around in all directions.

'Where's the family?' asked Charles.

'Your father is in the drawing room with some guests and your mother is upstairs in Lady Gwyneth's room preparing the young lady for the night ahead. Your sisters and brother are with her.'

'I'll go up to say hello then in that case. My trunk is in the carriage – please have it brought up to my room.'

Barton looked awkward. 'I'm afraid, sir, that due to the large volume of guests staying in the house tonight your room has been commandeered.'

'Commandeered?'

'Yes, sir, your room has been allocated to Lord and Lady Kinsale.'

'I see.' Charles' face was a mixture of surprise and irritation. 'And where am I to sleep, Barton?'

'Your mother has had a bed set up for you in your brother Harrison's room.'

'The whole thing is a bit of a nuisance, isn't it, Barton? Such a fuss over trying to marry a sister off. Let's hope the deed is done tonight and that's the end of it and we don't have to go through another season of Gwyneth trying to find a husband.'

'Indeed, sir.'

'Very well – have my trunk taken to Harrison's room.'

Charles looked around the expansive hallway. A wood fire was crackling in the marble fireplace. The house had been built by his grandfather Edward for his bride Lady Anna in the 1840s. Their portraits, along with those of other members of the Armstrong family, adorned the walls of the hall. At the front of the house to the right was the drawing room, and across the hall was a smaller family parlour. Behind this parlour was the dining room, which was splendidly furnished with mahogany chairs and a table capable of seating twenty-four people. Behind this room was the library, where his father Lawrence ran the estate. Across the hall from there and on the other side of the sweeping staircase, double doors led into a giant ballroom.

Charles walked across the hall and up the stairs. He passed two young female guests, neither of which he recognised.

'Ladies,' he said, nodding to them.

They smiled and nodded to him and giggled once he was past them.

Upstairs, he walked down the corridor to Gwyneth's room and, opening the door, stood for a moment unobserved, taking in the scene before him.

Gwyneth was sitting at her dressing table in front of the mirror, dressed in a resplendent gown, as two hairdressers styled her blonde hair. Lady Margaret stood beside them, supervising. All around the room were bouquets of flowers delivered from the guests that night for Gwyneth. Standing beside Margaret was her younger daughter Daphne, taking a keen interest in the

29

proceedings. Stretched out on a chaise-longue was their brother Harrison who was busy talking, while lying out on the bed was their youngest sister Emily who looked completely disinterested in what was happening as she read a book.

'Higher! Sweep her hair higher!' instructed Margaret as the hairdressers combed strands of hair.

'Well now, this is a pleasant welcome for a returning son and brother,' said Charles as he entered the room and closed the door after him.

'Charles!' said Margaret, leaving her supervision to come and kiss him. 'We were expecting you this morning.'

'I know, I got delayed,' said Charles.

'Well, at least you're here now,' said Margaret and she quickly returned to the dressing table to keep an eye on the work being done there.

Harrison got up and hugged Charles. 'It feels like such a long time since I've seen you.'

'Last Christmas,' said Charles.

He went over to Gwyneth and bent down to kiss her before then kissing Daphne. He glanced over at Emily who hadn't even looked up from her book since he arrived.

'Are you all prepared for tonight?' he asked as he sat down.

'It's been absolute chaos,' said Margaret. 'So much to organise and get ready. There will be two hundred guests. We've had a nightmare with accommodation. We've tried to accommodate as many as we can here at Armstrong House, while others we've put in Hunter's Farm and other houses on the estate.'

'I'm afraid we've had to put you in with Harri-

30

son,' said Gwyneth.

'So Barton told me,' said Charles. 'Let's hope, with all these strangers in the house, we aren't missing any silverware tomorrow.'

'Charles!' said Gwyneth.

There was a knock on the door and Barton came in with another bouquet of flowers.

'Bring them over to me,' said Gwyneth as she stretched out her hand to the side, unable to move her head due to the combing of her hair.

Barton brought them over and Gwyneth reached for the card and quickly opened it.

'Well?' asked Margaret.

'They're from Cecil Rotherham,' said Gwyneth, a note of disappointment in her voice.

Barton put the bouquet with the others.

'She's waiting for a bouquet from the Duke of Battington,' explained Harrison with a smirk.

'The Duke of Battington?' repeated Charles, looking impressed. 'You're setting your sights quite high, Gwyneth.'

'Why shouldn't she?' said Margaret. 'She would make a wonderful duchess. He would be lucky to have her.'

Gwyneth looked concerned. 'He hasn't sent any flowers and it's very late at this stage. He definitely said he was coming, Mama?'

'Yes,' said Margaret.

'But if he doesn't send flowers then he's clearly not interested.' Gwyneth's face creased with worry.

'Gwyneth, during the season in London you attended fifty balls, thirty lunches, twenty tea parties, and twenty breakfasts. I know, as I

31

attended every one with you, and the Duke went out of his way to attend as many of those occasions as possible, where he monopolised you for the whole time. He will be here, he will send flowers and he is clearly interested in you!'

'You hope!' Emily suddenly said without looking up from her book.

Margaret gave Emily a warning look. She looked at the clock. She was glad five of her children were now accounted for, but there was still no sign of her sixth child, her youngest son James.

'Barton, has Master James returned to the house yet?'

'I'm afraid not, my lady.'

'For goodness sake! I told him not to go gallivanting anywhere and to be back here in plenty of time. I have no patience for any of his tomfoolery tonight!'

'I think you know where he is if you want to find him,' said Emily, again not looking up from her book.

Margaret looked at Emily again and frowned before thinking hard and then saying, 'Barton, can you send a footman into town and collect Master James from ... Cassidy's public house.' She said the name of the establishment with a note of disgust.

'Very good, my lady. It's just–' Barton hesitated.

'It's just what, Barton?' snapped Margaret.

'It's just, if the young master is in Cassidy's, he will not pay any heed to a footman sent to bring him home.'

'For goodness sake!' Margaret's voice rose in frustration.

Harrison, seeing his mother's distress, stood up. 'It's all right. I'll go into town and collect him.'

'Oh, will you, Harrison? Thank you. And tell him I insist he comes straight back here. Don't take any of his nonsense.'

'If I have to throw him over my back and carry him out of that dive, I will do so,' said Harrison and left the room with Barton.

'I see some things never change,' said Charles. 'James is still giving trouble?'

'I really don't know what we're going to do with him. Expelled from two schools. No direction in life.'

'It's your own fault, Mama – you let him get away with everything,' said Gwyneth.

'Well, I've been so busy this year with you being a debutante and being in London for the season. Neither your father nor I have had the time to try and sort him out. But we will now, once we get you married.'

'*If* you get her married,' Emily pointed out.

Charles sat down on the chaise-longue. 'Perhaps you took too much on with this ball for Gwyneth. You could have just had an afternoon tea party for her in London. That's what most young women are having these days.'

'A tea party!' Margaret was horrified. 'I doubt a Duke would have too much interest in a young lady who had a tea party for her coming-out event!'

'Perhaps the Duke isn't that much interested in Gwyneth anyway after all this expense and effort,' said Emily. 'Maybe he stayed in his castle in England and didn't make the journey over here for tonight.'

'Emily!' snapped Margaret. 'Your comments are not being very helpful!'

'And perhaps Charles resents all this money being spent on Gwyneth,' Emily went on. 'After all, he is the heir and future Lord Armstrong – all this is coming out of his future coffers.'

'Emily, isn't it time you went and started getting yourself ready for tonight?' urged Gwyneth.

'Well, at least you won't have to worry about the expense of me being a debutante, Charles,' said Emily.

'And why is that?' asked Margaret.

'Because I'm not going to be one. Paraded around a lot of balls and lunches, waiting for a marriage proposal! It's no better than being a prize cow at a market fair. Disgusting!'

'You most certainly will be a debutante and, by the time I've knocked some sense into you, you'll be as popular as your sister Gwyneth on the circuit.'

'Anyway, I'd better go down and say hello to Papa,' said Charles.

'Yes, do that – he's in the drawing room with the Tattingers.'

'And who are the Tattingers?' asked Charles as he stood up.

'Sir George Tattinger and his wife Caroline. Sir George is the Governor of the Bank of Ireland and Harrison's boss.'

Harrison hadn't opted to go to university but had chosen a career in finance where he worked for the bank in Dublin.

'They are here with their daughter Arabella as Harrison's guests,' explained Gwyneth.

'Harrison's guests?' asked Charles.

'Yes, Harrison and Arabella's courtship has become quite serious,' said Margaret, looking delighted with the situation.

'Harrison is seriously interested in someone?' Charles was amazed.

'Not just someone, but Arabella Tattinger – quite a catch,' confirmed Gwyneth.

'But he's too young to be serious about anyone!' said Charles.

'Harrison always knows what he wants and always gets it,' said Margaret. 'I wish all my children had the same direction,' she added, giving Emily a displeased look.

Surprised by this news, Charles took his leave and as he opened the door Barton came in with a bouquet of flowers.

'The Duke of Battington has arrived, my lady, and sent these flowers for Lady Gwyneth.'

Gwyneth pushed the hairdressers away and, jumping up, went quickly to the flowers and took the card excitedly.

'I told you he would send flowers,' said Margaret.

'Yes,' said Gwyneth, smiling.

Emily raised her eyes to heaven.

'Barton, have all these bouquets of flowers taken down to the ballroom and arranged at the entrance,' said Margaret.

'All except this one,' said Gwyneth, taking the Duke's bouquet and holding it close. 'I'll be holding this bouquet when we greet the guests.'

Margaret moved over to her. 'Are you sure? You know holding the Duke's bouquet is telling everyone, including the Duke, you've chosen him?'

'I'm sure,' said Gwyneth.

Margaret nodded and smiled. 'Very good.' She sighed as she looked at all the other bouquets. 'I feel sorry for all these other young men who have sent you flowers and come tonight in the hope you would choose them...' She looked at Daphne and Emily. 'Still, I've two more daughters they can meet tonight which will give you two a head-start for when you are debutantes.'

Charles was coming down the stairs when his eye was caught by a stunning young woman walking across the hallway. He continued down the stairs, his eyes not leaving her.

'Good evening,' he said, pausing in front of her.

She nodded and walked past him. He watched her as she climbed the stairs. Barton came hurrying down past her, carrying two large bouquets of flowers.

'Barton, who is that woman?' asked Charles.

Barton glanced up the stairs. 'I'm afraid there's that many young gentlemen and ladies staying at the house tonight, that I've lost track of who is who.'

'You're falling down on your duties, Barton,' said Charles with a smirk.

'That I am!' agreed Barton as he hurried with the flowers to the ballroom at the back of the hall.

Charles continued across the hall and, opening

36

the door, went into the drawing room where he found his father Lawrence standing talking to a distinguished middle-aged man and a refined woman who was seated.

'Ah, my dear son!' exclaimed Lawrence, quickly going to Charles and shaking his hand. 'I was wondering if you had got here yet.'

'I've been here a while. I was upstairs with Mama and Gwyneth and the others.'

'I'm staying safely out of the pandemonium,' smiled Lawrence.

'Very wise,' agreed Charles.

Lawrence led him into the room which was painted a deep red and furnished elegantly with large couches and chaises-longues.

'May I present my son and heir, Harrison's brother Charles,' he said to his two guests. 'Charles – Sir George and Lady Tattinger.'

Charles kissed Lady Tattinger's hand and shook hands with Sir George.

'Another fine young man you have,' said George.

'Yes, we're all very proud of Charles. He's just finished university this year at Oxford.'

'Well done,' said George.

Lawrence went to the drinks table and poured Charles a glass of wine and handed it to him.

'Sir George is Harrison's boss at the bank,' Lawrence informed Charles.

'Really?' said Charles. 'I hope he isn't getting too much in the way there?'

'On the contrary, Harrison has been such an asset since he started with us,' said Sir George. 'We're expecting great things of him. We imagine he will rise to the very top.'

'Well, he will with your guidance and help, Sir George,' smiled Lawrence.

Charles sat down. 'I hadn't realised Harrison was so industrious. I imagined he was buried as a bank clerk somewhere.'

'His star started to shine as soon as he joined us,' said George.

'We're all terribly fond of him,' said Caroline.

'Isn't everybody?' smiled Charles.

'We've been meaning to visit Armstrong House and meet Harrison's family since his courtship of our daughter became serious, but we kept putting it off,' said Caroline.

'I'm afraid my wife was quite nervous about coming to Mayo with this awful Land War going on,' explained George.

'Well, it is the epicentre of the whole thing, isn't it?' said Caroline.

'The Land War did start here in Mayo, yes,' agreed Lawrence sadly, 'and has been a focal point for it since.'

'So many awful stories you read in the newspapers,' sighed Caroline. 'Landlords being murdered, crops being destroyed, agents attacked,' said George. 'Wasn't Captain Boycott, who was ostracised, here in Mayo?'

'Yes, he was, unfortunately,' said Lawrence.

'I don't know how you sleep easy in your beds at night with all that going on. Give me the leafy avenues of Dublin any day,' said Caroline.

'Well, we've had no trouble whatsoever here on the Armstrong estate, Lady Tattinger,' said Lawrence, 'so you are quite safe here I can assure you.'

'That's good to know, Lord Armstrong.'

'Out of the many social occasions myself and Lady Margaret have hosted here at Armstrong House, we've never lost a guest yet, you'll be pleased to know!' There was a hint of mockery in Lawrence's voice at Caroline's urban prejudices.

'That's comforting, Lord Armstrong.' Caroline laughed lightly as she admired the hand-carved oak fireplace. 'And it is a pleasure finally to stay here when this house has one of the finest reputations in Ireland for hospitality.'

'And how have you avoided being embroiled in the Land War?' asked George.

'We've always had an excellent relationship with the tenant farmers here. Even during the famine when my father and mother, Edward and Anna, were alive there wasn't one eviction and my mother worked tirelessly for famine relief.'

'Yes, Lady Anna was renowned for her good works,' nodded Caroline.

'And we have kept relations very good throughout the years. I don't mean to criticise my own class but a lot of them have nobody to blame but themselves for this Land War. They see their estates as nothing more than moneymaking devices to be squeezed for every drop of blood they can get. Ruthless evictions and whatnot. And then so many now are absentee landlords living the high life in London, barely ever visiting their country estates here in Ireland. The whole thing was bound to explode one day.'

'I believe you spent a good part of the year in London this year yourself, Lord Lawrence,' said Caroline.

'Yes, but only under duress. I had to attend the season because of Gwyneth. I'm delighted the whole thing is over and I'm back home at Armstrong House where I belong and am happy.'

'And what of you, Charles, now you've finished university?' smiled Caroline.

'Well, Charles will naturally be coming back to Armstrong House to learn the running of the estate and ensure its continual smooth and successful running into the future,' smiled Lawrence.

'Indeed,' smiled Charles, taking a sip of his wine.

Harrison's carriage pulled up outside Cassidy's pub in the main street of Castlewest. There was loud music, laughter and merriment coming from inside as he walked up to the door. He pushed it open and stepped in.

Inside, the pub was packed with a very jovial crowd, most of whom looked inebriated, with a strong swirl of tobacco and turf smoke from the blazing fire in the air, while a group in the corner played lively traditional music.

He peered through the crowd, looking for his brother, and finally spotted him sitting in an alcove, an arm around a young woman, with a crowd gathered around him.

Harrison pushed through the crowd till he reached the alcove.

James was whispering something in his female companion's ear that caused her to erupt in raucous laughter.

'James?' Harrison said, leaning forward.

James looked up and smiled. 'Harrison! Pull up

a chair and have a drink!' He nodded at the young woman beside him. 'This is Dolly Cassidy – her father is the publican.'

Harrison looked at the young woman who was dressed cheaply and provocatively as, with a cheeky smile, she said, 'Pleased to meet you, I'm sure.'

'Yes,' Harrison nodded. 'Likewise. James, you're to return with me at once to Armstrong House.'

'For what?' James said dismissively.

Harrison leaned forward and spoke forcefully. 'For Gwyneth's party, of course.'

'*Pah!*' James spat dismissively and sat back, folding his arms.

'Mama insists!' Harrison said.

'Oh well, if your mama insists, you'd better toddle along!' said Dolly and she roared with laughter.

'Come on, James, don't make this difficult. You have to attend. If I have to physically drag you back to Armstrong House, I will.'

'I'd like to see you try!' James taunted. Then he sighed loudly and stood up, throwing back the last of his drink.

'Leaving me so soon?' Dolly said, jumping up and draping her arm around his neck.

'Duty calls,' said James as he removed her arm.

Outside Harrison was already waiting in the carriage as his brother climbed in. He looked at James and shook his head as the carriage took off.

'Your carry-on is disgraceful. Lord Armstrong's son going into a place like that and flirting with a woman like that Cassidy girl! Why do you do it?'

James looked at him as he lit his cigarette. 'Same reason you hang out with a bunch of boring Dublin bankers – because I enjoy it.'

Charles brushed his hair, surveying himself dressed in his immaculate, tailed dinner suit in the full-length mirror in Harrison's room. He turned and looked at the temporary bed placed there for him and frowned.

'I'm so late – damn James!' snapped Harrison, rushing in.

'Did you find him all right?' asked Charles, still brushing his hair in the mirror and not looking too interested in the answer.

'I found him, his arm draped over some tart in Cassidy's pub,' Harrison informed him.

'Anyway, you were there to rescue the day, as always... What's this I hear about you being all very serious about some young girl?'

Harrison stopped and smiled. 'Who told you about her?'

'Well – everyone! In fact, I've just been introduced to her parents. Go on, tell me all about her!'

'Her name is Arabella. Our paths crossed through work as she's my boss's daughter.'

'Very tactical of you.'

'I wouldn't care who she was – my feelings about her would be the same,' said Harrison, looking shy.

Charles sat down on a chair and studied him. 'You have that stupid look of a man in love on your face. Tell me, little brother, that I won't be hearing the sound of wedding bells ringing soon?'

Harrison looked sheepish. 'Yes, you will.'

'But – but you haven't really lived yet! You haven't met all there is to meet, seen all there is to see – tasted all there is to taste.'

'What's the point in doing all that meeting, seeing and tasting, when I was lucky enough to find what I was looking for straight away?'

'Well, I look forward to meeting this – incredible – girl.'

Harrison looked at his watch. 'I'd better get ready very quickly. Arabella and her parents are waiting for me to escort them in to the ball.'

All the bouquets of flowers had been arranged at the entrance of the ballroom and Gwyneth stood just inside surrounded by them, beside her mother, as the guests were being announced. The ballroom had been set with long meticulously arranged tables.

Barton stood at the door and announced the guests as they entered.

'Lord and Lady Kinsale!' Barton called.

'Lady Margaret, good evening,' said the couple together.

'I'm so glad you could both be here tonight,' Margaret said, then indicated Gwyneth. 'Lord and Lady Kinsale, may I introduce my daughter, Gwyneth?'

Gwyneth curtsied deeply.

'Your daughter looks most beautiful tonight,' said Lady Kinsale with a smile, and then they walked on into the room and were shown down to their seating by a footman.

Charles looked on as this procedure was repeated over and over again with each guest who was shown in. He was standing by his father at the row of French windows that lined one wall.

'It's so good to have you home again,' said Lawrence.

'And good to be home,' smiled Charles.

'And I need you now more than ever – on the estate. Now the children are becoming adults, I've been taken away from estate business as you know. Gwyneth's coming out meant I had to be in London for weeks. I need to know the estate is in reliable hands when I'm not here.'

Charles shrugged. 'I don't know how reliable my hands would be. I don't really know too much about running this place.'

'Exactly, and now it's time you learnt.'

'You see, I hadn't planned on coming back to Armstrong House quite so soon,' explained Charles.

'I don't understand,' Lawrence was perplexed.

'I was going to stay in London for a while.'

'London! And what would you be doing there?'

'Oh, I don't know... Relaxing for a while.'

'Relaxing!'

'Yes, well, you see, university was such hard work.'

'Your grades didn't reflect much hard work!' snapped Lawrence.

'I know, but imagine how much worse they would have been if I hadn't put the work I did in!'

'And where do you propose to live in London?'

'I thought I'd open the house at Regent's Park.'

'My house, you mean? And what do you expect to live on while you – "relax" – in London?'

44

'My allowance naturally.'

'Your allowance was for when you were studying, not for partying in London!'

Charles remained cool but his eyes glared. 'So you are denying me my allowance while you squander all this money on frocks and balls for all my siblings?'

'The money spent on your siblings is so they will obtain good positions in life. Everything else goes to you as my heir .... that is the natural order of things.'

Margaret was beckoning Lawrence over to her.

'Your mother needs me – we will discuss this later.'

Lawrence made his way across the ballroom to his wife and Gwyneth, his smile disguising his anger and worry after his conversation with Charles. His worst fears had been confirmed after those few words with his son. Charles' lack of interest in the estate was obvious and from what he could see his son was intent on living the life of an absentee landlord in London – a breed Lawrence despised.

He reached his wife and Gwyneth.

'Lawrence, I've asked Barton to make a quick rearrangement with the seating. I'm placing the Duke of Battington at the head table with us and placing Charles with Harrison and the Tattingers.'

'Why are you putting the Duke with us?' Lawrence looked confused.

'For obvious reasons!' whispered Margaret. 'Oh dear, I feel sorry for all these young men who made the journey here only to discover Gwyneth has decided on the Duke.'

Charles looked on as the long lines of tables filled up with guests.

'Seemingly you are to be removed from the head table to make room for the Duke,' said a voice beside him and he turned to see Emily there.

'I'm beginning to wonder why I made this trip home for this ball at all,' said Charles. 'I seem to be shuttled around like unwanted luggage.'

'Well, you know Mama and Papa. They always like to get their priorities right. And tonight's priority is the Duke.'

'Really?' Charles looked unimpressed.

'That's the advantage of being the youngest – I'm last on their list of priorities,' said Emily.

'Perhaps, but I imagine you are highest on their list of concerns.'

'Oh, no, *you* are top of their concerns, with all their plans for you,' said Emily teasingly.

He studied her and put his arm around her shoulders. 'And tell me, favourite sister, what *have* Mama and Papa planned for me?'

Emily stood on her tiptoes and started whispering into Charles' ear while he listened intently. 'You are to remain here at Armstrong House and start immediate training for your role in life as dutiful son and heir of the Armstrong estate!'

'Anything else?' he asked, his expression clouded at the thought of it.

She got on her tiptoes again to whisper. 'You are to be married off to a young lady with impeccable breeding and unquestionable character forthwith.'

'Do I have any say in these matters?' he asked, irritated.

She shook her head.

He looked around at the tables, which were now almost full as the last of the guests took their seats. The noise level was high with chatter and laughter as an army of staff glided through the tables serving the hors d'oeuvre of smoked salmon and caviar.

'This house can drive me mad,' Emily said. 'Even with Harrison in Dublin most of the time and with Gwyneth soon to be married, there is James and Daphne and Mama and Papa... I always feel under Papa's control here.'

Charles suddenly saw the beautiful woman he had passed in the hallway, walking through the aisles between the tables. To his surprise he saw she was walking alongside Harrison, and behind Sir George and Lady Tattinger. He realised she must be Arabella Tattinger.

'That is Arabella Tattinger?' he checked with Emily, with a discreet nod over at the young woman.

'Yes, that's her.'

He gazed at Arabella, her dark-chestnut hair groomed high, dressed in a long ivory satin dress with the bodice embroidered in gold. 'What is she like?'

'Friendly, but keeps her distance. Quite proud of herself, I imagine.'

'Well, let's not miss the first course,' Charles said abruptly and left Emily.

He strode confidently to his appointed place at

the Tattingers' table.

'This is my seat, I believe?' he said, pulling out the empty chair beside Arabella.

Harrison was sitting on her other side while her parents were across the table.

Harrison stood up and greeted his brother. 'Ah, there you are, Charles! I believe you've already met Sir George and Lady Tattinger ... and this...' he paused as he smiled proudly, 'is Arabella.'

Arabella smiled at him and held out her hand, which he took and held tightly before bowing and kissing it briefly.

'A pleasure to meet you,' he said.

'Harrison speaks so much of you, I feel I already know you,' she said.

'And I feel I already know you,' he smiled.

He took his chair and nodded smilingly to Arabella's parents.

'Charles was to be seated up at the main table, but the Duke of Battington has displaced him as the...' Harrison paused and pulled a funny face, '*special* guest.'

'I was wondering whose bouquet she was holding,' said Caroline Tattinger, looking impressed as she observed the Duke sitting at the top table talking privately to Gwyneth. 'Is the deal done?'

'Looks like it – he's mad about her – she's mad about him. My parents are ecstatic – his family are delighted. It's as happy as a tennis match on a sunny afternoon!' Harrison laughed.

'And when are *you* to have your debutante ball?' Charles asked Arabella.

Arabella turned and smiled at him. 'I'm not having one.'

'Not having one?' Charles looked at her incredulously.

'I've been going to parties and functions since I was sixteen. I think there's no need for me to have one all to myself.'

Harrison leaned over and touched her hand lightly. 'Especially now.'

Charles watched the secret glances, rich in nuance, that passed between his brother and Arabella.

'Imagine, your sister will be a duchess!' said Caroline.

Charles laughed lightly. 'We've been used to having a duchess in the family since the day Gwyneth was born!'

'Yes, she's very regal,' agreed Caroline, her eyes fixed on Gwyneth.

Charles tried to engage Arabella in conversation throughout the dinner, but she seemed more interested in chatting to Harrison.

'So what do you do in Dublin all day long?' he inquired over the main course of baron of beef and lamb.

'The same as most young women my age do everywhere, I imagine,' she smiled at him.

'Do you have many brothers and sisters?'

'One brother, one sister – I'm a middle child,' she said before turning quickly to Harrison. 'Don't forget we're going to the Gaiety on Thursday night.'

'How could I forget? You've reminded me five times today already.'

'You're a fan of the theatre?' asked Charles.

'Yes, I adore it,' she said.

But not as much as you adore Harrison, thought Charles as he observed them enter into another whispered deep conversation.

'When do you return to Dublin?' asked Charles, interrupting their private chat.

'We are going back on Sunday,' said Arabella.

'I'm taking Arabella on the grouse shoot tomorrow,' said Harrison. 'She has never been on one before so I promised to take her.'

'Are you going on the shoot, Charles?' asked George.

'Well, if everyone else is – why not me?'

'Well, I'm not and neither is George. We don't enjoy rural pursuits,' said Caroline.

After dessert was served and then coffee and liqueurs, the tables were cleared away and the orchestra took up position at the top of the ballroom. As they began to play people moved onto the dance floor.

As the evening wore on, Charles was increasingly irked by Arabella's indifference to him. He set about gathering a handful of young beauties he knew around him. Most of them were daughters of his parents' friends who he had known over the years. Their attention was all very well as they circled around him, laughing at his conversation, but his own attention was on Arabella who was either dancing or deep in conversation with Harrison.

Eventually Charles walked over to Harrison and Arabella who were speaking with the Tattingers.

'Ah, Charles, perhaps you could settle an argument for us,' said Sir George. 'Do you think the whole Home Rule question is dead now Charles

Stewart Parnell has disgraced himself with this affair with the married woman?'

Charles thought quickly – he hadn't given either topic any thought. 'Em, no, I don't suppose it is.'

'My thoughts exactly!' said Sir George. 'The way I look at it, this is an ongoing thing since Catholics got the vote and the agitation after the Famine. It won't stop until the Irish get an independent country.'

'Well, hopefully that will be a long time off,' said Caroline. 'I can't imagine Dublin not being part of the United Kingdom.'

They continued their discussion in depth and Charles wondered if this was all they talked about in the parlours of Dublin.

'Arabella, could I ask for this dance?' asked Charles.

Arabella looked at him in surprise. 'Eh ... I'm afraid I'm too tired after all the earlier dancing so I'm afraid not.'

'Nonsense!' laughed Harrison. 'Off you go!'

'I'd really rather not. It was such a long journey from Dublin today,' said Arabella.

'Oh don't be so silly, Arabella! Go dance with Charles,' urged Caroline.

Arabella looked awkwardly at Charles as he indicated the dance floor to her.

Then she stepped unsmiling onto the floor and Charles slipped his left hand into her right and his right arm around her waist. They then joined the other couples swirling around the dance floor to the loud music. He held her firmly, as she tried to keep her distance.

He was going to try to enter into conversation

with her but, as she looked off coolly into the distance, he knew he would only get one-word answers till the dance ended.

'Thank you for the dance,' she said, nodding politely when the music stopped before quickly walking back to Harrison.

Emily sidled up beside him.

'They make a beautiful couple, don't they?' she smiled and indicated Gwyneth and the Duke of Battington.

'Yes, they do,' said Charles, but his eyes were focused on Harrison and Arabella.

Charles made his way to the back of the hall behind the grand staircase and through the door that led down to the servants' quarter. He passed startled staff who were rushing up the stairs to the ballroom with trays of drinks and bottles of alcohol.

As he entered the kitchen which was an extensive semi-basement at the back of the house, he saw it was a hive of activity with servants rushing around. The head cook Mrs Carey was there giving orders and she got a start to see Charles.

'Mr Charles! What are you doing down here?' she asked.

'Oh, don't mind me, Mrs Carey, I'm just looking for your medical supplies. Slight headache, you see,' explained Charles.

'Follow me, sir,' said Mrs Carey as she marched to one of the small rooms off the kitchen.

'Now ... what have we got for headaches?' she mused, perusing the shelves of bottles.

'Mrs Carey, I'm being a bore and a chore. You

52

have enough to be doing with the ball – you get back to your work.'

'No, it'll just take me a minute,' she said, peering at the bottles.

There was a sudden large crash in the kitchen and a scream from a kitchen maid.

'What on earth?' snapped Mrs Carey as she rushed from the storage room to the kitchen.

Charles closed the door and started examining the bottles.

As the ball carried on into the early hours, the alcohol continued to flow as the joviality became louder. Charles waited for his moment, carefully scrutinising Harrison as he finished his glass of champagne and then offering to refill it for him. Making sure he was unobserved he quickly took out the bottle he had got from the kitchens and poured a part of it into the glass before filling the glass to the top with champagne. He then gently shook the glass, making the liquid swirl inside, before heading back to Harrison and handing it to him with a smile.

He then watched Harrison chatting happily to Arabella as he drank from the glass.

'I'd better not have too many of these,' laughed Harrison. 'The grouse shoot starts at eleven in the morning. I don't want to have too bad a head for it.'

It was four in the morning before the last of the guests went to their rooms or made their way to the awaiting carriages which would take them to their accommodation. Charles was the last to leave the ballroom as he drank back his champagne and placed the empty glass on a nearby table.

He walked upstairs and down the corridor to Harrison's room. He opened the door and walked in. Harrison was sitting on his bed bent over double, his face contorted in agony.

'Harrison! What's wrong?' said Charles, rushing over.

'I don't know! I started getting these pains in my stomach an hour ago. I feel like I'm going to be sick all the time.'

'Probably too much champagne,' said Charles.

'I feel wretched.'

'Maybe mixing the wine with the champagne?'

Harrison suddenly jumped up and, placing his hand over his mouth, he went racing to the door and down the corridor.

Charles casually walked over to the door and closed it.

'Looks like I won't be sharing a room tonight after all,' he said aloud.

CHAPTER 2

The next morning the servants were up early putting the house back into its normal spick-and-span condition as Margaret issued them orders. It was nearly noon and the grouse-hunting party had set off an hour before. Arabella and her parents sat in the dining room, having finished a cooked breakfast of eggs, bacon and sausages. Arabella was dressed warmly for the day of shooting ahead in a dress with a dark-grey knitted V-line top over it.

She looked up at the clock. 'Where has Harrison got to?'

George chuckled. 'I imagine he's sleeping off a hangover, my dear. He did knock back the drink last night.'

At that moment Harrison and Charles walked into the dining room.

Arabella took one look at Harrison, who was as pale as a ghost and shaking, then rose to her feet and rushed over to him.

'What's wrong, Harrison?'

'I haven't been to bed all night. I've been throwing up for most of the night.'

'A hangover?' suggested George.

'No, it's more than that,' objected Harrison as Arabella felt his forehead.

'Perhaps something he ate,' Charles suggested.

'Well, whatever it is, you need a doctor immediately,' said Arabella.

'No. The worst of it is over. All I need to do now is go to bed and sleep. I'm exhausted.'

'My poor darling!' Arabella stroked his cheek.

'But what about you?' said Harrison.

'What about me?'

'You were so looking forward to going on the shoot.'

'Oh, it's not a worry. I'll just stay here in the house,' said Arabella.

'But you'll miss the shoot!'

Charles stepped forward. 'Well, you can accompany me, Arabella. I'm setting off to join the others shortly.'

'No, thank you,' said Arabella firmly.

'But that's a great idea,' said Harrison. 'Thank you, Charles, that's very good of you.'

'I couldn't possibly burden you with me for the day,' insisted Arabella.

'No burden at all,' said Charles.

'Thank you but no.'

'Oh, don't be silly, Arabella,' interjected Caroline. 'You wanted to go and here is your opportunity.'

'But...'

'That's decided then,' said Charles happily. 'I'll get the groomsman to bring our carriage to the front. I'll meet you there in – say – twenty minutes?'

With that he turned and walked out of the room

Arabella walked out the front door of Armstrong House and took in the view. It was a clear late-August day and she looked across the expansive forecourt beyond which was a series of terraced gardens leading down to the lake, which stretched out for miles to the other side.

She couldn't see Charles and strolled across the forecourt then turned and looked up at the house. She took in the majesty of the baronial three-storey granite house. The third storey was tucked just under the black tiled roof. A flight of stairs led up to the front double doors and the windows were tall and gothic.

She heard a horse and carriage approach and saw a smiling Charles enter the forecourt in a phaeton two-seater carriage.

He waved at her and smiled.

'It is a good day for the shoot,' said Charles as he jumped down from the carriage and assisted her up.

She nodded as she sat down.

He jumped up beside her, turned to her and smiled broadly. He shook the reins and the horse took off down the long avenue.

Arabella was entranced by the beautiful views as they rode through the narrow roads of the estate.

'It is exactly as beautiful as Harrison described it,' said Arabella. 'You're very lucky.'

'Am I?'

'Well, all this is going to be yours as the future Lord Armstrong.'

'Yes but, having said that, with it comes responsibility, or so my father is always insisting. I think the younger children of peers have it easier.'

'Do you?'

'Yes, they are free to choose whatever they want in life. I envy that.'

'I can't see you working in a bank like Harrison,' Arabella said.

He was surprised she had made any judgement of him at all as she seemed to pay no attention to him.

'But Harrison doesn't have to work in a bank. He can do anything he wishes but he chooses to work there. It's that choice I envy.'

'Well, I'm sure you'll be more than compensated with an eight thousand-acre estate and all the other benefits you'll get... Ah, there are the others, see!' She pointed at the crowd scattered across a hill, walking along with dogs.

'Yes – I see.'

Charles parked the carriage and they walked towards the others to join the shoot. As they did so she kept her distance from him.

'Is Gwyneth on the shoot today?' she asked.

'No. She will be in Armstrong House dissecting the success of her debutante ball with anyone who will listen to her.'

'She's entitled to talk about it.'

'She'll be married to the Duke in a few months and go to live in Battington Castle or Battington Palace or whatever he owns. And there she will stay forever in her ivory tower, deigning to come amongst us mere mortals only on special occasions.'

Arabella glanced at him. 'You sound contemptuous.'

'Not contemptuous. Just disappointed in people that they take an easy route, and Gwyneth has taken the easiest route of all … but then she was always going to.'

'She's just following her destiny, like you are yours.'

He stopped and looked at her. 'Is that what you think of me? I want a lot more than just taking over from my father here in Armstrong House.'

She stopped and glanced at him. 'I'm sure I don't think of you at all.'

Arabella held the gun shakily while Charles got into position to guide her. He stood close behind her, putting both arms around her arms and holding the gun with her.

'You watch your prey very carefully,' he said in a low voice as they watched the grouse in the distance. 'Then you follow it with your gun until you have it in your sights...What's the real reason you're not having a debutante ball?'

She was startled with this sudden question. 'I was going to have one this year but it was cancelled.'

'And why was it cancelled?'

'Because I had met Harrison by then, and knew we were meant for each other. Can we just concentrate on the shooting?' she urged.

He pulled his arms closer around her as he tightened his grip on the gun.

'I'd have thought a girl like you would have had many options.'

'I do.'

'Then why Harrison?'

She was becoming incredulous. 'Why not Harrison?'

'I just thought you'd have aimed for something a little...' he tilted the gun upwards as a grouse came into view, 'higher.'

He suddenly pressed his trigger finger over hers and the gun fired a shot into the distance. The shot missed its target and the grouse fled.

He didn't move from the position he was in.

'We missed,' she said eventually. She pulled away from him quickly and faced him. 'I'm quite glad actually – I don't think shoots are for me.' She handed him the gun back. 'Let's go back to Armstrong House.'

'But I bet you're glad you tried it!' he called

after her.

Most of the guests that had attended the ball had left by the Saturday evening and Lawrence and Margaret hosted a dinner party for close friends in the dining room that night. The Tattingers were among the twenty present. Charles found himself that night at the polar end of the dining table from Harrison and Arabella. He found it hard to keep his eyes from straying to observe them constantly.

'Well, congratulations, Lady Margaret, on a magnificent ball,' complimented Caroline Tattinger as she enjoyed her duckling.

'We're well used to entertaining at Armstrong House – but I was so busy introducing Gwyneth.'

'Introducing her to everyone she already knew,' said Charles.

'That's not the point, Charles. I was officially introducing her as a young woman come of age,' said Margaret.

'I meant to say before,' Sir George interjected, 'I met friends of yours at a function recently.'

'Really? Who?' asked Lawrence.

'The Earl of Galway and his wife.'

Lawrence looked displeased. 'Yes, the Galways were friends of ours. But we never see them any more.'

'Why?'

'I'm afraid the Galways live in their London house permanently now. Their manor in Galway is left in the care of an elderly housekeeper and their estate left to the running of a particularly nasty land manager. They have joined the ranks of those absentee landlords who see their estates as nothing more than moneymaking devices to squeeze every last penny from, to fund their extravagant lifestyle in London.' Lawrence shook his head in disgust.

'Maybe they are just scared to spend too much time on their estate with the Land War going on?' said George.

'If they are targets, then they have made themselves so!' snapped Lawrence.

Caroline was surprised. 'We found them very agreeable.'

'Now, Lawrence,' cautioned Margaret firmly, 'what the Galways do is really none of our business.'

'But–' began Lawrence.

'And the Countess of Galway had impeccable table manners, from what I remember,' Margaret smiled and nodded at Caroline in an approving way.

Arabella was sitting at the end of the table, engrossed in conversation with Harrison.

'Well?' asked Harrison. 'What is your verdict so far? Is Armstrong House what you expected? What do you make of everyone?'

'It's exactly as you described it. And everyone is exactly as you described them. Everyone is lovely,' said Arabella.

Harrison smiled proudly. 'It won't be long before we have a beautiful home and family too.'

She reached forward and stroked his hand in delight.

Harrison looked worried. 'Although I'm not sure how I'm going to afford to give us a beautiful home just yet, not on my wages.'

'Father says you'll continue to gallop up the ranks of the bank.'

'Still – in the meantime that doesn't help us. I spoke to my own father and he said we can live in his Dublin house on Merrion Square for however long we want.'

Arabella started laughing lightly with a slightly mocking tone.

'What's so funny?' he asked, confused.

'You! You are a silly goose! Don't you realise my parents have given me a substantial dowry? One large enough to buy us the house of our dreams in Dublin?'

Harrison looked shocked. 'No, I didn't! I never even thought about such a thing.'

Arabella smiled lovingly. 'I know. And that's one of the reasons I love you as much as I do.'

She glanced down the table and saw Charles was sitting back in his chair observing them. The intensity of his eyes unnerved her. Then he smiled at her. She nodded at him and quickly looked away.

She had found the Armstrong family utterly charming. Lawrence and Margaret were overly welcoming and kind, if Margaret was somewhat neurotic. The children had all been sincere and friendly, although James was unruly and Emily had a rebellious streak. But it was Charles that had caused her concern. Harrison had nothing but high praise for his brother. He had said Charles was charming, fun and intelligent. And Arabella agreed he was all those things. But there was more to him. She felt Charles' charm was self-serving, his fun side might be dangerous, and his intelligence used to get his own way. She believed Charles was too aware of his charm, his looks and his intelligence. She was wary of him. She was sure he had attempted to flirt with her, which she found very unsettling. Harrison had said Charles was planning to return to London without much delay. Arabella was glad. She thought the less she had to do with him the better.

Lawrence suddenly chinking a fork against his crystal glass brought a hush to the room as he rose to his feet.

'Family and friends, this has been such a wonderful weekend at Armstrong House. And I have some wonderful news to share with you. Harrison asked Sir George for his daughter's hand in marriage during the week. Sir George and Lady Tattinger have agreed and I am delighted to announce the engagement of my son Harrison to the very lovely Miss Arabella Tattinger.'

There were gasps of excitement and applause around the table as the footmen quickly refilled everyone's glass with champagne. Harrison and Arabella held hands tightly while they grinned at each other.

'And I would like you to join me in a toast,' said Lawrence as everyone rose to their feet. 'To Harrison and Arabella!'

'To Harrison and Arabella!' everyone chorused.

Arabella nodded appreciatively at everyone who was smiling happily at her, except for Charles whose cool eyes continued to stare at her.

On the Sunday the Tattingers and Harrison were

at the front door of Armstrong House saying their goodbyes.

'Thank you so much for a wonderful time and no doubt it won't be long before we see you again,' said Caroline as she kissed Lawrence and Margaret goodbye.

'Well, see you soon,' said Harrison as Charles walked him and Arabella down the steps to the carriage.

'Yes, indeed.' Charles turned to Arabella and, smiling, took her hand and kissed it. 'Until the next time?'

Arabella nodded. Harrison handed her up into the carriage, then stepped back to allow George and Caroline to join her, before getting in himself.

'Safe journey,' said Charles as he closed the carriage door after them.

He stood in the forecourt as he watched the carriage move away and make its way down the long driveway. Turning, he looked up at the house, then climbed the steps up to the front door and entered.

'Charles!' called Margaret from the drawing room.

He walked across the hallway and into the drawing room where his parents were sitting with serious looks on their faces.

Charles crossed over the room and poured himself a glass of whiskey from the drinks table.

'Thank goodness that's all over,' said Lawrence. 'Now we can get on with the business at hand.'

'Charles, your father has been telling me of your plans to live in London,' said Margaret.

'Charles, it's simply not allowable!' insisted Lawrence. 'This is going to be your house, your estate and you need to take responsibility for it!'

Charles turned around and saw the distress on their faces.

'I'm sorry, Mother, but there seems to have been a misunderstanding. I'm not returning to London.'

'You're staying here at Armstrong House?' Lawrence asked, confused.

'Of course – where else would I be?' He smiled at them.

Margaret and Lawrence looked at each other, visibly relieved.

CHAPTER 3

There were many villages scattered through the Armstrong estate but the one nearest the house was a model village that had been built by Lawrence's father, Edward, at the same time he built Armstrong House. It was a beautiful little village with stone houses around a village green which had a little clock tower in the middle of it and a church in pride of place.

That day the green was a hive of activity with many stalls set out as there was a turnip competition being judged. Charles found himself walking down the rows of stalls looking at turnip after turnip. He paused at the next stall to look at a particularly large specimen.

The farmer's wife picked up the turnip and held it out to him.

'Would you like to hold it, sir?' she asked with a smile.

He glanced at the vegetable which looked as if it had barely been washed.

'No, it's quite all right, thank you.' He nodded at her and moved on to the next stall, looking. He looked at his watch and wondered how much longer he would have to stay.

He looked around and saw his mother and Gwyneth nearby, eagerly engaging with a farmer about his fertilising methods.

Margaret saw him and, coming over, said, 'Well, I think it's a close race between farmers O'Donovan and O'Hara. What do you think?'

'To be honest, they all look the same to me. Once you've seen one turnip you've seen them all!'

Margaret looked irritated. 'It's not about the turnips, Charles. It's about morale and good relations in the estate.'

'Oh, is that the point of it all?' Charles didn't hide his sarcasm.

'Gwyneth understands the point of it, so why can't you?' She observed her daughter with pride as she moved effortlessly amongst the people, chatting. 'She has such a way with her. She'll be such an asset to the Duke on his estate.'

Gwyneth came over to them. 'Well, I think we should give it to the O'Donovans. They lost one of their children this year and I think it would give them a boost.'

'What do you think, Charles?' asked Margaret.

66

'Do you know, I couldn't care less! Can we just give the bloody prize and get on with it!'

'Charles! These people have gone to a huge effort to try and impress you, their future landlord,' said Gwyneth.

'All right, and I'm impressed as I ever could be about a turnip!'

Margaret was annoyed. 'In that case, as Charles has no objection, O'Donovan is the winner.'

The three of them went up on the stand and everyone gathered around.

'Well, get on with it,' Charles hissed at his mother.

'No, you have to make the speech, Charles – it's you they're expecting to hear.'

'For goodness' sake!' snapped Charles.

'And be enthusiastic and complimentary,' Margaret advised. 'Let them know you appreciate the lengths they have gone to. Reward them with your words and win them over.'

Charles raised his eyes as he stepped forward. 'Eh, thank you, everyone, for coming today...' He looked down at all the expectant, curious and excited faces. He glanced back at his mother and Gwyneth who were smiling encouragingly at him. 'And the winner is O'Donovan!'

Charles stepped back and stood beside his mother, looking bored. 'Charles! That was hardly worth the effort!'

'Short and sweet, Mother, short and sweet.'

'Short and nothing!' snapped Margaret.

The crowd applauded as O'Donovan stepped on the platform and Gwyneth presented him his prize and offered warm congratulations.

Lawrence ran the estate's business from the library at Armstrong House. It was an endless parade of meetings with the farm managers, accountants, tenant farmers, all of which Charles found he was expected to attend. His mind drifted to what his friends were getting up to in London, and to Harrison and Arabella in Dublin, and he found it hard not to doze off as he listened to the minutiae of the matters being discussed.

'And O'Reilly is how long in arrears now?' Lawrence was asking the estate manager.

'Four months, your lordship. If it was any other estate he would be evicted by now.'

'No, I want no evictions. Bring O'Reilly to me during the week and I'll see what he has to say for himself and see if we can come to some arrangement.'

'Very good, your lordship.' The farm estate manager left and Lawrence sighed loudly.

'If he's not going to be able to pay now then he never will,' said Charles. 'The longer it goes on, the more arrears he will be in and the less chance of him catching up. Drinking his money in a bar, no doubt.'

'But he has always been a good payer in the past. And don't be so judgemental, Charles. Being a landlord of an estate like this takes humanity and understanding – you should keep that in mind.'

'Oh, I will, Father, I will!' Charles said sarcastically as he got up from the chesterfield and sauntered over to one of the large windows that overlooked the courtyards at the back of the house. In the courtyard he saw James standing there with some groomsmen, ordering them about while exchanging banter with them at the same time. James was dressed as casually as the groomsmen.

'What is James up to now?' said Charles as he observed him.

Lawrence got up from behind his desk and came and joined him at the window.

He smiled. 'James loves the land. Loves working on it.'

'Hardly the correct thing for a gentleman to be doing.'

'Ah, your mother and I have had to accept what James is. School and university would be wasted on him.'

James was saying something to the groomsmen and suddenly they all burst out laughing.

'And he has a great way with the people. He loves them, and they love him.'

'Still, he's making a show of the family. I hear he goes socialising with the peasants in the town bars.'

'But he has a great heart. And I don't think anybody knows this estate as well as he. He will be a great asset to you when it comes to running this place.'

'A great asset or a great embarrassment?' said Charles before sauntering out of the room.

Lawrence glanced after Charles, surprised, before returning to his desk.

James came through the front door of Armstrong House, a rifle in one hand and some shot rabbits in the other. He flung the rabbits on an ornate side table.

'*James!*' screamed Margaret who had been coming down the stairs. She rushed over to him.

'What?'

'That is eighteenth-century Italian!' She pointed to the side table.

'So?' James looked unimpressed.

Margaret turned and tugged the bell pull with zest.

Charles sauntered down the stairs as Barton came hurrying along.

'You called, my lady?' asked Barton.

'Barton, take these rabbits quickly down to the kitchen to Cook or somebody and away from my side table.'

Barton reached out and took the rabbits. Holding them out in disdain, he carried them away, with Margaret in quick pursuit issuing orders.

'Use the back door in future when you bring in game, James!' Margaret called over her shoulder.

James started laughing to himself.

Charles looked James up and down condescendingly. 'Maybe you should use the back door all the time in future.'

'And what's that supposed to mean?' James asked, his laughter suddenly gone.

'Well, it's just if you want to dress like a peasant, act like a peasant, then use the back door like a peasant.'

'I don't need you to tell me what I should or shouldn't do,' James said angrily.

'Why? You need somebody to tell you. Your habits were very endearing when you were younger, I'm sure, but now you're just becoming a joke.'

James came up to him. 'I have an interest in what goes on around here, which is more than you'll ever have.'

'Pity you don't have as much interest in what you look like, isn't it?' Charles turned and went back into the drawing room, leaving James staring after him.

The family were gathered in the drawing room in the evening. Emily was walking up and down the room with a book balanced on her head and a displeased look on her face.

'Can I stop now?' she asked.

'No, Emily,' said Margaret. 'Keep walking and concentrate! Shoulders back and head kept level.'

Emily gritted her teeth and kept walking back and forth.

'Any word from Harrison?' asked Charles who was stretched out on the couch.

'No, he's probably far too enraptured with his young lady and the Tattinger family to give us a second thought,' chuckled Lawrence.

Margaret smiled. 'Arabella is such a fine young woman – so beautiful – and her parents so impressive.'

'Aren't they just?' agreed Charles then waited a while before speaking again. 'I might go up and visit him next weekend.'

'Go to Dublin?' Lawrence was surprised.

'Yes, I miss Harrison. It would be nice to spend some time with him.'

'You never missed him when you were in England. Harrison said you never even bothered to write,' said Emily.

'Why don't you just be quiet and concentrate on your posture, Emily,' warned Charles.

'Yes, it might be nice for you to go to Dublin,' said Margaret.

'That's what I was thinking,' said Charles.

Daphne came rushing into the room, waving a card.

'A ball, I've been invited to a ball!' she said excitedly.

'Where?' asked Margaret.

'At the Bramwells' – I'm so excited.'

'The Bramwells?' Lawrence's face creased in concern. 'I'm afraid you can't go, Daphne.'

'But why ever not?' Daphne was horrified.

'Because the Bramwells' estate is caught up in the Land War. There is much hatred felt towards them.'

'But what's that got to do with me?' Daphne was aghast.

'It's simply not safe for you to go,' said Lawrence. 'Anything could happen.'

'Mother?' Daphne appealed the decision.

'I'm afraid if your father says it's unsafe then you can't go.'

'This stupid Land War!' snapped Daphne. 'It's ruining all my fun!' She threw the invitation into the fire and stormed off.

'Such a pity! The Bramwells were always such a nice family,' sighed Margaret.

'They weren't nice to their tenants, especially during the famine,' said Lawrence.

'The famine was forty years ago, Father,' Charles pointed out. 'Isn't it time we all moved on?'

'It will take a long time to move on from that. It changed this country and changed our class's position forever. Before the famine families like ours were invincible. Now we can't take our power or position for granted.'

The book fell off Emily's head on to the floor.

'Emily! You aren't concentrating!' snapped Margaret.

Emily reached down, snatched up the book and threw it at the wall. 'What's the point in being able to walk properly if we are all going to be killed in our beds some night by rampaging peasants!'

'Emily!' Margaret said. 'Go to your room!'

'Good! At least there I won't have to parade around like a peacock!'

Charles laughed as Emily ran off.

'Oh dear!' sighed Margaret. 'Two disgruntled daughters under the same roof on the same night!'

CHAPTER 4

Charles got the train from Castlewest to Dublin and from there got a hansom cab to take him to their house on Merrion Square. As he looked out the window of the cab he inhaled the atmosphere of the busy streets, the traffic, the amazing Georgian architecture. He was excited about the prospect of meeting Arabella.

The cab pulled up outside the house in Merrion Square. He got out, walked up the steps and knocked loudly on the door. The house was a four-storey-over-basement townhouse. His father had bought it some twenty years before. For a family that was as distinguished and wealthy as the Armstrongs, it was important for them to have homes in Dublin and London, and his parents had hosted many functions in both houses over the years. However, the visits by his parents to Dublin were now cut short with Lawrence's obsession about being on the estate as much as possible and avoiding any label of being an absentee landlord.

The butler opened the door.

'Ah, Mr Charles, it is good to see you again,' he said, taking his suitcase.

'You too. Is my brother home?'

'No, Mr Harrison usually returns from work around half five, sir,' said the butler as Charles followed him up the stairs as far as the drawing room on the first floor.

'Unpack my case in my room, will you?' said Charles as he walked into the drawing room and lit a cigarette.

On the mantelpiece there were four photo-graphs of Arabella arranged in frames. He walked over and taking one of the photos in his hand, studied it intently.

An hour later he heard the front door open and slam and somebody taking quick steps up the stairs. Harrison came into the drawing room and came to an abrupt halt when he saw Charles standing there.

'Charles! This is a nice surprise!' He strode over to Charles and gave him a hug.

'I thought I'd pay you a visit.'

'How long are you staying?'

'Just the weekend. Going back on Monday.'

'And what are your plans?'

'I have none. My appointment book is empty and I'm yours for the whole weekend.'

'Excellent! I'm meeting Arabella for dinner tonight. She'll be delighted to see you.'

Arabella walked up the steps of The Shelbourne Hotel and through the ornate foyer to the restaurant.

As she was being shown through the restaurant, she nodded and said hello to people at different tables who were friends of her family. She saw Harrison and smiled at him. She then spotted somebody else sitting at the table and her eyes widened in shock as she realised it was Charles. Her stomach knotted at the sight of him, as she wondered why he was there.

Both men stood up as she reached their table.

'Look who's here, Arabella,' said Harrison happily.

'Yes, I can see. Hello again, Charles,' she said as she sat down.

'You are looking as lovely as before,' Charles complimented her as he sat down.

'You flatter me, Charles,' she smiled.

The waiter handed her a menu.

'You deserve flattering,' said Charles.

'I thought you were in London?' said Arabella.

'No, remember I told you Charles decided to

stay at Armstrong House,' said Harrison.

'Oh, yes, of course. And how are you finding life down on the farm?'

'Oh, you know! Life goes on there the same as always. Dinner parties and shoots.'

'The hunt season will be starting soon – that's always fun,' said Harrison.

'Yes, the hunt balls can be entertaining all right ... if I hear the words Home Rule or Land War again, I think I'll scream!' Charles started laughing.

'Politics doesn't interest you?' asked Arabella.

'Not really. I can never understand people who spend their lives caught up in what's going on with society. I think they are trying to escape something in their own lives.'

'"No man is an island",' said Arabella.

Charles took up his menu. 'Shall we order?'

Arabella managed to get through the evening. There wasn't much for her to contribute as Charles dominated the conversation with hilarious stories and anecdotes. At least Harrison found them hilarious – she remained on guard, smiling and nodding only when she needed to.

She found the next day that she and Harrison were expected to nanny Charles again when he showed up with Harrison for a garden party they had been invited to. The garden party was being hosted by friends of Arabella who lived in a house on a leafy street in Rathgar. The back garden had been laid out with a series of round tables with crisp white tablecloths on which were silver teapots that glistened in the early-October warm sunshine.

Arabella walked to her table and Charles hurried after her.

'Allow me?' he said as he pulled out a chair for her.

'Thank you,' she said as she sat down.

The afternoon passed in a leisurely enjoyment of company over neatly cut triangular sandwiches, scones with strawberry jam and cream, and an array of cakes.

'I'm not even going to *look* at another cream cake or I may as well say goodbye to my figure forever!' Arabella declared.

Charles bent forward to her and whispered, 'But you have an amazing figure.'

She ignored him and continued to chat to the others.

Charles soon went and circulated among the other guests. She watched from afar as he charmed and entertained them throughout the afternoon.

She had to put up with him only for one weekend, she reminded herself.

On the following Monday afternoon Arabella was sitting in her bedroom in front of her mirror as she tried on necklaces. The maid knocked and came in.

'Miss Arabella, Mr Armstrong is here to see you.'

Arabella turned around as she fastened the clip of the necklace at the back of her neck.

'Harrison didn't say he would be calling over.' She stood up. 'Tell him I'll be down in a couple of minutes.'

'Em, it's not Master Harrison. It's a Mr Charles Armstrong to see you,' explained the maid.

'Charles?' Arabella was confused and surprised. 'Tell him that I'm with guests, and can't see him.'

'Very good, my lady.' The maid turned and left.

Arabella sat down at the dressing table again and stared at her reflection, lost in thought. What did he want? Why did he want to see her without Harrison? Her suspicions of him increased even more.

CHAPTER 5

The following Friday evening Arabella had arranged to meet Harrison in Stephen's Green for them to go out to dinner. As she alighted from her father's carriage at the top of Grafton Street, she smiled as she saw him waiting for her. Her smile dropped as she saw Charles standing beside him.

'Charles, what a surprise!' Her smile did not carry to her eyes.

'I thought you were returning to Armstrong House last Monday?'

'I did and I caught the train back to Dublin today,' said Charles.

'Whatever for?' She couldn't keep the irritation out of her voice.

'For the theatre!' said Harrison. 'Charles has

got us three tickets to see the new play at the Gaiety tonight.'

'But I've already seen it,' said Arabella.

'Oh, dear! I wanted to repay you for being such hospitable hosts last weekend,' explained Charles.

'There *really* was no need,' insisted Arabella.

'Every need!' said Charles in a sing-song voice.

'I really wish somebody had warned me about this. I'm not dressed for the theatre...'

'But you look beautiful,' smiled Charles as his eyes bored into her.

'I'm not even in the mood for the theatre tonight,' she said.

'Arabella!' said Harrison, smiling, but with a cautious look on his face. 'You're almost being ungrateful to Charles.'

'No, it's all right, Harrison, if Arabella would prefer not to go...' said Charles.

Arabella forced herself to smile and spoke earnestly. 'Of course it's fine. Don't mind me, Charles – I'm just not good with surprises.'

'In that case, shall we make our way to the theatre?' said Charles with a broad smile as he held out his arm for Arabella to take.

Arabella hesitated before taking his arm and they walked down the street, with Harrison alongside them.

Arabella was positioned between the two brothers in the theatre. She was glad she had seen the play before, because that evening she would have been unable to concentrate on it. She felt extremely uncomfortable so close to Charles. She tried to keep away from him as much as she could, but it

79

didn't stop her feeling his leg through the many layers of her gown, or his arm pressed against hers. Like Harrison, Charles was a tall man leaving Arabella feeling her personal space was being invaded. What's more, his aroma was overpowering and intoxicating. She was delighted when the play was over and they all stood to clap for the actors.

The audience then made its way to the foyer where it congregated.

'Drinks?' smiled Charles.

'A glass of white wine, please,' said Harrison.

'The same for me,' said Arabella.

Charles made his way through the crowded foyer to join the queue at the bar.

'I have to say you could have been a bit politer to Charles earlier,' whispered Harrison.

'I told you, I don't like surprises,' she said.

'I mean, he made the journey all the way up from the country to bring us here tonight,' Harrison pointed out.

Her temper gave. 'For goodness' sake! Do you want me to apologise to him or something?'

'Of course not – it's just quite unlike you to be so rude!' said Harrison.

She forced herself to be quiet.

'What time does your parents' soirée start tomorrow night?' asked Harrison.

'Eight,' Arabella informed him as she spotted people she knew across the foyer and waved and mouthed hello to them.

'Fine, we'll be there in plenty of time.'

Arabella stopped waving and looked at Harrison, concerned. 'We?'

'Yes, myself and Charles.'

'*Harrison!*' she shrieked, causing people to look round.

'What on earth is wrong with you?' snapped Harrison.

'I just wish you could have consulted me beforehand. I don't want to lumber extra guests on my parents without them agreeing beforehand.'

'It's not extra guests, it's just Charles. They always have loads of people attending their drinks parties who they hardly know. I'm sure my brother won't be a burden to them.'

'Well, they won't be given the opportunity now to decide, will they?' she snapped.

'Well, I could hardly leave him at home on his own while we're off enjoying ourselves, could I?'

Arabella was saved from saying something she might regret by the reappearance of Charles with a waiter carrying a silver tray of three wineglasses. They took their glasses from the tray.

Charles raised his glass and smiled. 'Is everyone having as charming an evening as I am?'

Arabella took a large gulp of her drink.

The cab pulled up outside the Tattinger house on Ailesbury Avenue and Harrison and Charles alighted.

'This is Arabella's home,' said Harrison proudly as the two walked up the driveway of the imposing redbrick house.

'Very nice,' commented Charles, giving no indication he had been there the previous Monday when Arabella had refused to meet him.

They climbed the steps and Harrison pulled

the doorbell.

'Good evening, Molly,' said Harrison as he and Charles handed over their hats and coats.

'They're in the drawing room, sir,' said Molly as she put their garments to one side. She led them across the hall and opened the door for them.

The room was filled with well-dressed people as two footmen circulated and served drinks.

Charles spotted Arabella immediately. She was looking radiant and standing out from the crowd.

Harrison led Charles over to her parents.

'I'm sorry we're somewhat late,' said Harrison. 'Sir George and Lady Tattinger, you remember my brother Charles?'

'Of course, delighted to see you again,' smiled George. 'And how are your parents?'

'Very good, sir. I believe the price of wheat has gone up which has made my father exorbitantly happy!' said Charles, causing George and Caroline to laugh.

'I say, that's Charles Armstrong, isn't it?' said Sophia, a close female friend of Arabella's.

'Yes, Harrison's brother. Do you know him?'

'No. But my brother does. He was in university with him.' Sophia had a look on her face that was a mixture of excitement and horror.

'I don't know him that well,' said Arabella.

'Maybe it's just as well!'

'Why?'

'Well, he had quite a reputation at university.'

'In what way?' Arabella demanded.

'Well, he wasn't at university to study by all accounts but to drink, gamble and carouse. I believe trouble seemed to follow him around like a bad smell around a pig! But he's so smooth and devious he always got away with everything. My brother said he's not quite the charmer he presents to the world. On one occasion...' Sophia looked quickly around to make sure nobody was listening before leaning into Arabella's ear and whispering the rest of the story. 'He was courting four girls at the same time, and all four girls had their names ruined by him!'

Arabella's face turned red as she heard this. 'I don't believe it!'

Arabella found herself being drawn to looking at Charles for the rest of the night. Again he seemed to be seeking out her company and she continued to try to avoid him, even more so after what she had heard from Sophia. But she eventually found herself cornered by him.

'Your parents were so good to invite me,' said Charles.

'They didn't actually,' she said curtly. 'Harrison invited you.'

'What?' He looked surprised and then embarrassed. 'I'm so sorry. I had no idea. I assumed your parents had extended the invitation. I should leave.' He turned to go.

'No! Wait!' she said quickly. 'What I meant was they weren't aware you were in Dublin to invite. If they had been, they would naturally have invited you.'

'Are you sure?' he said. 'I would hate to stay where I wasn't welcome.'

'You are very welcome here, Charles,' she said politely.

'Oh good!' he smiled and moved on.

Caroline immediately came over to Arabella. 'I'd forgotten how nice Charles was!'

'Easily done,' Arabella muttered.

'What did you say?'

'Nothing!'

Caroline looked at her daughter, exasperated, then decided to let her rudeness go. 'I've invited him to our dinner party here next weekend.'

'But he'll be returning to the country on Monday!' Arabella was astounded.

'No, he said he'll make the journey up especially for the dinner party! Isn't that nice of him?'

'Mama!' Arabella snapped loudly. 'I wish you had discussed it with me before you asked him.'

'What is there to ask? You're going to be part of his family after all.' Caroline was puzzled.

'And I get stuck with him for yet another weekend,' Arabella whispered under her breath.

At the dinner party the following Saturday Arabella made sure to sit at the furthest end of the table from where Charles was positioned. It didn't matter as Charles' loud and gregarious conversation dominated the table and captured everyone's attention.

'I came into the drawing room at Armstrong House and my mother had my youngest sister Emily imprisoned on the couch, giving her elocution lessons, getting her to repeat over and over again *"The cat sat on the mat"*,' said Charles. 'My mother was reprimanding her, telling her she wasn't concentrating on her consonants –

"The *cat sat* on the *mat*,'" emphasised my mother. To which dearest little Emily jumped up in a fit of rage and screamed: "Who gives a damn where the bloody cat sat!"'

The whole table erupted in laughter mixed with shocked gasps.

'Poor Lady Armstrong!' said Caroline, shocked at his repeating Emily's bad language.

'I'm sure Emily will mature into as fine a lady as your sister Gwyneth,' said George.

'Yes, and any news of Gwyneth's wedding to the Duke?' inquired Caroline.

'They are talking spring,' said Charles.

After dinner, the party walked through the double doors into the front drawing room where the banter continued unabated. Arabella kept to the back of the room, where she hoped Charles wouldn't notice her. On the contrary, as the night wore on he made a beeline for her.

'Thank your parents for being wonderful hosts tonight,' said Charles.

'Why don't you thank them yourself?'

He smiled at her. 'We must meet up for tea during the week, perhaps Monday if you're free, before I return to the country.'

She looked at him, alarmed. 'But Harrison will be at work.'

'So?'

'I'm not in the habit of meeting men I don't know well, unchaperoned.'

'Well, as we are going to be family, I think we should get better acquainted.'

She studied him. 'You called to our house a while back asking to meet me. Why?'

'Ah yes, it was a Monday afternoon if I remember. It's quite simple: I was returning your glove.'

'Glove? What glove?'

'The glove you left behind at our house in Merrion Square over the weekend when you were there.'

'I wasn't missing any glove. It wasn't mine,' she said firmly.

'Oh, I see. I wonder then in that case whose it was?'

'I don't know and really don't care.'

'I hope Harrison hasn't been entertaining a young lady there behind your back.' His eyes glinted mischievously at her.

'Don't be ridiculous. And how dare you say such a thing!'

'I'm sorry. I've offended you.'

'Charles, you flatter yourself if you think you could ever provoke any reaction from me other than disinterest.' She turned and pushed past him to join the others.

CHAPTER 6

Weekend after weekend passed and Arabella became used to Harrison turning up to nearly every event with Charles but she was increasingly unhappy with the situation. The man seemed to know no boundaries, she thought. He continued to try to flirt with her, to capture her alone, to get her attention.

Charles was on horseback and was setting off for a ride around the estate.

'Charles!' cried a voice and he turned around to see Emily galloping towards him on her horse.

He waited for her to catch up.

'Mother will kill you if she sees you're not riding side-saddle,' he warned her.

'Mother will kill me anyway. I've escaped from her tuition for the afternoon.'

'Where are you going?'

'With you!' She looked imploringly at him.

'Come along then,' he sighed and the two of them set off, riding through the countryside, chatting.

'If it's not table manners, it's elocution. If it's not elocution it's walking practice. She wants to turn me into a walking, talking doll!'

Charles laughed. 'I suppose we have to take on the roles that are given to us in life.'

'You always please yourself. You're nobody's puppet. It's what I love about you. You're the only one here who really understands me.'

'Poor Emily!' he mocked.

She looked at him curiously. 'Where do you go at the weekends, Charles?'

'You know where I go – to the house in Dublin.'

'Are you sure that's where you go?'

He looked at her, confused. 'Check with Harrison if you don't believe me... Why, where do you think I go?'

'I'm not sure. But I know you, Charles, and I just don't buy you coming back to Armstrong House to take over your position here. You're up to something. You've got a secret.'

He started laughing. 'What secret could I have?'

'Does it involve a woman? I think it does. I think you're in love with a woman.'

'And who am I in love with?' he asked.

'I don't know... But it isn't straightforward. It's complicated, that's what I think... There's something holding you back from being with her and it's driving you mad ... is she married?'

'Emily!' Charles looked at her, shocked.

'Oh, I wouldn't mind if she was!' said Emily quickly.

'Well, the good lady's husband might!' said Charles.

'If she were married, I wouldn't judge you, honestly. I'm very open-minded.'

'Are you indeed?'

'Absolutely. In fact, I can't understand why everyone is horrified that Charles Stewart Parnell is having an affair with a married woman. I don't know why he's being ruined by it.'

'You'd better not let Mother hear you say that.'

'All I'm saying is, if you are in some – situation – with a woman that's ... complicated ... I can help you. I'm a very loyal ally, Charles. And if you need me to help, to cover up, to carry messages – anything at all – you can trust me.' She looked adoringly at him.

'Don't live your life through other people's lives, Emily. Live your own life.'

'Are you in love, Charles?'

He sighed. 'I don't know... I'm not sure... I haven't thought it through properly.' She was staring at him, burning with curiosity, and he smiled at her. 'No, there isn't anybody – I'm only teasing you. Now, shut up and let's go down to the lake.' He dug his heels into his horse and took off quickly.

Walking into the restaurant, Arabella spotted Charles sitting at the table alone and felt agitated, wondering where Harrison was. 'Where's Harrison?' she asked straight away.

'Ahh, I'm afraid he's been held up at work,' said Charles.

Arabella looked annoyed. 'I really wish he would tell me if he's going to be late.'

'Well, he knew you would be in safe hands with me.' She ignored him and picked up the menu.

'I took the liberty of already ordering your starter for you... Well, you always order scallops for starters, so it was no mystery.'

The waiter arrived with two plates of scallops and placed one in front of Charles and the other in front of Arabella.

Arabella looked at the scallops. 'Could you take this away please?' She glanced at the menu. 'I'll have the French cheese tartlet instead.'

'Very good, my lady.'

'Why don't you want scallops tonight?' asked Charles.

She said nothing.

He paused before asking, 'Is it because I ordered them?'

She ignored him and continued to look around the restaurant. Charles sat back and studied her. 'You don't like me much, do you?'

'I'm sure I neither like nor dislike you.'

89

He sat forward. 'Have I ever been unpleasant or discourteous to you?'

'No.'

'Then what is your problem with me?'

She stared at him a long time. 'Have you no life of your own? Every time I turn to look, there you are. Don't you have an estate you need to run?'

'I've as much right to be in Dublin as anyone. I've every right to be in the house in Merrion Square as much as Harrison does. More in fact, as it will be mine one day as the future Lord Armstrong.'

'Don't you ever think myself and Harrison do not want you with us all the time?'

'Has Harrison said so?'

'No but–'

'Then it's you who doesn't want me.'

She leaned towards him and spoke quietly. 'I don't trust you. I don't know what you are up to or what you want, but I don't trust you. You might have everyone else fooled with your charm and your ways, but not me... *I do not trust you!*'

They glared at each other.

Just then Arabella saw Harrison enter the restaurant and whispered, 'And to answer your question – no – no, *I do not like you!*'

Harrison reached the table and sat down. 'I am so sorry! It's entirely your father's fault I am late, Arabella.'

'My father?' she said, smiling warmly at him.

'Yes. With this award he has been given.' He turned to explain to Charles. 'Sir George has been given a big award by the Bankers Federation of America. We were having a drink to celebrate at

90

work tonight.'

'How very nice for him,' said Charles coolly as he avoided looking at Arabella.

'That's right – my parents are thrilled with it.' Arabella spoke happily and lightly. 'They have to travel to New York next month for him to accept the award.' She felt as though a weight had been lifted from her since she'd told Charles her feelings about him.

'Next month! But that's December – will they be back for Christmas?' said Harrison.

'No, nor will I. I'm travelling with them,' said Arabella.

'No!' Harrison was crestfallen. 'But you can't leave me alone at Christmas, can she, Charles?'

'Indeed, it would be heartless,' said Charles as he gave Arabella a cold stare.

'What option do I have?' said Arabella.

'You can come and spend Christmas at Armstrong House with my family, can't she, Charles?' said Harrison.

Charles said nothing as he continued to stare.

'You are silly, Harrison – that is out of the question,' said Arabella.

'Why? There would be nothing inappropriate. My mother can act as your chaperone,' said Harrison.

'Harrison, I will *not* be spending Christmas at Armstrong House.' She turned towards Charles and they glared coldly at each other.

Charles was sitting on the train as he made his way back home after the weekend. He sat staring out the window at the passing countryside,

Arabella's words ringing in his ears – *'I do not trust you'*, and *'no – no – I do not like you!'* He had tried everything with her, but she was immune to him. It made him want her all the more. He would have to change tack, he realised.

CHAPTER 7

The following Friday Arabella arrived with her parents at the Mansion House where a ball was being given by the Lord Mayor. They climbed the steps and entered the grand foyer of the building in Dawson Street, where Harrison was waiting for them.

'May I take your coats?' said the concierge.

Arabella untied her silk cape and handed it over.

As her mother and father chatted to Harrison, they made their way through the elegant crowd to the main room. Arabella's eyes surveyed the crowd, searching for Charles.

'Where's Charles?'

'I don't know,' said Harrison.

'Is he not coming tonight?'

'He's not in Dublin, so I suppose he's not.'

'Not in Dublin? Why not?'

'I haven't heard from him.' He held out his arms to her. 'Shall we dance?'

She nodded and went into his arms and the two of them joined the couples swirling around the dance floor. As she danced, her thoughts were preoccupied with Charles. As she replayed the conversation they'd had in the restaurant, she knew her words had been cutting and unkind – she had meant them to be. But she thought they would have had as much impact on a man like Charles as water off a duck's back. She was sure Charles had been held up on estate business, and would be back in Dublin the following weekend.

But Charles wasn't in Dublin the following weekend either. Arabella had found herself wondering all week would he show up. And when he didn't arrive to join Harrison and her on their weekend activities, she realised it must be what she said that was keeping him away.

The following week, she found she did far more than just wonder if Charles would show up the next weekend. She did little else but think about it. She found herself waiting expectantly for Friday to arrive. And when there was no sign of him she was disappointed.

'Whatever has happened to Charles?' Arabella asked Harrison as they took tea in a tearoom on Grafton Street on the Saturday afternoon.

'Nothing, I imagine,' said Harrison as he took a bite from the Victoria cream cake.

'I just find it very strange that one couldn't turn without seeing him for weekend after weekend and now he has just disappeared.'

'Oh, well, that's Charles for you. Something grabs his attention and it's like it takes over his life. Then something else comes along, and he's off obsessing on that.'

'It's not a very balanced way to lead your life.'

Harrison laughed loudly. 'I don't think balance

is something Charles particularly wants in life... I imagine some young lady has turned his head. The hunt season has begun.'

Harrison's words didn't calm her: they seemed to set something off in her. Something she had never experienced before. An anger, an irritation that seemed to grip her heart. Was this jealousy? And why should she be jealous of this man she despised? Why should she worry? But she did worry. And what worried her most was her reaction.

Caroline looked in a full-length mirror at the sparkling ensemble she was wearing.

'What do you think?' she asked Arabella who was sitting on a chaise-longue.

'Very nice,' said Arabella absent-mindedly.

'Nice!' exclaimed Caroline. 'I don't want to look just nice! I need to look dazzling for New York!' She turned to look at her daughter who was staring off into the distance. 'Arabella! Are you even listening to me?'

Arabella was jolted out of her trance. 'Yes, of course. The dress is beautiful, Mama.'

Caroline went and sat down on the chaise-longue beside Arabella.

'Arabella, what is wrong with you these past few weeks? You're so distracted, and bad-tempered even.'

'Mama, I don't want to go to New York!'

'Don't want to go to New York? It's a wonderful opportunity to see it. And we'll be staying at The Plaza and—'

'I just don't want to go.'

'But why?'

'Because I hate travelling at sea – I hate steam liners – I'll be ill all the time.'

'The journey will last less than a week. Besides, you have no choice. We can hardly leave you without a chaperone for the whole time of Christmas.'

'I've been invited down to Armstrong House for Christmas,' said Arabella suddenly.

'Armstrong House?' Realisation dawned on Caroline. 'So this is all about Harrison, is it?'

'No, yes, it's about everything!' Arabella suddenly became upset.

Caroline put her arms around Arabella. 'But, dear child, Harrison will be here when you get back from New York.'

'You can't take anything for granted.'

'Well, I think you can take Harrison's love for you for granted – it's as plain to see as daylight.'

'Oh, Mama, please don't make me go to New York!' Arabella said, her eyes pleading. 'I can't bear to be away from him for so long. And I'll be well chaperoned at Armstrong House with Lady Margaret, and Gwyneth and everyone else.'

Caroline had always had a weakness for romance. She believed in the simplicity of true love, destiny, and happy-ever-afters. But as she spoke to her husband that night in their bedroom about Arabella's wishes, she knew he would be far more practical about the whole business.

'Never heard anything like it!' he dismissed. 'Not coming to New York indeed because she can't bear to be apart from Harrison!'

'Well, I don't think there's a point in pushing

her to do something she doesn't want to. She is an adult now, and soon to be married to Harrison.'

'We have always allowed her more freedom than most young girls her age.'

'Arabella was always such a sensible and mature girl that there was never anything to fear with her.'

'True!' sighed George.

'And Harrison is so sensible and mature as well.'

'True,' George conceded again.

'She couldn't have a better chaperone than Lady Margaret over Christmas. The woman frets if there is a knife out of place at the table, let alone anything else.'

'And what about the Land War?'

'Oh, I think we've seen for ourselves that the Armstrong estate is perfectly safe and outside the reaches of it. Arabella will be in no danger there.'

'Oh, very well,' George sighed again.

'You are the most marvellous man!' Caroline leaned forward and kissed him.

'Better than being stuck with a lovelorn sulky daughter for the whole trip!'

Margaret was opening her letters at breakfast in the dining room at Armstrong House.

'A letter from Caroline Tattinger,' she said as she read it quickly. 'She asks if Arabella could stay with us for Christmas while they are in New York.'

'How lovely!' said Gwyneth.

'Seemingly Arabella suffers from severe sea sickness and can't face the journey across the

96

'Atlantic.' Margaret put the letter back in the envelope.

'As Gwyneth said, it will be lovely to have her,' said Lawrence.

'Harrison will certainly be delighted,' said Margaret. 'You'd swear she was never coming back the way he's been so desolate in his letters at the thought of her going!'

'Is there anything as enchanting as young love?' smiled Charles. He sat back, thinking. His plan was working. He just had to be very careful now not to do anything to upset it.

Arabella was amazed when her parents consented to her going to Armstrong House. Amazed, delighted and then terrified. She had never thought they would have allowed it, and so the decision would have been taken out of her hands. She wouldn't have to see Charles again or confront what he had stirred in her. Now she was terrified of what seeing him again would provoke in her.

She was being silly, she then reasoned. This was for the best. She would see Charles again and quickly realise she had let her mind run away with her these past weeks. She would see him and know that she had built him up into something he wasn't, and built her feelings up into something they weren't at all. She was going to Armstrong House to confront her real feelings for Charles and discover they amounted to nothing. Then she would put the whole sorry experience behind her, and get on with life with Harrison.

The Tattingers set off to catch the steamship in Cork and a spinster aunt had been dispatched to the Tattinger home to mind Arabella until she was to go to Armstrong House on Christmas Eve.

Arabella was counting the days.

CHAPTER 8

On Christmas Eve, Harrison collected her from Ailesbury Road in a cab and they continued to the train station. Snow was beginning to fall as they made their way through the Dublin streets. It had become heavy by the time they reached the station and walked through the bustling crowd to the first-class carriage where they had reservations.

'Everyone can't wait to see you again,' said Harrison excitedly. 'Mother is putting you in the Blue Room. That's the best guest room.'

'Very kind of her.'

Harrison prattled on about what to expect over Christmas at Armstrong House.

'Christmas is always such a special time there. There's always the hunt the day after Christmas. All the gentry come from far and wide...'

Arabella barely listened as she looked out the window at the countryside turning white under the snow.

By the time the train pulled into the station at Castlewest, the snow lay thick on the ground. As Arabella followed Harrison across the train platform, she was hoping Charles would be at the station to meet them. The Charles she had known in Dublin would have been eagerly waiting for them, full of compliments for her. As a servant came rushing to assist with the luggage, she realised Charles wasn't coming.

Their carriage drove the several miles to Armstrong House carefully through the snow. It entered the main gates to the estate and travelled along the lakeshore up the long winding driveway until Armstrong House, a vision in the snow, came into view across the lake.

The carriage pulled into the forecourt and Harrison assisted Arabella through the falling snow and up the steps to the front door where Barton was waiting.

'Merry Christmas, Barton,' said Harrison as he took off his snow-covered cloak and handed it over.

'Same to you, sir, and Miss Tattinger,' said Barton as two footmen carried in their luggage and took it upstairs to their rooms.

Arabella looked around and saw the hall had been decorated in holly, ivy and mistletoe, and a giant Christmas tree stood in a corner, lighted candles twinkling on the branches. There was a roaring fire in the fireplace, with turf smells filling the air.

'The family is in the drawing room, sir,' said Barton as he led them across the hallway and opened the door for them.

Arabella held her breath as she followed Harrison in.

'There you are!' said Margaret, coming to greet and hug them. 'Arabella, we're delighted to have you!'

'And thank you for having me,' said Arabella, looking around the room.

There was Lawrence at the fireplace, smiling warmly as Gwyneth followed her mother to embrace them. Daphne was waving at them and smiling as she put the final touches to another giant Christmas tree in the corner of that room. Emily was sitting and observing them coolly and making no move to greet them. James was pouring himself a large brandy.

But no Charles. Where was Charles?

'Awful for you to be separated from your family for Christmas. You suffer terrible sea sickness, they say?' said Margaret as she led her to the couch.

'I'm afraid so,' said Arabella as she sat down.

'I hope it's not hereditary?' Margaret was concerned.

'Mother fears you may pass it on to her grandchildren when you and Harrison have children!' said Emily. 'Any slight disadvantage would be much disapproved of.'

'Emily!' warned Margaret.

Arabella started laughing. 'No need to worry, Lady Margaret. The rest of my family do not appear to share my dislike of sea travel.'

'Oh, good!' smiled Margaret. 'I often find people who suffer sea sickness can have a poor constitution. But come, my dear, I shall personally escort you to your room. You will need to rest and change before we have dinner.'

Arabella looked around the resplendent Blue Room which was at the front of the house and offered breathtaking views down the terraced gardens and across the lake.

There was a soirée that night and neighbouring gentry families would be attending, if the snow permitted. She had spent days choosing what outfits to bring with her. Now she changed into a deep red gown which was low-cut and exposed her shoulders and arms. As she looked at herself in the mirror, she knew it wasn't a dress to impress a future mother-in-law with Lady Margaret's tastes. But it was a dress that would grab a man like Charles' attention.

As she heard the merriment and laughter on the other side of the drawing-room door, she thought Charles must be there by now.

She walked in. As she made her way through the smiling guests, her dress attracted admiring and surprised smiles.

'Ah there you are, my dear,' said Margaret as she came over to her. 'And what a – remarkable dress.'

Gwyneth was full of admiration. 'I think it's splendid! I'm going to get one just like it.'

'Not until after the wedding to the Duke,' advised Margaret, looking at Arabella's bare shoulders. 'We don't want you catching cold.'

'It's from Paris,' said Arabella.

'Yes,' said Margaret. 'The French are always so *forward* with their fashion.' She then took Arabella by the arm and led her around. 'Mr and Mrs Foxe, this is Miss Arabella Tattinger, Harrison's fiancée. Mr and Mrs Foxe are from the neighbouring estate, Arabella.'

Arabella's eyes searched the crowd as she was

introduced to everyone. But there was still no sign of Charles.

The snow was still pelting heavily against the windows as Margaret ordered Barton to close the curtains in the drawing room. As the wine and sherry continued to be served, the party was becoming merrier. Christmas songs were being played on the piano and the conversation was loud and jolly around the room. Arabella looked at the clock on the wall and saw it was nearly ten o'clock.

'The last few months have been so busy,' Gwyneth confided in Arabella. 'Organising the wedding, you know.'

'I can imagine,' said Arabella.

'Myself and Mother returned from London last week where I did the final fittings for the wedding dress.'

'Spectacular, I'm sure.'

'The wedding will be here at Armstrong House, of course.'

As Gwyneth discussed the minutiae of her pending nuptials, Arabella began to realise there was a very good chance Charles was away for Christmas. Nobody had said he would be there, and she hadn't asked, only assumed.

'I was in a dilemma because the church in the village is small, and the Duke has such a wide circle who will need to make the journey here. We debated about being married at Battington Hall and having the service nearby at Salisbury Cathedral. But Mother said a bride must be wed at her family home, otherwise it looks as if she has something to hide.'

'Sound advice.'

'What arrangements have you decided on for your own wedding?'

'Where is Charles?' Arabella suddenly blurted out.

'Charles?' Gwyneth looked around the room, unaware he wasn't present. 'He set off this morning and hasn't been seen since. I hope he's not stranded somewhere with the snow.'

Arabella felt relief. At least he would be there for Christmas.

At that moment the door opened and in walked Charles, looking calm and cool.

'Charles! What kept you?' demanded Lawrence.

'Detained on estate business, Father,' explained Charles, as he joined the men at the fireplace and took a glass of brandy from Barton. 'The snow is settling in. I hope it won't affect the hunt.'

Just then Harrison appeared.

'Oh, hello, Harrison!' said Charles. 'Happy Christmas!'

'You too!' Harrison grabbed him and pulled him across the room. 'And look who is down with me!'

Arabella steadied herself as she saw Harrison lead Charles over to her.

'Look, Arabella, it's Charles!' announced Harrison.

'So I can see – Merry Christmas, Charles.' She nodded and smiled at him.

'Yes – indeed,' Charles said.

Arabella smiled at him. And she realised her worst fears were true. She had not imagined the feelings he stirred in her.

'If you'll excuse me, I have to see to my guests,' said Charles and he turned and walked away.

'*His* guests!' Gwyneth laughed. 'I thought they were Mama and Papa's guests!'

'Well, as their heir, I suppose he has a duty to them as well,' said Harrison.

'He certainly seems to be settling into his role here. I never thought he would,' said Gwyneth.

'Oh, I think Charles could settle into any role he wanted to, if he put his mind to it,' said Arabella as she watched him mingle and charm a circle of women.

It was after midnight before everyone drifted off home.

Arabella had noticed Charles had slipped off to bed without saying goodnight.

'Well, I think everyone should be making their way to sleep shortly,' advised Margaret. 'We don't need sleepy heads on Christmas morning.'

'Thank you for everything,' said Arabella.

'Goodnight, my dear.' Margaret kissed Arabella on the cheek before kissing Gwyneth and Harrison.

'Happy Christmas, my dears,' said Lawrence as he linked Margaret's arm to lead her from the room.

At the door Margaret turned. 'Straight to bed everyone, yes?'

'Yes Mother!' said Harrison and Gwyneth together.

'She's making sure we're not left alone!' laughed Harrison to Arabella.

'I hope she's not suggesting any impropriety

would take place?' Arabella was affronted.

'No. She's just taking being your guardian for the week quite seriously,' said Gwyneth as they left the room and walked across the darkened hall and up the stairs. The house was quiet, only the odd crackle from the fireplace in the hall disturbing the silence.

Upstairs, Gwyneth walked along in front of them down a corridor to her room.

'I can't tell you how happy I am you are here,' said Harrison as he paused at Arabella's door.

'Goodnight, Arabella!' called Gwyneth down the hall as she opened her door.

'Goodnight,' said Arabella as she opened her own.

Harrison looked at her and hesitated before reaching forward and kissing her very quickly and lightly on the lips. Then he hurried down to his room.

Margaret was putting on her face cream at her dressing table as Lawrence got into bed.

'I have to say that dress Arabella was wearing was quite risqué,' she said. 'And I do find it odd that her parents didn't insist she go to New York, sea sickness or no sea sickness. I wouldn't let Gwyneth go to Battington Hall before she was married unless I accompanied her.'

'Well, the Tattingers are a little less formal than us, I suspect.'

'Well, she will have to get used to our ways when she marries Harrison.'

Arabella looked at the dress which was now back

hanging in the wardrobe. It had failed to capture any of Charles' attention. She closed the wardrobe door and got into bed where she lay studying the flames from the fire flickering against the wooden panels of the wall.

CHAPTER 9

Margaret was quite relieved when Arabella came into the drawing room the next morning dressed in a traditionally elegant dress. As Arabella observed the Armstrong family excitedly open their beautifully wrapped presents from under the tree, she knew they were a tightly knit family with much love between them. Only Charles, regardless of being sociable and charming with them, seemed set apart from them. Even Emily with her stubborn streak and James with his wild nature looked very much part of the family.

'This is for you,' said Harrison as he handed Arabella a beautifully wrapped box. Arabella unwrapped the paper and, opening the box, saw a brooch sitting on a velvet base. She smiled her gratitude to him, but he seemed more excited about the brooch than she was. She gave him her present of cufflinks and he was delighted with them.

They all travelled through the snow to church in the nearby village in a series of carriages. Charles continued to ignore her.

In the afternoon in the dining room, when a

Christmas feast of turkey and goose was being served, Charles chose to sit at the far end of the table from her.

'Is the snow going to affect the hunt tomorrow?' asked Harrison, concerned.

'It will take place as normal,' said Lawrence.

'I'm looking forward to it,' said Arabella.

'You're going on the hunt?' Margaret was surprised.

'Oh yes, when I visit my cousin's estate in Kildare, I always go on the hunt,' said Arabella.

'Did you bring your riding costume?' asked Charles.

Arabella was surprised. It was the first time he had addressed her since she had arrived, apart from their initial greeting. She looked down at him and his eyes were cool and slightly mocking. 'Yes, I came prepared.'

After dinner the family went for their traditional walk down through the terraced gardens until they reached the lakeshore and then they walked along it.

Arabella purposely left Harrison behind talking to Daphne as she caught up with Charles and tried to engage him in conversation.

'Although I've attended hunts before, I'm not very good. I usually get left behind and have to make my own way back!' she said and laughed lightly.

'I'm sure you'll do just fine,' he said and walked on quickly to join Emily, leaving Arabella behind.

By that night Arabella was fit to explode. She couldn't bear Charles' indifference to her and his subtle rudeness. Whatever these feelings he had created in her, she couldn't let the situation continue. She needed to apologise and return their relationship to something somewhat civil, for Harrison's sake if nothing else.

On Christmas night, the family was in the drawing room playing parlour games. Arabella kept an eye on Charles throughout, waiting for an opportunity. She got it when she saw him get up, whisper something to his father, and leave the room. She waited a minute and then sneaked out.

She looked down the hall and up the stairs and saw no sign of him. She walked across the hall to the small parlour and opened the door to see him standing by the fireplace lighting a cigarette. She took a deep breath, walked in and closed the door behind her.

'Oh, this is where you are hiding, is it?' she smiled as she walked into the room towards him.

'Not hiding, just trying to escape being dragged into any more games,' he said.

'I just wanted to check how you are,' she said. 'We've hardly spoken two words since I arrived.'

'I'm very well, thank you.'

She felt terribly awkward. 'Charles, I really wanted to apologise about the last time we met.'

'Whatever for?'

'I said some things that were – unkind – and I had no right to say them.'

'You had every right to express how you felt, and you did.'

'But...'

'But what?'

'So it is as I thought then? You have stopped coming to Dublin because of what I said.'

'I'm not in the habit of staying in a place where I'm not wanted, or keeping the company of people who do not like or – *trust* – me. Those were the words you used, I remember.'

'And, as you said, the house in Merrion Square is yours and Dublin is a free city. I have no right to make you feel you can't go there. I'm sorry, Charles.'

He looked at her for a long time. 'You have no idea, do you?'

'Idea about what?'

'It's not Merrion Square or Dublin I wanted to visit.'

'Well, then – Harrison! I have no right keeping you from seeking your brother's company. He loves you very much and–'

'*It's you!*' His voice rose before returning to a whisper. 'It's *you* I wanted to see. *Your* company I was seeking. *You* I needed to see all the time.'

'I don't...' Arabella was trying to absorb the enormity of the words he was saying.

'Arabella...' He moved towards her.

Her hand suddenly rose into the air and she slapped him hard across the face, before turning and running from the room.

She quickly crossed the hall to the drawing-room door and waited for a while. She forced herself to become calm and steadied herself before opening the door and walking in. They were still playing games and playing music. She walked calmly across the room and sat beside Harrison on the couch.

'Are you all right? You look flushed?' he said, concerned.

'I'm fine, perfectly fine,' she said, smiling, as Charles walked casually into the room and went and stood by the fireplace. She could see the red mark on his face from her slap and hoped no one else would notice it. As he looked at her, she had to turn away as she felt her heart thump and her face redden.

CHAPTER 10

The Armstrong Hunt was one of the most renowned in the country and an invitation to it was like gold dust. As Arabella changed into her riding clothes the next morning, the hunt had already gathered in the forecourt. She'd had her breakfast delivered to her room, sure she couldn't sit at the same table as Charles. She fastened the buttons of her short black tunic over her white blouse and the long black skirt and put on her black top hat.

She had found it very hard to sleep the previous night as she relived the scene in the parlour with Charles, his words dancing through her mind over and over again. The words that disgusted and excited her.

She left her room and went downstairs and out to the forecourt. The forecourt was filled with riders on their horses, while the pack of hounds excitedly scurried around.

'Tom, bring Miss Tattinger's horse over,' commanded Lawrence when he saw her and he rode over to her.

The groom assisted Arabella up onto the horse.

'I'll probably slow you down!' warned Arabella, as she spotted Charles talking merrily to a few men.

'Nonsense, you're a fine horsewoman,' said Harrison, mounting his own horse.

Gwyneth and Daphne came over on their horses.

'Emily refuses to come,' said Gwyneth. 'As usual.'

There was much mingling and then suddenly the horses started trotting out of the forecourt and down the driveway.

'We'll head over to Knockmora, and then on to the meadows,' called Lawrence who was leading the hunt, and the horses started trotting off at a faster rate.

As the hunt gathered pace, Arabella tried not to look at Charles, but every time she looked at him she found him already looking at her. They all trotted through the countryside until the horn blew strong.

'We're off!' shouted Harrison as the hounds made a dash across the fields after a fox in the distance. The horses quickly took off after them.

Arabella found herself falling behind. Charles looked back and nodded to her and suddenly she saw him break away from the group and ride towards a wood. Nobody else seemed to have spotted him as they concentrated on the fox. Arabella saw him pause at the wood and look at her before his horse disappeared in amongst the trees. She was falling even further behind as she paused to decide what to do next. She pulled on

111

the reins and directed the horse towards the wood.

The wood was large and expansive, snow draped across the branches of the trees. She followed a pathway and continued further and further until she came to a small clearing and saw Charles standing there holding the reins of his horse, waiting for her.

'I wasn't sure you'd come,' he said as she approached him.

'I wasn't sure either,' she said.

He came to help her dismount and as he caught her by the waist she felt a thrill at his touch.

Standing, she gazed up at him. 'What you said last night...'

'I meant every word.'

'But it's impossible! What you said is impossible, in every sense.'

'Why?'

'You know why! Harrison. If the truth be told, I guessed you had feelings for me, but I wasn't sure how deep. I thought you were playing games with me.'

'Never!'

'And I was frightened of my own feelings for you... But the truth is – since you stopped coming to Dublin, there's been a huge gap in my life, in me. I didn't understand it at first. I thought it would go away. But no matter what I did, the gap got bigger. And nothing could fill it, not parties, or my family, or a trip to New York, or even Harrison ... especially Harrison!'

His eyes began to sparkle as he heard the words. 'So what are we going to do?'

'What can we do? Nothing. We have to fight these feelings and get on with our lives. It can go nowhere, for obvious reasons.'

'Why then – why did you come to Armstrong House for Christmas if you wanted to ignore what was going on between us?'

'I – I – don't know... I have to go. Harrison will be wondering where I've got to. Come and help me mount.'

He came quickly behind her, turned her around and began to kiss her forcibly.

She escaped him for a second, and then she grabbed the back of his head and started to kiss him back.

'*Arabella! Arabella!*' they heard faintly in the distance. Arabella quickly pushed Charles away. 'It's Harrison!' she said and turned to mount.

'When will I see you again?' he asked urgently as he helped her.

'At dinner tonight, I expect.' She turned the horse around.

'You *know* what I mean!' he insisted.

She tapped her whip against the horse's flank and it took off through the wood.

As she emerged from the wood she saw Harrison surveying the rolling countryside, luckily with his back to her. She trotted in his direction.

He turned as he heard her approach. 'I've been looking everywhere for you!' he called.

'I'm so sorry, Harrison. I got left behind and was totally lost.'

'Come on, let's join the others. They lost the fox – they're gathered on the top of the hill.'

Back at the edge of the wood, Charles smiled to

himself as he watched them ride off. His plan had worked spectacularly.

After the hunt everyone came back to Armstrong House for food and drinks.

Arabella sat shivering in the drawing room even though the fires were blazing as Gwyneth wittered on about the Duke and her wedding. Arabella wasn't listening to a word as she sat bewildered about what had happened with Charles in the wood.

Harrison came over to her. 'You're very quiet this evening, are you all right?'

'I'm fine.'

'Do you want me to get you anything?'

'No.'

'You're shivering!' he said, putting an arm around her.

'I'm just a little cold.'

'I'll fetch you a shawl.'

'No need.'

'Every need.'

'For goodness sake, Harrison, *stop fussing!*' she snapped. 'You're worse than your mother!'

Harrison's face clouded with hurt.

'I'm sorry, Harrison. I just don't feel very well... I think I'll go to bed early.' She got up and left the room.

Margaret saw Harrison looking concerned and walked over to him, asking, 'Where is Arabella going?'

'To bed. I think she must have caught a cold out on the hunt.'

'More likely from the dress she was wearing the

114

other evening!' mused Margaret.

Arabella dimmed the lights in her room and tried to block out the noise coming from the party downstairs. As midnight came and went the laughter and chatter petered out.

She looked out her window and saw the last of the carriages and horses of the guests leave as the snow started to fall again. The house fell into silence as everyone went to bed. She paced up and down as the fire in the hearth kept the room in a warm glow. She would cut short her stay at Armstrong House and return to Dublin first thing in the morning. She had treaded into very dangerous territory and she had lost control.

There was a quiet knock on her door. Startled, she ignored it. The knock came again. She walked across the room and opened the door.

Charles was standing there.

'Charles! Are you mad, somebody will see!' she hissed, glancing up and down the corridor. He quickly entered the room and closed the door behind him.

'Charles, if anyone should discover you here, I'd be ruined!'

'I can't leave, not without knowing what is to become of us.'

She started pacing up and down again. 'Nothing will happen, because nothing can happen. I'm to marry your brother next year. We have no right. I blame myself as much as you – more so, in fact – I should have kept away.'

'And how would you have filled that gap in your life you were telling me about?'

115

'I would just ignore it.'

'Until it became bigger and bigger and would end by swallowing you up.'

'It is, as I said, impossible. If I had met you first, maybe we might have had a future. I wish I had met you first – *I wish I had never met you at all!*'

She stopped pacing and stood looking into the fire, rubbing her hands against her temples.

He walked slowly to her and carefully put his arms around her.

'Go. Charles, please just go! We can never be together.'

He turned back and locked the door. Then he led her over to the bed, kissing her, and whispered: 'This might be the only way we can be together.'

Charles heard the clock down in the hallway chime six times. He was lying on his back in Arabella's bed, her hand lying across his chest as he held her close. The fire was dying in the fireplace as the snow outside continued to fall against the window.

'I'd better go – the servants will be up soon,' he said.

'Do you feel ashamed and guilty?' she asked as she concentrated on the dying embers in the fireplace.

'No – why should I?'

'Because Harrison is fast asleep a few rooms down from here.'

'What do you want me to say? That I do feel guilty? Then that makes me a bastard. And if I

116

say I don't? Then that makes me a bastard as well!'

'And I wonder what it all makes me?'

He kissed her forehead.

'I'm trying hard to feel guilty and ashamed myself,' she said.

He pushed her away and got of bed and started to dress.

'Promise me one thing, Charles?' she said, sitting up frantically. 'Promise me Harrison will never find out.'

'Of course he can never find out!' He bent over and kissed her and then left.

Arabella didn't know what the night had made her. All she knew was she had smashed every rule in the rule book. Torn it up and thrown it into the fire. She wasn't sure how it all had happened. Yet as she dressed to go down to breakfast, she felt happier than she had in a long time.

Harrison was full of concern in the dining room. 'How do you feel this morning?'

'Oh, much better, thank you,' she said, smiling at everyone at the table.

'You probably just needed a good night,' smirked Charles from across the table, and he continued to read his newspaper.

Later, in the drawing room, Arabella was standing at the window looking out at the newly fallen layer of snow.

'They've all gone skating down on the lake – a good part of it is frozen over,' said Charles as he came up behind her and stood at her side.

'So I believe.'

'I need to see you tonight,' he whispered.

She paused for a few moments and then said, 'Yes.'

'You'll have to come to me.'

'*What?*'

'Your room is too risky. It's too near the stairs – there are too many people up and down. My room is at the end of the corridor, much safer... Well?'

'All right,' she said.

That night Arabella waited until half twelve before she slipped out of her room. She looked up and down the corridor and, seeing it was empty, with her heart pounding she hurried down the corridor and knocked gently on Charles' door. There was no answer and she knocked again louder.

'Charles!' she whispered through the door.

Eventually the door opened, and she rushed in.

'What took you so long? I could have been spotted!' she said, shivering with nerves at the thought of being caught.

'Sorry, I must have dozed off.'

They stood there looking at each other, and then she rushed to him.

The days passed over the Christmas period at Armstrong House with a series of lunches, dinners, walks along the lake, or horse riding. But the nights were all that Arabella could think of as she waited for them to arrive. By the end of the week, Arabella realised her infatuation with Charles had almost become a fever with her. As she observed the Armstrongs she realised what a happy family they were in their privileged world. She realised what she was doing with Charles could blow this happy family to smithereens, and yet she continued with the secret glances and snatched clandestine conversations with Charles during the day. And continued to make the journey down to his room each night when she was content the house was silent and everyone had gone to their rooms. It was only for the week, she told herself. A quick affair that would burn itself out and she would go back to life as normal with Harrison. And yet her feelings were so strong she already knew this could never happen. She had crossed barriers she never thought possible for her.

It was the night before New Year's Eve. He stroked her hair as she lay in bed and they heard the clock downstairs chime six times, the sound she had come to dread as she knew it indicated the time she had to leave him.

Emily was in her room, tossing and turning. She had been unable to get to sleep that night. She wondered if the cook was up yet and whether she could make her some warm milk to lull her to sleep for a few hours at least.

I suppose I could always try making it myself – it can't be that difficult, she said to herself as she got out of bed and put on her dressing gown. She opened her door and walked down the corridor. She loved Armstrong House at this time in the early morning. There was so much activity during the day with people coming and going, and now there was just silence.

She was surprised to hear a door open and turned to see who else was up.

To her astonishment she saw Arabella come out of Charles' room, in her dressing gown. She watched in shock as Arabella closed the door after her and began to hurry down the corridor.

Arabella stopped and stood rigid as she saw Emily standing there glaring at her.

The two stared at each other, both standing stock-still and silent.

Arabella was the first to move. She quickly continued to walk down the corridor, past Emily who she didn't acknowledge, to her room which she entered, closing the door firmly behind her.

Emily continued to stand stock-still in shock and she tried to comprehend what she had witnessed.

It was ten the next morning and Arabella was sitting on her bed, her face in her hands. She knew they were all having breakfast downstairs, no doubt wondering where she was, but she couldn't face going down and seeing Emily. She felt pure panic at the thought.

There was a knock on her door. 'Arabella!' Harrison called. 'Aren't you coming down for breakfast?'

'Just coming!' She tried to sound happy as she stood up and went to the door.

Harrison was waiting for her.

'I said to let you have a lie-in, but Mother said you needed to eat breakfast to set you up for the day,' explained Harrison as they walked along the corridor to the top of the stairs.

'What, to play more card games and discuss Gwyneth's wedding plans again?' she asked.

Harrison was embarrassed. 'I didn't realise we bored you!'

As they reached the hall at the bottom of the stairs she stopped and looked at him. 'I'm sorry, Harrison, that was ungrateful of me. I've enjoyed the week immensely.'

He nodded and led her into the dining room where the rest of the family were finishing their breakfast.

'Good morning!' said Margaret.

'I'm sorry I'm late,' said Arabella.

Arabella looked down the table. Emily was sitting at the end of the table, her face pale, staring at the food in front of her.

'Emily! Sit up and eat up!' ordered Margaret.

Emily straightened her shoulders and, picking up her fork, started to play with her food. Then she suddenly pushed her chair back and rushed from the room. 'Emily!' called her mother but she was gone. 'That girl!' she sighed. 'I despair of ever teaching her any manners!'

Arabella's heart sank at Emily's lack of control – she felt it was only a matter of time before she exposed her.

After breakfast she approached Charles in the hall.

'I need to speak to you urgently!' she whispered.

'What about?'

'Where can I meet you that we can talk in private?'

'Go for a walk into the gardens of the first terrace. I'll meet you by the fountain at two.'

Arabella found it hard to escape Harrison's constant attention for the day. She pretended she needed to have a lie-down in the afternoon, but instead quickly put on her coat, hat and gloves and headed for the rendezvous point with Charles. She walked along to the extensive gardens that led from the first terrace to the maze of footpaths and shrubberies until she found the fountain, which was frozen over and still covered in snow. She waited impatiently for him, walking round and round the fountain until he arrived.

'What's wrong?' he asked, seeing her panic-stricken face.

'Emily! She saw me coming out of your room this morning!'

'Are you sure?'

'Of course I'm sure! She stood there staring at me as if she had seen a ghost!'

Charles spotted a gardener tending to some snow-covered plants.

'Let's walk,' he suggested and they set off, walking through the pathways of the gardens.

'What are we going to do, Charles?' Arabella pleaded. 'If she tells anybody, I'll be ruined, and Harrison will be destroyed and your whole family will be–'

'She said nothing?' he interrupted.

'Not a word. She just stared at me in silence.'

'At least it wasn't Gwyneth or Daphne who saw you.'

'But what will Emily *do?*'

'I'll go and talk to her.'

'Charles, we've been playing with fire and now we're going to burn!' said Arabella and turning she put her hand on his chest.

'Arabella, the gardener!' Charles nodded over at the man who was wheeling a wheelbarrow nearby. Arabella quickly removed her hand and they continued walking.

Charles hovered outside Emily's door before knocking. There was no answer and so he knocked again.

'Emily – it's Charles,' he said through the door.

He waited and a moment later heard the door being unlocked. It opened slightly. He pushed it back and stepped inside.

Emily was standing at an easel, painting.

'What are you painting?' he asked.

'Why don't you see for yourself?' suggested Emily who didn't look at him once as she continued her work.

Charles walked over and saw she was painting a portrait of him.

'I didn't realise you were painting me,' he said, surprised.

'I've been working on it for a couple of months.'

'It's very good – if a little flattering!'

He walked around the room and picked up a book written by Karl Marx.

'Marx!' he exclaimed. 'I didn't realise you were a communist.'

'I find his thoughts interesting.'

He put the book down. 'Emily ... what you saw

this morning…'

'Arabella coming out of your room in her dressing gown?'

'Eh – yes – it's not what it may seem–'

'I know exactly what it seems and what it is.' She stopped painting and put down her paint brush. 'You've been seducing her behind Harrison's back!'

'You don't understand–'

'Don't I? Because it all looks very clear to me.' She walked over to him. 'Harrison is engaged to her, Charles. How could you?'

'Do you think I planned any of this?'

'How long has it been going on?'

'Only this week. Just this week, I swear.'

'Harrison has to know what kind of a woman he's mixed up with.'

Charles became panicked. 'Emily, you must never tell anybody what you saw, do you understand me? There's too much at stake. Nobody can ever find out, do you hear me?'

'But–'

He turned from her, walked to the window and looked out. 'I thought you and I were always the closest. I thought we understood each other.'

'Yes – but this is different!'

'So were you lying to me that day when we went out riding?' He turned and looked at her, his face full of hurt. 'Remember? When you said I could always rely on you. And you thought I was seeing a married woman and said you would cover for me, help me, act as a go-between even.'

'But that was before I realised the wronged man was Harrison!'

'So you're choosing him over me?'

'No – but–'

He picked up the Marx book. 'And everything you pretend you are – unconventional, rebellious – that's just all an act, is it?'

'But you must see!'

'I see I'm in love with Arabella and she is in love with me.'

Emily sat down on the bed. 'Oh Charles! Of all the women to fall in love with!'

'We couldn't help it. And now she is returning to Dublin in a couple of days and I might never see her again, only at family occasions when she's married to Harrison.'

He sat down on the bed and put his face in his hands, then reached up and grabbed her hand.

'Oh Charles!' Emily put her arms around him and held him tightly.

'I know she's Harrison's,' he said. 'I know they can never break up, because it would destroy him. All I'm asking for is some time with her – is that too much to ask?'

'I suppose not...'

'And what Harrison never knows won't hurt him.'

'But it's so dangerous!'

'I can't keep away from her, Emily. Not yet.' Charles started sobbing.

'All right – you know you can rely on me. I will cover for you. I'll say nothing. And when she returns to Dublin, she can write to me to plan your assignations.'

'Emily! I can't ask that you do that!'

'I insist. As you said, there's no point in me

pretending to be something if I don't follow it through. You and Arabella are in love, and I will help you. I told you before I would help and now I will – even if it is with Harrison's fiancée.'

'Thanks, Emily,' he said, wiping away a tear.

There was a knock on Arabella's door that night. She put on her dressing gown and went to open it.

'Charles!' she said as he quickly entered and closed the door behind him.

'Did you speak to Emily? What did she say?' she asked frantically.

'It's fine. Calm down,' he said, putting his hands on her shoulders.

'Is she going to tell Harrison?'

'No, we're safe. She has no intention of telling Harrison or anybody else.'

Arabella's body visibly relaxed. 'How can you be sure?'

'Because I know my sister. She understands what we're going through, she's quite sympathetic.'

'Is she?' Arabella was puzzled.

'I explained to her we are in love and in an impossible situation.'

His words surprised and delighted her. She was hugely relieved that he felt the same as she did.

She sat down on the bed. 'I couldn't have coped if he found out... So I suppose this is it ... we return to Dublin tomorrow.'

'It doesn't have to be the end.'

'It has to be. What we had was very special and now must end. We must go back to our normal lives.'

'We don't have to. Emily has agreed to cover for us. We can arrange to meet through her.'

'No, I couldn't continue with this, Charles. I couldn't continue to deceive Harrison. I've been in a state of terror all day fearing exposure.'

He sat beside her and smiled. 'And isn't that half the fun? The risk involved? The secrecy of it all. And now with Emily's help we can continue.'

'No!' she snapped and got up and looked out the window.

'Then I'll go. And we won't make contact. Is that what you want?' he asked, moving towards the door. He had his hand on the door handle and was opening it when she turned around.

'I don't want you to go – stay.'

The footmen were bringing Harrison and Arabella's luggage out to the waiting carriage as the family stood on the steps to say goodbye.

'You're in plenty of time for the train in Castlewest. It always runs late anyway,' said Lawrence.

'Thank you for everything,' said Arabella as she kissed Lawrence and Margaret goodbye.

Daphne and Jack were next to be kissed then she found herself in front of Charles.

'Goodbye, Charles,' she said as she kissed him quickly on the cheek and moved on to Gwyneth.

'Don't forget my wedding is in March. Put it in your diary,' said Gwyneth.

'I will.' Arabella moved on to Emily, feeling herself blush. 'Goodbye, Emily.'

'I wish you a safe journey back to Dublin.' Emily fixed her with a knowing look. 'We'll write to each other.'

Arabella nodded and quickly walked out the front door with Harrison.

'Write to each other?' asked Margaret. 'I didn't think you spoke two words to each other when Arabella was here.'

CHAPTER 11

Suddenly Emily found her life had a new sense of purpose. Excitement and danger had entered it in the most unexpected way. She was now so much more than just a troublesome youngest daughter. She had a secret. A scandalous, terrible, wonderful secret that would shock everyone if they knew. And she was being entrusted with it. She had always worshipped Charles, always sought his attention, longed for his approval. And now he needed her desperately.

She found him looking at her through new eyes. He respected her now. Together they plotted and planned their next move with Arabella.

'Why don't I write to her and tell her you're coming to Dublin this weekend?' suggested Emily as they rode side by side through the estate.

'The trouble is, in Dublin at weekends she's with Harrison all the time. We won't have any time together. And then she has to stay at her parents' at night obviously.'

'Hmmm...' Emily thought hard. 'The reality is Armstrong House is the best destination for a rendezvous. You are both staying under the same roof, so there are more opportunities.'

'Well, she and Harrison are not going to make the trip down here every weekend. I don't think her parents will permit it now they are back from New York. Besides, it might be suspicious.'

'Yes, you're right. I'll write to her and tell her you'll be in Dublin this weekend.'

Arabella was in a state of shock when she arrived back home. Shocked with herself. She had broken every convention and rule. She'd had intercourse before marriage. She'd had intercourse with a man she was not even betrothed to. And he was the brother of her fiancé. Her betrayal of herself, her family and most of all Harrison overwhelmed her.

Her family arrived back from New York in joyous spirits and laden down with presents for her. She found it hard to even look them in the eye.

And yet Arabella found herself anxiously awaiting the post each morning for something from Emily.

When one morning she saw a letter addressed to her in writing she didn't recognise, she knew it was from Emily. She grabbed the letter and raced to her bedroom and locked the door. She tore open the envelope and began to read the letter.

Armstrong House
12th January 1889

Dear Arabella,
It was so lovely to have you here at Christmas. I really hope you enjoyed your stay as much as we did. The hunt season is in full swing now. The Seymours'

hunt was at the weekend...

Arabella read the letter quickly and saw it was full of idle chat about happenings at Armstrong House and then she read: *What news is there from Dublin? Charles says he misses Dublin considerably. In fact he is due to travel to Dublin this weekend...*
Arabella threw down the letter. She was over-joyed at the thought of seeing him again. But did he expect things to be like they had been? Did he think he could just accompany her and Harrison to the theatre and restaurants and carry on as if nothing had happened, waiting for snatched moments when they could be alone together? Charles might be that good an actor, but she wasn't.
She quickly went to her writing bureau and started writing. As Emily had done she filled the letter up with non-consequential items and then she wrote: *It's so nice Charles is coming to Dublin this weekend. Unfortunately I have a packed itiner-ary with Harrison, so we won't be able to meet him. I'll be exhausted by the end of it! I plan to have a nice relaxing day on my own on Monday. I'm going to The Shelbourne Hotel for afternoon tea at two o'clock.*

Emily showed Charles the letter when she re-ceived it.
'You're to meet her in The Shelbourne at two on Monday,' she informed him.
'The Shelbourne for afternoon tea!' said Charles dismissively.
'These are her terms obviously. She doesn't want to or can't see you over the weekend.'

'Write back to her and say The Shelbourne on a Monday sounds like a superb way to pass the time.'

Arabella requested a corner table in The Shelbourne and sat nervously as the waitress poured tea from the silver teapot into a china cup and cut her a slice of the Victoria sponge that sat on a cake-stand on the table. Looking at the other tables filled with elegant people chatting, she wondered what they would all think of her if they knew the reason for her being there.

She saw Charles enter the tearoom. He surveyed the room and, seeing her, came over.

'Arabella, what a pleasant surprise! Fancy meeting you here! Do you mind if I join you?'

'Please do,' nodded Arabella and he sat on the seat opposite her. She poured him tea.

'So how are you?' he asked in a lower voice.

'As good as can be expected.'

'I could have come for the whole weekend.'

'I wrote to Emily that you were not to.'

'I know. Why not?'

She looked at him incredulously 'Why not? Why do you think, you fool! I can't gad around town with you and Harrison like we used to. I'm consumed with guilt as it is! Every time I look at him, I am so ashamed. Don't you feel guilty?'

'No. I don't. The only thing I care about is seeing you.'

She shook her head in despair. 'So you want this – affair – to continue?'

'Of course I do!' He reached over and took her hand.

She quickly pulled it back and looked around to make sure nobody had spotted the action.

He sat back. 'I've booked a room upstairs. You can follow me there. Room 132.'

'You expect me to go to a hotel room with you, like some – some common streetwalker!'

'No. A streetwalker would be on the street, and not in a luxurious boudoir.'

She shook her head at him. 'How can you be so flippant?'

'Because that's who I am.'

They sat in silence.

'I'm expected home for dinner at six,' she said then.

'That's fine. I have to catch the seven o'clock train back to Castlewest.'

She sat there in disarray, her heart thumping, while he gazed at her assessingly.

At last he spoke. 'It's a choice between an afternoon of champagne, strawberries and the man who loves you, or...' he glanced down at the cake sitting on the table, '...an afternoon of Victoria sponge on your own.'

He stood up and walked out of the tearoom.

Arabella waited ten minutes, then paid the bill, and left the tearoom. She slowly walked through the hotel foyer and reception. She walked up the stairs expecting somebody to stop her and ask her to leave. Hoping somebody would. But they didn't. She got to Room 132, hesitated, and then knocked quietly on the door.

CHAPTER 12

Emily came into Charles' room holding a letter.

'What news from Arabella?' asked Charles.

'She says that she and her parents are going to the races in Kildare next weekend, and that Harrison won't be with them.'

'What an opportunity!'

'She writes they are staying at the Imperial Hotel.'

'Sounds like an invitation to me, Emily! Go choose your best frocks. We're off to the races!'

'We?' asked Emily, her eyes opening wide.

'Of course, you need a bit of excitement too. Besides, you'll be the perfect cover for us.'

'Mama will never allow it,' Emily cautioned, excitement overcoming her at the thought of escaping for a couple of days from Armstrong House.

'You just leave Mama to me.' He winked at her.

The race course was packed with people as Charles and Emily made their way through the crowd.

'Any sign of them?' he asked, peering through the people.

'There they are!' exclaimed Emily, pointing.

Caroline and George were walking through the throng, with Arabella, who was wearing a cream dress with a tightly fitted bodice and carrying a cream parasol.

'Charles!' exclaimed Caroline, seeing them.

'You distract the parents,' whispered Charles to Emily.

'We didn't know you were coming to the races,' said George.

'Last-minute decision. And look who's with me – dearest little Emily!' said Charles, as Emily stepped forward.

Caroline was delighted. 'Arabella, it's Emily. You've become such good friends, haven't you? There's often a letter waiting for Arabella from Armstrong House on the sideboard.'

'Hello, dear Arabella!' Emily said in an overly friendly sing-song voice.

'Hello,' said Arabella, trying to keep the nerves out of hers.

'Where are you staying?' asked George.

'At the Imperial,' said Charles.

'So are we!' said Caroline.

'Oh, what a lovely brooch, Lady Tattinger,' said Emily as she moved towards her to examine the piece of jewellery.

'Thank you! I got it in New York.'

'Tell me all about New York,' said Emily as she cornered George and Caroline.

Charles went and stood beside Arabella.

'What room are you staying in?' he asked in a whisper.

'Room 22.'

'I'll come to you tonight.'

'No! My mother will be in the next room!'

'Well – when then?' he asked impatiently.

'We are to go out to dinner at nine. I'll tell them

I have one of my headaches and won't go with them ... come to my room then.'

And the letters kept being sent, and the meetings kept on being arranged, and the weeks flew by. Emily's approaching birthday offered another opportunity.

Arabella was in the dining room having breakfast with her parents. Caroline was opening her post.

'Here's a letter from Emily,' said Caroline in surprise.

'Emily?' Arabella dropped her spoon.

'Emily Armstrong,' confirmed Caroline.

Arabella, thinking her mother had opened her letter by mistake, reached out to grab it.

'The letter is for me,' insisted Caroline, pulling it back from her daughter.

'What does she want?' asked Arabella, trying to conceal the fact that she was panic-stricken.

'It's her birthday next weekend and she's invited me, your father and you to her party. Isn't that nice of her? She says Harrison will be there and her mother invites us to stay at Armstrong House. I know Emily can come across as a bit surly, but she's a sweet girl, I believe.'

Arabella wondered what Charles was up to and dreaded the thought of going. Her snatched meetings with him were one thing. But to be in the same house as Harrison, her parents, his family? To brazenly face them all over breakfast, lunch and dinner and pretend nothing was happening between her and Charles? She had done it at the start of their affair, borne along by the euphoria of their newly awakened passion, but to return now and do the same thing deliberately and calculatedly was quite a different thing. Besides, she felt Charles was flaunting it in front of them, taking unnecessary risks and making an utter fool of Harrison.

'Well, we can't go,' stated Arabella.

'Whyever not? We've nothing pressing on. It would be rude to decline. They are practically family to you at this stage, Arabella.'

CHAPTER 13

Arabella tried to hide her concerns from her parents as they made the train journey down to Castlewest.

A carriage was waiting at the station to take them to Armstrong House where Margaret, Harrison and Emily were waiting for them when they arrived.

'What a lovely thought to invite us down for Emily's birthday!' said Caroline.

'Arabella!' said Emily happily as she embraced her and kissed her cheek. Arabella realised Emily was as good an actor as Charles as she awkwardly accepted Emily's over-the-top welcome.

Emily linked Arabella's arm and led her into the drawing room.

'It so nice that they have become such good friends,' said Caroline as the rest of them followed.

Charles was standing at the front window in the drawing room, gazing out across the lake as he smoked a cigarette.

'Charles, Arabella and her parents have arrived,' said Emily.

Charles casually turned around and smiled. 'Hello there!' he said, and came forward to greet them.

That evening the Armstrongs and Tattingers were served a sumptuous meal of roast suckling pig in the dining room. The families chatted away amicably and pleasantly like old friends, only Arabella, Charles and Emily knowing the reality of what was going on. Arabella found the whole experience excruciating, feeling like a fraud. There with their families, sitting next to Harrison and facing Charles across the table, their affair suddenly became real to her. And yet when she looked at Charles, when she could muster the strength to look at him, he seemed as relaxed as ever, with not a care in the world as he chatted away to everyone.

'Have you been to the theatre recently, Arabella?' asked Charles, looking at her directly.

Arabella tried to look back, but found she couldn't look him in the eye as she began to blush.

'No, not recently,' she said.

'Yes, we were, we were there last Saturday. We went to see *Hamlet*, remember?' corrected Harrison.

'Oh, yes, we went to see *Hamlet*,' she agreed.

She glanced at Charles, who was sitting back,

smirking at her.

Arabella was not staying in the Blue Room on this visit. She was put in a room that was right beside the house's master bedroom, Margaret and Lawrence's. Her parents were put in the bedroom on the other side of her.

Surely even Charles wouldn't dare come down to her with such an arrangement? And yet he was so unpredictable, so loving of danger, she feared he would come to her during the night, regardless of who was on the other side of the walls.

But he didn't.

'I was thinking we might go for a drive around the estate this afternoon,' suggested Emily to Arabella over breakfast.

'But I was going to take her into Castlewest today,' objected Harrison.

'Harrison! You have Arabella in Dublin all the time! She's down for my birthday, so I want to spend some time with her,' scolded Emily.

Harrison turned to Arabella and smiled. 'You know something? I thought I had you all to myself, but I think I have serious competition for you from my family!'

Arabella glanced at Charles and stood up quickly. 'I'd better go and choose what to wear on the ride later.'

That afternoon Emily was waiting for Arabella in a small phaeton carriage in front of the house when she emerged.

Arabella stepped up into the phaeton and as

138

soon as she had settled herself comfortably Emily slapped the reins on the horse's back and they took off rapidly down the driveway.

'I must admire your skill in driving this phaeton,' said Arabella. 'Even men find them quite tricky and dangerous.'

'I enjoy danger,' said Emily with a sideways glance. 'Don't you?'

Arabella looked away and didn't answer. Did she like danger? Charles certainly did.

She lapsed into an awkward silence for a while before saying, 'I know we write to each other all the time, but I feel I don't really know you that well.'

'Oh, I feel as if I know you,' said Emily with a smile.

Arabella looked at her for any sign of sarcasm or innuendo, but there was none.

'It was a nice suggestion to go for a drive,' commented Arabella as she looked at the leaves coming out on the passing trees.

'Oh, we're not going for a ride around the estate – I only said that to the others.'

'I see – where are we going?' Arabella asked, knowing now for sure that the whole expedition was a ploy arranged by Charles.

'To Hunter's Farm,' said Emily as she turned the phaeton down the road.

'What's to see at Hunter's Farm?'

'It's a small manor house on the estate. It's only used as a guest house. Nobody goes there otherwise. You'll be quite safe there.'

Arabella realised Charles was waiting for her at this Hunter's Farm. She stared ahead again in awkward silence. Emily turned the carriage into a short driveway and drove up to a pretty dowager house surrounded by sycamores.

'I'll come back to collect you this evening,' said Emily.

Arabella stepped down from the carriage then turned to look at Emily. 'Whatever must you think of me?' she said.

Emily just smiled at her, turned the carriage and sped away.

Arabella walked up to the front door and opened it.

'Charles?' she called as she stepped in and closed the door behind her.

Charles came from the drawing room, quickly took her into his arms and started to kiss her.

Arabella pushed him away and walked into the drawing room.

'What do you think you're playing at?' she demanded angrily as he followed her in. 'Managing me into this terrible situation of coming down here for the weekend? Having to be in the same room as all our families, and Harrison and you!'

'I thought you'd be delighted. It's given us an opportunity to spend some real time with each other instead of a few snatched hours here and there.'

'Have you no shame? How can you sit in your brother's company as if nothing was wrong, when you are sleeping with me?'

'I don't care! All I care about is being with you.'

'Well, I care! Poor Harrison–'

'Poor Harrison, my posterior! If you cared so much about Harrison, you wouldn't be here now.

You managed to get yourself out of a voyage to New York, I'm sure you could have got yourself out of a weekend at Armstrong House – if you really wanted to.'

Arabella said nothing for a long while before sighing. 'And there lies the problem ... I had to see you again. It's like a drug. And I don't care who I'm betraying in the process. I want to stop, but I can't... But I don't think I can go on for much longer with this. The pressure is too much. Having to smile and nod at your parents and family, and Harrison... And as for Emily! She's a young impressionable girl whom we are ruthlessly using for our own ends!'

He came over to her and put his arms around her. 'She's loving it! She's loving every moment of it. She's having more excitement with us than she ever thought possible.'

'It doesn't make it right,' said Arabella.

'All I know is what feels right,' he said, bending down to kiss her.

That night Emily sat playing the piano for everyone in the drawing room.

'She plays very well,' Caroline said to Margaret.

'Emily has been getting lessons.'

'She has come along in leaps and bounds since I met her last. You're doing a wonderful job with her.'

'Well, I've been working very hard on her, Lady Tattinger.'

'Well, it shows.' Caroline's eyes fell on Harrison and Arabella sitting side by side on a couch. He was trying to engage her in conversation, but she seemed to be gazing off into the distance. 'Has Harrison said anything about setting a date for their wedding?'

'Well, I know he's longing to get married, but they don't seem to have progressed with any actual plans or arrangements.'

'Hmmm, that's my understanding as well,' mused Caroline.

Margaret hesitated before speaking. 'He's confided in me that every time he broaches the subject with Arabella, she sidesteps it.'

'Really?' Caroline was surprised. 'Well, there's no point in them hanging around!'

'Yes... Perhaps Arabella is just a little nervous about assuming the responsibility of becoming a wife and running her own house?' suggested Margaret.

'With her dowry, they should be well set up and have no need to worry.'

'Perhaps we need to push them along a bit?' suggested Margaret.

On the Sunday afternoon Lawrence suggested that he and Harrison go for a walk. They went across the forecourt and down the flight of stone steps that led to the first terrace of gardens.

'Where has Arabella been all day?' asked Lawrence as they reached the end of the first terrace and walked down another flight of steps to the next.

'She set off with Emily first thing after breakfast and I haven't seen them since,' said Harrison. 'I'd hoped this weekend would be an opportunity for us to spend some relaxed time together. But

Emily has taken her away for most of the time.'

'You can't blame your sister if she is a little bedazzled by the glamorous Arabella,' said Lawrence.

'I couldn't imagine Emily ever being bedazzled by anyone.'

They reached the bottom of the terraces and the lakeshore and began to walk along the pebbled shoreline that gave way to stretches of sand.

'Your mother tells me you haven't settled on a date for the wedding yet?' said Lawrence, choosing his words carefully.

'No.' Harrison looked down to the ground in thought. 'I've tried to numerous times over the past few months. But every time I try, Arabella just changes the subject quickly.'

'Have you tried to ask her why?'

'No. There was no point in me pushing her to... For the past while, she seems distracted. It's as if I don't have her attention when I'm with her. We were never like that before ... we were so close. I'm worried.'

Lawrence slowed down. Harrison was always different from their other children. Ever since he was a child, he needed gentle encouragement. None of the others ever needed gentle anything as they all knew their own minds, often too much so.

'Harrison, I think you need to stop beating around the bush with Arabella. Set the date, the venue and get on with it. In my opinion she is seeing you as not being determined enough and is fearing you have the same doubts as you fear she is having!'

'Do you think so?' Harrison said.

'Yes, I do. It's Gwyneth's wedding next month and the Tattingers are invited. There's nothing like attending a wedding to make a young woman think about her own. It's your opportunity to tie the whole thing down.'

CHAPTER 14

The weeks flew by and Gwyneth's wedding was approaching fast.

Charles was preparing himself for another trip to Dublin and was brushing his hair in the mirror in his room as Margaret talked to him.

'There are going to be some very important people at Gwyneth's wedding. Important people with important daughters. And Gwyneth's marriage will be elevating us and putting you in a prime position to select a wife.'

Charles admired himself in the mirror. 'I wasn't really thinking of marriage quite so soon.'

'Well, when were you thinking of it?'

'I hadn't given it much thought... I'd better run, I don't want to miss my train.' He kissed her cheek and walked out of the room.

Charles came bounding down the stairs and into the drawing room where he saw Harrison sitting in front of the fire, legs up on a footstool. Harrison had taken some time off from work for Gwyneth's wedding and was relaxing for the week in Armstrong House as he thought about his next step with Arabella.

'What are your plans for the week?'

'Oh, just staying in, nothing planned.'

As Harrison observed Charles, dressed in an immaculate black cape, all set for a few days' fun in Dublin, he wondered would Armstrong House ever be enough for him.

'Well – have fun. See you in a couple of days!' Charles glided out.

The house was a hive of activity in the week leading up to the wedding with the door constantly being opened to receive presents from far and near. Margaret was in a spin as she rushed around, checking the final arrangements for everything from the flowers to the cake.

'It's exhausting, just exhausting!' she exclaimed as she entered the drawing room where all the family, except Charles, were gathered.

'Come and sit down, my dear!' said Lawrence, gesturing to the armchair beside his. 'You need to rest!'

'Rest?' Margaret demanded as she sank down beside him. 'There is so much still to be done!'

'Well, we've only another week or so of it, and then we're back to normal!' soothed Lawrence. 'But I do think Charles should have been here for the week to assist.'

Margaret looked over to where her five other children were chatting and laughing together. 'Soon Gwyneth will be married to His Grace, and then we will never be together as a single family again.'

Lawrence saw the sadness in his wife's face.

'You've done a wonderful job raising our family and, tomorrow, when our daughter takes her position at the head of one of the empire's great families it will be a reward for all that work.'

'After all this effort preparing for the wedding, it's hard to believe it will soon be all over.' Margaret shook her head in wonder.

'Well, come to think of it, you won't have much time to relax. From what Harrison tells me you'll be straight to work on his wedding with Arabella.'

She smiled at him happily and hugged him.

Charles had given the servants in the house in Dublin the week off as he entertained Arabella there with nobody to disturb them.

'Where do your parents think you are?'

'With my friend Mabel. I can't stay late tonight, Charles. My parents and I are heading down early tomorrow to be in good time for Gwyneth's wedding the next day.'

Charles grimaced. 'Oh, the wedding! It's costing a fortune. My parents keep insisting that, as she's marrying *His Grace,* we have to spend money accordingly and not let the side down. If my other two sisters cost as much with their marriages, there will be nothing left for me to inherit by the time I become Lord Armstrong!'

'I'm quite looking forward to the spectacle of it all,' said Arabella. 'And yet dreading it as well. Staying in Armstrong House again. Having to go through the game of charades with Harrison and our families again.'

Charles reached out and took her hand. She held it tightly.

146

CHAPTER 15

And what a spectacle it was! The morning of the wedding a fleet of carriages brought the guests to the church in the village. The cream of society from all around the United Kingdom had made their way there to celebrate the Duke of Battington's wedding to Lord Armstrong's eldest daughter.

As Lawrence and Gwyneth were brought to the church in an open-topped carriage the roads were thronged with local well-wishers clapping and cheering. Arabella and her parents arrived only just in time for the ceremony as Caroline mislaid her white lace parasol at the last moment and their departure from Armstrong House was delayed. Now Arabella watched from one of the middle pews as Gwyneth glided gracefully up the aisle on her father's arm to her awaiting groom, her twenty-foot wedding train being tended to by Daphne and six other bridesmaids. Emily had refused to be a bridesmaid, and no amount of bribes or blackmail changed her mind. As Arabella watched the Bishop officiate the service and looked around at the calibre of the guests, she realised the Armstrongs were now connected to the top tier of society by this marriage of their daughter. It made her feel a little insignificant. As she looked up at Harrison sitting in the first pew with his family, she thought he looked a little sad.

Unlike Charles beside him who looked very pleased with himself and the attention he was receiving as the Armstrong heir that day.

The service over, the bells rang loudly as the newly married couple walked down the aisle and the grounds around the church were swarming with guests and onlookers.

Harrison came rushing over to the Tattingers.

'I was worried you wouldn't get here on time,' he said. 'I'm so sorry I couldn't have waited at the house and accompanied you here.'

'Why wouldn't we get here on time?' snapped Arabella.

'Well, you *were* rather late... I wasn't sure whether you were being driven by a coachman or if Sir George had chosen to drive himself – in which case you might have got lost or–'

'Hardly! Do we look like imbeciles?' said Arabella, as she studied Charles who was flirting outrageously with some refined-looking young women.

Harrison looked embarrassed. 'Anyway, I'd better go, my family is waiting. I'll see you at Armstrong House for the reception.' With that, he turned and walked away.

'Arabella!' chastised Caroline. 'That was impolite of you.'

Arabella quickly turned her eyes from Charles and looked at Caroline, confused. 'Sorry?'

'Harrison was only making conversation. There was no need for that tone you used with him.'

'What? Oh, I was distracted... I didn't mean to be rude.' She quickly scoured the crowd in search of Harrison but couldn't see him.

148

Caroline watched Gwyneth and her Duke walk happily into Armstrong House followed by the family. 'Imagine, Arabella, your and Harrison's children will be cousins to a Duke,' she whispered.

Inside they circulated among the other guests in the hall where footmen dressed in dark-blue and white livery and white wigs served champagne.

'There's Harrison now,' said Arabella, spotting him in the corner of the crowded hallway.

Caroline took Arabella's arm and looked at her pointedly. 'Try and be nice to him today, Arabella. It's his sister's wedding.'

'Aren't I always nice to him?' Arabella was surprised by her words.

'Not always ... not recently. You've been very dismissive of things he says.'

'Have I?' Arabella was even more surprised. 'He hasn't complained.'

'There's a surprise! Harrison complaining about anything? Complaining about anything to you?'

Arabella looked at the floor as they made their way over to Harrison.

However, they were soon separated from him again for the lavish wedding banquet in the ballroom, as he was seated with his family at the top table. But afterwards he came straight back to the Tattingers and was an attentive host.

It certainly was the Armstrongs' day, thought Arabella, as people thronged around them. And Charles in particular was receiving a lot of attention. A lot of female attention that made her burn with jealousy.

Arabella forced herself to avoid watching Charles all the time and to concentrate on Harrison, but she found it difficult. And when Charles did come over to them to talk, she didn't find it awkward or feel guilt – she was just glad he was paying her attention.

'There you are, Charles!' said Margaret, rushing over to him and grabbing his arm. 'Oh, hello, Arabella dear!' She reached forward and kissed Arabella's cheek. 'I must chat to you and your parents later. Charles, come with me this instant! I need to introduce you to an earl's daughter who I have just met. She's about to be presented at court, so it's her first season; she speaks four languages, and has the most beautiful table manners I've ever seen! Quickly, follow me!' And she raced off.

Charles turned to Harrison and Arabella and smirked. 'Meeting this young lady really does sound like too good an opportunity to miss!'

Arabella stared after him as he walked off after his mother.

Ten minutes later and Charles was still lavishing all his attentions on the multi-lingual young woman.

'Arabella, it's warm in here, would you like to go for a walk?' asked Harrison.

Arabella tore her stare away from Charles. 'Yes, I think that's a good idea.'

The couple went out through one of the French windows and began to walk. There were other guests strolling through the parklands in the sunny afternoon.

'Your parents will be delighted – the day is a triumph,' said Arabella.

'They did put a lot of work and money into it.'

They said nothing more as they walked along, Harrison trying to think of things to say that would interest or entertain her, Arabella wondering if Charles was still charming the earl's daughter.

'You'll be returning to Dublin tomorrow, you said?' said Arabella at last.

'Yes, I can't wait to get back. All I know is, this past week here, all I've thought about is you and how I couldn't wait to see you again.'

'You talk too flippantly about feelings,' said Arabella, trying not to sound cutting.

'No, I just speak the truth. I missed you so much.'

'You shouldn't think about me as strongly as you do,' she said.

'Why not? I'm in love with you. We're going to spend the rest of our lives together.' He stopped walking and looked at her, puzzled.

'You deserve somebody much better than me, Harrison,' she sighed.

'They don't come any better than you.'

'Oh, yes they do. If you had any sense you'd get back to that wedding and get your mother to start introducing you to those young women she's rounding up for Charles as quickly as possible.'

'Arabella, what are you saying? Not one of them could even hold a light to you.' He stepped towards her.

As she looked at his loving kind face, tears sprang to her eyes.

'You don't even know me, Harrison.'

'Don't be stupid. I know you better than anyone.'

She started to wipe away her tears. 'I – I – don't think I can marry you, Harrison.'

'What?' He moved quickly towards her, put his arms around her and started to wipe away her tears. 'What's wrong?'

'Don't be nice to me – I really don't deserve it. If you only knew … the real me.'

'I do know you. And that's why I want to marry you. We've delayed too long. Let's set the date.'

'Harrison–'

'I was thinking before the summer's end – August maybe? Papa said we can get married at Armstrong House. But if you would prefer Dublin – whatever you want!'

She pulled away from him and dried her tears with her hands. 'I can't marry you, Harrison. I'm sorry.'

'What kind of a joke is that?' he said half smiling. 'We've already agreed to be married.'

'That was before!'

'Before *what?*'

'Just leave it, Harrison!'

'No! *Before what?*'

'Before I met somebody else!'

They stared at each other, both in shock at what she had said.

'Before I met somebody else,' she repeated. 'I don't love you any more, Harrison. I'm sorry, I really wish I did, but I don't. I did love you. But it's gone. And I can't deceive you any more.' She turned and started walking back to the house.

He ran after her and grabbed her arm. 'Who?'

'It doesn't matter.'

'Of course it matters! Who is he? Do I know him?'

She shook his hand off and continued walking. 'No!'

'Well, who is he then?'

She started crying again. She stopped, reached out and stroked his face. 'I would never have wanted to hurt you.'

'You're breaking my heart!'

She grabbed up her skirts and went rushing across the parklands towards the house.

He stared after her in disbelief.

Arabella came rushing into the ballroom and her eyes darted around the crowd until she spotted her parents. She went racing over to them.

'Quickly, we have to leave now!' she said.

'Whatever are you talking about? It's only getting into full swing!' said Caroline.

'Please! We have to return to Dublin immediately!'

Caroline looked at her daughter's distraught face 'All right. But what about Harrison?'

'We have to go now!' said Arabella as she walked towards the door.

Caroline shrugged at George and they both followed their daughter out.

Harrison stumbled through the French windows and just caught sight of the Tattingers leaving.

Charles was with Emily while he regaled a group of guests with stories of the tenant farmers on the Armstrong estate when Margaret came over to them and took them aside. She looked confused and distressed.

'Charles, I don't know what has happened but Harrison has taken to the bed upstairs. He is beside himself.'

'What's wrong with him?'

'Seemingly it's Arabella. He says she has broken off their engagement!'

Emily gasped as she heard this and stared at Charles, who ignored her.

'Broken it off?' he said. 'Surely there's a mistake? They were practically married.'

'I fear there's no mistake. I've searched everywhere for the Tattingers and seemingly they have already left for Dublin. She's ended their relationship all right.'

'Poor Harrison!' Charles was genuinely shocked at Arabella's actions and that he had received no indication of what she had planned to do.

'Charles, will you go to him and try to comfort him? I don't want to tell your father yet or Gwyneth. I don't want to ruin their big day with this *terrible* news.'

'Of course.'

'I'll go too!' said Emily and began to follow Charles.

'You will not!' insisted Margaret, grabbing hold of Emily's arm. 'You'll stay here and mingle!'

Charles steadied himself before knocking on the door and opening it.

He found Harrison inside, sitting on the side of the bed, the curtains drawn. Charles drew the curtains back a little and saw Harrison had his face buried in his hands.

'Harrison?' he said softly as he came over and sat on the four-poster bed beside him.

'She's left me, Charles. She walked out. She said she didn't love me any more.'

'I see!' Charles sighed and put his hand on Harrison's shoulder.

Harrison lifted his tearstained face out of his hands and looked up at Charles.

'She said there was somebody else. That she had fallen for somebody else.'

Charles felt a shiver, but his face remained emotionless as he took his hand off Harrison's shoulder.

'Did she ... did she say who it was?'

'No, but that's not the point! She's fallen for somebody else.'

'Maybe it's best she told you now, before you got in too deep?'

'Too deep! We were engaged! I worshipped her! She was my whole life! I couldn't get in any deeper!'

'Yes, I see that now,' said Charles, frowning.

'What will I do, Charles? What'll I do without her?' Harrison buried his face in his hands again.

CHAPTER 16

The news of Arabella's desertion of Harrison cast a shadow over the rest of Gwyneth's wedding as Harrison refused to come down for the rest of the day and night. The following day Gwyneth and the Duke were waved off on their honeymoon and the guests who were staying in the house or on the estate all departed.

Harrison was as pale as a ghost as the family tried to get him to talk about what he was going to do next.

'I think it's best you stay at Armstrong House with us and not go to Dublin on your own,' advised Margaret, worried about the state he was in.

'I think that's wise. I'll write to the bank and tell them you'll be taking some time off,' said Lawrence.

'The bank!' exclaimed Harrison. 'I'm never going back to the bank again.'

'You're giving up your job?' asked Lawrence.

'How can I go back there? And work for Arabella's father? See him every day after what has happened?'

'Are you sure? This is your career,' Lawrence pointed out.

'I've never been more certain of anything in my life.'

Everyone at Armstrong House had hoped Harrison might start being himself again. But he seemed to have entered a strange dark world and nobody could snap him out of it. He would spend all day in his room. He rarely came down to eat, but had food delivered to his room. Occasionally he would instruct a horse to be brought to the front of house and he would go galloping off through the estate for hours on his own.

Charles looked on, distressed to see how much the break-up had affected him. The glorious day of Gwyneth's wedding seemed to be overshadowed since there was a cloud over Armstrong House with Harrison's black mood.

'I should have realised there was something wrong with that girl when she wore that red dress last Christmas Eve,' said Margaret.

'All we can do is rally round him and support him as best we can,' said Charles.

In the afternoon Charles found Harrison sitting at his window staring out at the view across the lake.

'I just wondered if you fancied going into Castlewest?'

'No.'

'What about the two of us heading up to Dublin this weekend and painting the town red? Take in a show, see if there are a couple of parties to attend?'

'Definitely not – I might bump into *her*.'

Charles came and sat beside him and spoke gently. 'You're going to have to leave this room at some stage. You can't spend the rest of your life in here staring out that window.'

'She was my life. She was everything to me. I'm empty without her.'

Charles nodded and looked down at the floor. Then he rose and left the room quickly.

As he was coming down the stairs he met Emily coming up.

'I'm just on my way to see Harrison,' she said.

'There's not much point. I've just left him and he's completely despondent.'

'I know. But I'll sit with him anyway. Even though he doesn't speak. Oh, Charles, what have we done?' She became distressed.

'Shhh!' he said and led her downstairs where they went into the small parlour and he closed the doors.

The tears started falling down Emily's face. 'It was all just a bit of fun and excitement. I never guessed it would end up breaking Harrison.'

'None of us did.' He shook his head.

'What can we do?' she asked. She knew Charles always had the answers to everything.

'Nothing, there's nothing we can do.' Charles held her arms. 'Emily, look at me. Harrison can never find out the truth, do you understand me? He can never find out about me and Arabella. It would finish him off.'

Emily nodded and wiped away her tears. 'I understand... I'd better go to him. He might eat something for me today.'

Charles watched her leave the room and shook his head in disbelief. The whole situation had exploded before his eyes. He would never have guessed Arabella would have weakened and end up leaving Harrison. He realised he could never see Arabella again. If the truth came out, it would destroy him and blow a hole in his family forever.

CHAPTER 17

Arabella was sitting at her dressing table on which her morning's post was thrown. Again there had been no letter from Emily. She was expecting one every day.

Her mother came into her room, wearing the same worried expression she had worn since Gwyneth's wedding.

'Your father has received a letter from Lord Armstrong,' she informed her daughter.

Arabella spun around. 'What does he want?'

'Nothing, it was just to inform him Harrison will not be returning to the bank.'

'Oh, no! He didn't say anything about – how Harrison was?'

'No, it was short and impersonal.'

'I see.'

'I imagine Lord and Lady Armstrong are as shocked by all this as we are, Arabella.'

'I'm sorry for the trouble I've caused.'

Caroline sat down beside her, took her hands and looked into her eyes imploringly. 'Are you sure you're doing the right thing? Harrison worshipped you. I just don't think you'll ever find anyone like him again.'

'I can't go back to him. It would be unfair on

him. I've deceived him enough by continuing to see him when my feelings had changed for him.'

And still no letter came from Emily. She had expected Charles to make contact with her. She was free now. There would be no need for any further deception. She wasn't naïve enough to think they could be publicly seen together yet. But why was he breaking off all contact? After four weeks she could stand it no longer and opened her writing bureau to start a letter.

Emily came into the library where Charles was working on estate business, an opened letter in her hand.

He looked up from his paperwork. 'Who is that from?' he asked.

'It's from Arabella,' stated Emily.

'*What?*' Charles snatched the letter from her and started to read it. 'What does she want?'

'She fills the letter about mundane things, and then uses her usual code to say she wants to meet you in The Shelbourne on Saturday at three.'

'Is she mad?' Charles stood up. 'Doesn't she realise Harrison is upstairs destroyed?'

'Will I write back?'

'No – ignore her!' Charles crossed over to the fire and threw the letter in.

That Saturday Arabella waited two hours in the tearoom in The Shelbourne for Charles to arrive, but he never did. As two more weeks went by she wrote to Emily again. This time she used less coded language and said she needed to speak to Charles. That letter ended up in the library fire as well.

Then one day Emily came knocking on Charles' door, looking very worried.

'Charles, I got another letter from Arabella,' she said.

'For blazes' sake, does that woman not take a hint?' Charles exploded.

'I think you should see her, Charles. She's practically begging me to get you to meet her.'

Charles grabbed the letter and started to read it. 'Has she lost her mind? If this fell into the wrong hands!' He went to the fire and burned it.

'I think you have to meet her, Charles.'

'All right!' snapped Charles, furious at the thought of it all. 'Write to her and tell her to be in Stephen's Green by the bridge at two on Saturday afternoon.'

When Arabella received the letter from Armstrong House, she was overjoyed, but even more so relieved.

She waited by the bridge in Stephen's Green, looking at the ducks swim in the pond underneath as the sun shone that Saturday afternoon. She kept looking at her watch and then checking for any sign of Charles. Eventually she saw him walking towards her and she tensed as he reached her.

He made no attempt to take her hand or touch her in any way. 'Sorry I'm late. I got the train up from Castlewest this morning,' he explained.

'That's fine.'

'Will we walk as we talk?' he suggested and she nodded.

They walked over the bridge and along one of the footpaths that criss-crossed the park.

'How's everything at Armstrong House?' she asked.

He looked at her incredulously. 'How do you think they are? Harrison is devastated. He hardly leaves his room.'

'I never meant to hurt him,' she said, overcome with guilt.

'Well, you did! Whatever possessed you to end it with him, and to tell him you were in love with somebody else to boot!'

'It felt like the right thing to do. What we were doing to him was wrong ... perhaps you could live with your conscience, but I couldn't.'

'Very noble of you, I'm sure.' He raised his eyes to heaven.

'I was surprised when you didn't contact me afterwards,' she said.

'How could I? My family are in disarray over Harrison. Look, you ending it with Harrison has made it impossible for us ever to see each other again. You need to realise that.'

Arabella stopped still and stared at him in shock. 'But what was it all about? What was it all in aid of? Us seeing each other, creeping behind Harrison's back, where was it leading to?'

'My dear, it could never have led anywhere – because you were Harrison's fiancée.'

Tears of anger and frustration gathered in Arabella's eyes. 'But we love each other!'

Charles sighed loudly. 'We were infatuated with each other – there's a difference. And when I see the cold reality of Harrison's face, I know our

162

infatuation must stop.'

She felt dizzy and sat down on a bench. He sat beside her and took her hand. 'You always said we were in an impossible situation,' he said. 'Now it's become so much more impossible.'

'And we never see each other again?'

'I'm afraid we can't.'

'While you go off to the season in London to call on all those earls' daughters who were flirting with you? The ones who could speak several languages and do perfect tapestry?' Her expression hardened.

'Don't be bitter, Arabella.'

'Oh, I'm not bitter,' she said. 'I'm pregnant.'

He dropped her hand slowly. 'What?'

'I'm with child.'

He found it hard to speak but managed, 'How long?'

'A couple of months.'

'What are you going to do?'

'What am *I* going to do?' she asked disbelievingly.

'You need to tell Harrison immediately.'

'Harrison! It's not Harrison's, you fool!'

'How do you know?'

'Because nothing ever happened between me and Harrison as you well know! It's your bloody child!' She was nearly shouting, causing people to look over from the lawns.

He stood up and began to walk up and down. 'I don't know that. The child could be anybody's. I think we know what kind of a woman you are.'

She stood up and marched up to him. 'I have only ever been with you. This is your child and you have to accept responsibility for it.'

'You're insane! My brother will kill me and so will my family. I'll be disowned and–'

'And what will happen to me? I'll be ruined if you don't marry me. I and my family will be destroyed. My name will be filth. I'll be ostracised from society. And what of the child? The child will be a bastard.'

'You should have thought about all this before you abandoned Harrison. I always assumed that if you became pregnant you would have had the sense to ... to ... arrange things so he thought the child was his! And then married him promptly. What else could be done?'

She stared at him, horrified.

'Instead you have done the worst thing possible and left him,' he said coldly. 'But I have to go now to catch my train. I have to get back to Armstrong House.' He reached forward and gave her a kiss on the cheek. 'You see the situation I'm in. If it was anyone but Harrison ... but he can never find out. Your parents are kind and wealthy – I'm sure they will stand by you.'

She stared in astonishment as he walked quickly away from her in the park. She stood there for what seemed like hours, bewildered. Finally she turned and walked in a trance back through the streets to her home in Ailesbury Road.

'Watch out!' came a scream from a cab driver and she realised she was standing still in the middle of the street with a horse-drawn carriage coming straight at her. She quickly made her way to the footpath and continued her slow walk home. She was finished, she realised. Her life was

over. Her mind was a maelstrom of emotion, switching from hurt and rejection as she realised she was nothing more than a conquest for Charles, to terror and panic when she thought of the situation she was now in. Not just her, but all the Tattingers would be ruined.

She had always carried herself with pride and confidence and yet now she would be the talk of Dublin. People would snigger and laugh about her and call her a whore and a slut. She wouldn't be received into other peoples' homes any more and people wouldn't want to be seen with her. Even her closest friends wouldn't be permitted near her in case they were tarred with the same brush. Her father could lose his job, and definitely his position in society. As for her mother…

She got home and went to the store room and searched amongst the bottles until she found what she was looking for. She took the bottle of rat poison and walked up the stairs to her room where she locked the door. She then unscrewed the bottle and put it on her dressing table. She sat down, staring at her snow-white reflection in the mirror.

CHAPTER 18

Charles tried not to think about Arabella's situation when he got back to Armstrong House. The whole thing was far too distressing to give much thought to, he reasoned. When he compared the beautiful independent wilful Arabella who he had first met to the scared desperate girl in the park, it was hard to equate them. As if he could marry her! What on earth was she thinking? He hoped he had explained the situation adequately to her. He wondered what would become of her. As he had said, her parents were kind and wealthy. Perhaps they might find a lowly bank clerk with few brains who could be quickly cajoled into marrying her. Or there was the case of that daughter from a 'big house' they knew in Cork who was flirtatious and loved men's attention and who suddenly disappeared for one year off the social scene. Rumours abounded she was in a convent in France. When she returned she was a different girl who never went to parties and spent all the day doing tapestry, a hobby she had picked up in the French convent, they said, while she waited to give birth to her baby. What a stupid girl Arabella was, and he thought she had been so intelligent! She could have had the best of all worlds. Marriage to Harrison and the Armstrong name. And she could have had Charles until they became bored with each other. But she had played her cards ridiculously wrong and now could be destroyed.

Returning from a ride some days later, he dismounted in the forecourt of Armstrong House and gave the reins to a stable lad. Then he bounded up the steps and in the front door.

He threw his coat onto a sideboard and walked into the drawing room where he got a start. On one couch sat his parents and on the other couch

166

sat Arabella and her parents. All had stony solemn faces except for Margaret whose face was red and tearstained from crying.

'Come in, Charles, and close the door behind you. I've told Barton we are not to be disturbed,' said Lawrence.

Emily had been waiting for Charles in the small parlour across from the drawing room. She had seen Arabella and her parents arrive earlier from her bedroom window and, realising all must not be right, she had looked for Charles everywhere. Unfortunately a maid entered the room with a laden coalscuttle just at the wrong moment and the noise of her tending to the fire cloaked the sound of Charles' arrival. As the maid left Emily flew to the window and spotted Charles disappearing in the front door. She rushed out into the hall to warn him but she was just too late. She saw him entering the drawing room and close the door slowly behind him. She thought for a few moments and then seeing there was nobody about, rushed across the hallway and put her ear against the keyhole of the door to listen in.

A million thoughts went racing through Charles' mind as he closed the door and walked into the room.

'Take a seat,' ordered Lawrence.

Charles sat down in the armchair that had obviously been positioned there for him between the two couches.

In the silence and with the cold stares, Charles decided to take control and said, 'I can guess why you're all here.'

'Is it true?' asked Lawrence.

Charles knew there was no point in denying it at this stage. 'Yes.'

'Ohhh!' cried Margaret as her handkerchief came to her face and tears began to spill again. 'How could you, Charles, with your own brother's fiancée!'

'I have no excuse,' he said.

'And neither do you!' Margaret snapped at Arabella.

'Perhaps,' said Caroline sternly, 'if you kept a tighter control on what goes on under your roof, this would never have happened, Lady Armstrong!'

'*My* roof! Who said anything about under *my* roof?' Margaret was furious.

'Well, it must have happened when she visited here. When else could it have happened?'

'Nothing untoward has ever happened under my roof! From what I hear, your daughter is left without a chaperone a great deal of time!'

'I don't think it matters how the situation occurred,' said Lawrence in a powerful voice. 'All we need to concern ourselves with now is that it *has* occurred and what we do from here.'

'Well, we all know what needs to be done. *He* must marry her without delay,' said George in an equally powerful voice.

'Are they agreeable to this?' asked Lawrence, looking at Arabella and Charles.

'Who gives a damn if they are agreeable!' George's voice rose further. 'I will not have my daughter and name destroyed over this.'

168

'Nevertheless,' said Lawrence, 'we need their consent.' He turned to Arabella. 'Will you marry Charles?'

Arabella had been staring ahead unfalteringly since she arrived. She glanced quickly at Charles and said, 'Yes.'

Lawrence nodded and then turned to Charles. 'Are you willing to marry Arabella and accept this is your child?'

Charles glanced at the Tattingers who looked as if they were ready to have him killed. 'Yes.' He looked at Arabella. 'Of course I'll marry Arabella. It was never in question that I wouldn't.'

There was an audible feeling of relief around the room.

Margaret, who looked heartbroken, said between her sniffles, 'We'll try to arrange the marriage as soon as possible.'

'But what about the banns?' said George. 'Either the banns will have to be called, for three Sundays in advance of the wedding, or a special marriage licence obtained from the bishop.'

'Leave that to me,' said Margaret. 'The bishop is a close friend of ours who is, by the way, a most discreet man. I'll travel to see him this very day. He can officiate at the wedding himself in the chapel at the Bishop's Palace, hopefully on Monday morning.'

'That should give enough time to get the licence,' said Lawrence.

'We'll have nobody in attendance at the service but ourselves,' Margaret went on. 'Nobody must ever find out about this, for the sake of us all! Not even our other children.'

169

'Well, I imagine everyone is going to realise something is the matter,' said Caroline. 'When one minute she is engaged to Harrison, and the next minute married to Charles!'

'And then when the baby arrives too soon!' George pointed out.

'They can't return to Dublin or stay at Armstrong House. Everyone knows them here. They must go away for a while, until after the baby is born,' said Margaret.

'Where to?' asked Caroline.

'They can go and live in our house in London for most of the pregnancy. When it comes to near the time the child is to be born they must travel abroad and have the child delivered there. Then after a while return to London and register the child's birth incorrectly in order to arouse no suspicion the child was conceived before the marriage.'

'Fraud! Fraud on top of everything else!' shouted George, horrified.

'We have no choice,' stated Lawrence.

Arabella sat back, amazed at Margaret. The woman was obviously as efficient at organising a cover-up as she was at organising a ball or a wedding.

'And ... and what about after the baby is born?' asked Arabella meekly.

'You're to go to London and keep a low profile for a while, until it all blows over. Out of sight, out of mind,' said Margaret. 'Arabella was never presented at court or did the season in London so she's not known there like she is known in Dublin. They can stay there until so much time has elapsed that it won't matter any more.'

'It sounds the best way to avoid any scandal,' acknowledged Caroline.

Everyone sat in silence. 'Well, that's that then!' said George.

'Not for us, Sir George. We have the little matter of Harrison who will obviously need to be informed of Charles and Arabella's forthcoming wedding and how we are going to deal with him I do not know!' said Margaret.

Caroline nodded and coughed. 'I think everyone is in agreement that Harrison is the true victim here. We all feel sorry for him.'

Arabella's impassivity broke and she quickly wiped away a tear.

'There's just the other small matter of the dowry,' said Charles, sitting up.

'Charles!' shouted Lawrence in horror.

'You can speak about money at a time like this?' George nearly screamed.

'Well, I have to be practical. If I'm taking on the responsibility of a wife and child, I'll need funds. Father is in perfect health, so hopefully it will be some time before I come into the Armstrong estate and its income.'

'Unbelievable!' stated George in disgust.

'I need to know where I stand – under the circumstances.'

George stood up. 'I'll double her bloody dowry – under the circumstances. Is that enough bloody money for you?'

Margaret stood up, flushed and embarrassed. 'I'll have Barton make up some rooms for you for tonight.'

'No need!' said George unpleasantly. 'I wouldn't spend another night in this house. We'll stay in a hotel in Castlewest.'

George went storming out and Arabella and Caroline stood up.

'We'll see you at the wedding on Monday,' said Caroline curtly and she and Arabella quickly left after George.

'A May wedding!' exclaimed Margaret. 'We used to say – marry in May and rue the day!'

Margaret and Lawrence stared at Charles as he took out a cigarette and lit it, his hands slightly shaking.

'You've ruined your life!' declared Margaret.

'Have you anything to say in your defence?' asked Lawrence.

'I'm afraid not. Guilty as charged,' said Charles as he managed to take a drag of his cigarette.

'You've let us down terribly,' said Lawrence. 'But you've let Harrison down even more. I suppose I'd better tell him what's been happening,' said Lawrence as he looked at the fear on Margaret and Charles' faces.

Lawrence knocked on Harrison's door and entered. He found him lying on the bed.

'How are you today?' he asked, sitting on the bed beside him.

'The same as yesterday and the day before,' said Harrison.

Lawrence said nothing as he searched for the right words to tell Harrison what had happened.

'Were there visitors earlier?' asked Harrison in

172

a disinterested fashion. 'I heard some commotion downstairs.'

'Yes, there were ... it was Arabella and her parents.'

Harrison sat up straight, his face a mixture of excitement and confusion. 'Arabella! Why didn't you call me?'

'She didn't come to see you, Harrison.' Lawrence put his hand on Harrison's shoulder. 'Son, I need you to prepare yourself for what I'm about to tell you...'

Harrison became extremely agitated as Lawrence said nothing more. 'Well, *tell me* – damn you!'

'There's no easy way ... there's no easy way to say this... Arabella and Charles have fallen in love. They are to be married. I presume ... I presume that is why she broke off her engagement with you.'

Lawrence studied his son's face as it went from a strange deathly pale to a bright red in a few seconds. Suddenly Harrison leapt from the bed but his legs gave way from under him and he fell to the floor.

'Harrison!' shouted Lawrence, rushing to his assistance.

As Harrison lay on the floor, he suddenly started laughing hysterically.

'*Harrison!*' pleaded Lawrence, kneeling beside him.

'*Arabella and Charles!*' gasped Harrison through his laughter as if he had been told the best joke ever. Then suddenly the laughter stopped as quickly as it began and, as he scrambled to his feet with Lawrence's assistance, Harrison's face became a mask of distraught horror.

'She would never – he would never–' he stuttered.

Lawrence nodded sadly. Harrison tore himself away from Lawrence and raced from the room.

Charles was in the library holding a decanter of whiskey as he poured himself another full glass and downed it in one. Suddenly the door swung open and Harrison came rushing in like a madman.

'You fucking bastard!' screamed Harrison as he marched right over to Charles and punched him in the face. The decanter went flying through the air and crashed to the ground as Charles was knocked to the floor.

Harrison jumped on top of him, put his hands around Charles' neck and started to strangle him.

'You couldn't leave her alone, could you? You had to take her, even though you knew she was mine!' he screamed as Charles tried to remove Harrison's hands from around his throat.

'Barton!' shouted Lawrence as he came into the room and viewed the spectacle on the ground before him. He rang the bell frantically then rushed to his sons and tried to pull Harrison away from Charles, but his younger son was so overcome with anger it was impossible.

A few seconds later Barton came rushing in.

'For pity's sake, help me, man!' pleaded Lawrence.

Barton and Lawrence managed to pull Harrison away.

Charles sat up, choking and coughing.

Harrison pointed at Charles. 'I never want to see you again. You and that bitch are welcome to each other – you deserve each other!' Turning, he stormed out of the room.

Lawrence stood shaking his head as he observed Charles trying to gasp for air.

CHAPTER 19

Caroline came into her daughter's bedroom in the small hotel in Castlewest, holding a tray with a sandwich on it.

'I got the kitchen to prepare this for you,' said Caroline.

'I'm not hungry.' Arabella pushed the tray away.

'You have to eat something, Arabella – you're eating for two now.'

'Don't I know!'

Caroline sat on the bed and started stroking her daughter's hair.

'I received a note from Margaret. The marriage is to be tomorrow at eleven at the Bishop's Palace. As practical as ever, she's given excellent instructions how to get there.' She crossed over to the wardrobe and started looking through the three or four dresses Arabella had brought with her. 'We have to choose what you will wear.'

'Oh, does it matter at this stage?'

Caroline came and sat beside her again. 'You

know I always imagined you with a great big wedding, like the one Gwyneth had.'

Arabella's voice was heavy with cynicism. 'Sorry to disappoint you, Mama, but tomorrow is going to be a far cry from Gwyneth's. A pregnant bride, a reluctant groom and the guests being just the two sets of parents to ensure the whole damned thing takes place!'

'Hardly a reluctant groom, perhaps just a surprised one.'

'You didn't see his face the day I told him in the park. It's a shotgun wedding, pure and simple.'

Caroline sighed loudly 'You've been very stupid, Arabella, we all know that. And very cruel to Harrison. But what's done is done. And now luckily it's working out for the best.'

'Only because it's been forced on Charles.'

'But you do have feelings for him?'

Arabella nodded. 'Unfortunately, I love him... I hate him too, for what he's put me through with all this.'

'But you *do* love him, and tomorrow you are going to marry the man you love ... that's the important thing, no matter what the circumstances are.'

'Is it?'

'Yes, and you have to think of the future now. With this funny twist of fate you are marrying the Armstrong heir. You will one day be Lady Armstrong and this child you are carrying will also be the heir.'

'I don't care about any of that.'

'I know, but I'm just trying to make you realise you have new responsibility now and you'll have to live up to it. You might love Charles, but these past few days have shown you can never trust him or rely on his love. You'll have to be one step ahead of him at all times. Never take him or your marriage for granted. You're entering the Armstrong family under difficult circumstances. You have to show them and the world and, most importantly, Charles, that you are a great woman who deserves the title and position you will now get. You have to, in order to have a happy future.'

Arabella thought about Harrison. 'And can you have a happy future that has been built on somebody else's misery?'

Lawrence came into the bedroom that night and saw Margaret, looking exhausted, lying back in her pillows.

'I tried Harrison again, but his door is locked and he won't answer.'

'Do you think we should break the door down?' asked Margaret, sitting up, concerned.

'No, he just wants to be alone – he won't thank us for doing that.'

'I'm in shock, Lawrence. That we have gone from the highs of Gwyneth's wedding to this sordid secret affair in a matter of weeks... To think Arabella will be Lady Armstrong and be the head of this family one day. A woman like that!'

'You used to think she was marvellous,' he pointed out.

'That was before I realised what she was like. Your parents Edward and Anna, bless them, would be mortified if they were alive to see that the future of this family is now in her hands.'

Lawrence took Margaret's hand and tried to comfort her. 'My parents were very pragmatic about these things. They understood destiny and nature and let it take its course. And they would just see this as nature bringing the next heir to Armstrong House ... in its own way.'

'And what a way!'

That night Charles was the only one up in the house as he stood at the window drinking whiskey in the drawing room, looking at the moon shining its light across the lake.

Emily came creeping in, in her dressing gown, and closed the door after her.

'Charles! Is what I'm hearing true? You're marrying Arabella in the morning?'

'It's true all right,' he sighed heavily. 'How do you know?'

Emily stared at him. 'I was listening at the door when the Tattingers were here. I know everything ... that she's expecting your child.'

He looked surprised and then nodded. 'You're not to tell anybody.'

'Of course I won't. I'd never betray you like that.' She came over and hugged him.

'I'm afraid our little game has exploded in our faces, dearest little Emily.' He stroked her hair.

'I overheard you and Harrison fighting... What's suddenly become of us?'

'We've grown up, that's all, Emily – it happens in all families.'

'You picked the wrong girl to trifle with, Charles. She was too clever and her family too powerful to ignore. At least now you can be together.' Emily was studying him intently.

He smiled at his sister, not sure if she was being naïve or just testing him. 'True. And I'm getting to live in London, which is what I always wanted. And I'm getting a very substantial dowry which will keep us in the style that we need to be accustomed to... I guess you could say I got everything I wanted.' He bent down and kissed her forehead. She watched him saunter out of the room and up to bed.

The wedding took place in the chapel in the Bishop's Palace at eleven. The Bishop was a little amazed with the whole promptness and mystery that clouded the event. He had been sworn to secrecy by Lady Armstrong not ever to reveal any details of the marriage. As he stood at the altar looking at the groom Charles with a big black eye, the bride Arabella in a plain cream dress and hat, the only guests being both sets of parents positioned on opposite sides of the aisle, he could only imagine what was going on. As the bride and groom both confirmed 'I do', their respective mothers burst out crying. Caroline out of relief and Margaret out of sorrow.

Armstrong House seemed quiet that night with Charles and Arabella already left for their new life and all of the drama the Tattingers brought with them gone. Lawrence and Margaret sat in a kind of disbelief, as if the past three days had been a strange and awful dream and they would wake up and everything would be back to normal.

179

To their surprise Harrison came in, looking pale and drawn.

'Have they gone?' he asked.

'Yes, they got the train this afternoon,' said Lawrence, who had informed Harrison of their plans to go and live in London.

Harrison laughed bitterly. 'I've been doing a lot of thinking – I need to get away.'

'Excellent idea,' said Lawrence. 'I'll arrange a holiday for you ... somewhere you can take the waters... Switzerland maybe.'

'No, I mean get away for good. There are too many bad memories in this country and I need a brand-new start.'

'Go away!' Margaret was horrified.

'To New York. I'm going as soon as I can.'

'But for how long?' asked Lawrence.

'For ever,' he said bitterly. 'For ever.'

CHAPTER 20

Present Day

There was a lull of some days in the filming and Kate decided to take advantage of the time to try and see if she could find out more about the mysterious photographs that were hidden in the police file.

One evening Kate and Nico opened a bottle of red wine and sat in the drawing room, the black-and-white photographs glaring at them from the coffee table, contradicting what was in the official inquiry. They were studying the family's statements in the police file.

'All the family's statements given to police are exactly the same as what the inquiry reported,' said Nico. 'That he was shot in the carriage while travelling on his own. And the policeman investigating the case, a Sergeant Kevin Cunningham, in his official report here also wrote this and as we know later gave the same evidence to the inquiry.'

Kate threw a pile of papers on the coffee table. 'There are pages and pages of statements from locals and in the town talking about the lead-up to the shooting and the Land War Charles was involved in.'

'But why would they not just say Charles was in the automobile?' Nico's mind was trying to come up with a solution. He picked up the pile of papers she had flung down and began to go through them again.

He suddenly stopped at one of the crumpled handwritten papers.

'This is a statement from another police officer, Tadhg Murnahan,' he said.

Kate reached forward, took the paper and started to read aloud. *"'On the morning of December 9th, 1903, I was on night duty at the Castlewest Police station. At seven o'clock in the morning an official from the hospital came and reported that Lord Charles Armstrong had been admitted to those premises the previous night with a significant gunshot wound to the chest. I rode out to the Armstrong Estate. On reaching the estate I found an automobile abandoned at the gateway. There was a bullet-hole through the windscreen and the interior of the automobile was stained with a considerable amount of blood. I set up my camera and took photographs of the scene. I called to Armstrong House where Lady Margaret Armstrong confirmed there had been an incident and requested my superior, Sergeant Kevin Cunningham, to come at once.'*

Nico and Kate looked at each other.

'So why did Sergeant Cunningham ignore this evidence his officer reported?' asked Kate.

'Sloppy police work?' suggested Nico.

'Very sloppy! In fact, too sloppy. It's no wonder they didn't capture this chief suspect Joe McGrath before he absconded to America.'

'But this says something else as well,' Nico pointed out. 'Lady Margaret, Charles' mother, was not only the first at the scene of the shooting the previous night, as her statement says, but she was also at Armstrong House in the morning by daylight. She must have been aware of the damaged car and for whatever reason said it was a carriage.'

'So, if she could get such a blatant thing wrong, then her statement that she saw a peasant rushing past Hunter's Farm with a shotgun – in the dark, mind you – can't be trusted either. Indeed, her sighting of that man seems all too convenient, doesn't it?'

'Yes – and it's always struck me as peculiar that the culprit would rush down the road past her house anyway, waving a shotgun, when he could just cut across country.'

'You're right. He wouldn't stay on the road.'

Kate suddenly jumped up from the couch,

went over to her desk and opened her laptop sitting there.

'I'm just thinking,' she said. 'McGrath was supposed to have fled to America. If he did, then all the records for Ellis Island are on the website and we can see if he actually did go there.' She started tapping on the keyboard.

'But there will have been millions of people passed through Ellis Island on their way to their new life to America,' Nico objected.

'Yes, back in the early 1900s it would be almost an impossible task to track a fled criminal to America, but now with the wonders of the internet ... everything has been uploaded and a few seconds away. I've tracked a lot of my relatives who emigrated through this.'

Kate typed in: *Joseph McGrath – Castlewest – 1903*.

After a few moments she began to read from the screen. *'Joseph McGrath, aged 30. Residence – Castlewest. Ship – Oceanic, Port – Queenstown. Destination – Queens. Date – 9th of December 1903.'*

Kate and Nico looked at each other.

'Well, one thing for sure is Joseph McGrath, despite what Lady Margaret testified and the police report said, did not shoot Charles because he was about to dock into New York at the time,' said Nico.

The old Victorian hospital in Castlewest which Charles had been admitted to in 1903 was long closed down. Kate drove back into town and inquired at the local library about the records.

'They were all forwarded to the National

Archives of Ireland in Dublin,' the librarian informed her.

Kate found gaining access to those files was not an easy task as she was told that generally they were not available for public viewing and she would have to obtain permission from the Health Service Executive. But she wasn't going to give up that easily. She had uncovered too much already that made her believe something sinister happened with the Armstrong family all those years ago.

She contacted a friend who worked for the Health Service Executive and finally got permission to view them but only with the permission and signature of Nico, Charles' great-grandson.

'I don't know why you're bothering to look at that file,' said Nico as he signed the consent form for her. 'You said you had to sign a confidentiality agreement as well.'

'True,' she said as she happily put the consent form in her handbag.

'Well, you won't be able to use anything you found for the film then,' Nico pointed out.

Kate just smiled, delighted she had secured permission.

The guide in the National Archives walked her down long corridors of shelves stacked with files.

'We've got many of the files from around the country stored here,' said the woman, whose name was Gillian. 'There are some very interesting cases, from the lunatic asylums particularly.'

Kate nodded and smiled at her. 'What kind of records do you have?'

'Oh, a lot of management minutes, operational records – case books and theatre records as we move into the twentieth century,' said Gillian.

Kate nodded, becoming more excited.

'Here we are,' said Gillian. 'These are from the hospital you are inquiring about. Can you tell me the information you have?'

'Yes. Lord Charles Armstrong was admitted on the night of the 8th of December 1903 or early morning of the 9th,' said Kate.

Kate waited patiently as Gillian sifted through the files for what seemed an eternity.

'Here we are!' said Gillian, taking a file box from the shelf.

Kate followed her over to a desk and they put the box on the table.

The two women sat down at the desk and Gillian put on white cotton gloves and handed Kate a pair, then opened the file and started going through it.

'This man was admitted to the hospital at twelve thirty the morning of 9th of December. He was signed in by a Harrison Armstrong,' said Gillian.

'That's all correct from what I know,' said Kate. 'What I'm trying to discover is exactly what kind of injury? What caused it?'

Gillian looked through the file. 'Let's look at his theatre record... He was admitted for surgery that night ... and a single bullet was removed from his chest ... severe internal injuries, ruptures to the–'

Kate leaned forward and gently took the report from her. 'It definitely says a single bullet?'

'You can see for yourself,' said Gillian.

'Yes, I do...' Nico was right. A shotgun wasn't used to kill Charles. A handgun was – leaving a single bullet, not pellets from a shotgun.

Kate and Nico were having a meeting with the director Brian while they ate dinner at their kitchen island. In front of them was all the evidence Kate had compiled about Charles' shooting.

'There's no doubt something peculiar was going on,' agreed Brian.

'I want to get to the bottom of it, Brian,' said Kate.

'But how does this affect the filming?' pushed Brian.

'Well, I was hoping we could delay things while I do more research,' suggested Kate.

'Delay things! Kate! Our budget won't allow that.'

'Well, at least to film around the shooting for now. We can concentrate on the other areas of the documentary. The social life here, the politics of the estate. Stuff we're already sure of.'

'We thought we were sure about the shooting!' Brian pointed out.

'But imagine if we put all this new stuff into the film and whatever else I can uncover – it would make it so much more engrossing.'

Nico took a sip of his red wine, not at all liking the direction in which Kate was manipulating the documentary.

Brian nodded. 'But where else can you go with this – what's your next step?'

'I want to go through all the documents and

journals that are being stored here at Armstrong House from the period,' said Kate. 'See if there's anything there. When this house was evacuated during the War of Independence, everyone left in a hurry and a lot of the personal items were abandoned here.'

'But you already researched all that stuff before you began the documentary,' said Nico, becoming irritable.

'I know, but I wasn't looking for anything in connection to a cover-up. I was just looking for indications of what life was like here at the time.'

Brian nodded as he finished off his lasagne. 'Okay, we'll film around it for now. But I can't allow this to cause any delays – there's a limited amount of time allotted to the project, Kate. You should know that.'

'I do!' she said, smiling happily. 'We'll work round the clock on it, won't we, Nico?'

Nico gave her a displeased look.

BOOK TWO

1890–1897

CHAPTER 21

The carriage drove up the curve of Regent Street as Arabella held her baby close. Charles sat beside them. They had all just returned from the Continent and were on their way home to the Armstrong family's house in London. As Arabella looked at her six-month-old baby she marvelled how the months had passed. She had been dazed those first few weeks when they moved to London as she contemplated how much her life had changed overnight and how close she had come to utter ruination. What amazed her in equal measure was Charles during those first few weeks. The whole experience hadn't knocked a feather out of him. He didn't seem one bit upset or concerned or confused by the events. He behaved as if it were all the most normal thing in the world as he went about with his usual cheerful disposition. He didn't seem one bit concerned about Harrison knowing the truth at last or his parents' knowledge of events. He seemed immune to it all.

He arrived back one day with an exquisite mink coat for her and told her happily that her father's dowry had cleared successfully into his bank account.

'The one you coerced Papa to double,' she said evenly to him.

'Yes, very clever of me, don't you think? Let's

face it, all your parents' wealth will go to your elder brother, and so clever of me to negotiate an extra share now for you when we had the opportunity, was it not?' He bent down and kissed her and she raised her eyes to heaven as he happily went off to his club.

When the time came close for her to give birth they travelled to France where they rented a house in the south near Cannes. There was only a midwife present at the birth as they didn't want any doctor registering it.

Arabella gave birth to a baby girl.

'A daughter!' exclaimed Charles as he held the baby with a bemused look on his face. 'To think of all that fuss and bother, and not even a son!'

'Sorry to disappoint!' said Arabella sarcastically.

'What are we to call her?' he said as he peered curiously down at her.

'Prudence,' said Arabella.

'Prudence!' exclaimed Charles. 'Why on earth Prudence?'

'A favourite aunt of mine was called Prudence. The name has happy connotations for me.'

'I never imagined a child of mine would be called Prudence. I can't imagine a child of mine being prudent!'

'All the more reason to call her that. I don't want her to follow in our footsteps. I want her to be careful and sensible and practical and never to get into any bother. I hope she is prudent in life.'

Charles made a face as he handed the baby back to Arabella.

They had waited a couple of further months in France and Margaret had registered Prudence's birth as two months later than it actually was in a little backward town hall in a small provincial town where the elderly official asked no more questions. Armed with their daughter's new birth certificate, they arrived back in London.

The carriage continued as far as Regent's Park, then pulled into the private driveway in front of Hanover Terrace. Hanover Terrace was a long row of four-storey terraced townhouses that looked across the road to the park. Lawrence owned the end house, which was the most spectacular of all the houses on the terrace. Charles got out of the carriage and reached to take Prudence from Arabella.

As Arabella alighted, she looked up at what would be their home for the foreseeable future.

The end house had a fleet of steps leading up to it onto a terrace which had three arches along it. Upstairs was a balcony terrace with pillars that rose to the third and fourth floor and at the top of the building was a Grecian-style triangular pediment with statues adorning it.

Arabella and Charles walked around to the side of the house where the main door was located and knocked loudly on the door.

The butler opened the door and welcomed them as they walked inside.

Margaret had never really interfered with the original antique interior of the house and, as Arabella stepped inside, she got a shock. The whole interior had been refurbished. The hallway divided the ground floor in half. To the left was a study and a staircase that led upstairs and one that led downstairs to the kitchens and servants' quarters.

On the other side of the hallway double doors led into the dining room which was at the front of the house. The windows here were French windows that led onto the terrace. As Arabella looked around she didn't recognise the gentle elegance that had been there before they left for France. In its stead was highly polished new walnut floors, a stone staircase with cast-iron balustrades, and Venetian crystal chandeliers.

'Charles?' she queried as he smilingly opened the doors into the dining room. Again, the inside had been transformed into an arena of opulence with thick pile carpet, a new Grecian marble fireplace and a gigantic oak table with ornate curved-back embroidered chairs.

'Well?' asked Charles proudly.

'But who organised all this?' she asked, concerned.

'I did, of course!'

'But do your parents know?'

'No.'

'But it's their house, Charles!'

'And it's going to be mine one day, so why not invest in it now when we have to live in it now?' he said as he led her out of the dining room and up the stairs to the first floor, which was mostly taken up with an L-shaped drawing room. Arabella walked in and marvelled at the polished walnut floor, the gold mirrors, the extravagant drapes at the two French windows that opened up onto the balcony at the front of the house, offering stunning views across Regent's Park.

'It's all from Paris,' declared Charles proudly. 'I met with the interior designers before we left for the Continent and told them what I wanted.'

'But how much did all this cost?' asked Arabella, still in shock.

'Who cares? It's only money and we can afford it.'

'Thanks to my dowry!' she said, crossing over to the French windows and inspecting the drapes.

'Don't be so suburban Dublin, Arabella!' he chided. 'We're going to be part of London high society now and need a home to impress.'

'But I thought your parents said our move to London was to be temporary until all the fuss dies down and we return to Armstrong House?'

'Pah!' he said dismissively. 'There will be plenty of time for me to return to Armstrong House when I'm Lord Armstrong. Until then I plan to live a little. And now we have the means to do so.'

'Well, I don't know what your parents are going to say about it all,' said Arabella.

He smirked at her. 'I shouldn't worry too much what they think. I can guess already what they think of us both at this stage.'

'Don't, Charles,' snapped Arabella, going red with embarrassment as she always did when she thought of Margaret.

Charles went over and tugged the bell pull and a minute later a young dark-haired woman entered in a nanny's uniform.

'Arabella, this is Mademoiselle Isabelle.'

'*Bonjour, madame,* so pleased to meet you,' Isabelle said, doing a little curtsy.

Arabella nodded at her, confused.

'I think Prudence. needs a sleep after all the travel, Mademoiselle. Take her to the nursery,' instructed Charles.

'*Oui, monsieur,*' said Isabelle as she went over to Arabella and reached out to take Prudence from her.

'I'm sorry, but who exactly are you?' asked Arabella as she refused to hand her child over.

Isabelle looked at Charles, concerned. 'But I am the new baby's nanny, *naturellement!*'

'The new baby's nanny! But I never employed you!' said Arabella.

'*Non* – Monsieur Charles interviewed me,' the girl explained.

'Oh he did, did he?' said Arabella, glaring at Charles.

'Yes, before we left for the Continent... Arabella dear, hand the child to *mademoiselle* and let her take her to the nursery,' said Charles.

Arabella reluctantly handed over Prudence and Isabelle left the room.

'Charles, I wanted to interview the nanny.'

'Well, I saved you the bother.'

'I didn't want a foreign nanny! I wanted an English or Irish one!'

'Trust me, my dear,' he said as he examined the fine whiskey in the decanters and poured himself a glass.

As she looked at him in exasperation, she felt she could never trust anyone less.

CHAPTER 22

'Another letter from Gwyneth,' said Charles over breakfast in the dining room. 'She wants to come and see her new niece.'

It had been a few weeks since they had arrived back in London and they still were lying low. They wanted some time to pass before people saw Prudence so nobody would spot she wasn't a newborn.

'Oh Charles, put her off for another while,' said Arabella, dreading the thought of meeting her.

'I'm afraid she insists. She is coming down from Battington Hall next week to London.'

'Not to stay here?' Arabella was alarmed.

'No, the Duke has a villa nearby, don't you know.'

'I don't want to see her, Charles.'

'Why? I think it's time we stopped shutting ourselves away.'

'What must Gwyneth think of me? One minute with Harrison and the next married to you,' Arabella said.

'I'm sure she'd think much worse of you if she knew the real truth!' chuckled Charles as he put the letter back in the envelope.

'And of you!' retorted Arabella.

'Anyway, we need to get on with life now... I'm getting bored.'

Charles threw his hand of cards down on the table.

'I can't believe it!' exclaimed Tom Hamley. 'You win again!'

The other four men around the table shook their heads in resigned admiration.

'What can I say?' laughed Charles. 'Lady Luck is being good to me! Another round?'

'No!' said Tom. 'That's me out for the count.'

They were in a panelled room in Tom Hamley's house. Tom had been at university with Charles and was an old friend of his. All the men present were friends of Charles from his school and university days, and all were avid card players. The butler came over quickly and began to fill their balloon glasses with cognac.

'I think we'll call it a night ... same time next Friday?' asked Charles as he took a cigar from the wooden box being offered by a footman.

'To win more money from us?' asked Tom mockingly.

Charles sat back and lit his cigar. 'I'm sure your luck will change.'

'Yours will have to change first!'

Charles looked around happily. He had missed this in Ireland. These friends, this scene.

'Tell me, Armstrong, when are we going to meet this wife of yours?' asked Michael Darnton, another friend.

'Well, you know, she's been busy with the baby,' said Charles.

'I think my mother met her during the week in Regent's Park,' said Tom. 'They ended up talking by the boating lake. She was with your French nanny and the baby.'

'Yes, they go for a walk in the park every morning, weather permitting.'

'She said she was very beautiful and very nice,' said Tom.

'Oh, it was definitely her in that case!' laughed Charles.

They continued talking and drinking into the night.

'What we need is some new blood to join this card game. Somebody who's not as good a player but has plenty of money to lose,' said Charles.

'What about your new brother-in-law, the Duke of Battington?' suggested Tom.

'Are you joking me? *His Grace* is far too sensible and stoic ever to get mixed up in gambling. He's much too concerned with his prize heifers on his estate.'

'Well, he must have a large circle of wealthy friends whom you could plunder?' suggested Tom.

Charles dragged on his cigar. 'Gwyneth is visiting me this week. I'll keep a look out... Of course, we have to be careful ... baccarat is illegal, gentlemen.'

Gwyneth marvelled at the décor of the house in Hanover Terrace as she was shown through the hallway and up the stairs by the butler.

'The Duchess of Battington,' announced the butler as he opened the door in the drawing room and she entered.

'Duchess!' declared Charles as he came over to her and gave her a hug.

'Charles – you're looking well,' said Gwyneth. 'The Riviera obviously suited you.'

'Oh, it did!' he said.

She saw Arabella sitting on the couch with the baby in a cot beside her.

'Hello, Gwyneth,' said Arabella, unable to keep her voice from sounding nervous.

Gwyneth walked over to her and then bent down and kissed her on the cheek.

'It's good to see you again, Arabella.'

Arabella nodded and smiled at her.

'And this must be Prudence,' said Gwyneth, turning her attention to the cot. She reached in and picked up the baby. Charles came and stood beside her.

'Well?' he asked.

'What a lovely baby!' said Gwyneth.

She was surprised. The baby looked like neither Charles nor Arabella. This baby was quite plain, Gwyneth thought, unlike her two good-looking parents.

Gwyneth sat down beside Arabella as she cradled Prudence.

'I was giving up hope of ever meeting my niece,' laughed Gwyneth. 'I thought you were going to keep her all to yourselves.' They spent some more time discussing the baby and then Isabelle came and took her away and the butler brought tea.

'I hardly recognised this place,' said Gwyneth, as she examined the ornate gold-framed couch she was sitting on, wondering where all the money was coming from. 'I'm just back from a visit to Armstrong House. It was the first time I was home since I married His Grace.'

'And how is everybody there?' asked Charles.

'More or less the same. Papa still going on about the Land War, Mama still trying to train Emily, James still doing whatever James does.'

'I imagine the house is quieter now without you and Charles,' said Arabella, afraid to mention Harrison.

'Well, life goes on in Armstrong House much as it always has ... though I daresay life is going to become even quieter there now.'

'Why?' asked Charles.

'Daphne has got engaged.'

'Really?' Charles was surprised. 'To whom?'

'To Gilbert Hatton.'

'He's a son of one of those Dublin brewery families, isn't he?' asked Charles.

'Yes, that's him.'

'Mama must be delighted,' said Charles.

'It's certainly got their blessing,' said Gwyneth as she looked uncomfortably at Arabella.

'Unlike my marriage to Arabella,' said Charles with a knowing look.

Gwyneth cleared her throat. 'I won't deny we got a shock on hearing you two had married.'

The butler knocked, came in and said, 'Your lordship, there's a gentleman downstairs to see you – Mr Arbuthnott.'

'Ah, he's come to give me my winnings from a card game I played with him last weekend – I'll be back in a short while,' Charles said as he followed the butler out.

Arabella and Gwyneth sat awkwardly together.

'It's all right,' said Arabella. 'We don't expect your approval.'

'I can't speak for the rest of the Armstrongs, but I think you did a very brave thing in ... in letting Harrison go.'

'You do?' Arabella was surprised.

'If you didn't love Harrison, it would be far more cruel to have gone ahead and married him.'

'That's kind of you to say, but I don't think anyone else is thinking like that... We're in a kind of exile here in London. Our parents thought it best for us to live here for a while because of the scandal.'

'I won't pretend that your dumping Harrison and marrying Charles hasn't been the talk of the drawing rooms of Dublin and the big houses around Ireland. But the thing is, did you do the right thing in marrying Charles? Are you in love with him?'

Arabella nodded and smiled. 'Yes, I am.'

'Well, then, does anything else matter? Besides, looking at Charles, he looks as if he is enjoying this exile immeasurably. Card games indeed! I don't think he was ever cut out to be a country gentleman, much to my father's chagrin.'

'And what about Harrison? Have you heard how he is? I understand he went to New York?'

'Yes, he's still there, working in a bank. He has no plans to return.'

Charles came in, counting an amount of money.

Gwyneth stood up. 'I'd better be getting back. We're having a party at our house in London on Saturday. You'll both be able to come?'

'Wouldn't miss it for the world!' said Charles gleefully.

Arabella came down the stairs on the Saturday evening dressed in an extravagant ball gown she had bought in Bond Street during the week. She felt nervous about the evening ahead at Gwyneth's but as she walked into the drawing room Charles seemed overly excited at the prospect of the night.

'Will I do?' she asked self-consciously.

He looked her up and down and then took a drink of his cognac. 'Very well indeed.'

He walked over to her and kissed her. She put her hand around the back of his neck and kissed him before pulling back and smiling. All the trauma was worth it for moments like this.

'The carriage awaits!' he said as he offered her his arm.

They made the short journey to the Duke's London residence on Prince Albert Road. It was a four-storey detached villa up a short drive. As their carriage pulled up outside, Arabella could see the rooms inside full of elegantly dressed people.

'I think we're a bit late,' said Charles as they climbed the steps to the front door.

'There's a surprise!' said Arabella, who had become accustomed to Charles' lateness.

A footman was waiting at the door and showed them in.

'Charles!' said Gwyneth as she spotted them and came over.

'A nice small gathering!' remarked Charles sarcastically as he took in the crowd.

Gwyneth kissed Arabella on the cheek. 'Come, and I'll introduce you to everyone.'

Charles and Arabella caused quite a stir that

night. The young Irish aristocrat and his wife offered what most of them wanted to be associated with: youth, beauty, money, class, family connections and one of the finest addresses in the city. Arabella noticed Charles lapped it up as people flocked to them. She noticed he seemed to be almost on a mission to ingratiate himself with as many people as possible.

On the following Monday Arabella and Charles were in the dining room waiting for breakfast. There was a stack of envelopes in front of Charles which he was feverishly opening. Prudence was sitting in her high chair close to Arabella.

'And another invitation to a party next Saturday night!' said Charles with relish.

'You were obviously quite a hit at Gwyneth's,' remarked Arabella.

'Yes,' he said absent-mindedly as he read another request for their company at a cocktail party. He looked up at her quickly. 'We were a hit, my dear... I'll have to study these invitations and see which ones we should attend.'

'Don't I get a say in this?' she said with a mixture of incredulity and bemusement.

'Of course, I'll leave out the invitations I think we should attend and you just tell me if you have any objections.'

'Charles!' snapped Arabella. 'You can leave out *all* the invitations and I will go through them myself in my own time!'

He smirked at her. 'As you wish.'

The butler came in with a large tray which he deposited on the sideboard. Then he approached the table carrying two plates which he put in front of them, looking embarrassed.

Arabella looked down at the burned bacon and eggs.

'What is this?' she asked, surprised.

'I'm afraid the kitchen maid isn't a very good cook,' he said.

'The kitchen maid! Why is she cooking breakfast? Where is Mrs Glover?'

The butler glanced down nervously at Charles. 'I'm afraid Mrs Glover is no longer with us.'

'Well, where is she?' Arabella demanded.

The butler started coughing as he looked down at Charles.

'Charles?' said Arabella, looking for some kind of explanation.

'I'm afraid I had to give Mrs Glover her marching orders. Don't worry – I gave her an excellent reference.'

'Marching orders! But why?'

'Because she could only cook plain fare.'

'Plain fare!' She looked down at her plate. 'I think I would prefer plain fare to burned fare! Besides, Mrs Glover was an excellent cook.'

'Yes, if you like a continual diet of Brussels sprouts and boiled bacon!'

'And who is to do the cooking now, as it is obvious the kitchen maid is not up to the job?'

'Monsieur Huppert.'

'And who is Monsieur Huppert?' demanded Arabella, her disbelief increasing.

'Monsieur Huppert is one of the finest chefs in London. He worked in the Ritz.'

'The Ritz!' Arabella's voiced rose further

decibels. 'You have employed a French chef to be our cook?'

Charles put his hand down on the stack of envelopes. 'Well, we are going to be doing a lot of entertaining. We want our house to be associated with good food and not Brussels sprouts!'

Arabella turned to the butler. 'Could you take away my plate, please. I'm no longer hungry.'

'*Moi aussi!*' said Charles as he pushed his plate away. The butler quickly took the plates and left.

'Charles, you mustn't do everything without consulting me!' Arabella said.

'Yes, dear!' said Charles as he got up from the table and sauntered out. Arabella stared at the closed door and then in a fit of temper took up her fork and threw it at the door. The clatter caused Prudence to start bawling.

'For goodness' sake!' said Arabella as she took the child and started to soothe her. She went and tugged on the bell pull and called, '*Mademoiselle!*'

CHAPTER 23

The weeks flew by into months and Charles and Arabella found they soon became one of the most sought-after couples on the London social scene. It wasn't long before they started to host dinner parties and occasions at the house on Hanover Terrace, and an invitation there became a coveted prize. Charles would select the wittiest and most connected people to gather at their home as he had a clear ambition for their house to gain a reputation as one of the most talked-about houses in the capital.

One evening Arabella and Charles were having dinner with guests.

'Arabella, that was simply delicious,' said David Chester, a young guest at the table.

'Thank you, David,' said Arabella.

Dessert was being served and the footmen placed white bowls in front of the diners. In each bowl was a large solid sphere of chocolate. The footmen then went around with silver jugs of piping hot cream. They poured the hot cream over the chocolate spheres which caused them to dissolve instantly and out of the middle of each one oozed raspberry.

'That's not a pudding – that's art!' declared another guest as she looked down at the sudden creation of a swirl of melted chocolate, raspberry and cream.

'That looks too good to eat!' said David as he smiled down at the dessert.

Arabella picked up his silver spoon, handed it to him and said, 'I insist!'

David was a young man who had suddenly come into a large inheritance and moved up from the country to enjoy London. His family was known and he was welcomed on to the social scene. He was slightly naïve and awestruck since coming to the capital, and Charles had befriended him at a few events and invited him to dine at Hanover Terrace a couple of times. David was very grateful as he felt lost in the big city.

'Any luck in finding a house to buy yet?'

Charles asked David.

'I'm afraid not,' said David. 'I've been going around with an agent but can't find anything suitable.'

'Why don't you let me help you?'

'I'd be very grateful, Charles,' smiled David.

After dinner the women retired to the drawing room while the men stayed at the table to enjoy cigars and port.

Charles opened a cigar box and offered one to David. 'Try one of these – imported from Cuba.'

'Don't mind if I do,' said David, taking one.

'They're excellent, I assure you.'

After he had lit up David said, 'Thanks again for the offer to help find a house, Charles. Some of these estate agents can be real shysters.'

'Yes, they can. It's all about who you know in London.'

'Yes, I'm finding that out.'

'I mean, having lots of money is all very well, but it's connections that matter.'

'Yes, I see that ... and thank you, Charles – you've introduced me to a lot of important contacts.'

'My pleasure. I say – are you any good at playing cards?'

'Eh – not bad. I was the best in my school!'

Charles lowered his voice and neared him. 'I'm a member of a small circle which meets to play cards once a week.'

'Really?' David's eyes opened wide.

'If you wish I could see about the others letting you attend once or twice.'

'Do you think they'd agree?'

'I don't know, it's a fairly select circle. These are serious players playing for serious money...' Charles shook his head and turned and looked out across the park again. 'No, forget it – it wouldn't be for you.'

'No, Charles, please ask them at least. I'd be very grateful!'

'Well, I can't promise anything – but I'll try if you insist.'

'Thank you, Charles!'

Charles reached forward and put out his cigar in an ashtray. 'Right, shall we go and join the ladies upstairs?' he suggested smiling.

Charles and Arabella were at the London Palladium in a box beside the royal box, watching a show. In the main audience a man and a woman were sitting in one of the aisles. The woman looked up and, spotting Charles and Arabella, turned to her companion.

'Who are that couple beside the royal box?' she asked.

The man peered up. 'Lord Armstrong's son, Charles, and his wife from Dublin.'

'Oh, that's them, is it?'

'They've quickly become a must-have at any party worth its salt.'

'I've heard they serve the best food in London at their dinner parties.'

'Yes, it's all caviar from Russia, champagne from the best French vineyards. Money seems no object to them... Of course you heard the rumour?'

'No?'

'She ditched the spare for the heir.'

'Sorry?'

'Seemingly she was engaged to the younger brother and left him to marry Charles.'

The woman took out her binoculars and studied Charles. 'Clever girl! Do you know them?'

'I've spoken to Charles a couple of times.'

'You just *have* to introduce me to them after the show. I'd love to get an invitation to their house. I believe it's quite breathtaking if also somewhat vulgar!'

CHAPTER 24

At Armstrong House Margaret was reading through a letter from a friend of hers in London. It was after dinner and Daphne, Emily and Lawrence were enjoying the summer evening with her in the drawing room.

'Penelope's whole letter is about Charles and Arabella!' said Margaret as she continued to read through it.

'What does she say?' asked Lawrence, concerned.

'Well, she merely repeats what other people have been telling us. That they appear to be having a wonderful life, get invited to all the best places and seem to be rolling in money!'

Margaret was due to travel to London soon with Daphne to have her fitted for a wedding dress.

Lawrence sat thinking. 'I think I shall go to London with you and Daphne, otherwise our grand-daughter will be in pigtails before I meet her.'

'It might be wise, Lawrence, to see what is actually going on there.' Margaret was consumed with concern.

Emily sat in a dreamlike trance as she always did when news came of Charles and Arabella's life in London. She could only imagine the glamorous time they were having there. She desperately missed Charles. And even though she knew the whole fiasco nearly ended in disaster, she hadn't had a moment's excitement since her secret part in Charles and Arabella's affair.

'I'll go too in that case. I don't want to be left here on my own,' said Emily.

'You won't be on your own,' Margaret shot down her suggestion. 'You'll have James and a household of servants.'

'But, Mama!' objected Emily.

'You'll stay here, Emily! And concentrate on your German grammar!' insisted Margaret.

David Chester placed a winning hand of cards down on the table at Tom Hamley's house.

Charles shouted in irritation. 'You win again!'

There was a chorus of annoyed groans around the table. It was the fourth time David had joined Charles' gambling circle.

David was almost embarrassed but very excited. 'It must be beginner's luck.'

'Beginner's luck, my arse! You're a bloody natural!' sighed Charles as he rose from his chair. 'Anyway, I'd better be getting back home – it's after one already.'

'I'll get my butler to call you a cab,' said Tom as he tugged the bell pull.

'Come on, David, I'll drop you at your hotel on the way home,' offered Charles.

'Thanks!' said David, also getting up.

'Until next weekend, gentlemen,' said Charles with a wink as they left.

'Male-female-male-female ... female...' said Arabella. 'I'm one male guest short to make up the table for the dinner party this Saturday.'

She and Charles were sitting in the drawing room where Arabella was making the table plan.

She looked up at Charles. 'Why don't we invite David Chester? He's always very pleasant company.'

Charles looked up from his newspaper. 'No – actually David has left London. He's returned home to Wiltshire.'

'Returned home! But I thought he loved it here.'

'Evidently not. He missed home. I think he made a couple of unwise investments as well.' Charles returned to reading his paper.

'What a shame! He was such a nice character.'

David Chester was sitting in a train-carriage looking despondent as he travelled back to the country. He was trying to figure out what had gone wrong. A few weeks earlier he had arrived in London with a large inheritance and the city at his feet. Now he was travelling home having lost most of his money in a game of cards.

CHAPTER 25

Arabella was dreading the visit from her parents-in-law. Meeting Gwyneth regularly was different: Gwyneth didn't know the truth. But Margaret and Lawrence did and that was an entirely different matter. The servants had been working non-stop to ensure the house was spick and span for their arrival. Prudence was dressed in her best outfit from Harrods. They waited in the drawing room.

The butler was showing Margaret, Lawrence and Daphne up the stairs.

'It is good to see you again, Lord Lawrence and Lady Margaret,' said the butler.

'And you, Burchill? How have things been?' asked Margaret.

'Eventful, Lady Margaret, eventful,' Burchill said as he reached the top of the stairs.

'I can imagine,' said Lawrence as he inspected the new banisters.

'We have so many French staff employed here, I'm afraid there's hardly anybody left for me to speak English to downstairs, my lady,' said Burchill.

'Poor Burchill!' said Margaret, as he opened the drawing-room door and ushered them in.

'Lord and Lady Armstrong and Lady Daphne,' announced Burchill.

'Charles!' said Margaret as she went to hug and

213

kiss him.

'Mother!' said Charles, embracing her warmly. 'And Father and Daphne!' He embraced them all.

Arabella stood up.

'Hello, Lady Armstrong,' said Arabella.

'Please, dear, call me Lady Margaret,' said Margaret, giving her a polite kiss but fixing her with a steely look.

'And this must be little Prudence!' said Lawrence as he picked her up.

They all swarmed around Prudence.

'She has a strong determined look about her,' said Margaret, realising Gwyneth was correct in describing the child as plain.

'She's quite a good baby,' said Arabella. 'She never cries or is contrary.'

'Well, that's a blessing – at least,' said Margaret, eyeing Arabella.

'Goodness, I hardly recognise my house,' said Lawrence, looking around at the décor.

'Very ostentatious taste,' said Margaret.

Arabella felt herself go red. 'I hope you don't mind–'

'Of course they don't mind!' said Charles quickly. He turned to his parents. 'Your house is all modernised and it didn't cost you a penny.'

'I imagine it cost *you* a very pretty penny,' said Margaret pointedly.

'And what's it all for?' asked Lawrence. 'A house that is only used for a couple of months for the season and will be unoccupied for the rest of the year.'

Arabella decided to change the topic quickly.

'We've prepared lunch for you. You must be starving after the journey.' She went over and tugged the bell pull.

'Pheasant!' said Charles. 'Roast pheasant for lunch.'

As Charles and Arabella followed his parents out to go downstairs to the dining room, she whispered to him, 'Thank you for not claiming full responsibility for the refurbishment and for letting them think I was behind it!'

'Of course – I couldn't take the credit for all this décor myself!'

Luckily Margaret was preoccupied with Daphne's wedding dress and arrangements during their stay, which Arabella was glad of because her mother-in-law constantly got subtle digs in at her when they were together. It was obvious to Arabella that Margaret had no intention of letting her forget her past. Lawrence was kind but kept his distance from her, and seemed more preoccupied with his son's lifestyle in London than anything else.

The night before they were to return to Ireland Margaret and Lawrence were speaking in their bedroom.

'They have mentioned nothing about returning home!' said Lawrence.

'They have no excuse any more. Prudence is older and nobody will doubt the facts of her birth... We'll have to tackle them tomorrow before we leave.'

'Yes, I'll speak to him and you can speak to her,'

said Lawrence.

Margaret raised her eyes to heaven. 'I suspect she's somebody who doesn't bend too easily. She's far too stubborn for her own good... She never once asked about Harrison.'

'Do you know, I haven't gone out to inspect the gardens even once since I arrived,' said Lawrence.

'Oh, they are being very well tended to,' Charles assured him. 'We have an excellent gardener.'

'Is he French as well?' Margaret asked sarcastically.

'Come, Charles,' said Lawrence, standing up. 'We'll go and take a walk outside.'

Charles shrugged and followed his father out of the drawing room, leaving Margaret alone with Arabella.

Margaret smiled over at Arabella. 'I'm glad we have this time to talk.'

'Yes?' said Arabella, shifting uncomfortably.

'I wanted to discuss your plans for the future.'

'I don't think we have any, Lady Margaret.'

'That was what I was afraid of ... you know, it's wonderful to have a townhouse, but all this,' Margaret waved her hand in the air, 'is only a townhouse to spend a few weeks in during the season. The same as the house in Dublin caters for the family for visits in the winter. But our real home is Armstrong House.'

'Yes.'

'So when will you be returning?'

'Well, Charles has no plans to return. He quite likes living here.'

'Then it is your duty to convince him otherwise.'

'I don't think anyone can convince Charles to do anything he doesn't want to.'

Margaret spoke slowly and patiently. 'A wife's role is to advise, guide and encourage her husband. That's what you must do now, in order to return to Armstrong House and start training for your roles in life.'

'Our roles?'

'Arabella, you will be Lady Armstrong one day, and it takes a lot more than just sitting around in pretty frocks to assume that role. You need to return to Armstrong House where I can start directing and training you so that you are ready when the time comes.'

'I'm not Emily!'

'I'm not suggesting you are – and what do you mean by that?'

'I'm not a project for you to mould and create.'

'My dear, you will learn a lot from me,' Margaret spoke assuredly.

'And where would we live during this – training?'

'In Armstrong House, of course.'

'All under the same roof!' Arabella said.

'If you prefer you can live in Hunter's Farm for now. Hunter's Farm is a very pretty–'

'I know what Hunter's Farm is!' snapped Arabella, thinking of her secret liaisons there with Charles before they were married.

'I must say I have huge concerns about the fact that you will one day be the matriarch of our family,' Margaret said. 'You very nearly brought destruction, not only on yourself but the whole Armstrong and Tattinger families as well.'

'I'm trying to put all that behind me now.'

'Easier said than done. You destroyed poor Harrison.'

'I know what I did to Harrison, and accept full responsibility for it.'

'Good! Somebody needs to! You behaved despicably and without conscience or morals.'

'And from what you are saying you will obviously never let me forget it, will you? I will always be a fallen woman to you. A woman who had intercourse before marriage. Who got pregnant before marriage. A whore!'

'You are only reaffirming my opinion that you are not worthy to be Lady Armstrong.'

'And you are reaffirming my opinion that we cannot return to Ireland to live. Live under the same roof as you? And put up with your constant disapproval?'

'I can see there is no talking sense to you.'

'I will always be grateful to you and Lord Lawrence for your intervention at the time, but I need to get on with my own life now – with Charles, with Prudence and with the child I'm carrying.'

Margaret blinked a few times. 'You're pregnant again?'

'Yes... Nobody knows yet – I haven't even told Charles.'

'I see!' Margaret was taken aback by the news.

Arabella's face softened. 'I want us to be friends, Margaret. But you don't. You want to punish me for the past.'

The garden was a long straight one with a mews house at the end.

'You see, Father, nothing to worry about, the garden is in full bloom,' said Charles.

'Yes ... of course, maintaining a small garden in London is one thing – maintaining an eight-thousand-acre estate in Ireland is another.'

'Which you do excellently.'

'But I need help running it, Charles.'

'You have James.'

'James isn't my heir, you are. And ... well ... this arrangement of living in London was only ever temporary, as you know.'

'And suggested by you.'

Lawrence felt himself become annoyed. 'Suggested to get you out of the ridiculous circumstances you and that girl in there found yourselves in.'

'And a wonderful suggestion it was too. It's worked out perfectly.'

'So?'

'So what?'

'So when are you coming back to Armstrong House now the situation has blown over?'

'I'm not coming back, Father. I enjoy life here too much.'

'But this is not your destiny! Your destiny is Armstrong House and the estate.'

'And destinies wait until we are ready for them.'

'You think you are very clever, don't you? I find it all irresponsible.'

'You find everything irresponsible.'

'This is still my house you are living in here,

even though you've done it up like a bordello and filled it with French waiters!'

'Would you like us to leave? We will if you would prefer. I'm independently wealthy now.'

'Don't be ridiculous, you're still my heir. But you might find, however large your wife's dowry is, money quickly goes when you run through it like you do.'

'Well, you don't need to concern yourself with that.' Charles looked up at the sky. 'I think it's going to rain – shall we go back inside?' He turned and walked back to the house.

Lawrence hurried after him, full of anger.

'Arabella has some news,' said Margaret as Charles and Lawrence walked into the room, Charles relaxed and smiling, Lawrence with a face like thunder.

'Yes?' asked Charles.

'I'm with child.'

'Oh!' said Charles and then he smiled happily, went to her and embraced her. 'What wonderful news! This calls for a celebration.' He went over and tugged the bell pull.

The butler appeared promptly.

'Champagne, Burchill! The very best we have!'

'Of course, why not?' sighed Lawrence.

'Just think, Father, this may be a son. A future Lord Armstrong,' smiled Charles happily.

'At least this pregnancy won't involve a conspiracy of silence!' said Margaret.

Later Margaret and Lawrence sat stony-faced in their carriage as Daphne waved goodbye to

Charles and Arabella who were standing at the door.

'See you at my wedding in Armstrong House next year!' Daphne cried as the carriage pulled away.

Arabella and Charles went inside and stared at each other in silence for a while.

'Well,' said Charles, 'at least that's over.'

Then they both erupted into laughter and fell into each other's arms.

CHAPTER 26

The cards were being dealt with around the table at Tom Hamley's house. Their card-playing circle had grown considerably, mainly due to Charles' connections and his subtle recruiting through them. The butler opened the door and a tall broad man entered whom Charles immediately observed was dressed expensively. He was nearly dressed too well for a card game on a Friday night.

'Mr Hugh Fitzroy,' announced the butler before taking the man's cape, gold-crested walking stick and top hat.

'Good evening, gentlemen,' said Hugh as he nodded to everyone at the table.

'Ah, Hugh, you managed to find us all right?' said Tom, getting up and shaking his hand.

'Yes, you gave my driver good instructions,' said Hugh. 'Good! Good!' said Tom and he proceeded to introduce him to each person at the table.

When it came to Charles' turn, Hugh stared at him intently with dark, almost black eyes then nodded.

Charles nodded back politely.

Hugh took his seat and the cards continued to be dealt.

'Any word of David Chester?' asked Tom.

'I believe he has returned to wherever he is from,' said Charles.

'Who's David Chester?' inquired Hugh.

'A young man who arrived from the country a while back with more money than sense ... and has returned to the country with considerably less money and hopefully a lot more sense!' said Charles, causing everyone to laugh.

Hugh nodded knowingly. 'Card-playing is for fools, unless you know what you're doing.'

'Isn't that the truth?' said Charles as he turned his cards over.

Charles continued to observe Hugh Fitzroy during the night. He guessed him to be a good but cautious player. The man seemed to have the trappings of wealth: gold cufflinks, gold cigarette case, plenty of money to bet with. But the man was obviously not of their class. He tried hard to disguise it but his manners were unpolished, his etiquette uninformed, his education not obvious. It was his accent that most intrigued Charles. Hugh clearly had a common accent that he was trying very hard to hide.

'Who is he and where on earth did you find him?' Charles asked Tom during the break as Tom refilled Charles' wineglass.

'Hugh Fitzroy is a very, very wealthy man,' said Tom.

'But I've never heard of him,' said Charles.

'You wouldn't have. He's from somewhere down the East End.'

'The East End!'

'Yes. I don't know much about him. I met him through an acquaintance of mine. He's completely self-made seemingly.'

'And how did he make his money?' Charles was becoming more intrigued by the minute.

'Who knows? He doesn't give much away.'

'I'm surprised you're allowing him into our circle,' said Charles as he watched Hugh eat canapes clumsily.

'Why not? His money is as good as anyone's, isn't it?'

'Call a cab for me, will you?' Charles asked Tom's butler, as they were all putting on their coats and hats to leave.

'Can I give anyone a lift? My driver is outside,' offered Hugh.

'I'm going to Regent's Park, if that's on your way?' said Charles.

Hugh put his hand out to indicate to Charles to go first. Charles walked down the steps from Tom's house and found a large ornate carriage waiting for them.

'Go first to Regent's Park,' instructed Hugh to the driver. He turned to Charles.

'I'm staying at Claridge's. I have a suite of rooms there.'

'But Regent's Park isn't in your direction at all!

I'm taking you out of your way,' said Charles.

'No matter,' said Hugh.

There was a heavy fog as the carriage drove through the London streets.

Charles found Hugh socially awkward and almost a little nervous as they chatted, but he suspected this man was no David Chester. He imagined him to be very tough.

'Tom said you were related to a duke?' Hugh said.

'That's right – my sister is the Duchess of Battington.'

'And you're the son of an earl?'

'That's right,' Charles chuckled. 'My father, the present Lord Armstrong, wants me to go back to Ireland and assume my position, but I'm having too much fun here!'

Hugh nodded as the carriage pulled up outside Charles' house.

'Well, thank you for the lift,' said Charles. 'Er, I'm having a card game here at my house next Friday evening, starting at nine, if you're free. Tom Hamley and the rest from this evening will be here.'

Hugh seemed surprised at the invitation and just nodded. 'See you then. Drive on!' he shouted at the driver.

'I'm having some friends over tonight. We'll be down in the dining room and so won't be bothering you,' Charles informed Arabella the following Friday in the drawing room.

'Shall I have Burchill prepare food?' asked Arabella.

'No need. I'll have something light sent up from the kitchen when they are here.'

Later that evening Arabella watched from the balcony of the drawing room upstairs as Charles' friends arrived one by one. She was struck by an oversized carriage that pulled up. Unlike the others, who arrived in cabs, this was obviously a private carriage as the man got out and the driver made no move to leave.

As the man made his way up to the front of the house he looked up, inspecting it. He stopped still when he saw Arabella standing there looking down at him from the balcony and stared at her. Arabella got an uncomfortable feeling and turned and went back inside.

As the hours of the evening passed by Arabella sat in the drawing room reading. She became curious as there wasn't a sound coming from downstairs. Finally she decided to go and investigate. She went downstairs and over to the dining room. Opening the door, she walked in. She found the group of men sitting around the table playing cards.

Seeing her, the men all stood up and bowed.

'Good evening, Tom ... gentlemen...' she nodded at them and gestured that they should sit down.

She saw the man from the carriage at the end of the table, again staring at her and making her feel uncomfortable.

'Can we help you, dear?' asked Charles who hadn't bothered to stand up. He was looking none too pleased at her entrance.

'Charles, could I speak to you for a moment?'

she asked.

'Is it necessary?' he asked, annoyed.

'Yes, it is!'

He mumbled under his breath, put down his cards and followed her out, closing the door behind him. She walked across the hall to the study. They both entered and he closed the door.

'Well?' he asked impatiently.

'What do you mean by having a game of baccarat in my house?' she demanded.

'I think you'll find it's my father's house.'

'In my *home* then in that case?'

'Why shouldn't I have a game of cards here? I'm always having games in the others' houses.'

'I don't care what you have in the other houses, but I will not have you play illicit games here,' she insisted.

'Whyever not?'

'Because I don't want to be associated with something like that! Gwyneth would never have a game of cards in her house or any other of the ladies we know.'

'I think we are already aware from your past that you are not like the other ladies we know,' he said mockingly.

His words were like a slap across the face. 'No, you're right. I'm not like the other simpering wives we know. I think we're both aware of what I'm capable of.'

'Arabella–'

'You brought me to the edge of destruction once before and I will *never* allow you to risk mine or my children's futures again.'

She marched across the room to the door.

He grabbed her arm. 'Where are you going?'

'Let go of my hand!' she snapped.

He held her tightly. 'Answer my question.'

'I'm going across that hall and I'm going to tell those men to get out. And I won't be telling them politely.'

She shook him free and continued to the door and across the hall.

'Arabella!' he hissed. 'All right! I'll tell them to go.'

She turned and faced him. 'You've got five minutes to get them out of here.'

She walked up the stairs. He looked after her angrily before turning and walking into the dining room.

'Sorry about this, chaps – I'm afraid we're going to have to call it a night.'

CHAPTER 27

The next day Arabella and Charles were sitting in an uneasy silence in the drawing room when Burchill came in carrying a huge hamper.

'What's that, Burchill?' questioned Charles.

'A hamper from Harrods delivered for Mrs Armstrong,' said Burchill as he struggled to put it down on the floor. 'There's a note attached.'

He handed the note to Arabella and left.

She opened the note.

'Well?' asked Charles.

'It's from a Hugh Fitzroy.' She struggled to read

the almost illegible scrawl. 'He says... *"Sorry for the embarrassment last night".'*

'He must mean your hissy fit at the card game,' said Charles as he opened the hamper. 'But this is crammed with the very best food.'

'Who is he?' asked Arabella, knowing he was the man who had been staring at her.

'I met him through Tom Hamley. Filthy rich apparently – bit rough around the edges though,' said Charles as he unscrewed a jar of caviar and sniffed at it. 'Maybe you should cause a scene more often, if it gets these results!'

Arabella looked at the hamper, feeling uneasy.

Hugh Fitzroy became a regular with Charles' card-gaming set. Charles found him never outspoken or loud. He was polite to everyone, but could be rough to staff. He was a strange mixture of confidence and insecurity. He was always keen to display the trappings of his wealth to everyone present. He seemed to focus in on Charles a lot and listened intently as he spoke about people he knew or parties he was attending. Soon Charles began to realise that if he discussed Armstrong House and his family or the Duke of Battington, Fitzroy seemed to become awestruck.

'You have to realise he's never met aristocracy before,' said Tom as they discussed him one evening.

'Well, money opens doors, no matter how uncouth he is,' Charles said.

Charles had an appointment with the bank manager, Mr Jones, and set off on foot to the meeting. He walked down Regent Street and through Piccadilly Circus until he reached the bank.

'I'm afraid money has been pouring out of your account,' warned the bank manager, handing over the figures.

Charles stared at the amount left in his account in shock.

'But there must be some mistake! The money deposited from my father-in-law on my wedding was ten times this amount.'

'There's no mistake, I'm afraid to say... The bank did write to you many times to update you on your ever-dwindling account.'

'But ... but...' Charles couldn't think what to say. He never read post from banks.

Mr Jones observed Charles. The young aristocrat's lavish lifestyle had become notorious around London.

'I should think there is no need to worry,' he said. 'With an estate as large as your father's which one day will be yours ... several thousand acres, isn't it?'

'Eight thousand,' corrected Charles, still feeling dazed.

'If I could suggest you dramatically cut back on your expenditure. I believe you employ a French chef? Myself and my wife have just employed a girl up from Sussex who is extremely reasonable and quite adequate – she can boil a perfect egg.'

'I imagine you and your wife do not have the same calibre of guests that we do,' snapped Charles unpleasantly. 'You can keep your Sussex girl – I'm sure she is adequate – for Wimbledon, or wherever you live!'

Mr Jones sat back, surprised, and his voice became colder. 'In that case may I suggest you go and speak to Lord Armstrong? Hopefully he can provide funds for the life you have become accustomed to.'

Charles was confused and angry over the next few weeks as he tried to understand how all the money had gone so quickly. He knew he had been on a losing streak with the cards for a long spell, and he had lost huge amounts. But that was temporary and his luck would change soon.

Arabella walked into the study, holding a menu.

'Charles, can you take a look at the menu Monsieur Huppert has prepared for the dinner party next Saturday? He's suggesting quail and doing the most extraordinary thing with it involving olives. But Lady Hollander is coming, and I think it won't sit well with her – you know she's very fussy–'

'Oh for goodness sake, Arabella! Can't you see I'm too busy to be bothered with those trivial things!' he snapped.

She looked down at the bare desk in front of him. 'Doing what exactly?'

'I've far too many things to organise to be discussing Lady Hollander's faddy tummy!'

'What – like organising your next card game?' Her voice dripped sarcasm.

'Just leave me alone, and let Huppert sort out the bloody menu – he gets paid enough!'

'Right, I will! I'll tell Monsieur Huppert to go ahead with the quails and bugger Lady Hollander's stomach. You know, I don't understand what's been wrong with you lately – you're in foul form.'

'I have a lot of responsibility, you know,' he defended himself.

'Not according to your father – he thinks you're very good at avoiding it,' she said, before turning and leaving him.

He stood up from behind the desk, went to the window and looked out at the long garden.

'All those assets that will one day be mine, and here I am worried about money!' he said to himself. 'All those assets...'

Charles marched into the bank manager's office.

'Good news, Mr Jones, good news!'

Jones looked up, surprised. 'It's always good to hear good news. What is it exactly?'

'I have corresponded with my father and he's agreed to raise a mortgage on his house at Hanover Terrace. The money is to be paid into my account.'

'Right!' Jones was surprised.

'It looks like we won't have to be relying on Sussex girls and boiled eggs just yet. Prepare the mortgage documents at your earliest convenience, Mr Jones, and I will have them signed by my father when I return for my sister Lady Daphne's wedding in Ireland. Good day to you, Mr Jones!' Charles turned and strode happily out of the office.

CHAPTER 28

Charles was in the study the morning they were due to depart to Ireland for Daphne's wedding. He was sitting at his desk and was reading through the new mortgage documentation. All seemed in order. He only needed his father's signature to release the funds into his account.

Arabella came into the study.

'Charles, the cab has arrived to take us to the train station,' she said.

Charles quickly tidied the paperwork away into a small leather case and locked it.

'Just coming now,' he said, standing up.

Arabella was heavily pregnant at this stage, with only a little over a month to go, and wasn't looking forward to the long trip to Liverpool, the sea journey across the Irish Sea and another long journey from Dublin across Ireland to Armstrong House.

At least she wouldn't be confronted by Harrison. It had been confirmed by Margaret prior to Charles and Arabella even being invited to the wedding that Harrison would not be returning to Ireland for the event.

They quickly walked out of the house.

'Have a good journey,' said Burchill as he and the driver put their trunk on to the back of the carriage.

'Thank you, Burchill,' said Arabella as she got

232

into the carriage with Charles' help.

'*Au revoir! Au revoir!*' sang Isabelle as she handed Prudence into the carriage. Arabella had agreed that Isabelle should take the opportunity to visit her family while they were away in Ireland.

Burchill sighed as he waved the carriage off.

'Monsieur Burchill! You look relieved they go,' Isabelle chastised him as she saw him rest against one of the Roman pillars in front of the house and light himself a cigarette.

'I'm delighted that circus has left town for a couple of weeks,' said Burchill cheerily. 'You have to remember this house was only opened for a couple of months every summer before them two arrived. It was nice and relaxing around here before it became their party house with their posh awful nosh ... first thing I'm going to do now is order me in some good old-fashioned Irish stew!'

'Irish stew!' Isabelle looked horrified. 'Monsieur Huppert will *not* allow!'

'Monsieur Huppert can stick it up his Versailles, for all I care!'

Arabella observed Charles' smiling face as he played with Prudence in the carriage.

'Well, at least you seem in better form recently,' commented Arabella.

'I am, dear, I am!'

'It must be the thought of seeing all your family again at the wedding,' she mused.

'It must be, it must be!'

'All your family except Harrison,' she said.

'Nobody is keeping Harrison away. It's his

choice if he doesn't want to attend his own sister's wedding. Selfish, if you ask me.'

She stared at him, trying to figure him out. 'It's quite obvious why he isn't coming – he doesn't want to see either of us! Or put the rest of the family in a compromising position. We were only invited after Harrison declined.'

'Nonsense! Do you know, you can be quite deluded at times. As if I wouldn't be invited to Daphne's wedding!'

'I wouldn't test their loyalties, Charles, not after everything that's happened,' she said, turning and looking out the window.

When their carriage pulled up outside Armstrong House, Charles helped Arabella descend and she looked up at the building with trepidation.

The front door swung open and Emily came rushing out, shouting 'Charles!' as she jumped into his arms and hugged him.

'Well, this is a welcome home!' said Charles.

Emily turned to Arabella who was holding Prudence and smiled at her. 'Hello again, Arabella.'

'You're looking very well, Emily. Say hello to your Aunt Emily, Prudence.' Arabella held the toddler out to her.

Emily looked at the child with disinterest.

'What do you think of your niece?' asked Charles.

'*There was a little girl, who had a little curl, right in the middle of her forehead– When she was good she was very good indeed, but when she was bad she was horrid!*' sang Emily, before holding on to Charles' arm tightly and leading him up the steps to the front door. 'I'm so glad you're here, Charles. You can rescue me from all this *wedding* talk around here!'

Arabella raised her eyes to heaven as she followed them into the house.

Arabella found Margaret courteous but inclined to keep her distance, her smile not carrying to her eyes. Lawrence was as pleasant as ever. Emily fawned over Charles, and Daphne was too wrapped up in her wedding arrangements to be concerned about anything else.

That night Charles and Arabella joined the family in the dining room.

'Gwyneth hasn't arrived yet?' asked Arabella.

'No, she and His Grace are coming the day before the wedding, along with the other guests,' said Margaret.

'The Foxes aren't coming,' said Daphne.

'Why not?' asked Charles.

'The Land War!' snapped Lawrence. 'Have you forgotten about that while busy being a socialite in London?'

'Of course not, Father. I just wonder why it's stopping the Foxes from coming.' He looked at his father challengingly.

'Because their estate has become embroiled in it,' said Margaret.

'They are being boycotted, you see,' said Emily. 'They had to bring in workers from England to save the harvest.'

'And all their house staff walked out. Mrs Foxe has had to send for a cook from England through an agency.'

'How terrible!' said Arabella. 'Is there nothing you can do to help?'

'Of course there isn't!' snapped Margaret impatiently. 'Or else we'd get dragged into the cursed war ourselves! Your gilded life in London seems to have made you forget the harsh realities of the politics of your home country.'

Lawrence sat back and drank from his glass of wine. 'The Foxes are probably our oldest friends in the county, but they know they can't expect us to come to their assistance. If I sent some men over to help with their work, we would end up being boycotted too.'

Arabella nodded sympathetically. With all the grandeur, power and lavish socialising at Armstrong House she knew it wouldn't take much to have hatred spill out against them and put them under siege.

'They felt it would be unfair on us if they came to the wedding as we would be seen to be siding with them, and so they have diplomatically chosen to stay away.'

Margaret fixed Arabella with a steely look as she thought of Harrison in New York. 'And they are not the only ones not attending out of diplomacy.'

Charles waited until he was sure everyone was asleep in the house before he got out of bed and slipped on his dressing gown. He then went to the wardrobe and took out the leather case hidden there. He left the room, crept along the corridor and down the stairs to the library.

The room was still dimly lit from the embers in

236

the fireplace and he crossed over to the oil lamp and lit it. Putting the case on Lawrence's desk, he crossed over to a shelf. He picked a book on trout fishing and placed it open on the desk. If anyone came upon him he would say he couldn't sleep and had come downstairs for a book to read. Then he took a file down from another shelf and brought it to the desk where he opened it. He studied Lawrence's signature on some documents inside. Taking a sheaf of paper from his case he copied the signature again and again. Then steadying his nerve he took the documents for the new mortgage he had arranged for the house in London out of the case and forged Lawrence's signature on them. Finally he closely compared the forged signatures with the originals and was confident there was no telling them apart. He then put back the file, put out the oil lamp, took the case and returned upstairs to bed.

CHAPTER 29

Returning to Armstrong House brought back all the memories to Arabella: coming there with Harrison when they were in love, meeting Charles there, the beginning of their affair and on to the horrible confrontation that resulted in their marriage. Over the next few days she took a back seat and watched while the Armstrongs did what they did best – entertaining on a grand scale and organising a big social occasion to perfection.

On the day of Daphne's wedding they made their way down to the church in the estate village which was crammed with wedding guests. As she watched Daphne and her bridegroom exchange their wedding vows, she couldn't help but marvel at how opposite this occasion was to her own meagre rushed and absent-of-ceremony marriage. But as she looked at Charles sitting beside her in the pew and contemplated her life, she was happy with her present state, even though it had been a rough journey to get there.

The rest of the day passed in a whirl of excellent food, amusing speeches and dances back at Armstrong House.

Margaret observed Daphne dancing with her bridegroom in the ballroom and turned to Gwyneth who was seated beside her.

'Well, that's two daughters successfully launched and happily married,' said Margaret.

'Yes, they make a lovely couple,' said Gwyneth.

'Daphne is such a social butterfly she accepted every invitation going and had the good sense to meet and fall in love with a brewery heir without ever even needing to be presented and do the season in London.'

'It seems a love match all right.'

Margaret sighed. 'There will be no such luck with Emily. She accepts no invitations that come her way. I sometimes despair of her. She definitely needs to be presented in London for her to find a suitable husband. I had hoped to take her to London next year.'

'Well, why don't you? Her education seems

complete to me.'

'She's flatly refusing to go! Silly girl.' Margaret looked over at Arabella who was chatting amicably with guests. 'If we do go, I don't fancy living at Hanover Terrace for the summer months with Arabella and Charles and their French cook either.'

'It's your house – you shouldn't feel uncomfortable staying there,' objected Gwyneth, concerned.

'Well, I do! Arabella was quite rude to me on our last visit there.'

'Arabella – rude? I can't see that.' Gwyneth was surprised.

'Well, more outspoken.'

'You didn't provoke her, did you?' Gwyneth eyed her mother knowingly.

'I just tried to talk to her about the future … of course it's very hard to discuss the future with someone when all you can think about is her past.'

Gwyneth heaved a sigh. 'Mama, I meet Arabella regularly in Regent's Park when we are walking the babies, and she's lovely.'

'She's good at putting on acts all right... I can never forgive her for what she did to this family, what she did to Harrison.'

'It was all very unfortunate, but the past is the past. She fell in love with Charles and unfortunately that meant breaking Harrison's heart.'

'If that was all she did!' snapped Margaret bitterly.

'What do you mean?' asked Gwyneth.

Margaret had an overwhelming desire to tell her trusted and most adored daughter about the affair and the pregnancy but knew she could never tell the truth, even to Gwyneth. 'Just poor Harrison!'

'Any word from him?'

'No. We write to him all the time, but he hardly ever responds. We got a card at Christmas. And then he wrote to Daphne saying he was unable to attend the wedding. It's like he switched off from us all after what happened. I wanted myself and your father to go to New York to see him.'

'Well, why don't you?'

'We can't with all the trouble now at the Foxes. Your father won't leave in case the mess spills over to our estate.'

Emily linked her arm through Charles' as they walked through the gardens.

'I miss this – the walks and horse rides we had together,' she said. 'I wish you'd move back.'

'Well, you'll be married yourself soon with your own house and family, if Mother has anything to do with it.'

Emily pulled a face. 'Mama can force me to do many things, from German grammar to needle-work, but she can't force me to say "I do" before an altar.'

'Don't destroy your own life in trying to be dis-obedient to Mama.'

'Destroy my life? I can't think of any better way to destroy my life than getting married to some fool I don't love and churning out child after child.'

'Not necessarily.'

'Do you know Felicity Keane? She got married

three years ago and has had three children in that space of time! It's an awful life! Stuck in some marriage and having baby after baby like a prize heifer. And that's what Mother has tried to make me into.'

'What's the alternative, Emily? Stay here a spinster minding Mother and Father into their old age?'

Emily sighed loudly. 'I just want to be free.'

'Unfortunately freedom costs a lot. We'd better be getting back to the wedding,' he said, turning around and heading back to the house.

Arabella had not being feeling well all afternoon and as the evening progressed she began feeling worse. She turned to Charles at the table.

'I think I might go upstairs to lie down,' she said.

'If you must,' said Charles, feeling anxious. He had signed many cheques before leaving London and was anxious to get back as soon as possible to execute the mortgage and have the money put into his account for fear they would bounce.

'I won't drag you away from the fun,' said Arabella sarcastically, standing up, irritated that Charles hadn't offered to walk her up.

She set off walking across the dance floor, but suddenly the room started to swirl and she blacked out.

Charles waited anxiously with his parents and Emily in the drawing room while the doctor tended to Arabella upstairs.

'You know, I always suspected she may have a

weak disposition. Do you remember that sea-sickness nonsense she claimed to have?' said Margaret. 'I only hope the baby is all right.'

'It was probably the journey over was too tiring for her,' suggested Emily.

'I'm sure it's something or nothing,' Charles said, not looking too worried.

The doctor came in.

'Well?' asked Charles.

'She needs rest, and plenty of it until the baby is born. I've advised her not to come down for the rest of the day and to try to get some sleep.'

'See – as I said it's something or nothing,' dismissed Charles.

'Well, I wouldn't call it that either. It's important she gets rest and stays off her feet as much as possible,' contradicted the doctor.

'And I'll make sure she does just that when we get back to London,' Charles assured him.

'Oh, there can be no returning to London until after the baby is born, I'm afraid,' said the doctor.

'*What?*' shouted Charles.

'Oh yes, I'm afraid that's out of the question. She'll have to stay here – she can't risk that journey back to London.'

Emily was delighted at the prospect of Charles staying and volunteered, 'I'll help mind her.'

'You'll do no such thing!' snapped Margaret.

'But, doctor, it's paramount I get back to London as quickly as possible!' said Charles.

'You'll have to delay all such plans. Travel at this point would endanger both your wife and the baby.' The doctor turned to go. 'Enjoy the rest of the wedding day.'

Charles stared into the fire in a mixture of fury and annoyance.

Margaret leaned over to Lawrence and whispered, 'That girl can't seem to have a pregnancy without attaching the greatest drama possible to it.'

Charles went up to check on Arabella and found her sleeping in their bed. He then returned to the wedding where he caught up with old friends. The doctor's statement that Arabella was unfit to travel worried him greatly. He simply could not be stuck in Armstrong House for another month. He had to get back and get that money into his bank account before those cheques started to bounce. Everything from the staff wages to the money he owed to his gambling circle would bounce and how would he explain it all? What would Arabella say if she found out? He needed to get back as soon as possible.

Charles was the last to go up to bed that night. As the staff finished clearing up and went themselves exhausted to bed, he walked out to the forecourt and had a cigar while he contemplated what he must do. Then he went up to their room.

To his surprise he found Arabella awake and sitting in her dressing gown beside a roaring fire.

'How are you feeling now?' he asked as he sat on the bed.

'Still very weak. I'm mortified that I collapsed in front of everyone like that.'

'Not half as mortified as I was. If you were feeling so unwell, why didn't you go up sooner?' he said with irritation.

She looked at him angrily. 'Your concern is touching, Charles! If you had bothered to get up and walk me out I might not have collapsed so spectacularly!'

'Had I done that you would have brought me down with you!' he said.

'I don't think you'll ever need any assistance to bring yourself down,' she sneered.

Both sat fuming for a while and then Charles said, 'The doctor says you can't travel.'

'I know. I'm annoyed with being trapped here as much as I'm sure you are.'

'Felicity Keane was out on a hunt the week before she gave birth, my mother was saying.'

'Well, you should have gone and got *her* pregnant then, shouldn't you?'

Arabella sat back and closed her eyes.

'Well ... you should be quite all right here with Mother and Father, and Emily has said she'll wait on you hand and foot.'

Arabella's eyes sprang open. 'And where do you suggest you'll be?'

'I have to return to London – pressing business which I can't delay.'

'Return to London!' Arabella's voice rose.

'There's nothing I can do. I'll be back before the birth, naturally.'

Arabella stood up and walked towards him. 'Do you honestly think you are going to walk out on me for a second time while I'm pregnant?'

'I'm not walking out on you – don't be so ridiculous.'

'Forget it, Charles! You're going nowhere!'

'I have to!'

'And leave me here with your horrid mother and ... and...' Arabella rarely cried, and certainly never in front of others, but the tears started to well up in her eyes. But as she glared at Charles she knew she must never let him see her cry and she willed the tears to go away.

'I'm going and that's an end to it!' His voice was raised now.

'You are not going – and that's an end to it!' she screamed at the top of her voice.

He looked at her in horror and shouted back, 'You're going to wake the bloody house up!'

'I don't care – you selfish bastard!'

They stared at each other angrily.

'You don't understand, I've made no arrangements to be away, the staff wages, the...' He stopped speaking, aware he could not let her know the predicament they were in financially. He couldn't let anyone know.

'You can post them cheques. I take it you brought your cheque book? You take it bloody everywhere with you.'

'I forgot it!'

'Well, tough! Write to Jones in the bank to sort it – but you are *not* walking out on me. Not when I'm about to give birth to your heir! Not now – not ever!'

She went and stood by the window, staring out at the lake.

He watched her for a long time.

He put his hands up in the air. 'In that case – I won't go. I'll stay and hold your hand and mop your brow and do everything else–'

'That a good husband should do!' she spat.

He walked towards the door.

'Where are you going now?' she asked.

'Downstairs for a glass of claret. *If* I'm allowed to do that?' He walked out and slammed the door behind him.

Margaret and Lawrence were sitting up in bed, listening intently. Arabella's screaming had awoken them.

'He's gone downstairs,' said Lawrence hearing Charles trot down the steps outside.

'Maybe I should go down and see if he's all right?' said Margaret, getting out of the bed.

'No, you don't!' said Lawrence, grabbing her and pulling her back. 'Stay out of it.'

'How can I stay out of it when they nearly took the roof off with their screaming? And all the wedding guests here to hear!'

'It's none of our business. Charles and Arabella have both said they don't want our interference.'

'Well, there's something wrong with that marriage, I can tell you that!' said Margaret as she lay back on her pillows. 'And why wouldn't there be when it was built on the shakiest foundations known to man. And I know the problem is her!'

CHAPTER 30

Arabella and Charles kept a cool distance from each other after their row.

She took the doctor's advice and rested a lot, only joining the family for dinner in the evenings if she felt able for it. It was obvious from the embarrassed looks some people gave her the next day that they had heard their argument. She was angry with Charles that he would have abandoned her without a second thought. Angry but not surprised. Because she knew her husband. She never kidded herself that he was really in love with her. Oh, he was proud of her and enjoyed her and did love her in his own way. But she feared Charles could never really love anybody, except perhaps himself and the good life. He was very good at convincing others that they were the centre of his world, and maybe in that passing moment when he was being entertained by them, they were. But when push came to shove, Charles suited himself, he always had and he always would.

After a month at Armstrong House Arabella went into labour and in the early hours gave birth to their son.

Charles looked delighted as he held him.

'Well, it's good to see you with a smile on your face at last,' said Arabella cynically.

'I'm getting to choose the name this time. I'm calling him Pierce. Lord Pierce Armstrong, it has a nice ring to it, doesn't it?' said Charles.

She nodded and smiled. 'Yes, it does.'

He bent down and kissed her.

The family gathered around later on in the day.

'It's fitting that my future heir was born in Armstrong House,' said Lawrence, delighted that the succession was secured.

'He is the most beautiful baby I've ever seen,' said Margaret, amazed as she had half expected the child to be as plain as Prudence. But this child had a combination of the best of both his parents' looks.

CHAPTER 31

When they arrived back to London, Charles was confronted with an army of disgruntled French staff and even a sour-looking Burchill.

'It is not right to disappear off to Ireland and leave us with no funds to run the house or pay wages,' objected an irate Monsieur Huppert in the study where Charles was going through a pile of letters, all of which were complaining about cheques that had bounced.

'Well, I couldn't help it if my wife took ill,' said Charles, only half listening as he opened another demand letter.

'I've worked in the best hotels in Europe and never have I been left in such awkward circumstances as these past few weeks.'

Charles suddenly looked up and glared at him. 'You're forgetting your place, Huppert.'

'But–'

'I don't want to hear another word – get out of my sight!' Charles glared angrily.

Huppert was stunned at the outburst from the usually cheerful Charles.

'I'm sorry if I have offended,' said the chef as he exited quickly.

Charles took all the correspondence and locked it in his desk and then headed to the bank as quickly as possible to hand in the forged mortgage documents.

'Congratulations – I believe you had a son,' smiled Mr Jones.

'Yes, never mind all that. These are the mortgage documents signed and my father wants the money transferred into my account as soon as possible, as you can see from his letter.'

Charles never was so relieved as when the money was transferred and managed to start breathing again normally. He quickly reissued cheques for debts that were outstanding and letters of apology saying it was unavoidable due to being stranded because of his wife's illness.

Now all he had to do was face his friends. He had given cheques to a considerable number of his card-playing friends and those cheques had bounced as well. He was more concerned about this than the other bills. Firstly, they were friends he could not afford to be ostracised from and, secondly, if word got around that he wasn't good for his money he would never again be allowed at a gambling table in London.

He arrived, trying to hide his nerves, at Tom Hamley's house for a scheduled game of cards. He had left for Ireland without settling substantial money he owed to his card circle. He knew only too well the etiquette with gambling debts and that they needed to be paid immediately. Now, with having been delayed for over a month in Ireland, he could only imagine how irate and angry his card-playing comrades would be. He was shown in to Tom Hamley's parlour and braced himself.

'Armstrong!' shouted somebody straight away, giving him a fright. 'Congratulations! The best of wishes to your son and heir!'

'Yes! I offer my warmest congratulations as well,' said Tom Hamley, coming to him and shaking his hand warmly. He turned to his butler. 'Get the best bottle of champagne to wet the baby's head!'

As Charles accepted the good wishes from everybody, he was confused. Surely these men could not be so happy and forgiving over such a long-overdue debt?

'What are you going to call him?' asked Tom as he chinked his glass against Charles'.

'Pierce,' informed Charles.

'Lord Pierce Armstrong – a fine name,' acknowledged Tom, nodding approvingly.

Charles lowered his voice. 'Eh – Tom, about the debts I owe. Sorry for leaving you all in the lurch for so long.'

Tom looked at him, confused. 'But Hugh Fitzroy covered all your debts with everyone here.'

'Fitzroy?' Charles was mystified.

'When you didn't show for a couple of weeks, he said you had arranged the payments with him and he paid everyone.'

Charles smiled broadly. 'Of course he did! I just want to check nothing is still owed to anyone?'

'All paid up to date,' confirmed Tom. 'And how is Arabella?'

As Tom spoke on, Charles tuned out as he tried to figure out why Fitzroy had done as he did. His eyes scanned the room looking for Fitzroy and spotted him in the corner, looking over at him as he spoke to some others. Charles nodded over to him and Fitzroy nodded back.

At the end of the card game, when everyone was going home, Fitzroy came up to Charles.

'My carriage is outside,' he said. 'If I could offer you a lift home?'

'You really are too kind,' said Charles, looking at him cautiously as the butler helped him on with his cape.

The two men chatted inconsequentially as they left Tom's house and walked through the swirling fog to the carriage.

'Regent's Park,' instructed Hugh to the driver as they got in.

As the carriage made its way through the densely thick fog Charles waited for Hugh to bring up the subject of the money. But he didn't broach it.

Finally Charles said pleasantly, 'I believe I owe you a debt of gratitude.'

'Ah yes. They were all getting a little concerned when you didn't return from Ireland so I covered it for you, to save any embarrassment.'

251

'I can only thank you. My wife became ill and we were stranded at Armstrong House.'

'I thought it would be something like that.'

'I will immediately forward you a cheque to cover the full amount.'

'In your own time, there's no rush,' Hugh assured him.

Charles stared at him, trying to fathom him out. Why would he do such a thing for a relative stranger, with no guarantee Charles would return to London let alone with the money?

The carriage pulled up outside Hanover Terrace and Charles got out. He turned and spoke through the window.

'If you can give me your address – for the cheque?'

'Just send it to Claridge's.'

Charles nodded. 'If you are free next Saturday, my wife and I are having a dinner party here.'

Hugh stared at him.

'Only if you're free, of course,' added Charles.

Hugh nodded quickly and shouted, 'Drive on!'

Charles watched as the carriage drove away and was swallowed up by the fog.

'Hugh Fitzroy?' Arabella studied the guest list curiously. 'Isn't that the man who sent the hamper?'

'The very one,' confirmed Charles.

They were in the drawing room during the week. Charles was reading the paper as Arabella went through the details of the forthcoming dinner party. Prudence played on the floor beside her while Pierce slept in a cot close by.

Arabella remembered the man with the staring eyes. 'I didn't realise you knew him that well?'

'He seems like a nice fellow. Filthy rich.'

'So you said before ... hmmm,' said Arabella, studying her table plan. 'I'll put him beside Lady Hollander.'

Charles looked up, alarmed. 'Not a good idea. She's far too pernickety. And he doesn't seem to be a great conversationalist.'

'Well, where will I put him then?'

'Beside you.'

'Me!'

'Yes, why not?'

'But why are you inviting him if he's not a good conversationalist?' she asked. 'I thought you wanted this house to be filled with witty and entertaining company. I've never heard of this Hugh Fitzroy socially.'

'Maybe not – but I've a feeling you might in the future.' Charles looked at her smugly and sat back to read the newspaper. He looked up again. 'Speaking of entertaining and witty company, any luck in getting Oscar Wilde to accept our invitation yet?'

Arabella raised her eyes and concentrated on her table plan.

CHAPTER 32

By the time Hugh arrived on the Saturday night the other guests were already in the drawing room having sherry.

'Mr Hugh Fitzroy,' said Burchill as he showed him in.

'Hugh!' said Charles, shaking his hand and leading him into the room. 'Let me introduce you to my wife. Arabella, this is Hugh Fitzroy.'

'I'm so glad you could make it tonight,' smiled Arabella, shaking his hand.

'Thanks for inviting me,' said Hugh.

Arabella was slightly unnerved by his staring eyes, which she imagined observed everything very quickly. She noticed his clothes were of the finest quality but nevertheless he immediately stood out from the others in the room. He was very ill at ease and uncomfortable as she brought him around and introduced him to everybody. He seemed relieved when she deposited him back with Charles, who quickly engaged him in conversation.

When dinner was served Arabella took Hugh's arm and led the other guests out of the room and down the stairs to the dining room.

'You're seated next to me, Mr Fitzroy,' she said.

She led him through the dining room and sat at the end of the table. She gestured to the chair beside her and Hugh awkwardly sat down. Charles took his seat at the top of the table.

As everyone took their places they viewed Hugh suspiciously. Arabella tried to engage Hugh in light-hearted conversation as the appetiser and then soup courses were served. She found him hopelessly out of his depth even talking about the most mundane things.

'Fitzroy?' questioned Lady Hollander from down the table. 'I don't think I've ever met your family socially before, have I? Are you anything to do with the Fitzroys in Halifax – they are mill-owners – wool?'

'Eh, no, I don't think so.' Hugh shook his head.

'Perhaps distant relations?' suggested Arabella as the footmen entered and put large white bowls of lobster bisque in front of everyone.

Arabella saw Hugh look down at the array of cutlery in front of him and saw the confused horror on his face. She grimaced as he took up his dessertspoon and started eating the lobster bisque with it.

As the table chatted away about the theatre, Arabella tried to involve Hugh in the conversation, but he seemed to have nothing to contribute.

As the empty bowls were taken away Lady Hollander said, 'You looked like you enjoyed that, Mr Fitzroy?'

'Yes,' said Hugh. 'I like tomato soup.'

'Tomato soup!' Lady Hollander laughed like a neighing horse. 'Dear man! It was lobster bisque!'

Hugh went bright red as a wave of embarrassment went around the table.

'Actually,' said Arabella sternly, 'you are quite

wrong, Lady Hollander. Mr Fitzroy is not fond of lobster and so I had chef prepare tomato soup for him.'

'Oh, I see,' said Lady Hollander quickly as she turned to talk to the guest beside her.

Arabella smiled at Hugh who nodded back his thanks.

As the main course of roasted beef was served, Hugh looked at the array of forks and knives, exasperated. He finally picked up the pastry fork.

Arabella caught his eye and shook her head and then discreetly pointed to the correct fork to be used. He nodded his thanks again.

As the night progressed and the conversation switched from art to politics to opera, both Arabella and Hugh realised he was hopelessly struggling in the company. She tried to smooth the conversation over for him, but it was next to impossible. As Hugh spilled the gravy from the beef down his shirt, she looked down irritated at Charles who seemed oblivious to the situation as he was his normal jovial self.

'I do find gravy most tiresome,' sympathised Arabella as a footman assisted Hugh in cleaning up the mess.

At the end of the dinner, as the women were standing to go upstairs to the drawing room, Hugh took the opportunity to make his excuses and said he must leave.

'Thank you for a very enjoyable night,' he said to Arabella, almost heaving with shame.

'It was very nice to meet you. Charles speaks very highly of you,' said Arabella, glad he had elected to go early.

'Are you sure you won't join us for a cigar and port?' said Charles, lounging back in his chair at the head of the table.

'No, I have to go,' he said and quickly left.

Arabella joined the women upstairs and watched from the balcony as Hugh's elaborate carriage drove off. She felt relieved he was gone.

That night in their bedroom, Arabella was annoyed as she put on her face cream at her dressing table.

'Honestly, Charles! Whatever were you thinking of inviting Hugh Fitzroy tonight? You shouldn't have!'

'Whyever not?' he said, getting into bed.

She turned around and faced him. 'The poor man was humiliated. He hadn't a clue how to behave or act or talk. And as for his table manners – it's lucky your mother wasn't there to witness it – she'd have fainted on the spot! And that accent!'

'Nonsense! He was perfectly fine.'

'As ever, you are showing the social sensitivity of a bull!'

'The other chaps at cards think he's all right.'

'The other *chaps* are probably too greedy swindling him out of his money to care! He's from a different world, and it's unfair to try and bring him into ours.'

'He's probably richer than anyone at that table tonight.'

'And where did he make all this money?'

'Don't know.'

'Very dubious.'

'Well, I think he's a find.'

'Not so much a find as a lost cause! I think we should leave him off the guest list in future, for his own sake, if no other reason.'

'I think he's an important contact, and could be very useful.'

'I don't care how useful he is! Besides, there's something about him that's slightly scary. Those eyes! We don't know anything about him, where he's from or how he got his money. He might be all right for your card games, but not for my dining table.'

CHAPTER 33

Burchill came into the drawing room one evening during the following week.

'A delivery for Mrs Armstrong,' he said, handing over a beautifully wrapped box from Asprey of Bond Street.

'Have you got me a surprise?' Arabella called to Charles who was smoking out on the balcony.

He came in as Burchill left. 'Certainly not. It's not your birthday, is it?'

She raised her eyes to heaven. 'No – do you even know when my birthday is?'

'December?'

She shook her head in resigned despair as she untied the ribbons on the box. 'June, for the record. Harrison always remembered my birthday. In fact, he used to shower me with gifts whether it was my birthday or not.'

He grinned at her. 'Perhaps this is from him then!'

Arabella gave him a dirty look and opened the velvet box inside the wrapping. She stared in amazement at the beautiful diamond earrings inside.

'Whoever could have–?' She quickly took the card and read it. 'They are from Hugh Fitzroy! Thanking me for the Saturday dinner party.'

'Now that is what I call a thank-you!' said Charles, taking the earrings and examining them closely.

'But why should he feel the need to send these? I can't possibly accept them. I'll have them returned to him immediately.'

Charles looked at her in horror. 'You most certainly will not! If you won't accept them, then I will on your behalf! I wonder how much I'd get if I sold these on?'

'You're so cheap, Charles!' she snapped at him.

'Well, I can afford to be cheap when I've got such rich and generous friends as Hugh Fitzroy.'

Arabella was walking through Regent's Park on a sunny morning with Isabelle by her side pushing Pierce in the perambulator as Prudence tottered along beside them. They met Lady Hollander coming in their direction with a young female companion.

'Good morning,' said Lady Hollander.

'How do you do, Lady Hollander,' said Arabella.

'My, Prudence is getting big, isn't she?' observed Lady Hollander and then she peered into the pram. 'It's as everyone says – what a really beautiful baby he is!'

'Thank you,' said Arabella gratefully, but also a little concerned. Pierce seemed to always grab all the attention and poor Prudence never seemed to get a look in.

No matter how many pretty dresses and ribbons she put on Prudence, it didn't seem to attract any positive comments. She was worried that Prudence would become jealous of her little brother.

Lady Hollander took her head out of the pram. 'Thank you for a really wonderful night last Saturday. Much enjoyed by us all.'

'It was lovely to have you,' smiled Arabella.

Isabelle and Lady Hollander's companion took the two children over to the boating lake to see the swans.

'What an extraordinary chap that Mr Fitzroy is – wherever did you find him?' said Lady Hollander.

'He's an acquaintance of Charles; I'm not sure how they met,' said Arabella, not wishing to divulge her husband's card-playing obsession to the conservative Lady Hollander.

'I have to tell you,' said Lady Hollander as the two women strolled along the pathway, 'that a Harrods hamper was delivered to me on Monday. When I read the note it was from Mr Fitzroy thanking me for being such, and I quote, "wonderful company" at your dinner party.'

'Really?' Arabella was taken aback.

'Yes, and I hardly spoke two words to him the whole night, so I was quite flabbergasted.'

'He's a very generous man,' said Arabella,

260

wondering why on earth Fitzroy would send gifts to the other guests.

'I mean to say,' Lady Hollander gave a little laugh, 'I didn't say much to him, because I didn't feel we would have anything in common, and I don't mean to be cruel, but *common* is the word I would use to describe him. I don't think I've ever met anyone from the working class who wasn't a domestic servant or some such before.'

'Maybe it's time you broadened your horizons a little in that case,' said Arabella, not bothering to hide the note of sarcasm in her voice.

'I would, however, like to send a note to the man to thank him for the hamper – perhaps you could get his address from Charles for me?'

'Just send it care of Claridge's, Lady Hollander. I'm sure they'll deliver it safely to him.'

'Claridge's?' Lady Hollander was even more curious.

'Yes, he lives in a suite of rooms there, I believe.'

'What – permanently? Well, that would cost a pretty penny! Where on earth did a man like that come into such money?'

'Charles tells me Mr Fitzroy is successful on the stock market,' said Arabella, becoming tired of Lady Hollander's new-found obsession with Fitzroy.

'It's so – extraordinary! I mean we're just getting used to the middle classes having all this affluence, and now it's finding its way to the working classes as well!'

Over the following days, Arabella checked with all their friends who had attended their dinner party the previous Saturday, and all confirmed they had received a Harrods hamper from Fitz-roy.

Charles had no intention of following Arabella's advice and avoiding Hugh Fitzroy in the future. Who cared if he slurped his lobster bisque and mistook it for tomato soup? He felt he had the measure of Fitzroy. Rich, shrewd but desperate for acceptance in polite society. He could be Hugh's ticket into polite society, and in exchange Hugh could be his meal ticket.

The two men were having lunch at Claridge's.

'Arabella loved the diamond earrings you sent to her – she said to say thank you,' said Charles.

Hugh's face lit up in delight. 'Did she really?'

'Loved them, I tell you.'

'She's a very beautiful and nice lady – you're a lucky man.'

'Yes – she's all those things. You'll have to come to dinner again.'

'I wouldn't want to embarrass you...'

'Embarrass me? But how?'

Hugh said nothing as he scraped his plate with his knife and licked it.

Charles pulled a face. 'You won't be embarrassing me. But you might embarrass yourself with table manners like that.'

Charles looked around the restaurant and clicked his fingers. The head waiter came over.

'Now I want you to bring all your cutlery out and place it in front of Mr Fitzroy and tell him which course each is meant for,' said Charles to the astonished waiter.

Hugh sat back, mortified and angry.

262

'Oh come on, Hugh!' said Charles, standing up and smirking. 'If you don't ask, you'll never learn. Anyway, better dash – have to get to my club.'

CHAPTER 34

Charles opened doors for Hugh and didn't mind doing it. Through him, Hugh was invited to many events. He took it very slowly at first but then he nominated Hugh to be a member of his club.

The other members looked on curiously at the outsider who seemed awkward and ill at ease and who nobody had ever heard of. But when Charles went to pay his own annual subscription fee to the club, he found it had already been taken care of by Mr Fitzroy. In fact, when Charles went to pay for anything he found it had already been paid for by a grateful Mr Fitzroy.

'You really need to do something about that accent,' Charles recommended one day to Hugh.

Hugh went bright red with embarrassment.

'I know you try to disguise it, but you don't do it very well, and people laugh at you behind your back because of it,' said Charles. 'My mother knows this woman who gives the best elocution lessons. I'll set it up for you.'

The next time Hugh was invited to Hanover Terrace for dinner, Arabella found him more relaxed and self-assured than before.

As she sat next to him at the dinner table she was preparing herself again for a spectacle of discomfort. She was surprised and relieved to see he suddenly had mastered cutlery etiquette.

'How are your children, Mrs Armstrong?' asked Hugh.

'Very well, thank you, Mr Fitzroy. Thank you for the rocking horse you sent to them, they were very pleased with it.' Arabella wasn't as pleased as the children to receive it. 'You're getting a reputation of being the most generous man in London.'

He smiled.

After dinner, Hugh did not rush off like last time but stayed with the men downstairs for port and cigars as the women went up to the drawing room. Later, after the men joined the women Hugh came over to talk to Arabella.

'I have a friend who runs a fashion shop in Bond Street. Any time you want a dress, let me know, and I can organise it for you,' he told Arabella.

She managed to smile. 'Thank you, Mr Fitzroy, but–'

'Hugh,' he insisted.

'Thank you – Hugh – but that's completely unnecessary,' she said coolly.

'There would be no charge,' he informed her.

'Thank you, but no. If you excuse me, I need to see to my other guests.' She nodded and moved to the balcony where the others were gathered.

Hugh stared after her, feeling angry that he had been rejected.

Charles came over and filled his glass of port. 'Enjoying the evening?'

'Eh, yes.' Hugh was staring at Arabella as she laughed over some anecdote told by one of the guests.

'Good. My sister, the Duchess of Battington and her husband are having a garden party next month. They've invited you along.'

Hugh looked at Charles, delighted.

'A garden party!' Arabella raised her voice in alarm after all the guests had gone home and she was alone with Charles in the drawing room. 'What on earth would Hugh Fitzroy be doing at a garden party?'

'Doing what everyone else is doing, I imagine – enjoying himself?'

'Oh come on, Charles, you're putting Gwyneth and His Grace in an awkward position bringing Fitzroy. There will be members of the royal family there.'

'But he's come on in leaps and bounds, I'm sure you'll agree?'

'You can't polish coal, Charles.'

'You are being a snob – you'll be turning into my mother next.'

'It's not that...'

'What is it then?'

'I don't trust him.'

'On what grounds?'

'He's using you. He thinks he can get anything he wants with his money.'

'Sounds good to me!' Charles said flippantly.

'I'm being serious, Charles. You might think you're coming off well in this arrangement you have, but I doubt it. You're introducing him to everyone and getting him into society. He's clever. He's not the likes of David Chester and those others you and your friends played for fools.'

'I never played anyone for a fool.'

'You play anybody for a fool you think you can! And you think you're playing Fitzroy for a fool, but he's playing you!'

Arabella tried to avoid Hugh Fitzroy at the Battingtons' garden party. She felt he was taken aback at first by the calibre of guests there. But Charles introduced him around and he happily got acquainted. She wondered how many of these people would be receiving Harrods hampers first thing on Monday, courtesy of him. And even though the others were sniggering and talking about him behind his back, they were really only interested in his money.

CHAPTER 35

The seasons came and went in Armstrong House and, though Emily and James were the only children left there, life went on much as it always had.

The house ran like clockwork. Margaret would meet the housekeeper in the morning and issue the orders for the day. If there were guests coming to lunch or dinner, she would discuss the menu with the cook. She would meet the butler and his staff and go through the order of the day. Lawrence and James would be tied up with the running of the estate.

And this really left Emily with little or nothing

to do. Her education now completed, Margaret felt there was no more to teach her. Now with Daphne left to live in Dublin and already pregnant with her second child, Emily began to feel somewhat isolated and not sure what she could do with the rest of her life. Margaret had almost given up on her and didn't nag her about going to London to be a debutante any more. She attended all the social events at Armstrong House, but she began to dread them. The guests viewed her as a curiosity. The unmarried daughter who didn't seem to want to *get on* with her own life as a young woman would want to.

There was a dinner party at Armstrong House and she overheard two guests talking about her in the drawing room.

'She must be such a disappointment for poor Lady Margaret.'

'Especially after such triumphs as Gwyneth and Daphne.'

'Why doesn't she want to get married?'

'Who knows? It's quite tragic. She has turned into quite a beauty. It's a waste.'

'Well, she only has a couple of years left to be a debutante and then it's all behind her. Opportunity lost.'

Occasionally, she would go to a hunt ball in one of the neighbouring gentry's houses. But it was the same old faces, which bored her.

Emily longed for the visits from her siblings. When either Gwyneth or Daphne visited she enjoyed the company and they could catch up on the gossip. Of course, she loved it when Charles came back on one of his sporadic visits. She particularly liked it when he came back without Arabella and the children and she could have him all to herself.

She remembered Charles' words to her: she could end up a spinster minding Mama and Papa into their old age. She didn't want to get married but she dreaded this other destiny for herself.

One night in February she observed herself in the mirror in her bedroom. Maybe she didn't have her sisters' easy charm, but she was as beautiful as her sisters, she thought. She envied Harrison in New York, being able to escape everything. She thought of all their siblings living their lives to the full. She thought of what the two guests at the dinner party had said – another couple of years and it would all be behind her. She wanted to live life while she still could. She wanted to experience life while she had an opportunity.

The next evening she came into the drawing room where Margaret and Lawrence were chatting.

'I've been thinking – I would like to go to London as a debutante when the next season starts,' she announced.

'*What?*' shrieked Margaret, nearly falling off her chair.

'A debutante – next season,' Emily verified.

'Hallelujah!' Margaret jumped up and embraced her daughter. 'I'd nearly given up hope!'

'Are you sure?' said Lawrence.

'I'm sure!' said Emily.

Margaret started rushing around. 'Excellent! We must invest in a new wardrobe of clothes for you. And jewellery. I'll notify all my friends in

London that we are available to go to all their breakfasts, lunches, dinners and balls. And that you are – at last – on the market. And start organising the schedule. Now you're related to the Duke of Battington, they'll be queuing up for you!' Margaret clasped her hands together in delight.

Emily nodded happily. She would go to London and be a debutante and go to all the parties and functions and spend time with Charles and at last be able to see life. And at the end of the season, she didn't have to marry anybody.

The doctor examined Margaret who was feverish and confined to bed.

'I'm afraid it's a case of pneumonia,' he said.

'Pneumonia!' Margaret was horrified. 'I knew I shouldn't have gone out on that walk at Easter.'

'How bad is it?' asked Lawrence, full of concern.

'Well, she will need plenty of rest to recuperate. The fires must be kept at full blast at all times. Plenty more blankets.'

'But, doctor, I'm going to London with my daughter soon to present her at court.'

'The court will have to wait, Lady Armstrong, your health will not. I'll come by tomorrow to see how you are progressing.'

The doctor packed up his case and, with a bow, left.

Lawrence reached out and took her hand. 'You look very poorly, darling.'

'But what about Emily doing the season in London? If she doesn't go this year, she might never go. I simply have to go!' She struggled to sit up.

Lawrence gently pushed her back against the pillows.

'It's out of the question, Margaret, you're just too weak.'

'But...'

'Emily can still go to London. Gwyneth can be her patroness. Gwyneth is so connected and respected Emily couldn't have a better patroness to introduce and show her off, except yourself of course. And then there's Charles and Arabella – they can look after her and present her as well.'

'Arabella!' Margaret managed to squawk. 'I will not entrust the care of my daughter to that woman. Goodness knows what would happen if Emily was left to her considering how she conducted herself as a single woman!'

'Relax, darling – Gwyneth will be a magnificent guide for Emily. I'm just saying Charles is at hand to ride through the parks with her and for other outdoor events.'

'Well,' Margaret sighed. 'What choice do I have?'

Arabella and Gwyneth were walking through Regent's Park together as the nannies walked the children ahead.

'Mama is very poorly by all accounts,' said Gwyneth. 'It's strange to think of her ill when she's usually so strong. But Emily will be coming to London to be presented anyway. I've already made the application to Buckingham Palace for her.'

'She's lucky to have you,' said Arabella.

'Well, applying for her to be presented is the easy part. It's the endless rounds of events I'll have to accompany her to that is concerning me.' Gwyneth gave a weary sigh.

'Oh – why?' Arabella had never known Gwyneth not to take any social occasion in her stride before.

Gwyneth turned and smiled at Arabella. 'I'm with child'

'Oh, but that's wonderful news!' She hugged Gwyneth.

'Of course it is. But I found my last pregnancy so difficult, and I'm finding this one the same. In fact His Grace and I were going to go and spend the summer months at Battington Hall and just rest and not attend the season at all this year. But now with Mama being unable to travel, I've no option.'

'But, Gwyneth, you must put your health first.' Arabella was full of concern.

'But what can I do?' Gwyneth asked.

'You must rely on me and Charles – we'll look after Emily. I'll bring her to the parties, and Charles will ride with her through the parks.'

Gwyneth looked concerned. 'I'd thought of that. But...'

'But what?'

Gwyneth looked embarrassed. 'I'm sorry, Arabella, but you know Mama's opinion of you.'

Arabella nodded. 'Lady Margaret is a stubborn woman, and I realise I'll never change her opinion of me. But I'll not sit back and let you risk your health and your baby by doing too much. What Margaret doesn't know won't harm her. You will be Emily's official patroness, but I'll do all the work. By the end of the summer Emily will have made a brilliant match, and Margaret will be none the wiser.'

Gwyneth linked Arabella's arm. 'I hate deception, but ... yes, thank you, Arabella. His Grace has so many friends eager to meet Emily, it should be an easy job all round.'

'That settles that then. And it'll be our secret.'

They continued to walk. 'I saw in *Tatler* an article about Charles' friend Hugh Fitzroy. He's sponsoring a charity gala.'

'Yes, he's always sponsoring something,' said Arabella. Usually Charles, she thought cynically.

'I believe he's a regular visitor at your house?'

'Oh yes,' Arabella nodded resignedly. 'Speaking of patrons, Mr Fitzroy found his very own patron in Charles to present *him* to society.'

CHAPTER 36

It was evening time and Hugh was in the drawing room with Charles as Charles refilled his crystal glass with red wine.

'I meant to say – thank you for covering my loss last week at Tom Hamley's card game,' said Charles, sitting down opposite him.

'My pleasure – as always,' said Hugh.

'I don't know what's wrong with me lately. I've been on such a losing streak with the cards. And I was doing so well last year.'

'Your luck will change soon,' comforted Hugh.

'Hopefully. I could do with a winning streak... I'm not leaving you any way short with those losses you've covered for me?'

Hugh burst out laughing. 'No, not at all. It would need to be a lot more than that to leave me short of cash.'

Charles smiled and sat back and studied Hugh. 'How much are you actually worth? Where did your money come from?'

'The stock exchange. I've told you before.'

'I know that's what everyone says. But you didn't just arrive in and start making money on the stock exchange. You must have had considerable money before,' said Charles.

'What makes you say that?'

'Let's face it, Hugh, a man like you from your background, whatever your background is, wouldn't even know how to find the stock exchange, let alone know how to invest in it.'

Hugh hid how Charles' derogatory words insulted him. He suddenly stood up and downed his drink.

'What's wrong?' asked Charles.

'You want to see where I made my money – then come and I'll show you.' He turned and abruptly walked out of the room.

Charles stood up and followed him.

Charles looked out the window of Hugh's carriage. Gradually the great Regency and Victorian buildings were being left behind, and the carriage was making its way through narrower streets.

'Where is this?' asked Charles, concerned as he saw they were travelling through streets that were becoming dilapidated and dimly lit.

Hugh's eyes were staring at Charles. 'Welcome

to darkest London,' he said.

Charles looked out the window with increasing concern as he realised he must be in the East End. They passed by bars that were full to overflowing with music blaring out of them, and through streets that seemed full of rowdy drunken people.

The carriage stopped and Charles stared out at the sight before him. He spotted a young woman leering at him.

She came sauntering over. 'Looking for some company, Mister?'

She looked into the carriage and saw Hugh and suddenly her face became scared and she backed off and disappeared into the crowd.

'What are we doing here?' demanded Charles, feeling unsafe.

'Answering your questions,' said Hugh as he opened up the door and stepped out. 'Come on.' He beckoned to Charles.

The two men walked down through the narrow streets. Charles could only stare at the people who caroused and fought as they passed.

'You introduced me to your world, and now I'm introducing you to mine,' said Hugh.

A beggar came up to them and Hugh pushed him aside as they continued on their journey.

'Your world?' asked Charles.

'I was born and raised in a tenement like that.' He pointed to a rundown building.

'And how did you escape?'

'I fought my way out. I did everything I had to do. I made money any way I could. You wouldn't understand that, coming from your background.

You wouldn't understand what desperation feels like.'

They turned a corner and started walking down some dark quiet alleys.

'Should we really be getting so far off the beaten track?' suggested Charles as the street gaslights disappeared.

'We're safe,' said Hugh.

Suddenly three men came rushing out to them. One of them went to hit Hugh then stopped suddenly, apparently recognising him, and shouted at the others. They rushed back into the darkness.

The incident didn't seem to bother Hugh who just continued on his way.

Charles saw they were approaching the docks. Feeling decidedly frightened at this stage, he said, 'Arabella is going to wonder where I've got to. I should be getting back.'

'We're nearly there,' Hugh assured him as they reached some big warehouses. Hugh walked up to one of the giant warehouses and taking out a key he opened a door and they stepped in. Hugh turned on the gaslight inside and the warehouse lit up.

Charles walked around. The warehouse was filled with boxes stacked high.

'What is this?' said Charles.

'Opium,' said Hugh.

'Opium!' said Charles, going over and inspecting it. 'But this is illegal.'

'I know – don't worry, it doesn't belong to me. I don't trade in opium, at least not any more. I own the warehouses, and most of the property around here. I rent it out. If the police ever discover what's been shipped through, I'm clean as a whistle – nothing to do with me.'

'But you are making money from the drug trade then?'

'I prefer to see myself as a casual observer of the drug trade.'

Charles was amazed. 'And this is where all your money came from?'

'In the beginning, yes. And then I got advisors who invested in the stock exchange and it went on from there. But money can't buy me what you were born with. Respectability, acceptance, being part of society.'

'Well, you're sure giving it a damned good try!'

'Only with your patronage. Without you pushing me, those people wouldn't entertain me. But I want their acceptance. And I'll get it.'

As Charles looked at Hugh he was unnerved by the mad determination in his eyes. Did Hugh not realise those people would never really accept him?

'Come on,' said Hugh roughly as he turned off the lights and started leading him through the maze of streets that led from the docks. They went down a long cobbled street with all the doors firmly closed. Hugh went up to one and knocked loudly with his cane. A minute later a window in the door opened and shut quickly. A moment later the door opened and Hugh walked in, followed by Charles.

Charles was immediately struck by the strong odours circulating.

'Good evening, Mr Fitzroy, how are you

tonight?' asked a young Chinese woman who took their cloaks.

'Good,' said Hugh, following her down a corridor.

Charles was amazed by the inside of the building. Outside it looked like any other rundown tenement in the area. But inside was done up like the finest hotel with purple velvet drapes, and thick pile carpets. They were brought into a gigantic room in the centre of the building which was again decorated sumptuously. To Charles' alarm there were people stretched out on velvet chaises-longues everywhere while they smoked through long pipes.

'An opium den! You've brought me to an opium den!' he said, shocked.

'Of course. Why not?' said Hugh, going to an empty chaise-longue and stretching out on it. He snapped his fingers and straight away two women came over and set him up with an opium pipe.

Hugh gestured to Charles to take a sofa across from him. Charles sat down on the sofa and observed all around him.

There were both men and women smoking. What amazed him was the customers weren't the same as the people out on the streets – instead they seemed affluent and well dressed. He remembered people talking about slumming. The rich going down to the East End to enjoy the drugs and free-for-all lifestyle there that contrasted so much to their own society's late Victorian rigidness.

A Chinese woman came over and began to set him up with an opium pipe.

He started carefully to inhale as he observed all around him. A man got up from his couch and went up the stairs holding hands with a young woman. What kind of a place had he been brought to?

'Do you own shares in this business as well?' asked Charles.

'I own all the property on this street,' said Hugh.

The woman who had given him the opium pipe indicated Charles should lie out on the sofa and Charles stretched back as she undid his shirt.

'What made you trust me to bring me here?' asked Charles. 'Why do you think I won't tell everybody what you're involved in?'

'Because I do trust you,' said Hugh. 'Besides, you can't.'

'Why not?'

'Because you've come here with me – you've become part of this world now.'

Hugh looked on as another man went up the stairs with a young woman.

'Being here for a couple of hours doesn't make me a part of this world,' said Charles.

Hugh looked over at him and smiled broadly. 'Besides, you couldn't possibly betray my secrets.'

Charles was curious. 'And why not?'

'Because you owe me far too much money.' Hugh sat back and closed his eyes as the woman massaged his temples.

Charles felt a shiver go down his back as he heard these words. Hugh thought that he was in his power.

Charles suddenly stood up and pushed the opium pipe aside.

'I have to go,' he said.

'But I've just started to enjoy myself,' said Hugh. 'Sit down and relax.'

'No, I really must go right now.'

'But you don't know the way back.'

'I'll find it,' said Charles as he headed for the door.

'If you can find my driver get him to take you home ... *if* you can find him,' said Hugh and he started to laugh – a hollow laugh that echoed in Charles' ears as he hurried from the building.

Charles seemed to take hours negotiating the maze of streets trying to find where the carriage was parked. The streets looked all the same and he was constantly accosted by beggars and prostitutes and jostled by people he suspected were thieves. Finally he found the carriage parked on a street corner.

'Take me back to Regent's Park – quickly as you can,' Charles said to the driver, then added, 'Mr Fitzroy has given his permission.'

Charles sat back in the comfort of the carriage, the images of all the things he'd seen swirling through his mind.

CHAPTER 37

Emily was so thrilled to be going to London, she wondered why she hadn't thought of the idea of exploiting being a debutante before. Margaret's health was improving, but Emily couldn't help being glad it hadn't improved enough for her to accompany her to London. Four whole months away from Armstrong House beckoned, and now without the watchful eye of her mother correcting everything she did.

When she reached London she was brought to the Battingtons' villa where Gwyneth gently explained that due to her pregnancy Charles and Arabella would assist with her during the season – did she mind?

'Mind?' said Emily. 'Of course not!' She was over the moon. It meant she would be spending even more time with Charles.

'Of course we mustn't tell Mama that Arabella will be involved for fear of upsetting her health,' Gwyneth insisted.

Emily readily agreed.

Emily was then deposited to Hanover Terrace where she embraced Charles tightly.

'Welcome to London, my dear,' said Arabella, kissing her on the cheek and smiling at her.

'I want to go to art galleries, museums and parks,' said Emily. 'And restaurants, and I want to go on the underground – Mama never let me when I was here with her. I want to go on a boat down the Thames, and–'

'But your mother and Gwyneth have already put your schedule together for you,' said Arabella, holding up the paperwork.

'Yes,' said Charles. 'Breakfast on Monday at the Hansons', lunch at the Whitbreads' – they've a second son they want to marry off. Then a dance at the Howards'. Tuesday, breakfast at the Lascelles' – they have a French cousin they want you to meet.'

Emily crossed over the drawing room and took up the paperwork.

'Mama has organised this with military precision!' objected Emily. 'When do I ever get any time to do the things *I* want to do?'

'I believe you are here for a purpose,' Charles pointed out, looking bemused.

Emily flung the paperwork on the table. 'Well, I can't possibly go to half of these – I'd be exhausted! Where's my room? And where's this French chef I hear all the talk about – can he cook me steak with Béarnaise sauce for my dinner?'

As Arabella looked on she realised that dealing with Emily as a house guest was not going to be an easy feat, and the girl had obviously come to London on false pretences. She had no interest in finding a husband.

Arabella did try to take a firm hand with Emily and force her to go to the events arranged. But Emily was headstrong and, if she didn't want to go, then she didn't. Arabella realised that if the indomitable Margaret had failed to marry Emily off so far, what chance did she have?

Emily was presented at court, together with the mandatory ten-foot train on her debutante dress.

'At least the curtsy was correct,' said Gwyneth who had managed to make it to the palace to observe.

The ironic thing was that Emily was in great demand from her first event on. News quickly spread about Lord Armstrong's beautiful young daughter who had everything going for her, from her rounded education to impeccable relations. The trouble was, Emily found them all a bore.

Emily had been invited to dinner at the Lascelles' and Arabella and Charles accompanied her. The Lascelles were trying to match her with their cousin Henri from France. Emily sat bored as both Henri and his family discussed his merits and qualities.

'My father is the Count de Chavan. We are one of the oldest and most respected families in France,' said Henri.

'How did your family escape the guillotine?' questioned Emily, causing a surprised murmur around the table.

Henri continued undaunted. 'My father is a very wealthy man. He owns the de Chavan vineyard in the Loire. Our wine is the best in France.'

'In fact,' interrupted Mrs Lascelle, 'this wine is from the vineyard.'

'Oh? It's just a little bitter for my taste,' said Emily.

The table fell into silence for a while before it was broken by Arabella. 'Emily speaks fluent French, Henri. Perhaps you would like to speak in French together for a while?'

'Oh no, you're mistaken, Arabella. My French teacher said I had the worst pronunciation she had ever heard ... my German isn't bad though. Do you speak German, Henri?'

'*Non!*'

'Not surprising ... the French lost the Franco-German war, didn't they?'

Henri looked insulted but continued unabated.

'My family have one of the largest chateaus in the Loire, and I as their only son and heir–'

'I'm sorry!' said Emily, holding up her hand. 'I'm sorry – but if you are so wonderful, then why haven't you been taken already?'

The whole table looked on shocked, except for Charles who burst out laughing.

One part of being a debutante Emily loved was Saturday afternoons when the debutantes were expected to ride through Hyde Park with a male relative to show off their riding skills and beauty to passing suitors. She had Charles all to herself for a few hours as they rode side by side.

'This is like putting yourself in a shop window,' said Emily as she trotted beside Charles.

She was attracting a lot of attention from the passing people and Charles expected they would have many calling cards and invitations left in on Monday for Emily.

They stopped along the way to chat to passing people and for Charles to introduce Emily.

'Isn't this just like the old times, Charles? Remember when I was your confidante?'

'I remember well,' he said, nodding, remembering the unfortunate hand Emily had in the start of his relationship with his wife.

Suddenly Charles saw Hugh Fitzroy riding towards them on his stallion. Charles had tried to keep a distance between himself and Hugh since their journey that night to the East End. The whole experience had unnerved him considerably. He realised there was a lot more to Hugh than he had imagined. And that lot more was unsavoury and could be dangerous. The trouble was he had so ingratiated himself with Hugh by this stage that keeping that distance was proving very hard.

'Hello, Charles,' said Hugh, stopping beside them.

'Good afternoon, Hugh. I didn't realise you'd taken riding lessons?'

Hugh looked at Emily quizzically.

'Hugh Fitzroy, may I introduce my sister, Lady Emily,' said Charles.

Hugh looked at Emily, surprised.

'Delighted to meet you,' said Hugh.

'A pleasure,' said Emily.

'I didn't know you had another sister,' said Hugh.

'Yes, I'm the youngest,' said Emily. 'I'm usually buried away in the Irish countryside, but they let me out for the season, on the promise I'm on my best behaviour.'

Hugh stared at the girl, taken aback by her cheeky talk. 'And how are you liking your time here?'

'Oh, I'm liking it very much, Mr Fitzroy. I feel like a prisoner let out after a life sentence,' she said lightly.

'I'm afraid we have to get on – Arabella is expecting us back,' said Charles.

'Of course,' said Hugh. 'Are you both free next week for lunch, my treat, Fortnum and Mason?'

Charles shook his head. 'Unfortunately not. Emily has a packed week of events.'

'No, I don't,' said Emily. 'Well, nothing that can't be cancelled. I haven't been to Fortnum and Mason yet, and it's on my list of things to do.'

'Well, then – Tuesday at one?' asked Hugh.

'See you then,' said Emily nonchalantly.

Hugh nodded and rode on.

'Who is he?' asked Emily.

'Just an acquaintance. You shouldn't have accepted that invitation.' Charles was annoyed. 'You're supposed to be having lunch with the Brewers on Tuesday.'

'That's the very reason I accepted it!' said Emily as they rode on through the park.

As Arabella and Charles walked into Fortnum and Mason they spotted Hugh immediately – he was sitting at a table and waved them over.

'This is a treat!' said Emily after they greeted each other and she sat down.

Hugh handed them menus. 'Please, order anything you want.'

Charles took the menu and sat back. 'Have you bought Fortnum and Masons as well, Hugh?' He didn't hide the cynicism in his voice.

'Not yet.' Hugh looked at him pointedly.

They ordered food and chatted away.

'You're over here as a debutante?' said Hugh.

'Yes, I've already been presented at court. Poor old Queen Vicky, I felt quite sorry for her. She looked as if she had less interest in being there than I had! The Prince of Wales seemed to be fun, though.'

Hugh looked at her, amused. 'Do you like London?' he asked.

'Oh, yes. But what I'd really like is to go to New York some time. Have you travelled much?'

'Yes, I've been to many places around the world.'

Emily sat forward, intrigued. 'Where's the most exotic place you've been?'

'I'd say Constantinople,' Hugh said.

Emily's eyes widened in amazement. 'Tell me what are the markets like – is it true you can buy anything in the world there?'

As Hugh talked about Constantinople, Charles wondered what reasons took Hugh there and guessed it would be something to do with the opium trade.

Emily found Hugh's stories captivating. She hadn't met anyone like him before – he was so different from the stuffy people she had met since arriving in London.

'Charles!' called somebody from another table and Charles excused himself to go over and talk to them.

Hugh looked at Emily and smiled and seemed suddenly embarrassed to be left alone in her company.

'So – what events have you lined up for the rest of the week?' he asked.

'I'm attending a ball at Lady Hollander's on Friday. Do you know her?'

'Yes, I sponsor a lot of her charity work.'

'I know she does a lot of good works. I know this because she never shuts up telling everyone about it!'

'I'm certain she'll have a lot of eligible suitors lined up to meet you.'

Emily looked at him and giggled before sitting forward. 'Can I tell you a secret?'

'Yes.'

'I have no intention of marrying any of them.'

'Sorry?'

'A lot of insipid bores. I'm over here to enjoy myself.'

'I see! But a girl like you could own the world,' he said, amazed at her attitude.

'Oh, I'm not like my sisters, Mr Fitzroy. I don't want to own the world – I just want to see some of it.'

He smiled at her. 'Please, call me Hugh.'

At Lady Hollander's ball Emily tried to be polite to the people around her and then found a quiet corner and sat down, wondering how long it would go on and when she could get home to her comfortable bed. Then she saw Hugh Fitzroy walking across the floor to her.

'Hello there,' he said.

'Good evening, Hugh. I didn't realise you were coming tonight.'

'Neither did I,' he said, looking awkward. 'Could you put me on your card later for a dance, if you would allow? That is, if you're not already booked up?'

She looked at him curiously and held up her dance card. 'My dance card is empty.'

Hugh looked at her, confused.

'I haven't accepted any dance invitations to-night, you see,' she explained.

'Oh, you don't like to dance?'

'No, it's not that,' she said, standing up. 'I'm free to dance now, if you wish?'

He nodded and smiled and led her out to the dance floor where they began to waltz.

'Why didn't you accept anybody's dance

invitations?' he asked.

'Because there was nobody here that interested me enough to dance with.'

He went red with embarrassment. 'But you accepted mine?'

She nodded and smiled. She found his eyes always stared and, when she was that close to him, it was impossible not to stare back.

'I'm getting some jealous looks from the men,' said Hugh.

'Who cares? They are not interested in me, not really. More interested in how big a dowry they can get from my father.'

'If I ... if I ever got married ... I wouldn't accept any dowry at all.'

She smiled at him, trying to understand him. 'Why not?'

'Because I'd just want her.'

Suddenly he stood on her toes.

'I'm sorry!' He was mortified. 'I'm so sorry. I'm not a good dancer at all. I've been getting lessons, but...'

She placed a finger against his mouth. 'It doesn't matter, not to me, how you dance.'

She went back into his arms and they continued to dance.

At the breakfast table at Hanover Terrace on the Monday morning, Emily was having breakfast with Arabella and Charles when Burchill came in holding a gift box which he laid on the table.

'For Lady Emily,' he said, before retreating from the room.

'What on earth is that?' asked Charles as Emily

opened the navy velvet box.

'It's a diamond necklace,' said Emily, astounded, as she looked down at the necklace sitting on its silk bed.

Arabella got up quickly and came around to look at it.

'Who is it from?'

Emily read the card. 'Hugh Fitzroy!'

Arabella looked at Charles with concern.

'Such a remarkable gesture!' Emily was taken aback.

'It certainly beats the normal calling cards that gentlemen send you,' said Charles.

'That man has more money than sense,' said Arabella, trying to calm Emily's obvious excitement. 'He's always sending lavish gifts to anyone who looks at him in London. He sent me diamond earrings once.'

'But I imagine they were nothing like this!' said Emily correctly, as they all started to mentally count the diamonds on the necklace.

CHAPTER 38

Arabella looked on with increasing concern as the summer months passed by. Hugh Fitzroy turned up at all the balls Emily went to and Emily spent most of the evenings in his company. Arabella decided she needed to act to avoid any misunderstanding on anyone's part. She was in the drawing room at Hanover Terrace in the late morning when Emily came happily in.

'What a lovely day!' said Emily as she went and looked out the windows. 'Do you fancy going for a walk in the park this afternoon?'

'Yes, that sounds nice. Emily, I've been meaning to have a word with you about Mr Fitzroy.'

'About Hugh?' asked Emily, turning around, smiling.

'Yes. I don't think it's wise for you to spend too much time in his company from now on.'

'Why not?' Emily's face soured.

'Because I think you might be scaring off other potential suitors by giving him so much attention.'

'Good! I want to scare off any potential suitors.'

Arabella became annoyed. 'And I don't think you're being fair to Hugh himself.'

'Why not?'

'Because – because you don't want to give him the wrong impression.'

Emily walked slowly over to the couch and sat down. 'And what wrong impression would that be?'

'That he might be in with any kind of chance with you.'

'I see ... and who says he's not in with "any kind of chance" with me?'

Arabella laughed derisorily. 'Of course he isn't! Because he's not in any way suitable – in fact I can't think of anyone less suitable.'

'I think Hugh is refreshing. He's different from the others. He's not caught up in what schools everyone went to and what clubs they are in.'

'That's only because he probably didn't go to

school and is only in any club because Charles nominated him into it!'

'Well, I'm sorry, Arabella, but I'm not going to shun Hugh in future. He's been incredibly kind to me. Kinder than anyone ever has been.'

Arabella looked cynical. 'He's good at deceiving people, Emily, and buying them and swamping them with gifts. That's not kindness – that's vulgar and insincere.'

'Well, I don't see how it's anything to do with you.'

'It's everything to do with me! While in London, you're my charge–'

'I'm not your charge! I'm supposed to be Gwyneth's charge, except she's not up to the job due to her pregnancy.'

'Exactly, and the job has fallen to me. Your mother and father would be horrified that you were even speaking to someone like Hugh Fitzroy, let alone accepting all these gifts and dancing all night with him. I owe it to them to ensure you conduct yourself properly while here.'

'They don't trust *you* of all people! Not after everything you did! You forget, Arabella, I was party to your deceitful affair with Charles. Everyone else doesn't know the extent of your deception and the lengths you went to and the depths to which you sank in order to hide your sordid affair. But I do. I was your go-between. And I will not be dictated to you by now about who is suitable and not suitable to socialise with. Not you of all people!'

'Emily–'

'No! You might like to go around now with all

your airs and graces. You and Charles, the toast of society. But I know it's all a façade, a game of charades to hide your real selves.' She stood up angrily. 'At least with Hugh you get what you see. Certainly he doesn't have the polite manners and upbringing everyone else has, but at least he's real – and that's what I like about him!'

Emily turned and stormed out of the room.

Charles was in the study reading a letter when Arabella walked in and closed the door behind her.

'Charles, I need to speak to you about Emily and this unsuitable friendship she's established with Hugh Fitzroy. It has to stop! I tried speaking to her about it, but you know how defiant she is. She pushed me away and dismissed me, in quite a rude way.'

Charles laughed. 'That's dearest little Emily for you.'

'It's not a laughing matter, Charles. She's never going to find a suitable match with him hanging around like a bad smell.'

'Come, come, Arabella! I think both you and I know Emily has no intention of making a match with anybody.' He looked at her, amused. 'Are you honestly suggesting she's contemplating Hugh in any way other than a casual entertainment?'

'You are forgetting, Charles, that Emily is a young and a very inexperienced girl. Just because she has a smart mouth and a stubborn streak does not make her in any way worldly wise. All she knows about the world she's read in books, but this is the real world she's in now, and she's completely uneducated in its ways.'

'Emily is much cleverer than you give her credit for. As if she has any real feelings for Fitzroy or ever could! She's an aristocrat; Lord Armstrong's daughter!'

'That's as may be, but you and I of all people should know how things can get out of hand. If your mother was here supervising Emily, she wouldn't even be allowed in the same room as Fitzroy.'

'What do you suggest I do about it?'

'Speak to Fitzroy – warn him to keep his distance.'

'I see!' said Charles, wondering how Hugh would take that.

'The more that man has infiltrated himself into society the more fantastical the rumours I've heard about him. Most of which I wouldn't sully my mouth by repeating. I don't want him near Emily again, or near you for that matter.'

'I can hardly just cut off a friend!'

'Yes, you can!' she said, her eyes blazing with determination. Then she turned and walked out.

As Charles turned his chair and looked out the window at the gardens, he thought how Hugh had become too powerful for anyone to tell what to do. But he knew Arabella was right. If she had known what he had witnessed that night in the East End, she would faint. The time had come to cut Hugh Fitzroy loose.

Charles had been summoned in to meet his bank manager. And as Charles sat down opposite him Mr Jones did not look in a good mood.

'We've been writing to you for months and our correspondence has been ignored,' said Mr Jones.

'It's Burchill the butler – he's always falling down on his duties. But he's been with the family for years, so it would be cruel to get rid of him at this stage.'

'Indeed. Well, quite simply you are behind months with the mortgage repayments for Hanover Terrace.'

Charles glared at Mr Jones. 'And why haven't you been taking the repayments from my bank account as usual?'

'There isn't enough in your bank account to cover the repayments,' Mr Jones said, handing over a sheaf of paperwork.

Charles looked through the paperwork with growing alarm. 'But – but – this can't be correct.'

'Quite correct, unfortunately.'

'But where did all the money go to? All the money transferred when I raised the money on the mortgage on Hanover Terrace?'

'Spent, I imagine. Money has been pouring out of your account like water over the Victoria Falls. Previously, when your account was nearly empty it was of no concern for the bank. But now, with the massive arrears you owe the bank, it's very much our concern.'

Charles continued to stare at the paperwork in shock. He knew their lifestyle was lavish but even they couldn't go through this amount of money, could they? Two fortunes lost in a matter of years – Arabella's dowry and the mortgage money.

And yet as Mr Jones droned on, he realised the

expense of everything in their life, not to mention that confounded gambling debt he had built up. Usually his winnings supplemented their lifestyle, but he had been on such a losing streak for such a long time.

'I'm afraid at this stage we have no alternative but to write to your father Lord Armstrong and inform him that unless immediate payment is made we will have to repossess his house at Hanover Terrace.'

Charles slammed the paperwork down on the desk.

'You will do no such thing!' he almost shouted. 'You will not write to my father under any circumstances regarding this!'

'But–'

'But nothing! You sit there in your cheap suit and with your tacky spectacles and dare to talk to me about such things!'

Mr Jones was taken aback and found himself getting angry. 'This is the bank's money, and we have a responsibility to our shareholders.'

'You should be honoured you have the Armstrongs as clients! You will leave this with me and you'll get your bloody money.'

'Very well. I'm aware your father has considerable assets and will obviously not want to lose his London house. But I'm warning you, if we do not receive full payment, we will repossess that house. Good day.'

Dazed, Charles walked along Regent Street. He had to concede he had been living like one of the richest men in London, when clearly he wasn't.

Charles realised Jones was not messing around and would start taking the necessary steps to recoup the bank's money. It would take only one letter to his father from the bank for his house of cards to come crashing down. His father and everyone else would find out about the fraudulent mortgage he had raised. Not to mention the fact he would be left penniless. He wracked his head trying to think of a solution. And then he thought of Hugh Fitzroy. His close and loyal and very rich friend. Hugh would lend him the money to stave off this disaster. What was the money to him? A drop in the ocean.

'This is unexpected,' said Hugh as he led Charles into the living room of his suite at Claridge's. 'You haven't been over for a while.'

'No – I've been busy chaperoning Emily around.'

'I see,' said Hugh, sitting down. 'Tea or something?'

'No, I'm all right for now.' Charles smiled over at Hugh. 'I've come to see you because I need your help with something.'

'Name it and I'll do it,' said Hugh.

Charles felt relieved. 'You see, Hugh, I've got myself into a bit of a pickle.'

'How so?'

'A financial pickle, I'm afraid.'

'Go on.'

'Well, I took out a loan from the bank and now they are demanding it back, greedy bastards.'

'I see,' Hugh said, lost in thought.

'I thought there was enough money there to

cover the loan, and when I checked the cupboard was bare, so to speak.'

Hugh said nothing as he studied Charles.

'A bit embarrassing really,' Charles rattled on. 'Power can really go to some people's heads. This little bank manager sat there lecturing me.'

'But your father is Lord Armstrong with that vast estate.'

'I know, but I can't really go to him, you'll understand. I'll obviously own it all one day, but tomorrow isn't today, and today is when I need the money. So I'd hoped...'

'That I would give you the money,' Hugh finished off the sentence.

'Lend it to me.' Charles smiled confidently at him.

Hugh took a long time to answer before saying, 'No, I can't.'

'I'm sorry?'

'I can't lend you any more money.'

'Any more?' Charles looked bewildered.

'Yes, you already owe me a huge sum from all your card losses. I've been covering you for months.'

'Yes, I know, but–'

'Those wagers I covered for you were only loans – you knew that?'

'Yes, but–'

'Tom Hamley has kept an account of everything you lost and everything that's owed to me from you.'

'*By* you,' Charles corrected his grammar.

'Money owed to me *by* you, in that case. You can check with Hamley – it comes to thousands.'

'And you waited until now when I come to you with money worries to throw this at me?' Charles felt himself become angry.

'Now's as good a time as ever. More so, when you've just told me you have no money left to pay me back.'

'I think I'll be going,' said Charles, standing up.

'Sit down!' commanded Hugh.

Charles looked at Hugh's glaring eyes and slowly sat down again.

'I'm calling in my wager now. I want my money back, every last penny,' said Hugh.

'I've just told you I'm not in funds at the moment.'

'And won't be for a long time, considering your father is in excellent health.'

Charles sat forward. 'Yes, you covered my wagers, but what have I done for you? You were nobody or nothing when I met you. No family would have you in their house. A card game at Tom Hamley's was all you could manage to be invited to and that was only because they all wanted your money.'

'Including you! I'm not saying you didn't put the key in the door for me, but I opened the door, or rather my money did. Are you sure you don't want that drink?'

'I don't want anything from you, considering you keep a record of everything owed!'

Hugh sat back and crossed his legs. 'I'm not saying we can't come to some arrangement.'

'What kind of an arrangement?' said Charles coldly.

'Emily.'

'*Emily?*' Charles nearly shouted.

'I'm very fond of her.'

'So?'

'So... I want to marry her.'

Through his anger Charles managed to laugh. 'You're insane! Marry Emily! She wouldn't even look at you.'

'I think you're wrong. I think she's taken with me.'

Charles sat forward and snapped. 'You're deluded!'

Anger flashed through Hugh's eyes. 'That's the last time you ever look down on me! I've had enough of you telling me I need to speak properly, eat properly, walk properly – you pass judgement on me and you can't even pay your bills!'

'It's quite out of the question. Put any thoughts you are entertaining of marrying my sister out of your head. My sister is a lady. She's one of the most well-connected young women around and you are nothing, I'm afraid.'

'I'm a millionaire.'

'Good for you, but that doesn't really cut it with families like mine. I suggest you go back to that disgusting place you brought me to and find a wife to suit your sort there.'

'In that case, you pay me back all the money you owe me by the end of the week. If not the bailiffs will be knocking at your door. And not just the bailiffs, but I know some persuasive people from that disgusting place, as you call it, where I'm from and where I have many contacts. You don't want these people coming and finding you or your lovely wife and children, I can guarantee you.'

'Are you threatening me?'

'I'm warning you.'

Charles softened his voice. 'Hugh ... what you're saying can never happen. You and Emily have nothing in common. My parents would never allow it.'

'For your sake it had better happen. I want you to smooth over this with Emily and your family. I want you to get Emily to marry me and for your family to accept it.'

'You're asking the impossible and I refuse to do it.'

'Then you'd better have all that money ready for me by Friday.'

Charles was shaken after his meetings with Fitzroy and the bank manager. He had been pushed into the tightest corner of his life and was now facing ruin. He couldn't sleep that night so he sat in the study thinking. He knew Hugh was not a man to joke around. He was owed considerable money and Charles didn't even want to think how he would react if he didn't get it. By the time the sun started to rise, he knew he had no option.

CHAPTER 39

Charles and Emily rode their horses through Hyde Park together.

'It's near summer's end,' said Charles.

'I know!' said Emily, disheartened.

'You'll soon be returning to Armstrong House.'

'I don't want to think about it. I suppose I can come back next summer and do the season again,' she said hopefully.

'Mama will never allow that – she'll have heard back from everybody that you made no effort to meet a husband this summer.'

Emily sighed heavily. 'I suppose not.'

'So – what are you going to do now?'

'What can I do? I've no money of my own. I'll have to remain at Armstrong House and...'

'Look after Mama and Papa into their old age, the spinster daughter.'

'Don't, Charles! The thought of it depresses me too much.'

Charles chose his words carefully. 'There are always options, Emily.'

'Not for me. Only two. Marry one of those awful boring men or remain a spinster.'

'Was ... Hugh one of those awful boring men?'

'No, Hugh is different. I enjoyed being around him. He's exciting.'

'He wants to marry you, Emily,' Charles said directly.

'*What?*' Emily turned to him, stunned.

'Oh, come on, Emily, you're not that naïve, surely? All the attention he paid you, presents he sent. Making sure he was at every dance you were at. What did you think that was all about?'

'I – I knew he liked me and, yes, I suppose I knew he was interested in me. But I never thought he would actually want to marry me. I just thought he was, I don't know ... but, Charles, he's not one of us.'

'I know.'

'Then I suppose I thought he would never contemplate a marriage with me, because he would never dream of marrying so much above his station.'

'Why not? He's worked hard for what he has and he believes social barriers shouldn't get in the way of what he wants – including you.'

Emily rode along in stunned silence for a long while.

'Well?' Charles asked eventually.

'I don't know, Charles. I never contemplated marrying anyone. But ... would I not be some kind of social outcast marrying a man like that?'

'Nobody will ostracise you with his money. Anyway, I didn't think you cared about what people think?'

'I don't! But there would be so much opposition. Mama and Papa would never allow it.'

'How could they stop it?'

'What do *you* think, Charles?'

'I think ... I think you could have a wonderful life with someone like Hugh. You could travel to all the places you want to. You could go anywhere in the world and stay in the best places. Anything you want, you could have. It's either that or returning to Armstrong House and doing nothing for the rest of your life but being the pitied unmarried younger daughter.'

Emily felt she was standing on the edge of a cliff, hearing this news. That she could so dramatically change her life forever.

'And he wouldn't have the expectations from you that marrying one of the sons of the aristocracy would have. You wouldn't have to host endless dinner parties, make small talk to people you don't like, and have child after child. Marrying Hugh would make you free ... isn't that what you've always wanted, Emily?'

'Out of the question!' Arabella shrieked.

'It's nothing to do with you!' retorted Emily.

'It's everything to do with me,' said Arabella.

They were in the drawing room at Hanover Terrace after Emily and Charles had just broken the news.

'Emily, you have no idea what you're doing. You'll ruin your life if you marry that man!'

'It's my life to ruin, nobody else's,' said Emily. 'Beside, I've said yes to him now, so it's too late.'

'Of course it's not!'

'I, unlike you, Arabella, do not break my promises. When I tell somebody I'm going to marry them, I'm not lying to him. Besides, Charles supports my decision.'

'Of course he doesn't, how could he?' Arabella turned to look at Charles. 'Charles?'

Charles shifted uncomfortably. 'Well, it's as

Emily says – it's her choice who she marries.'

Arabella stared at Charles, uncomprehendingly.

'See,' said Emily standing up. 'Now, I'm far too busy to be sitting around discussing something that's already been decided.'

'And who is going to break this news to your parents?' demanded Arabella.

'I will,' said Emily, heading towards the door.

'They'll never permit it!' Arabella shouted after her.

Arabella lay on the bed in a long ivory silk night-dress. She surveyed Charles who was beginning to undress.

'Tell me, Charles, what's in all this for you?' she said, looking at him coldly.

'For me? I don't know what you're talking about.'

'I know you too well, Charles. There's no way you'd permit this wedding unless there's something in it for you.'

He glared at her angrily. 'You'd want to watch what you say.'

She started laughing. 'You've sunk to a new low. That you'd betray your sister in this way, for whatever financial gain is in it for you–'

'That's a fucking lie!'

'I suppose it's not that surprising. I mean, you tricked your brother out of marriage with me, so it shouldn't be that difficult to trick your sister into a marriage with Fitzroy.'

'I tricked nobody out or in to anything. You couldn't keep out of my bed, from what I remember.'

304

'Charles, I'm begging you to stop Emily going through with this. If she means anything to you, do not allow her to marry Fitzroy.'

'As if Emily would listen to me!'

'You're the only person she *will* listen to!' Arabella's voice rose to a shout. 'She's doing this out of defiance to her parents and to her family. And you have to stop her!'

'As she said, it's nothing to do with you, so keep fucking out of it!' His face was contorted as he roared.

The door of the bedroom opened and Prudence walked in.

'Mama, Papa,' she said, rubbing her eyes.

Arabella gave Charles a filthy look and then went quickly to Prudence and picked her up.

'Sorry, darling,' she soothed. 'Did we wake you up?'

Prudence nodded.

Isabelle came rushing in. 'Mademoiselle Prudence! I'm so sorry, my lady – she slipped out of the nursery without waking me!' Isabelle took the child from Arabella and quickly went back to the nursery.

Arabella turned to Charles. 'I'll sleep with the children in the nursery tonight.'

'Good. I hope you'll be comfortable there!' Charles said as she left.

Charles pulled off his shirt and flung it across the room. Damn Fitzroy and his blackmail. He had no choice but to go through with the plan.

CHAPTER 40

Margaret went marching into the library at Armstrong House holding a letter.

'A letter from Gwyneth,' she announced.

'How is the new baby?' asked Lawrence smiling.

'Fine, fine. More importantly she writes that Emily has got engaged!'

Lawrence sat back, bowled over. 'I hardly believe it! To whom?'

'Well, that's just the point. To somebody we've never heard of before – a Hugh Fitzroy.'

'Who?'

'Exactly! Gwyneth writes that he's a friend of Charles, very rich. But...'

'But what?'

'I know my Gwyneth and she's not saying much about him. That's a bad sign, Lawrence. She's not enthusing about his virtues. She just says we should meet him as soon as possible.'

'That sounds ominous.'

'She was introduced to at least two hundred young men that we knew or who were recommended by our friends whose families we know and trust – how did she end up with this Hugh Fitzroy?' Margaret's face clouded with concern.

A flurry of correspondences scurried between Armstrong House and London following on this. Margaret inquired from all her friends what they knew of Hugh Fitzroy and a sketchy and unflattering image was created.

September 18th

Dear Lady Margaret,

Congratulations on Emily's engagement to Mr Fitzroy. I have to say we were all surprised to hear the news! You asked me in your letter what I know of Mr Fitzroy.

I'm afraid the answer is: not very much. He arrived on the scene in London some time ago and he has certainly made an impression, but, alas, not the best impression.

Although generous to a fault, he seems to think he can use his money to gain acceptance and influence in circles that he was obviously not born to. Although polite, his manners are somewhat primitive. I know Emily was always an independently minded girl, but this borders on being revolutionary-minded! I don't mean to concern you, but you did ask me to write candidly. All I can say is that if it was a daughter of mine, I would want to meet this man at the earliest opportunity. It's such a pity that the Duchess of Battington was so housebound during her pregnancy and not able to chaperone her sister adequately. The Armstrong family is such a respected family with such excellent breeding, it is a concern for all that you will be infiltrated by that man. I urge you to meet Mr Fitzroy at your earliest convenience in order to make up your own minds.

I remain your friend,

Lady Hollander

Margaret crumpled the letter in her hands as she screamed at the top of her voice, *'Lawrence!'*

Charles, Arabella and Emily were summoned to Armstrong House immediately and an invitation to Hugh Fitzroy extended.

On the day they were all due to arrive Margaret was in a state of near panic as letter after letter had arrived from friends who knew of Hugh and voiced their concerns to the Armstrongs.

'Now remember, Margaret, do not say anything negative about the wedding until after we've met Fitzroy,' warned Lawrence. 'If Emily sees we are against the match as soon as we meet her, she'll say we had already made up our minds about him before meeting him.'

'I will try to keep my mouth shut,' agreed Margaret.

Arabella sat with Charles and Emily in the carriage that had been sent to bring them from the station at Castlewest to the house. She was filled with dread. Hugh was due to arrive later that evening and she could only imagine Margaret and Lawrence's reaction to him. Charles and Emily seemed immune to the coming storm as they chatted and joked away beside her. She wished she could have their sense of lightness to life. But as the carriage circled around the lake and Armstrong House came into view, she realised she had always a sense of dread when she came to this place and she couldn't wait to return to London as soon as possible, to her life and her children who had been left in the care of Gwyneth there.

Emily raced into the drawing room and kissed her parents.

'Mama! How are you feeling now?' asked Emily.

'The doctor said I'm well on the road to recovery,' Margaret assured her.

She viewed Charles and Arabella coldly as they came into the room.

'Charles ... Arabella,' she greeted them, then briefly kissed them both.

Lawrence tugged the bell pull and ordered tea and sandwiches when the butler came.

'How are little Prudence and Pierce?' asked Lawrence.

'Oh, just fine. Prudence is way ahead of her years. She's into everything!' said Charles. 'I've never seen a child like her.'

'And Pierce?' asked Margaret.

'Pierce is an adorable child,' said Arabella. 'No trouble at all. He is literally mobbed by mothers besotted with him when I take him walking in Regent's Park.'

'I sometimes wish their roles were reversed,' laughed Charles. 'It should be Pierce who's into everything and Prudence admired.'

'Well, we can't help how our children turn out,' said Margaret, not leaving the bitterness out of her voice as she looked at Emily.

'What time is Mr Fitzroy due to arrive?' asked Lawrence.

'Hugh should arrive at Armstrong House this evening. He's very much looking forward to meeting you all,' said Emily happily.

'As we are him,' said Margaret.

'We're talking about going to South America for our honeymoon!'

'Well, let's not get ahead of ourselves,' warned Margaret.

That evening as the carriage pulled up in the forecourt in front of Armstrong House, Hugh stepped out and looked up at the regal building in awe.

The front door opened and the butler and footman came down to take his luggage.

'Lord and Lady Armstrong are waiting for you in the drawing room,' said the butler as Hugh entered the hall and marvelled at all the portraits of the Armstrong ancestors on the walls.

When Hugh was shown into the drawing room, Lawrence and Margaret made their minds up about him in ten seconds flat. This was a man who could never be allowed to marry their daughter.

'Mr Fitzroy, how nice of you to visit,' said Margaret, rising from her chair and extending her hand for him to shake.

'I'm pleased to meet you,' said Hugh.

'How do you do?' said Lawrence formally as he shook his hand.

Emily rushed to him and gave him a hug.

'Emily!' snapped Margaret. 'Remember yourself!'

'You see, I told you how stuffy they were! It's all protocol and manners around here,' said Emily, laughing as she sat down again. Arabella and

Charles came forward to greet him.

'Hello, Hugh,' said Arabella, feeling a knot of tension in her stomach.

'Arabella – Charles,' nodded Hugh.

'We've put you in the Blue Room – it has a lovely aspect out onto the lake,' said Margaret. 'We're serving dinner in an hour, so perhaps the butler should take you straight there so you can freshen up and dress for dinner.'

Hugh was surprised by this sudden order.

'If you care to follow the butler up,' insisted Margaret as she gestured to the butler standing behind him.

'Of course,' said Hugh and he turned to leave.

'Isn't he wonderful?' smiled Emily once he had left.

Margaret and Lawrence sat saying nothing and glaring at Charles and Arabella coldly.

A dinner of roast beef was served in the dining room that night. Lawrence and Margaret sat at either end of the table, Charles and Arabella to one side, Emily and Hugh to the other.

'I trust you had a good journey?' asked Lawrence.

'Yes,' nodded Hugh. 'I've never been to Ireland before.'

'Really?' said Margaret. 'I understood you had been to everywhere?'

'Not Ireland,' said Hugh. 'You really get the feeling as you travel across Ireland to the west coast here that you're going to the end of the world ... next stop America.'

'It might feel like the end of the world to you,

Mr Fitzroy, but it's the centre of ours. The Armstrongs have been here for three hundred years.'

'Yes, I've been reading up on Irish history,' said Hugh.

'Really? I wouldn't have taken you for a man much given to reading,' said Margaret acidly.

'Mother!' Emily protested.

Hugh glared at Margaret. 'I understand that most of the Irish aristocracy like yourselves were originally soldiers in the British army that the King couldn't afford to pay so he paid them with these vast estates where the land was stolen from the original Irish native owners, who are now your tenant farmers.'

Everyone, including Emily, stared at Hugh in disbelief at what he had said.

'The Armstrong estate is legally owned by me, Mr Fitzroy,' said Lawrence evenly. 'You have no need to fear that you are staying on any stolen property.'

'And the Armstrongs were never soldiers, Mr Fitzroy,' said Margaret, amazed at his rudeness. 'The Armstrongs have a pedigree going back many hundreds of years.'

'Of course... I'm just saying we're all the same, aren't we?'

'I doubt we have that much in common with you,' said Margaret.

'I'm just saying family fortunes have to be built somewhere by someone originally, and it usually comes at the expense of others,' said Hugh.

'And what of your own family, Mr Fitzroy?' said Margaret. 'You have the most unusual accent.'

'I'm from London,' stated Hugh.

'What part? Kensington? Chelsea?' Margaret looked at him condescendingly.

'No, further east,' said Hugh.

'A lot further east, I imagine,' said Lawrence knowingly.

'And do you have a large family?' asked Margaret. 'Will there be many at this wedding you are planning with our daughter? Is Armstrong House to be filled on the day by the good working people of Whitechapel?'

'I don't have much family, Lady Armstrong, and the few I have I'm no longer in contact with,' said Hugh.

'Indeed! Probably wise!' said Margaret.

'And I believe you live in a hotel?' asked Lawrence incredulously.

'At Claridge's, yes.'

'And do you propose that my daughter live at Claridge's as well if this marriage takes place?' questioned Margaret.

'Of course not. *When* I marry Emily, I plan to buy a house – perhaps in Regent's Park.'

Arabella could not finish the delicious food on her plate as the dinner continued to be a volley of subtle insults and she longed for the night to be over.

The next day Hugh was in the hall examining the portraits on the walls. Charles came down the stairs and approached him carefully.

'Your ancestors?' asked Hugh.

'Yes. This one here you are looking at is of my grandparents, Lord Edward and Lady Anna. He built this house for her as a wedding present.'

'What a lovely idea. Giving a house to your bride... I wonder will my portrait hang here one day?'

Charles looked at him, wondering how deluded he could be. 'Hardly. These are all the heirs, their wives and children who lived at Armstrong House. That will never be you. Eh, Hugh, about the gambling money I owe you?'

Hugh turned from the paintings and faced Charles. 'Oh, yes, consider it paid. I've already informed Tom Hamley to cancel it.'

Charles felt overcome with relief. 'And the matter of the arrears on the mortgage I owe the bank which I discussed with you?'

Hugh looked surprised. 'Yes, of course, I'll take it up with the bank. Can you send me the details of what is owed and who I should address about the matter?'

'Of course. It's a tiresome little man called Jones. I'll forward you the details as soon as I get back to London.'

Hugh stretched out his hand. 'Our deal is done.'

Charles looked at his hand and then shook it, feeling relieved.

Emily stood in the forecourt waving to Hugh as his carriage went down the driveway.

The butler came out to her. 'Lady Emily, your parents want to see you in the drawing room.'

Sighing she went inside the house and braced herself as she went into the drawing room where she found her parents and Charles and Arabella waiting for her. She felt relieved that Charles was there too. He would support her.

'Well, I have to say, you were incredibly rude to Hugh,' Emily said, deciding to go on the offensive.

'Rude!' said Margaret. 'It's you who has been rude bringing a man like that in to our home!'

'What do you mean – a man like that?' Emily said, getting angry.

'I mean he has no breeding whatsoever! And you the daughter of an earl marrying a man like that!'

'Emily, it's inconceivable that you should marry this man,' said Lawrence. 'Now he might be very industrious and ambitious, but he's as common as muck.'

'As you kept pointing out to him at any opportunity. I wonder about you – you go on and on about etiquette and manners and then give the most disgusting display of manners I've ever seen.'

'The engagement will have to end immediately. I will write to Mr Fitzroy and tell him it is over,' said Lawrence.

'You'll do no such thing!' said Emily angrily, her eyes filling with tears. 'I've made my mind up and I *will* marry him.'

'Right, Emily, you've played your prank on us now,' said Margaret. 'You've managed to prove yet again how far you'll go to show how independent you are. You've shown your contempt of both your family and society. But this is where the joke ends!'

'The wedding can't continue because I'll not give a dowry to that man,' said Lawrence.

'He doesn't want a dowry from you. He told me flatly he would refuse any money from you.'

Margaret looked at her husband, worried. 'We will not permit the wedding to take place in Armstrong House, so it can't continue.'

'We don't want to get married here. We've already decided we're getting married in St Paul's Cathedral or Westminster and we're having the reception at The Dorchester Hotel.'

'In a hotel!' Margaret was aghast.

'It's becoming ever so popular having wedding receptions in hotels – it's becoming all the rage,' said Charles.

'So you see, we need nothing from you,' said Emily.

'Well, your father won't give you away on the day and I won't attend, as I'm sure none of your brothers or sisters will either.'

'Don't come then!' Emily's voice rose further. 'Charles will walk me down the aisle and give me away, won't you, Charles?'

All eyes turned to Charles.

'Charles?' asked Lawrence.

'Yes, yes, I will. I will give Emily away,' confirmed Charles.

'Oh Charles!' sighed Arabella under her breath as she rubbed her forehead in distress.

'This wedding will take place and there's nothing you can do about it,' stated Emily. 'But you will come, Mother. You will come, Father.'

'What makes you think that?' demanded Margaret.

'Because you won't have the scandal of not attending. You will grit your teeth and pretend everything is perfect on the day. Because that's what you do. You cover up anything you don't like

316

for the sake of the family reputation. You'll go to any lengths to avoid a scandal. That's what you did when Arabella got pregnant by Charles!'

'*Emily!*' shouted Lawrence.

'Yes, I know all about it. I was listening at the doors. She was pregnant by Charles and you concocted the whole plan that she go to France and lie about when Prudence was born. None of you cared about Harrison – you were delighted he left and you could get on with your deception. You threw him out like the rubbish – he was just a casualty you sacrificed to cover up your sordid little secret! At least Hugh is honest, something none of you know anything about!'

She stood up and marched from the room, slamming the door behind her.

They sat in silence, stunned.

'I can't believe she knew all along,' said Arabella eventually, shaking her head.

'You may well shake your head – I hope you are shaking your head in shame!' said Margaret crossly.

'Now, Mother–' began Charles.

'I hold you, Charles, and you, Arabella, completely responsible for this debacle. I had no idea Gwyneth was so poorly and that you were stepping in as Emily's chaperone, Arabella. It was bound to end in disaster.'

'Well, I knew it was only a matter of time before I got the blame for all this!' said Arabella.

'Well, who else is to blame? She was in your home under your care, albeit not known to me!'

'I did try to warn Emily to stay away from Hugh,' Arabella defended herself.

'Well, you mustn't have done a good job warning her!' Margaret's voice rose.

'Margaret, calm down,' said Lawrence.

'I will not calm down! Not content with ruining Harrison's life, the two of you have now ruined Emily's as well!'

'Emily is a grown woman, who can make her own decisions,' said Charles.

'Emily is a fool who thinks she knows everything and knows nothing!' said Lawrence. 'What were you even thinking of, being acquainted with a man like that? How did you even meet him?'

'I met him through friends.'

'I can only imagine what kind of life you're living in London, hanging around with Fitzroy. Living the good life, no responsibility, when you should be here taking up your rightful position,' accused Lawrence.

'I'm disgusted beyond belief,' said Margaret. 'To have my beautiful daughter end up in a marriage with a man with no background, breeding, education – need I go on!'

'And what were you thinking of saying you'll walk her down the aisle?' Lawrence renewed his attack on Charles. 'You've given her your approval, Charles!'

'I'm afraid I need to go and lie down,' said Arabella.

'We all need to lie down!' countered Margaret.

Arabella left the room quickly.

The remaining three sat in silence for a long while.

'The reality is Emily is determined to marry him and there's nothing you can do,' said Charles at last. 'You need to accept her decision. If she doesn't marry Hugh Fitzroy, then she'll marry nobody.'

'I would so much prefer for her to marry nobody,' said Margaret.

Lighting a cigarette Charles walked across the forecourt and down the steps to the first terrace. He continued into the gardens where he found Emily walking on her own.

'You've caused quite a stir,' he said.

She held him tightly. 'Why don't they want me to be happy?'

'They've accepted your decision. They'll support your marriage to Hugh. They are very unhappy but I've smoothed it over with them.'

'Charles, I knew I could rely on you,' she smiled up into his face. 'We've always been able to count on each other ... we're as thick as thieves.'

'That's right,' nodded Charles. 'Thick as thieves.'

That night when Charles came into the bedroom he found Arabella lying awake in bed. She had stayed in the room all day, not even coming down for dinner and Charles had not gone up to see her.

'They've accepted her decision,' he informed her.

She looked at him coldly. 'Thank you for letting me take the blame for the whole thing.'

'I didn't let you take the blame. They hold me equally responsible.'

'Equally responsible!' her voice rose. 'I had no hand in this whatsoever! It's you that's behind it all.'

'I'm not behind anything,' he said angrily.

'Whatever the truth is, and only you know the truth, I hope you can live with yourself in the future, when Emily's life is miserable.'

'Travelling first class around the world? Doing everything she wants to? She's been given her freedom.'

'She's been given a life sentence.' Arabella turned away from him on to her side.

CHAPTER 41

Margaret and Lawrence kept hoping that Emily would see sense and call off the wedding, but as the weeks flew into months, they realised Emily was not for turning.

Finally the week of the wedding arrived. As Hugh and Emily had planned, they were to be married in London at Westminster Abbey with the reception at The Dorchester. The family were all staying at the house in Hanover Terrace for the event.

Invitations were issued to all the right people in London. But as Margaret expected only half were accepted.

'Well, if they don't want us, then we don't want them,' said Emily, unconcerned.

It was the morning of the wedding and the family was waiting in the hallway at Hanover Terrace for Emily to come down.

She finally appeared and came slowly down the stairs in her wedding dress with Gwyneth behind her.

'You look stunning,' said Charles, kissing her.

'We'd better get going,' said Margaret. 'We don't want to keep the congregation waiting too long – it was hard enough to get them there in the first place.' She wiped away her tears and kissed Emily. 'We'll see you at the church.'

'Good luck,' said Arabella, kissing her.

'You can come in our carriage, Mother,' offered Charles.

'No, thank you, I'd prefer to travel with Gwyneth,' Margaret sniffled as she left with her eldest daughter.

'We'll give you twenty minutes and then Emily and I will follow you,' said Lawrence as the family left.

Then he was alone with his daughter.

'Are you sure?' he asked one last time.

'Very sure!' she answered and he came and hugged her.

'You know your mother and I only want what's best for you,' he said.

'You want what is best for you, Papa, not me,' she said.

There was suddenly a loud knock on the door.

'Burchill! Get that, would you?' shouted Lawrence as Emily went to check her appearance one more time in the mirror in the hall.

'Probably a neighbour come to wish me luck,' said Emily.

'Can I help you?' asked Burchill, looking in confusion at the eight men standing there.

The men walked in past Burchill and the eldest said, 'We're from Matheson, Matheson & Sons.'

'You can't just walk in like this – what do you want?' demanded Burchill, shocked.

Lawrence stepped forward. 'Who on earth are you and what do you want? Leave immediately or I'll call the police!'

'No need for that, guvnor – we're here to take the furniture,' said the man as his colleagues started picking up furniture and walking out the door with it.

'You're obviously in the wrong house,' Lawrence shouted.

'No mistake,' said the man as he put down a chair he was carrying. He reached into his pocket and took out a notice which he handed to Lawrence. 'This is the house of Lord Lawrence Armstrong?'

'That's correct.'

'That's a court order on behalf of the bank to take all furniture and belongings from the house. We're to take everything immediately to Sotheby's who are selling everything as quickly as possible for the bank to get its money back,' said the man.

'Bank? Take possessions?' Lawrence read quickly through the order. 'But there must be some mistake. This is Jones at Coutts Bank who applied for the order?'

'That's right, sir.'

'I must go and talk to him straight away and see what on earth is going on,' said Lawrence.

'Papa! We have to get to the church!' said Emily, distressed, as the mirror she had been looking at was taken down and carried away.

Lawrence thought for a moment before crossing into the study. 'Burchill, follow me.'

Lawrence sat down at the writing desk and started to write a letter.

'Burchill, you're to take this letter immediately to the bank at this address and give it personally to the manager, Jones. You are to demand he write an explanation to me as to what is going on and bring me his letter to The Dorchester Hotel.'

'Very well, Lord Armstrong.'

'I'm outraged! What does the bank think it is doing?'

'Papa, we really have to go!' Emily demanded.

Lawrence got up quickly and the two made their way past the removal men and out to their waiting carriage.

Emily walked down the aisle, smiling, on the arm of Hugh who looked smugly at the guests. Lawrence had been unable to concentrate on the ceremony he had been so taken aback by the scene he had witnessed that morning in the house.

He immediately sought out Charles amongst the guests outside the Abbey.

'Charles, removal men arrived at the house just after you left and began to seize all the furniture. What is this about?'

Charles paled on hearing the news. 'I haven't a clue!'

'They produced a court order from the bank. I've sent Burchill to Jones to get a full explanation,' said Lawrence.

Appalled, Charles quickly searched through the crowd for Hugh and took him aside.

'I need to talk to you urgently,' Charles whispered to him.

'Charles! It's my wedding day, it'll have to wait,' said Hugh, moving away from him to the guests.

As the party moved back to The Dorchester for the wedding breakfast, Charles waited for his moment to get Hugh on his own. But Emily was beside him at all times.

'What's wrong with you?' Arabella asked Charles, noticing his agitation, as they sat at one of the head tables.

He ignored her as he saw Burchill arrive and discreetly make his way through the function room to the head table and hand Lawrence a letter. Charles watched as Lawrence tore open the envelope and read. Lawrence suddenly looked up and looked around the room, searching for Charles. Spotting him, Lawrence stared at him in fury.

Charles suddenly got up from the table and began to walk quickly to the door. Startled, Arabella saw Lawrence and Margaret get up from their seats and hurry after him. Arabella decided to follow and hurried out to the huge foyer outside the banquet room.

'Charles!' said Lawrence, waving the letter from the bank in front of him. 'Jones has written to say my house is repossessed for non-payment of a mortgage taken by myself on the property! That the furniture has been taken to be auctioned off tomorrow at Sotheby's as the bank wants its money back without delay!'

'What have you done, Charles?' demanded Margaret furiously.

'There must be some mistake,' said Charles. 'The repayments have been settled.'

'*What repayments?*' shouted Lawrence, causing the passing hotel staff to look over, concerned. 'What is this mortgage Jones is talking about. I have no mortgage on that house!'

Charles shifted uncomfortably before explaining. 'I took out a loan and offered Hanover Terrace as collateral.'

'*On my house, without my permission?*' Lawrence screamed.

'Lawrence!' whispered Margaret. 'Shhh!'

'It was only a temporary measure. And I had arranged for the repayment. The bank has made a mistake.'

'No, you are the one who has made a mistake!' said Lawrence. 'How did you secure a loan against the house without my signature on the documents?'

Charles said nothing as he stared ahead.

'You have surpassed yourself, Charles, and that takes some doing!' said Margaret.

'You are despicable!' said Lawrence. 'That house was bought by my father and you just gambled it away as if it were a bag of sweets! You've gone too far this time, Charles. I could put up with your fecklessness, your lack of responsibility, your greed. But now you can add fraud to your list of credits. You ruined Harrison's life, you've ruined Emily's life, and now you've lost our precious London home!'

Margaret stared at Arabella. 'And what part did *you* play in all this?'

'None! This is the first I've heard of it,' Arabella

defended herself, her head spinning from the revelations.

'I'm so ashamed of you!' said Lawrence, with tears in his eyes, then suddenly turned and walked off.

'This isn't over,' warned Margaret. 'Not by a long shot!'

'Charles?' said Arabella, looking for some kind of an explanation, but Charles just turned and walked away.

Hugh was chatting to some guests. 'Yes, my wife and I will be looking for a suitable residence as soon as we return from South America.'

'There's a house on my street for sale, if you are interested,' said a guest.

'No, the houses on your street are far too small for what Mrs Fitzroy will be needing,' said Hugh dismissively.

Charles grabbed Hugh's arm. 'I need to speak to you. *Now!*'

Hugh looked at him irritably and excused himself from his guests.

'What is it?' asked Hugh.

'The bank has repossessed the house – they've already taken all the furniture away. Did you pay them the money?'

'The money? Oh, you mean the money you owed them? No, I didn't.'

Charles erupted in anger. 'Well, why the fuck not? They've taken the house away, my father knows about it and I'm ruined!'

'I never said I'd pay off your mortgage with the bank. I just said I'd cancel all the money you owed me over the gambling debts.'

326

'But you said you'd make contact with Jones!'

'And I did, and then when he told me how much was outstanding I declined to pay it.'

'But why didn't you tell me?'

'Well, I've been busy organising the wedding.' Hugh surveyed the function room of well-dressed people. 'Look at them all, the cream of society at my wedding, eating my food and drinking my champagne. Are they finally accepting me? I don't think so, but I'm too rich and generous for them to ignore. But now with my new wife, I'm one of them. Lady Emily Armstrong. Oh, I know they will laugh and talk about me behind my back, but Emily is one of them and I'm now married to her and there's nothing they can do about it.'

'You've crossed me. I expected you to pay that mortgage off. Emily would never even have looked at you if I hadn't talked her in to it.'

'And I'm thankful to you. You've given me the respectability I craved.'

'You're a bastard.'

'In this case,' said Hugh, placing a hand on Charles' shoulder and whispering into his ear, 'it really does take one to know one – brother-in-law. Now I have to get back to my guests and my wife.'

'I'll get you back for this one day,' warned Charles as Hugh walked away.

Hugh was laughing as he went over to Emily and kissed her.

Arabella tried to act normally for the rest of the wedding day but she found it almost impossible as questions danced around her mind. Why did he take the mortgage? How did he manage it? Why did he need it with her dowry in place? And what would become of them now with their home gone? She would never forget the looks on Lawrence's and Margaret's faces: a mixture of disgust, horror and anger.

There was no sign of Charles and she realised he must have left the wedding. Typical Charles, she thought, running out and leaving her to deal with the mess. As what Charles did was related to the rest of the Armstrong family, she had to put up with their questions and their accusing eyes.

That evening it was arranged for Margaret and Lawrence to go and stay with Gwyneth. Gwyneth kindly agreed to take Prudence and Pierce with her as well, as Arabella desperately needed to talk to Charles and find out what was going on. As she sat in the back of a hansom cab on her way home she hoped Charles would be back in Hanover Terrace.

The cab pulled up outside the house and the driver helped her to dismount. She walked up the steps and knocked on the door. No one answered so, puzzled, she let herself in with her key. An eerie silence hung over the house as she walked through the empty hall. She looked through the open door to their once splendid dining room and she saw it had been stripped bare as well. She walked up the stairs and into the now empty drawing room.

She saw Charles standing there, staring out the balcony window.

'You're back?' he said seeing her reflection in the window pane before him.

'You should have told me you were leaving The Dorchester,' she said.

He turned to face her. 'I suppose I should have told you a lot of things.'

'It's true then ... they've taken the house... Why did you need a loan from the bank?'

'To fund our life of course,' said Charles.

'But my dowry – we have my dowry!'

'That, my dear, disappeared long ago.'

'*What?*'

'It's spent.'

'Lost at gambling tables around London, you mean!' Arabella was furious.

She walked around the room. 'Where are the servants?'

'Gone. I explained to them there was no money to pay them.'

'How much money have we got left?' She was almost afraid to ask.

'Nothing. The mortgage loan kept us going for a while but now that's gone too.'

'How did you ever let it get to this?' she demanded.

'There's no point in analysing what went wrong.'

'There is to me! But what are we going to do now?'

'I don't know.'

'Well, you'd better start thinking! Do you know something? One day somebody is going to kill you ... and it could very well be me.'

CHAPTER 42

Present Day

Nico's teenage daughter from his previous marriage, Alex, was at Armstrong House for the weekend. Kate loved when Alex was staying with them. She had built a close relationship with the girl. Having no children of her own, she relished her role of stepmother.

'Oh, Kate, I meant to ask you a favour?' asked Alex.

'Name it,' said Kate.

'I wanted to ask – would it be possible for me to have a cameo role in your docudrama?'

'I can't see any problem with that,' Kate assured her.

'What?' said Nico. 'No way!' He had been very concerned with Alex's recent revelation that she was interested in becoming an actress.

'Dad!' Alex protested.

'Alex, you have exams this year. You don't need any distractions from them. You need to concentrate on your grades so you can get into university and get a proper profession,' said Nico.

'Acting not being a proper profession?' Kate arched her eyebrow cynically at him.

Much to Nico's chagrin, Kate brought all the storage boxes from the attics down to the library to go through.

She sat at the desk in the library smoking a cigarette, examining all the photographs from Charles' time. She had previously selected the best-quality photographs for the film but now she started going through the pile she had discarded, looking for some detail that would help her in her quest. As she studied the photographs of Charles and his family, it was hard for her to equate this smiling handsome man with all the reports of him being cruel and ruthless. But everyone had two sides to them, she reasoned, and looks could be deceiving. She looked at the photographs of his wife Arabella. She was very beautiful but Kate couldn't find a photograph of her smiling. She didn't look sad either, but she seemed tense. And she couldn't find one photograph of just the couple together. And in the family photographs they didn't stand together, the children Pierce and Prudence being always positioned between them. As an actress she was used to reading people, looking at their faces and their body language and determining what kind of person they were, what made them tick, how they interacted. This did not look like a happy couple to Kate. She studied the photos of Prudence and Pierce. Prudence seemed a confident girl, always smiling with knowing eyes. Pierce appeared more reserved. Their body language when with their parents showed great affection towards them. She passed through the photographs and came across one of Charles in his car with the two children in the front seat beside him. She imagined the terrible impact it must have had on them when he was shot and their lives changed forever. She took up the photograph and felt sad looking at them. A family who could have had so much destroyed overnight, that night in December 1903.

Looking at the photograph she suddenly got a jolt. She got up and walked quickly to the police file and took out the photograph of the crime scene and compared them.

Kate went marching quickly across the hall and into the drawing room where Nico was stretched out watching television.

'Eh – do you mind?' he said as she took up the remote and turned off the television.

'Look at these photos!'

He took the photos and shrugged. 'So?'

'So, they are different cars! Charles' car was a different make to the one he was shot in. See – his car doesn't even have a windscreen. In fact most cars didn't have windscreens back then.'

'So what? He probably had another car.'

'Not very likely – there were fewer than three hundred cars in Ireland at the time – they were extremely expensive and a rarity.'

'What are you saying?'

'Charles was in somebody else's car the night he was shot. Perhaps a woman's car, because of the fox fur and high-heeled shoe that was left there.'

'I doubt any woman would be driving back then,' said Nico.

'Oh, they did. Not many, but you had the beginning of the suffragette movement by then and they were trying to prove themselves to be as

332

capable as men,' said Kate.

'So what are you getting at?' asked Nico, irritated by her detective work.

'It makes sense, because the gunshot is through the passenger's side of the windscreen, so Charles must have been sitting on the passenger side as somebody else was driving their own car!' Kate was delighted with her discovery. 'Where was Charles going that night with this woman, and who was the woman in the car? And why did the family go to such lengths to cover it up? Was that why Lady Margaret and the family said he was in a carriage because they didn't want it to be known whose car he was actually in?'

Nico flung the photos on the coffee table. 'Don't you think you're taking all this a bit far?'

'I haven't taken it far enough, Nico!'

'Did you ever hear the expression – let sleeping dogs lie?'

'I have, and I never liked that expression.'

'You wouldn't! You know, Kate, you're always trying to push things to the limit. The fact is, although all these people are long dead, they still have a right to privacy.'

'Not really, not if they covered up a crime they don't.'

'Well, I think they do. And I think at the end of the day it's immoral for you to start trying to sensationalise something for the sake of your film and getting it better publicity and ratings,' he said in a determined voice.

'I knew you weren't behind me on this! I knew you weren't happy about it from the start,' she accused.

'Well, if you knew, then why did you proceed with it?'

'Because – because I wanted to!'

'It's not the first time you've had an obsession with my family's past, and look where that led you before!' he said. 'We don't need any more unsavoury secrets to be uncovered!'

She looked very hurt. 'Thank you! Thank you very much for dragging all that up again.'

'I just don't want you getting carried away with this like last time,' he said.

'And you know something?' Kate went on regardless. 'Your surname might be Collins, but I think you have that same streak as your Armstrong ancestors did. I think you're as happy as they were to cover this up to protect the reputation of your family.'

'At the end of the day, Kate, this man you're investigating is my mother's grandfather. It's not that far back, and I know my mother would be horrified to know you were trying to besmirch her family name. She was very proud of it, you know.'

'Well, I'm sorry, Nico, but I can't stop now. I want to know what happened and to make sure justice was done.'

'Kate – the great crusader!' mocked Nico.

She stood up and grabbed the photos. 'And if you don't want to help me, then I'll do it on my own.'

He watched her walk out of the room then he put the television back on.

BOOK THREE

1897–1900

CHAPTER 43

It was nine o'clock in the evening in New York and all the employees of Union Bank had long since gone home as the chairman of the bank, Morgan Wells, left his office and walked down the corridor. He spotted a light on in Harrison Armstrong's' office. He walked over and opened the door to find Harrison inside at his desk, poring over paperwork.

'Are you still here?' asked Morgan, not surprised that he was.

'Yes, I need to finish this before morning – the client is coming in at nine,' explained Harrison, not concealing his irritation at being disturbed.

'Why not go home, get a good night's sleep, and get in early and finish it then?' suggested Morgan.

'I'll keep going, thank you,' said Harrison as his head went down and he continued reading.

To Harrison's further irritation, Morgan walked into the office, over to his desk and picked up some of the paperwork.

'Are you sure you want to stay?' asked Morgan. 'I can give you a lift home. My motor car is waiting outside.'

'No, thank you,' said Harrison.

'Any plans for the weekend?'

'No, yes – I've a few things on,' said Harrison.

'Me and my wife are having a dinner party on Saturday evening. We'd like you to attend if you're free?'

'I'm actually not free, but thank your wife for the invitation,' said Harrison curtly.

Morgan smiled. 'There will be a lot of interesting people there – some powerful people in banking. It could be good for you to attend.'

Harrison looked up. 'Is it an order that I attend?'

Morgan gave a little laugh. 'Of course it's not an order – just an invitation.'

'In that case, as I said, I've something else on,' Harrison said firmly.

'I see,' Morgan nodded and, turning, walked to the door where he paused and said, 'You know the expression, Harrison – "All work and no play"…'

'…gets the job done on time,' Harrison finished, giving the expression his own ending.

Morgan nodded and, smiling, left, closing the door after him.

Sitting in the back of the motor car as he was driven home, Morgan thought about Harrison Armstrong, as he had countless times before. Harrison had been with the bank for several years. He had started in a lowly position and through sheer hard work and dedication beyond the call of duty had risen through the ranks. From the beginning Harrison did not mix with the other employees. He did not attend any social function, not even the Christmas party. He never socialised with anyone and kept himself to himself. He was always polite but his attitude was often taken as aloofness and unfriendliness. It had been three years before it was revealed who he actually was. A visiting official from Dublin had spotted him at the bank and to everyone's shock exposed him as being the son of one of the United Kingdom's most respected families, related to lords and dukes and whatnot. Morgan remembered Harrison being furious when this was discovered. He became even more withdrawn when his true identity was known. Morgan worried about Harrison. It just wasn't natural for a young person to have no life outside that office he seemed chained to. Especially for a young man like Harrison who could have New York at his feet. Morgan had tried his best to nurture him into having a better life for himself. But he had to admit defeat on Harrison Armstrong and leave him to his own ways.

It was after ten by the time Harrison reached home, which was only a short distance from the bank. Letting himself into his apartment, he picked up the post that his housekeeper had left on the sideboard for him. He flicked through the letters and threw them back on the sideboard except for one whose writing he recognised as his sister Daphne's.

Walking into his sitting room he saw his housekeeper had left a cold meat salad for him before she had gone home. He ignored it as he sat on the couch and, smiling to himself, touched the neat handwriting on the envelope. He then carefully opened the envelope, unfolded the paper inside and sat back to read the letter from Daphne. It was the typical type of letter she and his family wrote to him. Full of news from home – gossip about somebody they knew growing up, chit-chat about relatives, hearsay about neighbours. Inconsequential news, but he relished hearing it all anyway. The letter finished as usual with a paragraph asking how he was, hoping he was looking after himself, saying how they missed him and would love to see him soon. His siblings and his parents wrote very regularly to him, regardless of the fact he rarely responded. When he left Ireland he knew he would never return. And writing to his family would only give them false hope that one day he would. It was better for them to get on with their own lives without him. They hardly ever mentioned Charles and Arabella in their letters, only in passing for some event like when their children Prudence and Pierce were born. The very thought of them sent him into a cycle of hurt, depression and shame. The shame of everyone in Ireland knowing how he had been made such a fool of. Charles, Arabella, Prudence and Pierce: he imagined the happy family.

He got up off the couch and ate the meal the housekeeper had left for him. Then he went straight to bed.

Morgan Wells looked exceptionally pleased with himself as Harrison sat down opposite him in his office.

'We've landed them! We've landed the Van Hoevans as a client … almost,' he declared.

Harrison sat back, impressed by this news himself. The Van Hoevans were one of those families who had built America. A name that sat alongside Vanderbilt or Rockefeller whose wealth and glamour had come to epitomise America during this gilded age. A family whose fortune was built on steel and railroads. Landing the Van Hoevans and their millions was a major coup for the bank.

'You said the word "almost"?' asked Harrison, concerned. He had been involved in too many deals that were almost done and that fell apart at the last moment.

'Yes, they've agreed to come to us in principle but we've no signatures yet,' explained Morgan.

'I see – and when do you think we'll get the signatures?'

'You know Oscar Van Hoevan's reputation. He likes to leave people dangling and often pulls out at the last minute when he gets a better deal or interest rate from somebody else.'

'So nothing is guaranteed with this deal?' said Harrison, disappointed.

'Not yet – and that's where you come in.'

'Me?'

'You're going up to Newport, Rhode Island to meet him on Monday, and you're not to come back until his signature is on all the paperwork.'

'I don't really want to meet or have to deal with Oscar Van Hoevan.'

'Why not? It could be entertaining for you. See how the other half live.'

'The other half doesn't live like the Van Hoevans. Only a tiny minority of people live like that... I think you should send Pratchford instead. He'd love all that and do a great job.'

'I don't want Pratchford to go, I want you to go,' said Morgan.

'But–'

'And that is an order, this time, Harrison.'

Harrison didn't hide his frustration. 'Very well.'

'You're to travel to Newport on Monday and you'll be staying at the Van Hoevans' house.'

Harrison stood up and left as Morgan sat back, satisfied with himself. Harrison Armstrong was the perfect man for the job. Anyone else would be overawed and intimidated stepping into the Van Hoevans' world. Harrison wouldn't give a damn. And Oscar Van Hoevan would lose respect for anyone in awe of him.

CHAPTER 44

The train pulled into the station in Newport and Harrison stepped off onto the platform where he was met by one of Van Hoevan's chauffeurs. As the motor car was driven through the streets of Newport Harrison observed the splendid palaces built by America's super rich to show off their wealth. Finally they reached the Van Hoevan mansion and drove through gigantic pillars and up a driveway. The house was an extravagant white building and Harrison realised that the rumour the Van Hoevans had based the design of the building on Versailles was not unfounded. In the distance he could hear the ocean. He followed the chauffeur up the wide sandstone steps and through the front door into a colossal hallway with white walls and white marble floor and a wide staircase with gold-encrusted balustrades, where he was met by a butler.

'This way, sir,' said the butler, opening ornately engraved double doors.

As Charles stepped into the next room he realised he was in the Van Hoevan famed Hall of Mirrors. It was a giant room with wooden floors and huge gold-framed mirrors all along the walls. The room was known for the elaborate parties held there.

Across the room he saw a woman approach him. As she neared him he saw she was a striking young woman with soft curled blonde hair and the most refined bone structure he had ever seen.

'And you must be Harrison Armstrong,' said the woman as she reached him. 'I'm Victoria Van Hoevan.'

He reached out and shook her proffered hand.

'Welcome to our home. I hope you enjoy your stay here. My father is waiting for you if you would care to follow me?'

She turned and started walking through the room and he followed her.

'Thank you for having me. I don't plan to impose on you that long,' he said.

'Really?' she said.

'I just need to get a few signatures from your father and then I'll be on my way back to New York.'

She smiled at him as she led him out of the room and through further hallways.

'You don't know what my father is like, Harrison. Getting a few signatures from him can be like extracting teeth, and often more painful.'

'Oh dear,' said Harrison under his breath.

'Yes, I'm afraid so. Don't bother trying to fight

it, just accept his ways,' she advised.

They reached another double door which was dark mahogany.

She leaned forward and whispered to him. 'Don't be intimidated by him, and don't let him bully you either. He can come across as a terrible grizzly bear, but he's really just a cuddly cub underneath.' She smiled at him and opened the doors.

'Don't you ever knock?' growled a deep voice from behind an expansive desk.

'Somebody is after getting out of bed the wrong side this morning,' said Victoria as she led Harrison in. 'Dad, Harrison Armstrong has arrived from New York.'

'Who?'

'The man from Union Bank, which you are investing with,' said Victoria.

'Which I *might* be investing with,' stated Oscar.

Harrison, on reaching the desk, put out his hand. 'Pleased to meet you, sir.'

Oscar ignored the hand. 'How do you know you're pleased to meet me? You might be very displeased to meet me once you see what I'm like.'

Seeing his outstretched hand was being ignored, Harrison awkwardly put it down by his side.

'Would you like a drink, Harrison?' asked Victoria.

Harrison started to open his case. 'No, thank you. I have the papers here and it's very straightforward really.'

'Sit down and have a drink,' commanded Oscar. 'And get me one while you're at it, Vicky.'

'Certainly, Daddy. I might even have one myself,' said Victoria, walking over to the drinks cabinet and pouring three gin and tonics.

She came back, handed the drinks to the men and sat down on the arm of her father's chair.

'To your good health,' said Oscar.

'And yours, sir,' said Harrison.

'So you're the guy who wants all my money,' said Oscar, studying him.

'Well, some of it anyway, sir,' said Harrison.

'What do you think, Vicky, should I give it to him?' asked Oscar with a smirk.

'Well, you see, I don't know why you ask me these things. I'll get no credit if it goes well, and get all the blame if it goes wrong,' said Victoria.

'That's why I ask you!' laughed Oscar. 'I don't want to blame myself if it goes wrong, do I?'

'Could you not just blame Harrison and keep me out of it?' Victoria laughed lightly back.

Harrison coughed, took the papers out of his case and handed them across the desk.

Oscar reached out and took the paperwork and then flung it to the other side of the desk. 'Paperwork bores me ... my grandfather, who started the Van Hoevan fortune, didn't make money out of paperwork, young fella,' he made it out of steel, blood, sweat and tears.'

'Usually other people's,' said Victoria.

Harrison coughed again. 'Indeed, but you need to keep that fortune well minded, and we at Union Bank–'

'Will mind it like a newborn baby, no doubt,' said Oscar.

'Daddy! Hear him out!'

'Why don't you two run along and let me get back to what I was doing,' said Oscar.

'But, sir,' began Harrison.

'We're being dismissed,' said Victoria, getting up off the arm of the chair. 'No point in arguing with him.'

'You could learn a few things from listening to her,' said Oscar.

Harrison felt bewildered as he stood up and followed Victoria out of the room.

'No need to look so puzzled,' said Victoria as she led him down the corridor. 'I told you he's a cuddly cub ... now let's get you settled into your room. We're serving dinner at eight tonight; Daddy is a stickler for time, so try not to be late.'

Harrison was completely confused as he hung up his clothes in the sumptuous guest room he was shown to. Oscar Van Hoevan didn't seem to have any interest in finding out anything about the Union Bank proposals. He really hoped he hadn't made a wasted journey. His room was at the back of the house and he went to one of the windows that looked out over an expansive lawn and the ocean just beyond it. He stayed in his room for the rest of the day, not daring to venture out in case he had to cope with Oscar's overly confident and peculiar daughter.

In the evening he dressed for dinner and headed down for eight sharp as instructed. A butler showed him into the dining room, which had the familiar theme of the house: huge and lavishly decorated.

'Ah, you managed to find us all right!' Victoria

said as he came in. 'You know, we had a guest here this summer who got lost in the house and couldn't find his way back to his room and ended up sleeping on a couch in a hall!'

'Uncomfortable for him, I imagine,' said Harrison.

'Well, he was half drunk on Daddy's best cognac, so I don't think he minded that much.'

Oscar was seated at the top of the table and had already started to eat the first course of salad.

A lady in her fifties, impeccably dressed and groomed with dazzling diamonds around her neck, was also seated at the table.

'Harrison, this is my mother, Tess,' said Victoria.

'Very nice to meet you,' smiled Tess. 'Victoria has been telling me all about you. You must sit beside me so I can interrogate you properly.'

Harrison nervously went and sat down where he was told to, which was across the table from Victoria. A footman poured him wine and he started to eat his salad.

'We met your sister and brother-in-law, the Duke of Battington, when we were in London last year – charming couple,' Tess said to Harrison's amazement.

'You're the son of an Irish lord, aren't you?' said Victoria.

Harrison nodded, becoming angry. He knew they must have been informed of all this by Morgan. It became apparent why he had been chosen to come to the Van Hoevans. Morgan had wanted to impress them with Harrison's family background. He wasn't there on merit but because Morgan felt Harrison's aristocratic connections would impress the Van Hoevans and land them as a client.

'We haven't been to Ireland, but we believe it's beautiful,' said Tess.

'Yes, it is,' agreed Harrison.

'Do you go home often?' asked Victoria.

'No.'

'Of course there's Irish in us somewhere,' said Victoria.

'Really? I thought you descended from Dutch with your name?' said Harrison.

'Dutch, Irish, German, French, we're a real melting pot – it's all in there somewhere,' stated Oscar.

'I'm surprised we've never met you socially before in New York,' said Tess.

'Oh, I believe Harrison doesn't like to go out much, do you?' Victoria said.

Harrison glared at Victoria, wondering who she had been talking to and what she had heard. He felt very much exposed and wanted to get away from them as quickly as possible.

Harrison turned to Oscar. 'I was hoping we could meet at the earliest opportunity in the morning, to go over the paperwork.'

'Sure, sure – what's my diary like tomorrow, Vicky?'

'A bit busy really, but I'm sure we'll manage to fit you in.' Victoria smiled over at Harrison.

Tess talked incessantly about her children – two sons and two daughters.

'Two of them are in New York at the moment, and Conrad – he's in San Francisco.'

He found Tess to be jovial and warm, Victoria

348

inquisitive to the point of being nosy and Oscar changeable from being warm to grumpy.

He waited for the earliest opportunity to get away from them that evening and go to bed.

The next morning he dressed and came down for breakfast. He was shown into the dining room where he found Victoria.

'Did you sleep well?' she asked.

'Yes, thank you.'

'The sea air here always gives people a good night's sleep... I'm afraid Daddy has had to go.'

Harrison looked up, alarmed. 'Go where?'

'Chicago.'

'*Chicago!* What's he doing there?'

'Building a railroad or something. An urgent message came for him this morning and off he had to go.'

'But what about our business together?'

'He said you weren't to leave until he had an opportunity to talk to you.'

'And when will that be?' Harrison was aghast.

'Who knows?' said Victoria shrugging. 'Everyone knows what Daddy is like... I'm sure you won't be bored here.'

'It's not a case of being bored. I've commitments back in New York with my job.'

'Very thoughtless of Daddy really, he can be like that, you know.'

'I – I – I just don't think I can stay waiting for him. My boss won't understand.'

'Oh, I'm sure he will. Relax – you might just enjoy yourself!' She smiled at him.

Five days came and went at the Van Hoevan mansion and there was still no sign of Oscar Van Hoevan returning, much to Harrison's dismay. He contacted Morgan who instructed him again under no circumstances to leave without getting his business done with Oscar. Oscar obviously thought that his wealth allowed him to inconvenience others with no regard, thought Harrison angrily. He spent his time in Newport trying to avoid Victoria who had taken it on herself to try and alleviate Harrison's boredom with suggestions of doing everything from sailing to horse riding, all of which he politely declined.

He dined with her and Tess most evenings. A couple of times he feigned a headache and had food brought to his room. He longed to be back on the train to New York.

One afternoon he went walking by himself down the long expansive lawn. At the end of the lawn was a cliff edge with a straight drop down to the ocean below, where the waves crashed continuously against the rocks. He walked past a gazebo and stood, staring out to sea.

'A penny for your thoughts,' said a voice and he turned to see Victoria.

'Oh, nothing – just looking at the ocean... My home is across that ocean, the west of Ireland... Armstrong House.' He gazed out at the sea.

Victoria studied him and then her usually happy face turned very sad. 'Do you know ... I think you're the loneliest person I've ever met.'

He turned to her, startled. 'I'd better get back to the house.' He turned and walked quickly across the lawn, leaving her staring after him.

Harrison came into the dining room that evening and found Victoria on her own there waiting for him.

'Where's your mother?'

'She's retired to bed early, she's not feeling well. Your headaches must be catching,' she said, smiling cynically at him.

Irritated, he sat down. It was bad enough having dinner every evening with them but at least Tess filled the conversation with talk about East Coast society.

The dinner progressed with Victoria trying to get Harrison to talk about his life in New York.

'So are you courting?' she asked, smiling at him.

'No, I'm not.'

'Why not? I'm sure you're not short of offers?'

'I'm very busy with work.'

'So I've heard.'

'What do you mean by that?' he snapped.

'Nothing. I just know you work very hard. I know some people at your bank.'

'Really? And why were you bothering to ask about me?'

'I'm interested in people. Aren't you?'

'No. I know all there is to know about people and I don't need to know any more.'

'And what do you know of people?'

'That they always look after themselves. That they only pretend to care about others. That if you're of some use to them, then they'll use you, and then drop you as soon as you're of no use to them any more.'

'That's incredibly cynical, Harrison!' Victoria

was taken aback.

'It's not, it's the truth. Even Morgan Wells used me, sending me up here to exploit my background to impress your parents. It's what people do, they use each other.'

'And you don't?'

'I've no need for people, so I don't use them.'

'You might have tried using me during the week to get my father to sign those papers for you when he returns.'

'If your father wants to sign them he will because there's something in it for him.'

She studied him. 'I'm trying to understand you. She must have hurt you very badly.'

'Who?'

'That girl who left you for your brother.'

Harrison's eyes welled up in anger and frustration. 'What do you know about any of that?'

'I inquired. I know people from Dublin. It caused quite a scandal at the time.'

Harrison threw his napkin on the table. 'Have you nothing better to do than go around spying on people?'

He got up from the table and stormed out.

The next day Harrison was walking through the Hall of Mirrors and saw Victoria sitting there on a couch.

He looked at her wearily.

'Good news, Harrison,' she said. 'My father is returning in the morning. Don't worry about your papers. I'll get him to sign them quickly for you and you can get a train back to New York straight away. You won't have to put up with me any more.'

'I – I didn't mean to be rude last night.'

'You weren't rude, Harrison – you were just being who you've become. So you can go back to New York and back to that lonely empty life you have.'

'You don't know anything about my life there.'

'Yes, I do, it's written all across your face. If you choose to let what happened in the past destroy the rest of your life, then that's your choice. If you don't want to reach out to somebody who's reaching out to you, then there's nothing I can do about it.'

'But why are you reaching out to me at all? Why do you care?'

'Don't you see that I'm mad about you? Haven't you seen all the signs I've given you this past week?'

'*What?*' Harrison was astounded. 'You don't even know me!'

'You don't want me to know you – you don't want anybody to know you. And that's so sad.'

'Let me just go back to New York and forget you ever met me – you'll be far better off. There's nothing to me – you'd only be disappointed.'

She got up and walked towards him. 'I wouldn't be if you just let me in.'

'I don't want to let you in,' he said. 'I don't want to let anybody in.'

'You had a terrible time, but I can help you. I can make it better,' she said, putting her arms around him and holding him tightly.

'Don't be nice to me!' he begged.

'Why not? You need somebody to be nice to you.'

'Don't – Victoria,' he said, gently trying to push

her away.

She held on to him tightly. 'You need somebody to hold you. Let it go, Harrison, let the past go.'

Harrison grabbed on to her and suddenly all the pent-up anguish was escaping in volumes.

'Let it all go,' said Victoria, stroking his hair.

CHAPTER 45

Charles, Arabella and the children moved back to Armstrong House. Quite simply, now that they were penniless and homeless there was nowhere left for them to go. Arabella dreaded the move. She knew that one day, when Lawrence and Margaret were gone and she and Charles were Lord and Lady Armstrong, the house would become theirs and they would be obliged to spend considerable time there. But she had thought that would be in the far-off future.

Lawrence was still enraged about the loss of his house in London as a result of Charles' deception and fraud. He saw it as an absolute betrayal by his heir, not only of himself but of the whole Armstrong family. Arabella noticed that Lawrence seemed to age overnight from the whole business as the anger and the stress caused by his son took its toll.

'You were given everything in life!' shouted Lawrence. 'But all you did was take without ever a thought for me, your mother, your wife or your children!'

'The house in London would be mine one day,' retorted Charles. 'All I was doing was raising some capital on it early.'

'One day, but not yet! All you think about is money and power and the good life and being ahead of everyone else.'

'What's done is done, and there's no point in you continually going over it,' said Charles.

'Well, I am going to make sure nothing like this ever happens again. I've put the house in Dublin on the market. The auctioneer expects it to be sold within weeks.'

'*What?*' Charles was horrified. 'You have no right to sell that house. You're throwing away part of the Armstrong fortune being held in trust for me and my son.'

'It's *you* that threw away our legacy with your flippancy. No – the house in Dublin is going. I don't want you distracted by the bright lights of any city in future. Your life and future are now here at Armstrong House and the estate where you will begin to fulfil your role immediately.'

Arabella was upstairs in the nursery with the children as Charles and Lawrence's shouts echoed through the house.

'Mama, why is Grandfather shouting at Papa?' asked Prudence, not seeming too concerned, unlike Pierce who looked disturbed by the shouting.

'Oh, they are just having a silly argument, nothing to worry about,' soothed Arabella as she stroked Pierce's hair.

'Oh, like when you and Papa row?' asked Prudence.

Arabella had to admit her children were well

used to the rows that erupted between her and Charles. Prudence, who seemed to have nerves of steel, never seemed to give them a second thought.

'Something like that. Now, will I read you a story?' smiled Arabella.

Arabella was sitting on the couch in their bedroom reading, in front of the fire, when Charles came in that night, his face dark with anger.

He walked over to the drinks cabinet and poured himself a whiskey from the decanter.

'Finished arguing with your father for the day?' she asked, not looking up from her book.

'I just walked out in the end, I couldn't listen to him any more.'

'Where did you get to for the rest of the day?'

'Out riding.'

She closed her book and put it on the couch beside her. 'I don't blame him in the least,' she said.

'Easily known *you* wouldn't support me!'

Arabella laughed sarcastically. 'Of course I don't! Squandering my dowry on whatever you squandered it on – French chefs and card games.'

'You didn't object when we were living the high life.'

'I would have if I'd had an inkling of the fact we were hurtling to financial disaster! But no, as with everything with you, you covered it up with a cloak of secrecy and lies.'

'*I* was the one deceived by everyone,' Charles said, as he bitterly thought of Fitzroy. 'But I never will be again, I swear that. Whatever I have to do,

I'll do it, but nobody will ever get the better of me again. I'm still the heir to all this. I'll still one day be head of this family. And nobody will ever cross me or cheat me again.'

As Arabella looked at him she was almost a little afraid. She knew how ruthless he could be, but this new determination frightened her.

Margaret came into the drawing room where she found Lawrence staring into the fire. She came over and hugged him.

'You know, I often think that this system of primogeniture is wrong,' he said. 'Why should the eldest son inherit the title and everything? Why should Charles, who is so unfit for it, one day be Lord Armstrong?'

Margaret looked worried. 'That is our system, Lawrence, and one that has worked very well through the centuries and one that will continue to work.'

'I know that. But my other sons would make much better heirs than him. I just can't trust him, especially after this latest situation.'

'Charles is our heir, Lawrence, and though we can do our best to guide and direct him, we must never doubt or undermine that position with him.'

Lawrence studied his wife. She was a bastion of tradition and continuity. She never questioned the order of things and the family name and reputation always came first. Even with all Charles' fecklessness and deceit, she in her own mind refused to really accept it was any of Charles' fault. Margaret was quite content to blame any falling down on Charles' part as being the result of a bad marriage to an irresponsible woman. Although Lawrence was as shocked as Margaret over Arabella's behaviour before marriage, he had come to feel quite sorry for her. It was obvious Arabella was still madly in love with Charles, and that love had led her into a life that she had definitely not been brought up to, but she had an inner strength that made her capable of dealing with it. Lawrence suspected most other women would have been broken by Charles long since.

In the dining room one morning Charles looked at a boiled egg in front of him with displeasure as he remembered the wonderful breakfasts conjured up by Monsieur Huppert. He looked across the table at Arabella spreading marmalade on her toast and at his parents at either end of the table.

'There's a problem with the harvest over at the O'Hara farm. I want us to go and look at it this morning,' Lawrence informed Charles.

Charles nodded as he cracked his egg open with a knife.

'And, Arabella, I'll be judging a beautiful baby competition in the village this afternoon – perhaps you'd like to join me as a judge?' said Margaret.

Arabella recoiled at the thought. 'I'm afraid I'll be busy with the children. Until we hire a governess I need to be with them.'

'We can bring them with us,' insisted Margaret 'The estate children will love to see them.'

Arabella was going to say something further but thought better of it. There was no point in offending Margaret. As they were going to have to share a house, she had better make an effort.

'Where have you applied for a governess?' asked Margaret.

'Through an agency in Dublin.'

'Although we can't afford much of a one with the meagre salary I'm allowed to draw from the estate,' bitched Charles. He wasn't sure if it was part of his punishment or if Lawrence was trying to train him into more frugal ways, but the salary he was being allowed was ridiculously small. He was sure James was on a much higher salary.

James had moved into a large farmhouse on the estate when Charles and his family returned to Armstrong House. Charles thought it looked like a peasant cottage, but didn't care as long as James wasn't under his feet any more.

'There's no need for you to draw a big salary,' stated Lawrence. 'All your needs are met here at Armstrong House.'

'And there's no need for you to use a Dublin agency for a governess,' stated Margaret. 'My friend Sally Bramwell will recommend somebody for you. She keeps almost a directory of nannies and governesses to be recommended.'

'I would prefer to do it this way and for the agency to send me down the governess to interview,' objected Arabella.

'Nonsense! Look at that silly French girl you employed in London. You need a good solid, no-nonsense woman, and Sally Bramwell will know just such a woman.'

'I need somebody caring and kind as well,' said Arabella.

'Solid and no-nonsense is what you need for those children, particularly Prudence.'

The new butler Fennell came in and gave the post to Margaret.

'Thank you, Fennell,' said Margaret and, once he had left, said, 'I was sorry to see Barton leave us, but he was simply too old to continue his duties here. You know, Fennell was quite a find. I hope he stays with us many years. I believe he's become quite serious with the cook's assistant, so hopefully they'll marry and it will be an incentive to stay ... ah, a letter from Gwyneth!' Margaret opened the letter and started to read it. Suddenly her face clouded over.

'What is it?' asked Lawrence.

'Seemingly Hugh Fitzroy has bought our house in London from the bank! Himself and Emily are moving in next week!'

'Unbelievable!' Lawrence was amazed.

Margaret became upset. 'The thought of our beautiful house in that man's hands!'

'At least it will still be in the family,' stated Charles with a cough.

'The family! He's not our family, he's filth!' stated Margaret.

'We'll be the talk of the place in London,' said Lawrence sadly.

Margaret got up from the table and hurried out, followed by Lawrence.

Arabella sat back in her chair and clapped slowly. 'Well done, Charles! I warned you about Fitzroy, I told you what you were dealing with and you just ignored me. You've given him your sister, you've given him your house – in fact you've given him your life. While you are left to look at bad harvests and I to judge baby contests.'

CHAPTER 46

Sally Bramwell did indeed forward a governess for the children, called Miss Kingston. And as Margaret requested, Miss Kingston was a solid, no-nonsense woman.

Unfortunately Prudence had a personality clash with her from the start.

'Mama, why do we have to eat with her all the time in the nursery? I want to eat with you,' objected Prudence in the drawing room one evening.

'Nonsense,' said Margaret. 'Children always eat with the governess.'

'We used to eat with Mama in London a lot,' stated Prudence.

'Well, you're not in London now, Prudence dear. Now run along or your dinner will be cold and Miss Kingston will be angry.'

'Miss Kingston is always angry!' said Prudence.

'Perhaps she is angry because you make her so?' Margaret suggested.

Arabella went to say something to Margaret but decided to bite her tongue.

'I'll be up to you after dinner,' said Arabella, smiling at Prudence.

'I know your parents were quite lax and indulgent with you growing up, Arabella. Children need to know they are loved but with strict guidelines. Otherwise we know where they can end up.'

Margaret smiled sadly at Arabella.

Arabella became angry at the obvious insult to her. 'Well, I presume you brought Charles up with love and strict guidelines, and he doesn't seem to have been too bothered with either all his life!'

'Arabella!' Margaret was shocked. 'A wife must *never* criticise her husband!'

Miss Kingston had tutored some of the best families in the country and so she was used to the aristocracy and their ways. She often found governesses were in a unique position. They had power and charge over the children who would one day be the establishment. She was looking forward to life at Armstrong House, with this very noble family. Her living quarters were lovely and the servants pleasant. She didn't have much to do with Lord Lawrence and Lady Margaret, but found them to have that commanding but kind dignity they were known for.

But it was the immediate family she worked for that she had problems with. The children Prudence and Pierce were quite extraordinary to her mind. They weren't like the normal children of their age she had dealt with who were all the things children were known for being: in turn kind, inquisitive, naughty, lazy or delightful. These children were different. Prudence was way ahead of her years – manipulative, clever, sly and smart-mouthed. Miss Kingston found it nearly impossible to win any argument with her, and they were usually instigated by the girl. Pierce was much quieter, happy living in his own world, in his sister's overbearing shadow, and yet because he was such a handsome child he was used to and expected people to flock and fuss around him. And then there were the parents, thought Miss Kingston. Charles was arrogant and too sure of himself and seemed bitter over a world that didn't worship him as he thought it should. Arabella, Miss Kingston thought, was a strong woman but she seemed unhappy and sometimes living on her nerves. Miss Kingston would hear the two of them rowing loudly into the night, oblivious to the fact others could hear in the house.

Prudence sat in the schoolroom with Pierce as Miss Kingston droned on about European geography. Prudence sat gazing out the window. Charles had gone off on estate business all day and she longed to be out with him rather than stuck in there.

'Prudence!'

'What?'

'I've asked you three times and you've ignored me. The capital of Germany?'

'Berlin!' Prudence snapped back irritably.

'Would you please drop that attitude!' Miss Kingston became angry. 'And how are you to answer questions to me? I've told you a thousand times? Berlin *what?*'

'Berlin is the capital of Germany!'

'No!'

'But it is!'

'I mean, you are to respond to my questions with the words *"Miss Kingston"!*'

'Oh I see!' Prudence said sarcastically.

'Now, let's try it again – what is the capital of Germany?'

'*Miss Kingston!*'

'Ahhh! You must answer: "The capital of Germany is Berlin, *Miss Kingston!*"'

'But if you knew that in the first place then why did you ask me?' said Prudence.

Miss Kingston shrieked in frustration as Pierce erupted in laughter.

Miss Kingston rushed over to her desk to take out a ruler to slap the girl. She opened the desk and saw a dead rat lying there. Screaming, she ran from the room leaving Prudence and Pierce in convulsions of laughter.

Miss Kingston sat stony-faced in front of Arabella in the small parlour across from the drawing room.

'I simply will not teach that child again. I hand in my notice as of today,' announced Miss Kingston.

'Which one of my children are you referring to?'

'Prudence, of course! Although if you forgive me for saying, there isn't much "prudent" about her. She's rude, insolent, conniving–'

'Yes, I think you've made your point, Miss Kingston.'

'I have never in all my time encountered a child who seems so sure of herself and so insolent and disobedient.'

'Thank you and goodbye, Miss Kingston.' Arabella tried to dismiss her.

'I sometimes wonder whether the girl is bad or slightly mad!'

'Thank you and good day, Miss Kingston! You were never my choice anyway! My mother-in-law thrust you upon us as she said you were "solid and no-nonsense". Although if a ten-year-old girl can have you running for the hills, that description of you is obviously false.'

'If you don't mind me saying, Mrs Armstrong, I think both your children are unsettled and I wonder, observing your marriage while here at Armstrong House, whether it is being caused by being brought up in a disturbed family.'

'How dare you!'

'It manifests itself in Prudence knowing no boundaries and poor Pierce going into his shell.'

'I want you to leave Armstrong House at once, without reference, Miss Kingston. I'll get Fennell to organise a carriage to take you to the train station.'

'It will be my pleasure to leave,' said Miss Kingston, departing.

Arabella realised she was shaking when Miss Kingston closed the door. She went over to the drinks cabinet and poured herself a strong drink.

The next week Arabella contacted a Dublin agency who sent down a new governess. Prudence had the new governess dispatched in three weeks flat. Arabella didn't see in her children anything to confirm the worrying reports of the governesses or indeed the overheard conversations of the servants or Margaret's criticisms. All she experienced was two children who loved and worshipped her and Charles unconditionally. Who longed for and adored being in their parents' company and were such a comfort to her when the going was tough with Charles.

Arabella was in the drawing room with Margaret in the morning as Margaret planned the day ahead. Fennell the butler stood there attentively.

'The Foxes are coming to dinner, Fennell, so I think we'll have lamb tonight – it was always Mrs Foxe's favourite.'

'Very good, my lady, I'll inform Cook,' said Fennell.

'And what dinner service to use?' Margaret looked at Arabella. 'What do you think, Arabella.'

'I'm not familiar with the dinner services,' said Arabella.

'Well, I've asked you several times to come with me and let me talk you through them, so it's your own fault you don't know,' said Margaret unpleasantly before turning to Fennell. 'You can leave us for now, Fennell. Send Cook up to me please before lunch and I'll go through the rest of the menu with her.'

'Very good, my lady.' Fennell retreated from the room.

'Honestly, Arabella, you need to know about all the dinner services and cutlery we have at Armstrong House. How else are you going to fill your role as Lady Armstrong when the time comes?'

'Forgive me, Margaret, but I really don't have an interest in plates and spoons!'

'Well, that's obvious. I often wonder what you *are* interested in? I thought you and Charles were supposed to have held the most exquisite dinner parties in London before you went bankrupt? How did you at all manage that with this disinterest you have?'

'It was mostly arranged by Charles and the staff.'

'While you just turned up looking pretty?' Margaret spoke sarcastically.

'Anyway, our time in London taught me how false all that is ... and besides, I was busy with my children.'

'If you don't mind me saying, busy not doing a very good job! I've been meaning to talk to you for a while about them. I've had reports back from Fennell that Prudence is practically turning the parlour maids' lives into torture with her, pranks while Pierce spends his time daydreaming, staring out the window.'

Arabella became annoyed. 'My goodness! What is wrong with all these servants who can't cope with a couple of children? They aren't made of very strong stuff, is all I can say.'

'Of course, it's not the child's fault,' said Margaret. 'She just isn't getting the proper upbringing. I think I shall take her in hand myself.'

'You might be able to dictate everything else in this house, but you will not dictate to Prudence and Pierce. I don't want you having any direct involvement in their upbringing, not after how your own children turned out.'

'I beg your pardon! I know how to bring up young ladies.'

'You can blame me and Charles as much as you want about Emily, but the truth is you emotionally battered and beat Emily into being what you wanted and limited her options so much that she practically ran away to marry Fitzroy to escape the life you made for her. I want my daughter and son to be free of all that. I don't care if Prudence doesn't know how to walk elegantly and speak German fluently. I don't care if she never gets married. I want her to have the freedom to be herself, and that's how I intend to keep it!'

Arabella stood up and stormed off.

CHAPTER 47

Charles rode his horse through the small gateway into the Doherty farmholding on the Armstrong estate. He found himself in a yard in front of a small thatched cottage typical of the homes on the estate. Hens were walking around the yard clucking as a stray calf pulled at a haystack in the corner of the yard.

'Good afternoon!' he called.

A moment later a woman in her thirties came out, wiping her hands on her apron.

'Hello, your lordship, you're very welcome,' said the woman.

'Is this the Doherty farm?'

'It is, of course, your lordship, sure what else would it be? I'm Nuala Doherty.'

'My father asked me to come and meet him here. Where is he?' asked Charles, just then spotting his father's carriage at the gable of the house.

'Isn't he up with my husband Denis – they're inspecting the high meadow, although to be truthful with you, sir, it isn't much of a high meadow with the bad weather we had and the bad harvest we're getting.'

'Indeed, quite. Did he say he would be long?' asked Charles impatiently.

'Ah sure, isn't this him coming back now!' she said, pointing to another gateway.

In through that gateway walked Lawrence accompanied by James and a farmer in his thirties.

'You finally managed to find the place all right then?' said Lawrence disapprovingly to Charles who was an hour late.

'I got lost down by the river,' said Charles.

'Charles, this is Denis Doherty – the farmer who rents this holding and who we were talking about yesterday.'

'Sure you're as welcome as sunlight on a rainy day, your lordship,' smiled Denis warmly.

Charles managed to smile and nod at the man.

'Anyway,' said Lawrence, shaking his head, worried. 'That harvest in the meadow is as bad as you said it is, Denis.'

'That it is, your lordship,' Denis nodded his head sadly.

'And we put that much shite on the ground, if you pardon the expression, we were expecting a bumper harvest,' said Nuala.

Lawrence smiled. 'I know how hard you worked – very disappointing for you.'

'So what do we do, that's the question,' said James.

'Won't ye come in for some tea to discuss it all?' said Nuala. 'I've the kettle boiling.'

'Very kind of you, Nuala,' said Lawrence

happily as he followed the Dohertys to their front door.

Charles raised his eyes to heaven as he turned his horse around. 'If you'll excuse me, I'll head back to Armstrong House.'

Lawrence turned quickly around and gave Charles a warning look. 'You'll do no such thing, Charles. Come in with us, we've business to discuss.'

Charles reluctantly jumped off his horse and followed them in. Inside he saw a kitchen with a door on either end, presumably leading to bedrooms. As Charles counted five children glaring at him in awe, he wondered where they all slept. The kitchen was clean with flagstones on the floor, a bed beside the open fire that was blazing and a dresser full of delph. There were holy pictures on the wall and a crucifix over the bed.

'Sit yourselves down here,' said Nuala and the men all sat down around a wooden table beside the small window.

Nuala made the tea and filled their tea cups. Then she cut large slices of soda bread and put it on plates, gave one to each of them and placed butter and jam on the table.

'Nuala, this soda bread is excellent!' complimented Lawrence after he had taken a bite.

'Ah thanks, your lordship, I made it myself and the jam and the butter.' Nuala was delighted.

'Well, I tell you, you could teach the cooks at Armstrong House a thing or two,' said Lawrence.

'I've another just baked this morning – I'll wrap it up for you and you can take it back to Lady Armstrong,' smiled Nuala.

'Most kind – we can have it tonight after our dinner as a special treat.' Lawrence made a grinning face at her, as Charles raised his eyes to heaven.

'Anyway on to the business at hand,' suggested James. 'That bad harvest has left you in a predicament, Denis.'

'That it has,' Denis nodded sadly.

'What chance have you to pay the rent this year?'

'Not much chance, sorry to say, not much chance at all,' said Denis.

'You're already in arrears from last year, Denis,' Lawrence pointed out.

'I know, sir … the child was sick last year and most of our money went on medical bills.' Denis pointed to what in Charles' mind was a fine strapping girl sitting on the bed.

Lawrence coughed and sat forward. 'Would you be able to pay half of what you owe this year?'

'I could manage that, sir.'

Lawrence nodded thoughtfully. 'What I propose is we write off what you owe last year and in exchange for that you'll do some harvesting work for us. Then with your rent this year we'll restructure your payments over the next two years so it won't leave you short and yet all your arrears will be paid up over a twenty-four-month period. How does that sound?'

Denis Doherty looked delighted. 'Your lordship is very good – that sounds grand. I won't let you down. I'll work every hour to catch up on me arrears.'

'Good man!' Lawrence patted his arm approvingly.

To Charles' horror one of the children jumped up on his lap and gave him a hug.

'Get down off his lordship's lap before you dirty his fine new suit!' warned Nuala, horrified.

'Too late, I'm afraid,' said Charles as he observed the big dirty imprint left on his jacket by the child.

Nuala quickly retrieved her child.

'He's just so happy we've come to an arrangement over the payment. This little one was worried sick and couldn't sleep – he hears all the stories about evictions and so on,' said Denis.

'No need to worry on that account.' Lawrence winked reassuringly at him before standing. 'And now we must get on. Nuala, thank you for a delightful tea.'

'Sure the pleasure was all ours. Sure the neighbours will be that jealous we got a visit from your honour.' Nuala gave a little curtsy.

Outside Lawrence and James got into their carriage and waved goodbye before taking off. Charles jumped on his horse, dug his heels into the horse's sides and sped off without looking back.

Back at the library in Armstrong House Charles sat at the desk looking through the rent books of the estate. Lawrence and James walked in.

'Well, I'm glad to see you're at last taking an interest in the bookwork of the estate,' commented Lawrence.

'Oh, I'm taking an interest all right. So far I reckon I've counted a fifth of the tenants who are in some sort of arrears,' said Charles, closing over the book.

'We have arrangements with them all so they'll catch up with their repayments,' said James.

'What, like the arrangement you came to with Doherty today, when you just wrote off last year's debt?' asked Charles incredulously.

'We haven't written it off,' said James. 'You heard he'll do work in exchange for it.'

'As I said – written it off!'

'Well, what would you suggest we do?' demanded Lawrence. 'That family is struggling and on its knees.'

'Struggling!' Charles was dismissive. 'They don't look like they're struggling to me, with their chickens walking around everywhere and their fine fat children. In fact, Nuala Doherty looks to me as if she could lose a few pounds.'

'You're being ridiculous,' said Lawrence.

'No, you're the one being ridiculous. They made a total fool of you. Can't pay the rent indeed, and he'll be off down in Cassidy's pub in Castlewest tonight spending our rent!'

'And what would you suggest we do with them?' asked Lawrence.

'Give them two weeks to pay everything or kick them out and get in somebody on their land who is willing to pay,' said Charles.

'Evict them!' Lawrence was horrified. 'The Dohertys have been on this land as long as the Armstrongs. Longer in fact as they were farmers here before our ancestors got this estate.'

'No wonder they're here that long when they don't have to pay any rent!' Charles said.

'Up until last year they were never late with

their payments,' said James.

'Well, I can assure you they will never be on time again, now they see how soft you are,' predicted Charles.

'We have to co-operate with the tenants otherwise we'll be at war with them, and they're not people you cross,' said Lawrence.

'You're afraid of them and they know it. You think you're in a partnership with these people and they respect you. They don't! They despise you! They hate giving you rent for land they think is theirs and that our ancestors stole from them.'

'Which is all the more reason to not rock the boat with them,' said Lawrence. 'I will not have our estate go down the same road as others in this country with hatred and mistrust.'

'The only way to run it is like a business! You two are living in the past when you thought all the gentry had to do was wave benevolently to the tenants and the estate would be profitable. Times have changed. You might mock people like Fitzroy, but they know how to make money in today's world and come out on top. It's all about making money and that's how this estate should be run,' Charles stood up and walked out, leaving Lawrence looking after him worried.

CHAPTER 48

Arabella and Charles were having drinks with Lawrence in the drawing room when Margaret came rushing in holding a letter.

'It's a letter from Harrison!' she announced and Charles and Arabella gave each other an uncomfortable look.

'Well, that's an unusual thing! How is he?' asked Lawrence, surprised.

'He's – getting married!'

'What? To whom?' asked Lawrence, standing up and rushing to his wife to see the letter.

'To a Victoria Van Hoevan,' said Margaret.

'Van Hoevan?' Charles asked, immediately recognising the surname and very curious to know more.

'Yes, Van Hoevan! As in *the* Van Hoevans!' confirmed Margaret excitedly. 'He's sent our wedding invitation and everything!' Margaret handed the invitation to Lawrence.

Lawrence took the invitation and started to read it. 'And the reception is in Newport, Rhode Island. Newport – it's *that* Van Hoevan family all right.'

'Yes, yes! Oh, Lawrence!' Margaret turned and hugged her husband. 'I've been so worried about him all these years, and frightened for him alone in America and how he was, with scarcely a card from him, and here he is marrying a Van Hoevan!'

She suddenly started to cry and Lawrence comforted her. 'Wipe away those tears, darling. You're being silly – this is good news.'

'Goods news! It's the best news ever. He's invited us all over to the wedding.' She looked at Charles and Arabella. 'Well, nearly all of us – he says he's inviting Gwyneth, Daphne, Emily, their husbands and James of course. I'm afraid he doesn't mention you, Charles and Arabella, and I presume no invitation came to you in the post.'

'Don't say he's still sore after all these years?' Charles said with an exaggerated sigh.

Arabella gave him a withering look.

Margaret and Lawrence hurried out to find James to tell him the news.

Arabella sat back and digested the news.

'Harrison marrying into one of America's richest families – who'd ever have thought?' said Charles.

'I'm not surprised. Harrison has many fine qualities. I hope he'll be very happy.'

'Aren't you jealous?'

'Not in the least. If anything I'm relieved. Harrison has been a huge source of guilt to me over the years, and I'm delighted he's finally settling down with someone.'

'Not just someone – a Van Hoevan.'

She looked at him pointedly. 'Well, he always had good taste, if I say so myself. Pity I didn't have as sound taste myself.'

He smirked at her and said mockingly, 'Well, it's not too late if you feel that strongly about it. You might be able to rush over and stop the wedding.'

'No, interfering in marriage arrangements is

your speciality.'

'Well, let's hope he has better luck, and taste, in choosing his fiancée this time round.'

'As you won't be allowed anywhere near his wedding I'm sure he'll have all the luck in the world,' said Arabella.

Although Lawrence was excited about seeing Harrison again, he was extremely concerned about leaving the estate in Charles' care as they headed off to America for the wedding. There wouldn't even be James there to keep an eye on things as he was naturally going to the wedding as well.

'Oh, he'll be all right,' Margaret reassured him as they got in to their landau carriage and waved goodbye to Charles and Arabella and the children who were standing at the door.

'I wonder,' said Lawrence.

'You said yourself he's taking a much keener interest in the running of the estate.'

'That's what's worrying me!' confided Lawrence.

Fennell was serving breakfast to Charles and Arabella.

'Do you know, I fancy salmon tonight,' said Charles. 'Tell Cook to prepare salmon and tell her to try and do something fancy and French with it.'

Fennell looked concerned.

'I take it Cook can't do something fancy and French,' smiled Arabella knowingly.

'Well, it's not that, it's just we haven't had

377

salmon all season. None has been caught from the river and delivered to the house.'

'Whyever not?' asked Charles. 'There was always fresh salmon caught in the river and served when I was growing up.'

Fennell shrugged.

'Ask the head gamekeeper to come and see me at twelve,' instructed Charles.

'Why is there no salmon being caught in the river this year?' asked Charles.

'I'm afraid it's a bad year for salmon, sir.'

Charles raised his eyes to heaven. 'Is it a bad year for everything this year around here?'

The gamekeeper shifted uncomfortably. 'His lordship gave instructions no salmon was to be fished in order to allow the salmon to restock.'

'A river that was so plentiful with salmon doesn't just run dry.'

The gamekeeper continued to shift uncomfortably.

'What else is going on with the salmon?' asked Charles coolly, seeing the gamekeeper was hiding something.

'Well, there's been a lot of poaching in the river lately.'

'Poaching!'

'Yes, sir. To be honest all the tenant farmers always do a bit of poaching and his lordship always turns a blind eye to it.'

'There's a surprise.'

'But this past couple of years you have a lot of poachers coming out from Castlewest and helping themselves as they know his lordship won't call the police.'

'I can't believe it! So we must starve while strangers feed on our salmon!'

The gamekeeper's eyes widened at Charles' exaggeration.

'I want you to gather your best men and we'll go down to the river tonight. We'll catch these bastards who are stealing our salmon.'

It was a moonlit night as Charles and four of the gamekeepers hid near the river behind trees. The men were waiting there with guns. It was cold and a bird called as the wind rustled through the branches. A couple of hours went by and Charles was freezing but he was determined to put an end to this plundering which his father had not only ignored but had encouraged by turning a blind eye.

Suddenly three men came down a laneway to the river and started talking to each other before they started casting their nets.

'When I count to three, rush them!' ordered Charles. 'One, two ... three!'

The gamekeepers came running out of the bushes, startling the poachers.

'Get the bastards!' shouted Charles.

They managed to grab two of the poachers but the third went racing into the trees.

The two frightened poachers were brought in front of Charles by the gamekeepers.

'Bring them down to the police in the town. Have them charged with theft and poaching,' ordered Charles.

The gamekeepers looked warily at each other.

'I don't think his lordship would want to involve the police, sir. He'd just want them well warned and released,' said the head gamekeeper.

'Do as I say – take these thieves down to the police station at once,' commanded Charles as he turned and headed back to Armstrong House.

CHAPTER 49

Arabella much enjoyed the few weeks that Lawrence and Margaret were away. It was nice having the house to themselves without Margaret's constant spying and criticisms and Charles' constant arguing with Lawrence and James. Her thoughts often drifted to Harrison and what his wedding would be like, what this Victoria Van Hoevan was like. She wondered if Harrison was the same as when she knew him. Was he still as lovely and trusting and kind? She hoped he was. Having lived with Charles for so many years those qualities of Harrison were much more endearing to her now than they had been to her as a young girl when her head was turned by charm and danger and intrigue.

Margaret and Lawrence arrived back from America full of talk about the wedding. As they handed presents to Prudence and Pierce in the drawing room the evening of their arrival they regaled Charles and Arabella with stories.

'It was simply amazing!' said Margaret. 'The wealth and extravagance was staggering! These

Van Hoevans certainly know how to live!'

'We travelled in a motor car!' said Lawrence. 'I don't mind telling you I was terrified.'

'The wedding reception was at the Van Hoevan house, their palace by the sea. The reception was on the lawn! In front of the ocean! Can you imagine!'

'A river of champagne ran the whole day, and I mean river!' said Lawrence.

'Everyone who was anyone in American society was there,' said Margaret proudly.

Charles stood at the fireplace, mesmerised with all the reports of glamour beyond anything he could ever imagine for himself.

'And what of Harrison? How was Harrison?' asked Arabella eventually.

'Oh, he's perfectly happy! Blissfully happy!' said Margaret, delighted to give this report to Arabella.

'He looked very well, and delighted we could all make it over,' said Lawrence.

'Even Emily and Fitzroy, although I don't know what American society made of *him*. He, of course, loved being amongst the nobs, but I'll tell you more about that later,' said Margaret, disgusted by the memory of him.

'And what of the girl? The girl he married?' asked Charles, his curiosity piqued to fever point.

Margaret sat back with a hugely satisfied look on her face. 'She's perfection, absolute perfection. Beautiful, cultured, educated and just a thoroughly nice person.'

'They said she came into a million-dollar trust fund on her twenty-first birthday,' chuckled Lawrence.

Charles suddenly dropped his glass of wine and it smashed to the floor.

'Are you all right, Charles?' asked Margaret, concerned.

'Yes, clumsy of me,' said Charles, tugging the bell pull to call Fennell to clean up the mess.

Lawrence sighed loudly. 'I'm absolutely exhausted. The trip back on the ocean liner was very tiresome. I'm going to bed.'

Arabella had to admit Lawrence looked aged and tired from the whole trip.

'I'll come with you too,' said Margaret, linking his arm.

'Yes, Victoria was a dream,' said Margaret as she left the room. 'Everything you'd want in a daughter-in-law, but so seldom get.'

Arabella and Charles looked at each other discontentedly.

Charles found himself lost in thought of Harrison and this fairytale bride he'd found. All Margaret and Lawrence seemed to talk about was Harrison and his wife. They seemed so proud of him. The whole thing only caused resentment in Charles. Resentment of Harrison who had been allowed to sail off to this fantastic new life. Resentment of his father who put such restrictions on his life. Resentment of Fitzroy who cheated him of his life and good name in London. And resentment of Arabella. Arabella whose marriage with him had been born out of avoiding a scandal. Arabella whose dowry paled in comparison to this Victoria Van Hoevan's. Arabella who made unpleasant comments to him and who rowed with him incessantly. He loved his children, but he remembered the all-consuming passionate desire and love he had for Arabella at the beginning, and he had to admit to himself that it no longer existed. Arabella carried herself well as a society hostess in London and he had enjoyed the envy she inspired in people. But she seemed no longer interested in being a society hostess since returning to Armstrong House, and he had to admit the opportunity to be one was greatly diminished in his parents' home. But she seemed uninterested in anything. She never went into town and, although Charles had accepted the drapers and haberdasheries of Castlewest could not compete with the delights of Bond Street and Knightsbridge, she could at least show some interest. Apart from walking through the gardens, she never ventured beyond that to the estate. She talked politely at dinner parties and social gatherings, but she was no great society hostess.

Charles came down the staircase, putting on his gloves and dressed in his riding clothes.

'Excuse me, Mr Charles, but his lordship would like to see you in the library,' Fennell informed him.

Charles tutted, took off his hat and gloves and left them on the sideboard. He headed into the library where he found Lawrence sitting behind his desk, looking angry.

'Tell me this isn't so, Charles?' asked Lawrence.

'What exactly are you talking about?' Charles asked irritably.

'Did you go and catch poachers while I was in America and hand them over to the police for prosecution?' demanded Lawrence

'Yes, I did,' said Charles, unconcerned.

'And what became of them?'

'They were put in gaol for a week and given a hefty fine.'

'How dare you – who gave you permission to do such a thing?' Lawrence's face was red with anger.

'I did! I was in charge and these men were breaking the law by stealing our best salmon and deserved prosecution,' Charles said assuredly.

'You stupid, stupid boy! Don't you know anything? Don't you understand anything?'

'I understand peasants stealing what does not belong to them and them needing to be taught a lesson and made an example of,' said Charles.

'You had no right! You have no understanding of our own family history. We've turned a blind eye to poaching on the river ever since the famine, when the fish stock there allowed many families to survive. It's an unwritten understanding between us and the locals.'

'The famine! The famine was fifty years ago – it's ancient history, I've told you before.'

'That famine built such a resentment towards our class from the locals that we have to at all times tread very carefully. We are a rich and powerful family but times are changing. This Land War has very much strengthened the peasants' rights. Some of the gentry families are already pulling out of Ireland, taking advantage of the land acts that enabled their tenants to buy them out. They don't want to stay here in a country that makes them feel unwelcome as it hurries to Home Rule.'

'Home Rule! They've been going on about Home Rule for the past hundred years, and they will be going on about it in a hundred years, but it will never come to pass.'

'Don't you see what I'm trying to tell you? My father successfully brought this great estate through the terrible famine, and I successfully brought it through the worst years of the Land War. And here you are, upsetting and risking those decades of careful politics and diplomacy by calling in the police over a couple of salmon being poached!'

'And why not? I see the way you flutter around those peasants and it makes me sick!' Charles adopted a mocking imitation of Lawrence's accent: '"Fine day, Mr Doyle, what lovely children, Mrs O'Hara, soda bread is simply thrilling, Mrs Kennedy!"'

'But that's what running an estate like this involves – good relations!'

'I piss on your good relations!'

'Charles!'

'They are peasants – filthy, uneducated peasants!'

'How can you say such a thing?'

'Because it's true!' Charles leaned forward across the desk, his face a mask of anger as everything came whirring through his mind at the same time from Harrison's marriage to Fitzroy's cheating to Arabella's arguments. 'You've let them take advantage of you all your life, but I won't let them do the same to me or my son. I'll run this place like a finely tuned business when my time comes. I won't be walked over and poached and taken advantage of by those wretched people we have nothing in common with!'

Lawrence stared at his son's angry face and felt fear. Not for himself but for the future of the family and the estate.

He sat down at the desk and sighed. 'You might have more in common with the peasants than you think.'

'Yes, we breathe the same air, and that's where it stops.'

Lawrence studied Charles' arrogant and angry face and knew he had to do something to divert the disaster that would come to the estate with Charles' attitude and actions.

'I want to tell you something – something I've never told a living soul, not even your mother, especially not your mother,' said Lawrence.

Charles looked at the strange expression on Lawrence's face.

'I've kept this secret for years, but as you are my heir you need to know the truth, and to keep the secret as well.'

'Get on with it!' said Charles unpleasantly.

'My mother, Lady Anna, told me this when she was dying. She told me that when she was younger and married to my father, Lord Edward, she had an affair. And that I was the result of this affair.'

'*What?*' Charles shouted.

'Edward never knew I was not his real son. When my mother told me Edward had already passed away. It weighed heavy on her conscience and so she told me – she had to share it with me.'

'And who then was your real father?' Charles

felt as if the whole world he knew was turning upside-down in front of him.

'A peasant,' confirmed Lawrence.

'*Noooo!*' screamed Charles. 'You're lying!'

'Why would I lie?' said Lawrence.

'I don't know – to anger me, to teach me some sort of lesson on humility.'

'I'm not lying, Charles. Lord Edward Armstrong, wonderful man and father that he was to me, was not my real father. I never knew who my real father was or even his identity, only that he wasn't from our class.'

'But – but – your whole life has been a lie, and you've made our lives a lie as well!'

'I only found this out when I was in my twenties. Edward had passed away and my mother was not far off it herself. My mother was so kind and loving to everyone and yet she always seemed haunted by something. When she told me this, I realised this was what haunted her.'

'And why didn't you keep this to yourself? Why have you told me? Can you imagine what effect this will have on me?'

'That's precisely why I *did* tell you. I'm so worried about your attitude and the way you behave to the tenants and even the staff in the house. You think you're above them and you need to understand you're not. You're part of them and they are part of you.'

Charles' face contorted in anger. 'You make me sick! I can't even bear to look at you! The result of a sordid affair, and you had the audacity to judge me when Arabella became pregnant!'

'I judged you over how you treated Harrison,

but if you remember it was I encouraged you to marry Arabella and accept fate. Ever since I found out how I was conceived I've understood that nature has its own way of dealing with things and pushing the human race on even though sometimes we don't understand it, I said this to your mother when she was distraught about Arabella being pregnant. I explained to her it was nature's way of promoting our family – in the same way my mother's liaison pushed the Armstrong family to the next generation.'

'But you weren't the next generation of the Armstrong family – you were some bastard of a peasant!'

'Charles!'

'It's the fucking truth!'

'Once you calm down you'll understand what I'm talking about.'

'I will *never* recover from this! You've robbed me of my identity. And if you think this will make me somehow bond with the locals then you're sadly mistaken. Whereas before I looked down on them, now I'll despise them. And my children will never find out this dirty family secret you've burdened me with!'

Charles turned and stormed from the room.

'Charles!' Lawrence shouted after him, but he was gone.

Charles went storming through the courtyards at the back of the house.

'Get me a horse – *now!*' he roared at a passing stable boy who ran into a stable and brought out a saddled mare straight away. Charles jumped on the horse and dug his heels into her so that she took off at high speed.

Charles raced down the avenue through the parklands surrounding Armstrong House. For the next couple of hours he rode the horse fast through the lanes and roads that crisscrossed the Armstrong estate. He jumped the horse over hedges and gates, scattering groups of children who fled for their lives as he passed by. He continued up into the hills and finally stopped when he got to the top of a high hill. He dismounted from the exhausted horse.

As the horse wandered off he stood on top of the hill. He used to come to that hill when he was a child. It offered a breathtaking view across the entire estate. He could see the hundreds of tenant cottages spread out like a patchwork. In the distance stood Armstrong House majestically on the shores of the lake that stretched out for miles beyond it. He had stood there like a prince all those times before, surveying the kingdom that would one day be his. Confident in his position in life as the heir to a noble family that had stretched back centuries. Even the area and the earldom were named after them. And yet that had been taken from him, stolen by a few words of honesty that afternoon from his father. As he surveyed the estate he realised his heritage didn't lie in the regal stonework of Armstrong House but somewhere in that patchwork of cottages that spread out like a plague of thistles across the land. He sank to his knees in despair. He had always studied the portraits of his ancestors that hung in the house, delighting in the fact that he was their descendent. And now he had been told they were strangers to him. He shared no blood with them.

It was night by the time Charles rode the weary horse back to Armstrong House. He handed the animal to a stable boy and made his way to the front door and let himself in.

'Charles!' said Arabella, rushing from the drawing room. 'Where have you been? We've been looking for you all day.'

'What's wrong?' he asked, looking at her ashen face.

'It's your father – he collapsed in the library this afternoon. Fennell found him lying unconscious on the floor.'

'Where is he now?'

'Upstairs with the doctor and Margaret. They've been up there for hours!'

At that moment Margaret and the doctor came down the stairs.

'If I could speak to you somewhere private?' asked the doctor.

'We'll go into the drawing room,' said Margaret, leading them in and closing the door.

James was already in there, pacing nervously up and down.

'Well?' demanded James.

'Lord Armstrong has had a major coronary attack,' said the doctor.

'Will he be all right, Doctor? What can you do for him?' asked Margaret in a surprisingly even voice.

'I'm afraid there isn't much I can do for him. He really shouldn't have travelled to America for the wedding, he wasn't well enough. I advised him not to go. He's been in bad health for a while.'

'He never said anything!' Margaret was shocked.

'He didn't want to worry you. He has been very stressed with one thing and another.' The doctor shot Charles a look.

'But he will recover?' asked Arabella, alarmed.

'I'm afraid not. He should last for a couple of weeks, but who can say after that,' said the doctor.

James sat down on the couch and buried his head in his hands as he started crying in a strange gasping manner.

Charles stood rigid, his face pale as a ghost.

But what astounded Arabella most was Margaret. She and Lawrence were so close, so loving, she expected her to collapse in tears or even faint. Instead she went to the bell pull and tugged it.

'We must send telegrams to all the children immediately. They all need to get back and see their father. I hope Harrison can get back from America in time.'

Fennell arrived in.

'Fennell, go to Castlewest immediately and have telegrams sent to London, Dublin and New York and tell all my children their father is dying and they are to come back immediately. I shall give you the addresses shortly.'

'Yes, my lady.'

'Send me in the housekeeper. We must have all the guest rooms aired and made up for their arrival. We'll put Gwyneth and His Grace in the Blue Room.'

'Yes, my lady.'

'Harrison and Victoria in the Red Room...'

Arabella could only look on in awe and shock as Margaret continued with the arrangements with military precision.

In London, Emily and Hugh Fitzroy sat eating their dinner in silence. She cringed as he ate his roasted duck with the worst table manners she had ever witnessed. As he slobbered over his food she found he was making her lose her appetite. He spotted the look of disdain on her face.

'What's the matter?' he demanded.

'Nothing!' she said as she delicately cut her meat with her silver knife.

He threw his fork down on the table and picked up what was left of the duck on his plate and started sucking it.

As she watched him she began to feel sick.

Marriage to Hugh had not been what she had expected. Oh, the travel was exciting at the beginning. South America and Europe and even as far as India. She had gluttonously fed on the sights and sounds of all the foreign climates she never had expected to see. But as the marriage continued, she realised there was no more foreign a sight than Hugh. As she became used to his ways she realised they had very little in common. And seeing him in his full ignorance, he sometimes repelled her.

Then there were other things, darker things, that she could only see shadows of but she feared ever seeing those things in the full light of day. He would go out at night and never explain where he was going. Sometimes he would disappear for days and leave her worried sick. And when he did come back he would look exhausted and wrecked and sleep for twenty-four hours without waking up. She tried to question him about where he went and what was he doing in these absences, but he would clam up and sometimes get angry.

She had never considered herself a snob in any way. She hated snobbery. She had hated her mother's and their circle's way of doing things. She had thought marrying Hugh would be an escape from all that, yet she often thought he was an even bigger snob than they were, the way he revered the upper classes and strained every nerve to aspire to being just like them. All the time he strove to be accepted by society. He continuously splashed his money around buying friendships with people who Emily could see viewed him with contempt. He loved attending the high-class functions with Emily and continually telling people that he was married to Lady Emily Armstrong as if she were some badge of honour he wore to impress people. Sometimes she thought he despised her. Sometimes she wondered if he despised her because he could see the disdain she held him in. Because she now knew that in spite of his money, marriage to him had cost her the position in society that she had taken for granted from birth. She dreaded attending all these social functions that Hugh insisted they went to, not because of the sniggers of people about Hugh, but because they were also sniggering about her. She had lost people's respect.

The butler came in. 'A telegram for you, my lady.'

'Get me a vodka!' Hugh barked at the butler as he wiped his mouth with his sleeve.

'I wish you wouldn't speak to him like that,' said Emily. 'It shows a lack of breeding when you don't address staff correctly.'

Hugh looked at her and then he roared with laughter. 'You're not at Armstrong House now – you're in my house – the house your family lost to the bank!'

Emily ignored him as she read the telegram. Her hand shot to her mouth.

'It's Father, he's not well. We have to go to Armstrong House immediately.'

Hugh flung the duck back on his plate. 'I'm not going to Armstrong House. I'm not giving your mother the opportunity to look down her snobby nose at me again.'

'Did you not hear what I said? He could be dying,' Emily said, reinforcing her message.

'You'll have to go on your own.'

'Right then, I will,' said Emily, rising from the table and walking out. She felt relieved that he didn't want to go.

CHAPTER 50

As Lawrence drifted in and out of consciousness the siblings arrived. First Daphne from Dublin, then Gwyneth and His Grace from London. Then a pale and tired-looking Emily. To everyone's relief Hugh had not come with her. Everyone sat around drinking tea and holding vigils by Lawrence's bed. Margaret was a revelation. She didn't falter once.

'Your mother is very strong,' said Arabella one night as she lay in bed with Charles.

'Not really. She's just treating death in the same manner she treats every occasion in her life. It's to be overseen with dignity and decorum.'

'But it's her husband!' Arabella still couldn't understand.

'It doesn't matter. The pride and reputation of the family comes first, and she will make sure this is done the correct way.'

'It almost sounds heartless,' sighed Arabella.

'It's not heartless, it's just her. You're not like that, so you'll never understand her.'

What Arabella really dreaded was the arrival of Harrison and his wife who had sent back a telegram saying they were coming straight away. She had never imagined she would see Harrison again. He was just an echo from her past. And yet soon he and his wife would be here at Armstrong House. She didn't know how she would behave to them or how they would behave to her. Would he still be angry and bitter? Would he ignore her? Would this new marvel of a wife insult her? Arabella gathered her nerve and prepared for the storm that was coming.

'Aren't you nervous about seeing Harrison again after all these years?' she asked Charles in bed another night.

'I'm curious if anything. Curious to see what he's become, curious to meet this wife.'

'I hope it won't be awkward,' she said.

'Of course it will be awkward! But don't worry, the little matter of Lord Armstrong's death will take all the attention away from you!'

Charles sat at Lawrence's side, watching him sleep. He continuously thought about the secret his father had shared with him. And as Charles watched him breathe slowly, he didn't see the great Lord Armstrong any more, he saw a man who had been a fake all his life, even to his wife.

Charles leaned forward and whispered, 'Why did you tell me? I didn't want to know.'

The family were gathered in the drawing room late one afternoon when they suddenly heard the most extraordinary noise coming in the distance. James got up and raced to the window.

'It's a motor car!' he said excitedly.

'Whoever is coming to us in a motor car?' said Margaret, getting up for a look.

The family all rose quickly and hurried to the window for a look as the motor car pulled up in the forecourt.

'It's Harrison!' declared Emily.

'Indeed – who else?' said Charles as he strained to get a glimpse of his brother and his wife.

'And Victoria is driving it!' exclaimed Emily.

Arabella remained seated. She had known it would be Harrison without even looking.

Outside, Harrison got out of the motor car and took off his gloves as he stared up at Armstrong House.

'Has it changed?' asked Victoria, coming from around the side of the car and resting against his arm.

'No, it hasn't changed, not one tiny bit,' he said.

The front door opened and the family came rushing out to greet them. Charles and Arabella stayed in the drawing room, looking out the window.

'The prodigal son returns,' said Charles.

'Harrison isn't a prodigal son – I'm sure he's never done anything wayward in his life,' said Arabella.

Charles turned to her. 'Aren't you going out to greet your boyfriend?'

'And aren't you going out to greet your brother?' She fixed him with a look.

As Arabella heard everyone come into the hall, she went and sat down and tried to compose herself. A few seconds later the drawing room door opened and in came Margaret with Harrison and Victoria, followed by the rest of the family.

Harrison stopped suddenly as he saw Arabella sitting on a Queen Anne chair and Charles standing beside her.

Victoria saw the stern look on Harrison's face and she quickly took in the couple already in the room. She suddenly broke away from the others, smiling as she crossed the room.

'Hello, I'm Victoria,' she said very warmly. 'You must be Charles and Arabella.'

'Yes,' Arabella managed, the impact of seeing Harrison again only hitting her now.

'Welcome to Armstrong House,' said Charles.

'I was so looking forward to meeting you both – it's unfortunate it's not under happier circumstances,' said Victoria. She reached forward and kissed Charles on the cheek and then bent down and did the same to Arabella.

It was such a tender kind kiss that Arabella suddenly felt like crying.

Victoria turned around to the others. 'Harrison, come and greet Charles and Arabella.'

Harrison nodded and slowly walked across the room.

'Charles,' he said on reaching them.

'Welcome home, Harrison,' said Charles and he put out his hand.

Harrison viewed the hand and for a moment it looked as if he would ignore it. But to everybody's relief he took the hand and shook it.

Harrison then looked at Arabella.

'It's good to see you again, Harrison,' said Arabella evenly.

Harrison nodded and bent down and kissed her cheek.

'You must be hungry – I'll get Fennell to bring in something for you immediately,' said Margaret. 'Of course we didn't know when exactly to expect you so we are not quite prepared...'

'Oh, please excuse us,' said Victoria, registering the mild complaint from her hostess. 'We really should have sent a telegram along the way. We docked the day before yesterday and set out to drive up here, staying in little Irish hotels on the way. As for food, we had a hearty breakfast this morning – rashers and sausages and this amazing thing called black pudding! So hearty I could hardly eat a bite when we stopped for lunch. So we can certainly last till dinner!'

Fennell came rushing into the room looking

panic-stricken. 'My lady, the doctor said you're to come at once to his lordship.'

Margaret turned and began to walk quickly from the room, saying, 'Harrison, quick, come with me, there mightn't be much time.'

Everyone rushed out of the room, leaving Arabella alone. She stood up and walked over to the fireplace, her mind lost in thought after seeing Harrison again.

CHAPTER 51

'It's the end of an era,' said Margaret that evening as they all sat in the drawing room.

'That it is,' said Gwyneth, wiping her eyes with her handkerchief.

'I'm so sorry he didn't get to see the new century in a couple of months. He was so looking forward to 1900, and seeing the twentieth century,' sighed Margaret.

'I'm just glad we got to see him in time,' said Harrison.

'First thing in the morning we'll start sending the telegrams. It will be a very big funeral,' said Margaret.

'Where will the service be?' asked Victoria.

'In the village church,' said Margaret. 'It probably won't be big enough to hold everyone, but it's tradition for the Armstrongs.' For a man who was never an Armstrong, thought Charles.

There was much crying echoing around the

house from the servants' quarters.

'Why do they have to wail and bellow like that?' asked Charles irritably.

'Nobody mourns like Catholics,' said Margaret. 'I went down earlier to give them words of comfort and they were all on their knees praying for Lawrence, bless them all.'

'He was obviously much loved by everyone,' said Victoria who was sitting on a couch holding Harrison's hand tightly.

James had been sitting in the far corner, his eyes red from crying.

'At least they know how to mourn him, Charles!' James suddenly said angrily, causing everyone to look at him. 'At least they cared about him, unlike you!'

'James, shut up, you're being ridiculous,' snapped Charles.

'No, I'm not! I heard you shouting at him in the library the afternoon he collapsed. I heard the screaming match you were having!'

'James, you know nothing about it,' snapped Charles, looking over at Harrison and Victoria who were listening attentively.

'You were always having rows with him, causing him stress. You lost him his prize house in London with your deceit and your tricks, which he never recovered from. You killed him!'

'His heart killed him, you stupid boy!' shouted Charles.

'You killed him as much as if you'd drowned or shot him!' shouted James as he rushed from the room and slammed the door behind him, leaving everyone to look uncomfortably at each other.

'I'm sorry, Victoria, what must you think of us?' said Margaret eventually.

'Oh, I never think anything of anybody at times like this – people say things when they are distraught,' said Victoria with a reassuring smile.

'Poor James,' said Margaret. 'He's taken it very badly – they were very close, you know.'

'James will be lost without him,' Arabella said, unsettled by the things James had said about Charles.

Charles wanted to say so much about James in his own defence, but as he looked at Harrison and Victoria he knew their presence was stopping him.

Victoria stood up. 'You know, I'm tired from all the driving – I think I need to go to bed.'

'Of course. In fact, I think we all need to go to bed – we have much to do over the next few days,' said Margaret, standing up.

Charles didn't go to bed with the rest of them. He stayed up drinking into the night.

At about two he opened the front door and walked across the forecourt and stood staring out at the gardens below him and the lake stretching into the distance. It was now all his, he was the new Lord Armstrong. He heard a noise behind him and turned to see Arabella walking towards him.

She stood beside him. 'Aren't you coming to bed?'

'I suppose,' he agreed.

'What was James talking about? A row you had with Lawrence?'

'Nothing, we had a disagreement over wheat-pricing, that's all,' Charles lied.

'I see,' said Arabella.

Charles turned and they began to walk across the forecourt together.

'Showing me up like that in front of Harrison and Victoria! James would want to realise who's in charge around here now and watch what he says.'

'I don't think anything James could say would influence opinions they have already formed about us,' said Arabella, as they reached the front steps of the house.

Charles paused and he held out his arm to her. 'Lady Armstrong?'

She smiled at him and took his arm, and they walked in and closed the door behind them.

True for Margaret, Lawrence's funeral was a huge occasion. Not only did dignitaries come from far and near but hundreds of locals thronged the green outside the church.

Gwyneth, who had announced she was pregnant again, left soon after to return to her other three children and duties waiting in England. Daphne returned to Dublin and her children. Emily seemed in no rush to return to London. She had purposely not sent a telegram to Hugh to inform him of Lawrence's death as she really didn't want him coming. She pretended to everyone that he was travelling abroad. But the reality was she couldn't cope with him arriving and showing her up in front of everyone with his brutish manners, the way he had when they went to Newport for Harrison's wedding.

She loved being back at Armstrong House in her old room. She realised she never appreciated what she had when she was there. Now she dreaded returning to her marriage. She had listened to Gwyneth and Daphne and Arabella discuss their children with joy, feeling like an outsider with none of her own. But the fact was she really didn't want any. The idea of having a child with Hugh had become repellent to her. Even for him to touch her repulsed her now.

She was out riding with Charles on the estate a couple of weeks after Lawrence's funeral.

He observed her sitting elegantly side-saddle and laughed.

'What's funny?' she asked.

'I'm laughing at you! You hated riding side-saddle and only did it when you had to. Why are you riding side-saddle now with nobody around to observe?'

'I always ride side-saddle nowadays. There's something very uncouth doing it the other way, I think.'

She seemed to have changed a lot, Charles thought.

'How's Hugh?' asked Charles. He had purposely avoided talking about Hugh as he was still so angry with him.

'Hugh is Hugh!' said Emily. 'I don't think he'll ever change, regardless of how much money he makes or how many dancing lessons he takes. Charles ... can I ask you something?'

'Of course!'

'There seems to be so much about Hugh that I

don't know, even now after being married to him. Do you know anything about him, being his friend?'

'I don't know if Hugh and I were ever friends, so no, I don't know anything,' said Charles, thinking back to that night when Hugh had taken him on that journey into the darkness of the East End of London.

'Don't tell anyone this... I know I can trust you ... sometimes he disappears for days and I never know where he's gone to.'

'I see,' said Charles, thinking of the opium den that Hugh had shown him.

'And then when he comes back he looks like he's a different person. Other times he locks himself in his bedroom, and won't come out for days, only allowing food to be delivered to his room.'

'*His* room?'

'Yes, we often have separate bedrooms. I prefer it like that, I think he does too, to be honest. I think I'm a terrible disappointment to him.'

'Surely not? He was desperate to marry you.'

'He was desperate to acquire a mill in Yorkshire last month as well. Once he got that, he never bothered talking about it or visiting it again either!'

'When are you going back to London?'

'Soon, I suppose. I have to get back or otherwise he'll arrive over here looking for me.'

Charles looked at his sister who seemed so miserable and remembered his part in her marriage.

'Come on,' he said, turning his horse. 'We'd better get back to the house.'

Victoria loved Armstrong House and Ireland. She had heard Harrison talking so much about it, but actually being there and seeing it was an entirely different matter.

There had been so much going on and so many people visiting Armstrong House in the aftermath of Lawrence passing away that they hadn't been alone much with Arabella and Charles, which was the thing they were dreading. But Victoria had observed the two of them from afar. She judged Arabella to be very beautiful with a refined manner. She had wondered over and over again since meeting Harrison what this woman would be like, this woman who had broken Harrison. She had thought Arabella would be some kind of ogre. But Arabella didn't come across like that. Victoria thought Arabella wasn't an open and carefree woman like Gwyneth and Daphne. But she imagined Arabella hadn't done anything on purpose all those years back, and had never intended to cause Harrison such hurt. The trouble was, watching Harrison near Arabella made her aware that he still didn't see it that way. He still viewed her with suspicion and contempt. The relationship between Harrison and Charles was beyond strained, Victoria thought, and was truly broken. It saddened her.

With the others gone, only Victoria, Harrison and Emily joined Charles, Arabella and Margaret for dinner that evening.

'Where's James tonight?' asked Harrison.

'Oh, James rarely joins us for dinner in the big house. He's off doing whatever James does,' said Charles.

'James works very hard on the estate,' said Margaret. 'Night and day.'

'He'll be a big help to you running this place,' said Victoria. 'It'll be quite a responsibility minding all these tenants.'

'Not at all, Victoria,' said Charles sitting back arrogantly. 'I'm very much looking forward to taking over. I've a lot of ideas how the estate should be run in the future. We need to move with the times.'

'Father ran this place excellently,' said Harrison coolly.

'Of course he did! I'm not saying that. I'm just saying we're on the cusp of a new century. It's going to be the twentieth century in a few weeks and we need to enter the twentieth century like the rest of the world.' Charles looked at Victoria. 'You know what I mean, Victoria, being an American. Americans aren't frightened of the future.'

'Oh, I don't know, Charles. My country isn't perfect either. It's all about profit. I think the way of life is so perfect here. I hope you don't do anything to tamper with life on the estate too much,' she said, smiling hopefully.

He smiled back at her and nodded.

'You might think it's all very quaint here, Victoria,' said Arabella, smiling, 'but you don't have to put up with the plumbing that takes hours to heat up. I'm sure you don't have that in Newport.'

'True! But I think I could put up with a little faulty plumbing to have this beautiful countryside on my doorstep,' smiled Victoria.

'How are your parents, Arabella?' asked Harrison.

Arabella got a start, it was the first time he had addressed or looked at her since they had arrived and she found herself going red. 'Very well, thank you. Papa has retired now so he has more time on his hands to do whatever he wants.'

'Tell them I was enquiring after them – they were very kind to me,' said Harrison.

Arabella nodded and quickly continued with her soup.

Victoria leaned over and kissed Harrison and held his hand.

Charles stood at the drawing-room window, watching Harrison and Victoria frolic around their Mercedes Benz. He observed them intently: they seemed so blissfully happy together.

Arabella walked in and came up to him just in time to see the motor car drive off from the forecourt.

'Where are they going?' asked Arabella.

'Who knows? Off on one of their day sojourns again. Quite remarkable, a woman driving a motor car like that!'

'She seems quite a remarkable woman full stop,' said Arabella.

'You wanted to see me?' asked James, coming into the library where Charles was sitting at the desk.

'Yes, take a seat,' ordered Charles and James sat across the desk from him.

Charles sat back and observed his brother. 'I'm willing to forgive your despicable outburst in front of the family, but I'm warning you nothing like that must ever happen again.'

James looked at him defiantly. 'You know what I was saying was the truth.'

'I know no such thing! I know that you have been allowed to run around this estate as if you own it. And I'm now making myself very clear that you don't. You might be my brother, but you're also my employee and I will not be disrespected by you like you have done in the past. Do I make myself clear?'

James stared at Charles with hatred.

'Well?' Charles pushed.

James nodded.

'Good, and now we can get on with the running of this estate. There's going to be changes, and big changes. Father let the tenants run serious arrears. I'm not going to allow that in the future.'

'You can't get blood from a stone, Charles! If they don't have money to pay rents, then they don't have it!'

'They have money all right. They have money for drinking in the bars in Castlewest every night and those dances they are always having. You should know, James, you go to enough of them with your lady friend from the town.'

James looked at him with contempt and surprise.

'Oh, I don't care what you get up to in your private life. Although I have to say you're letting the side down with that riff-raff. I don't know what Mother would ever say if she knew.'

'That is none of your business!'

'No, but my business is running this estate as I want it run. And you will co-operate with me... I think we understand each other.' Charles finished talking and began to look through paperwork.

James sat glaring at him in anger.

Charles looked up at him. 'Don't you have any work to do?'

James stood up and stormed from the library. Victoria was coming down the stairs and nearly bumped into him.

'James, is everything all right?' she asked, seeing he was close to tears.

James didn't answer her but stormed out the front door.

CHAPTER 52

Emily reluctantly got out of the hansom cab in London and looked up at the house in Hanover Terrace. She climbed the steps to the front door and knocked loudly. A minute later the butler answered.

'Oh Lady Emily, we weren't expecting you,' he said, surprised.

'No, I didn't wire ahead. Has everything been all right here?' she asked.

'Yes, eh, fine, Lady Emily.'

'My trunk is in the cab if you can have the footmen get it?'

'Certainly.'

'Is Mr Fitzroy home?' she asked.

'Eh, yes, I'll just go and tell him you are here,' said the butler, rushing for the stairs.

'No need,' she said, taking off her coat and gloves and putting them on a side table. 'Just get my trunk.'

The butler reluctantly went to find the footmen.

As she slowly walked up the stairs she got the strong smell of something she didn't recognise and something she didn't like. She crossed over the corridor to the drawing room and opened the door.

The room was dimly lit as she walked in. There, stretched across the couch, was a half-naked Hugh smoking an opium pipe. On either side of Hugh on the couch were two half-naked women, one white and one black.

Emily got such a shock she could only stand and stare.

'I think you have a visitor,' said one of the women, nodding over at Emily.

Hugh opened his bleary eyes and looked over at his wife. 'Ah, you're back, are you?' he drawled.

Emily turned and ran from the room. She could hear the three of them laughing loudly as she ran all the way upstairs. Reaching her bedroom she locked the door, leaning against it, panting in distress. She could still hear their cackling laughter downstairs.

Arabella sat at her bedroom window looking out at the terraced gardens as Harrison and Victoria walked down the steps to them hand in hand. They seemed so much in love, she thought. Harrison was such an attentive, loving husband. But then she wasn't surprised – he had been such an attentive loving fiancée to her. Watching them together was a stark reminder of how her own marriage was so different. She was so used to the arguments and deceit in her own marriage, she forgot how it could be otherwise. As she watched them walk off to the lakes she couldn't help but feel jealous. What would her life be like if she had never been seduced by Charles? Would she be in this kind of a loving marriage with Harrison now? She reached forward and poured another glass of gin for herself from the bottle on her dressing table.

There was a knock on the door.

'Lady Armstrong, may I speak to you?' came a shrill Scottish voice from behind the door.

Arabella was still finding it strange to be addressed as Lady Armstrong.

She quickly hid the gin bottle and said, 'Come in!'

Miss Kilty, the latest governess, walked in.

'Lady Armstrong, I'm sorry to disturb you,' Miss Kilty began.

'Well, why disturb me then?' asked Arabella, not in the mood for another lecture from a governess.

'Well, I have to – it's about your children.'

'And here was me thinking it was about the weather,' Arabella said sarcastically.

'Prudence or Pierce did not show up for their lesson today – they've been missing all day,' informed Miss Kilty.

'Missing?' said Arabella, shocked.

'Well, when I say missing, I know where they are. They've run off to accompany Lord Charles

411

on estate business.'

'Oh, I see,' said Arabella, relaxing.

'I don't think that you do, Lady Armstrong! The child Prudence is running wild!'

Arabella looked out the window and saw Harrison and Victoria kissing. She turned around and said, 'I do see very clearly, Miss Kilty. I see a woman who is supposed to be in charge of my children and not keeping close guard on them.'

'But–'

'My children are highly sensitive, intelligent children–'

'I wouldn't go *that* far,' said Miss Kilty, looking around the room dismissively.

'And they need a governess with those qualities, which you obviously don't have. You can leave at the end of the week.'

Miss Kilty nodded. 'As you wish, my lady.'

'I do wish!'

Miss Kilty turned and left.

Arabella grabbed the bottle of gin, refilled her glass and drank it while looking out at Harrison and Victoria getting into a rowing boat and rowing out on the lake.

CHAPTER 53

Charles knocked on the door of his parents' bedroom.

'Come in!' said Margaret. Charles walked in and found Margaret writing at her bureau.

'So many letters to answer, so many kind words from friends of your father,' said Margaret, putting her fountain pen down.

'Yes, I can imagine,' said Charles, looking around the bedroom.

'Can I help you with anything, Charles?'

'I wanted to speak to you about your plans for the future.'

'Well, I've no immediate plans. All my plans revolved around Lawrence and my children. And now that Lawrence is gone and all my children married off, nearly, what is left for me to do?'

'I was thinking that you probably would like your own space,' said Charles.

'I don't think I quite understand?'

'Well, this room is traditionally always taken by Lord and Lady Armstrong,' he pointed out.

'Oh, I see, you want my bedroom, do you?' She looked cynically at him.

'Well, I thought, and it's just a thought, that you would like your independence.'

'In what way?'

'Hunter's Farm is such a pretty house, don't you think?'

'Yes, it's a lovely old Georgian house,' she agreed, thinking of the small manor house a couple of miles away.

'Did you ever think about moving into it?'

'Well, I hadn't actually, no. But you obviously have!'

'I think it might be for the best in the future. It would give you independence and, to be honest, your presence here at Armstrong House will always undermine Arabella's position here.'

'Arabella's position? It doesn't exist! She doesn't do anything!'

'Exactly. The staff and guests will always see you as Lady Armstrong and not her. So I think it's a good idea if you move to Hunter's Farm.'

Margaret's face was stern. 'I'm not saying it's not customary for the Dowager to be moved on once her husband has deceased, but I didn't expect to be given my marching orders quite so soon!'

'Well, it's not me, Mother. It's Arabella. Let's face it, the two of you don't get on – and two women who don't agree under the same roof...'

'So *she's* behind this, is she?'

'I think it's for the best, don't you?' He smiled sympathetically at her.

Arabella was in the small parlour when Margaret came marching in.

'I'll be gone by the end of the week, you'll be glad to know!' announced Margaret.

'Gone where?' Arabella shook her head in confusion.

'I'm going to live in Hunter's Farm as you requested,' said Margaret.

'I didn't request any such thing – it's the first I've heard of it,' said Arabella.

'Oh come on, Arabella, don't lie to me and insult my intelligence. You know, you're such an ambitious woman, nothing gets in your way. I think it was always your plan to be Lady Armstrong. I think you used Harrison all those years back to get in with the family and then snare Charles. And you've been waiting your moment all these years so you can take over here, and now

414

your opportunity has come.'

'Margaret, you're being ridiculous.'

'Am I indeed? Well, you're welcome to it all, Lady Armstrong. I'll be quite happy down in Hunter's Farm away from you. We'll see how long you last running a house like this, a responsibility which you're completely lacking in ability for.'

Arabella stood up angrily. 'Do you know something? I had nothing to do with this plan of yours to move to Hunter's Farm – but I think it's an excellent idea!'

Arabella walked past her out of the room and got a start when she came out as she found Victoria standing there. Arabella walked past her and up the stairs.

Arabella waited for Charles to come home and then confronted him in the drawing room.

'Your mother is under the impression I asked for her to move out!'

'I wonder where she got that impression from?'

'From you, of course, you idiot!'

'Well, I said nothing – you know how she likes to blame you for everything.'

'I put her straight – not that she believed me.'

'Oh it's all for the best! You don't want her here checking on us all the time, undermining us. We're Lord and Lady Armstrong now, and everyone had better get used to it.'

'If they don't I'm sure you'll make them so!'

Charles walked into the library and found Victoria there looking through books.

'Oh, I'm sorry,' she excused herself, standing up.

'Can I help you with anything?' he asked, smiling at her.

'No, I was trying to find out about the history of the house and the Armstrong family. I love family history and you have such an interesting one.' She closed the books and put them back on the shelves. 'I know this is your place of work, so I'll get out of your way.'

'No, please, don't leave on my account. Take as much time as you want,' Charles urged.

'Have you seen Harrison anywhere?'

'I passed him on the stairs earlier – he didn't stop to chat.' Charles looked disappointed.

She studied his face. 'You know I've only ever heard Harrison's side of the story of what happened all those years ago, but I think it wasn't as cut and dried as people make out.'

'Is anything ever?'

'Not in my experience, no. I think you loved Arabella very much, didn't you?'

Charles nodded appropriately.

'I know Harrison used to adore you before all that happened. He held you in such high esteem, perhaps that's why it hit so hard.'

'And I adored Harrison. He was my best friend as well as my brother. I'd do anything to get that friendship back.'

'Give him time, Charles.'

'How much time does he want? It's over ten years.'

'But he's been away all that time, nurturing and analysing the hurt caused. If he stayed here he would have had to have dealt with it.'

'I don't think he'll ever forgive me.'

416

'I think he will, I think in his heart he already has, but is afraid to show it. He's afraid to trust you again... I for one, Charles, am very glad you did what you did back then.'

'You are?' he said, shocked.

'Of course! If you hadn't done what you did you wouldn't have your wonderful children Prudence and Pierce ... and I wouldn't have Harrison.'

Charles smiled at her.

'Anyway, we should be gone soon and out of your hair, you'll be glad to know.'

'Oh no, I very much enjoy you being here,' he said earnestly. 'Please stay for however long you want. Could I ask a favour though?'

'Of course.'

'I want to buy a motor car, having seen yours. Could you give me the name of the place you got it from?'

'Yes, my grandfather arranged it for us to collect it in Cork. I'll contact them and arrange it for you. They are very pricey though.'

'No matter – the price doesn't matter.'

Harrison and Victoria were walking along the shingled beach at the lake, their arms around each other's waists.

Harrison was recounting tales of his childhood. 'Christmas was always so special at Armstrong House. We were one big happy family.'

'It sounds idyllic. It's all exactly as you described it.'

'I don't think so. The closeness we all had seems to be going quickly, if not gone.'

'Harrison, I was thinking, we don't have to return to the States, you know.'

'Well, what else would we do?'

'We could stay here.'

'In Armstrong House?' he said incredulously.

'Of course not, but we could get our own house here. Rent a place for now.'

'Have you lost your mind? What about our life in America?'

'What about it? It'll be there waiting for us if we decide to go back. We're wealthy – we can do anything we want, live anywhere we care to.'

Harrison stopped and looked at her. 'I don't think you're thinking straight.'

'I always think straight. And what I see here is a family in crisis. I heard James and Charles argue terribly last week. I heard Arabella and your mother argue the other day. Emily is obviously miserably unhappy with whatever is going on in her life. And the feud between you and Charles is so destructive.'

'We've actually managed to be very civil to each other under the circumstances,' Harrison pointed out.

'"Being civil" doesn't constitute a good relationship, Harrison.'

'It's the best we can have under the circumstances.'

'Circumstances that happened years ago. From what I see he's trying to hold out the hand of friendship to you desperately and you're ignoring it.'

'That's because I don't want it!'

'Harrison!' She lost patience. 'Has Lawrence's

death shown you nothing? Life is too short not to be friends with your family. Because of this feud with Charles you've missed all these years with your father and you'll never get them back now. Do you want to have regrets in the future that you didn't spend time now with your mother and family, when they so desperately need you?'

'I don't think they need me.'

'They do. It seems to me, this family started falling apart when you left for America. You're such a balanced person, Harrison, and this family needs a balanced person. If you walk away from them now, I don't know where this family will end up in the future.'

'You know your problem, Victoria? You think you can heal everything and everyone.'

'I healed you, didn't I?' she smiled at him.

'But my family is not your problem to heal.'

'Harrison – what's my name?'

He looked at her confused and answered, 'Victoria Van Hoevan.'

'No! My name is Victoria Armstrong, and this family is my family, and I want to know them and love them.'

'But – but – could you really live here?'

'Of course I could. I love the people, the scenery, the food. And it would be a wonderful base for us to travel around Europe which we always wanted to do.'

'I don't know...'

'Maybe there's another reason you don't want to stay here?'

'Like what?'

'Arabella? Maybe you still have feelings for her.

419

I can see how you fell in love with her in the first place.'

'Don't be ridiculous, she means nothing to me!'

'Good – glad to hear it! Then there's nothing stopping us from living here,' she said, smiling at him.

CHAPTER 54

Arabella was sitting in the drawing room reading to Pierce and Prudence as Charles read the newspaper when they heard the sound of a motor car.

'Are Harrison and Victoria back so soon?' asked Arabella.

'No, it's Papa's new motor car!' shrieked Prudence excitedly as both children went rushing out the door.

'What new motor car?' asked Arabella.

Charles put down the paper and went to the window. 'Oh yes, they've delivered it up from Cork.'

'You didn't say anything about getting a motor car,' said Arabella, alarmed, as her husband's expensive tastes seemed to have returned in full force since he had come into his estate.

'Didn't I?'

'Where did you get it from?'

'Victoria organised it all for me, and she managed to get me a discount into the bargain.'

'Did she indeed?' asked Arabella, as she joined

her husband and viewed the vehicle which the children were now climbing all over.

'It's a fine job.'

'But you don't even know how to drive the thing!'

'Victoria said she'd teach me.'

'Does the girl have no limitations?'

'Are you coming out to inspect it?' he said, heading to the door.

'No, I'll give it a miss,' said Arabella irritably.

Charles got into the driving seat of the motor car and Victoria sat beside him. Harrison sat into the back, stoney-faced.

'Now what do I do?' asked Charles, smiling.

Victoria gave him instructions and he followed them. Harrison went to wind up the handle in front of the car and then quickly got into the back again.

'That pedal is the accelerator for going forward and that one is for going back, and that's the brake,' instructed Victoria.

'Easy-peasy,' said Charles confidently as the motor car took off in a series of jerks. Suddenly the vehicle rushed forward at high speed.

'Take your foot off the accelerator!' screamed Victoria as the car sped across the forecourt.

'Which one is the accelerator?' shouted Charles.

'The left!' shouted Harrison.

'The right!' corrected Victoria.

The car continued at high speed as Charles desperately tried to gain control. The car suddenly shot through the opening in the wall and started bouncing down the steps to the first terraced garden.

'The brake! Pull the bloody brake!' screamed Harrison.

The car continued through the next opening at the end of the terrace and bounced down the steps there as well.

'We'll end up in the bloody lake!' screamed Harrison as the car made its way to the next opening.

Charles suddenly swerved the car into a large flower bed and it came to an abrupt halt on top of it.

The three of them sat in dazed silence for a while.

'Not as easy as it looks!' said Charles eventually.

Victoria looked at him and then burst out laughing. The two men looked at her and then they started laughing loudly as well.

That night the family sat around the dining table having dinner.

'Honestly, Charles, you need to be more careful,' warned Margaret. 'We don't want to lose two Lord Armstrongs in a matter of months.'

'I think Charles has the making of being an excellent driver,' Victoria reassured him.

'The motor car lodged on top of the flower bed indicates otherwise,' said Arabella, drinking her wine.

'All he needs is a bit of experience. He's an excellent horseman and that shows he'll be an excellent driver,' said Victoria.

'Hope springs eternal,' said Arabella.

Victoria looked over at Harrison and he nodded

to her.

'We've got a bit of news ourselves,' smiled Harrison. 'We're not going back to the States, not yet anyway.'

'What do you mean?' asked Margaret.

'We've decided to stay here. We're going to rent a house and live here, see how we like it,' said Victoria.

'I can't believe it!' said Margaret, thrilled, tears coming to her eyes. 'I'm getting my son back!' She jumped up and hugged Harrison tightly before hugging Victoria.

'Well, that is excellent news!' said Charles, getting up and kissing Victoria. 'Isn't it, Arabella?'

'Wonderful!' said Arabella, unsmiling.

Charles walked over to Harrison. 'Welcome home, brother!' He stretched his hand out to Harrison. Harrison glanced over at Victoria who nodded encouragingly at him. He took Charles' hand and shook it, smiling at him.

'Won't you miss New York and Rhode Island?' asked Arabella, concerned.

'Not really. I love it here. And it gives me the chance to really get to know you all, which is what I really wish for.'

'You know, I'm going to help you find a place to live. I know all the places around here that are available,' said Charles.

'Would you, Charles?' said Victoria appreciatively.

'I don't think you'll find anywhere that will match what you're used to in Newport,' said Arabella.

'Oh, we don't want something palatial. Just

something quaint. Maybe we should move into a little peasant's cottage,' laughed Victoria.

'I can't see it somehow,' said Arabella.

Charles drove along the road with Victoria beside him and Harrison in the back seat.

'Where are we going, Charles?' asked Victoria. They had already travelled fifteen miles from Armstrong House.

'Nearly there!' said Charles as he drove through a gateway of a large white house with tall windows.

'What do you think?' he asked, getting out of the car and leading them to the front door which he opened with a key.

Victoria walked quickly through the large airy bright house.

'It's wonderful!' she exclaimed as she walked to the back of the long drawing room which had French windows. 'Harrison, look!'

She opened the windows and walked out. There was a long garden that backed onto a beach.

'That's why the house got its name – Ocean's End,' explained Charles. 'It's been for rent for a while, and I thought it would be perfect for you.'

'Ocean's End – it is perfect, Charles,' said Victoria happily.

CHAPTER 55

The last Christmas of the century came and went and everyone was excited as the dawn of the new century approached. Charles decided to have a ball at the house to celebrate the new century, and on New Year's Eve the house was a flurry of activity as everyone prepared for the ball that night.

Arabella was being helped to change into a glittering sequined violet ball gown by her dresser. She was sitting at her dressing table putting on her earrings when Charles came out of the dressing room, fixing his gold cufflinks on his shirt.

'It's started to snow,' he said, looking out the window.

She stood up and turned around.

'You look very beautiful tonight, darling,' he complimented her.

'Thank you,' she smiled.

He came over and kissed her. She sighed and kissed him back. If only it could be like this all the time, she thought.

Charles was in his element. It was the first ball at the house since he became Lord Armstrong. He had instructed the staff that no expense was to be spared. Arabella nearly trembled when she heard Charles use that expression as she remembered how his past extravagance had left them penniless and destitute. He offered her his arm and they left the bedroom and walked down the corridor and down the staircase.

Fennell was busy instructing the staff who were running here and there.

They heard a motor car outside.

'It looks like Harrison and Victoria are the first to arrive,' said Charles.

'Punctual as ever,' said Arabella.

Fennell opened the door and a few seconds later Victoria and Harrison rushed in, shaking snow off themselves.

'Happy New Year, everybody!' said Victoria, taking off her cape and handing it to Fennell.

'The snow is coming down in buckets out there,' said Harrison, shaking the snow off his hair.

'Happy New Year, Arabella,' Victoria kissed her, 'and Charles,' and she kissed him warmly.

'What you need is hot whiskey. Fennell!' said Charles.

Fennell arrived carrying a tray full of tumblers of Jameson.

'That's twenty-year-old malt whiskey,' said Charles.

'We'll all be a century older in a few hours,' joked Harrison.

Margaret came down the stairs. 'Happy New Year, my darlings!' She kissed Harrison and Victoria.

The sound of carriages came from outside.

'Looks like they're all arriving,' said Arabella.

'Do you know Colonel Tommy Radford is coming tonight with his new bride?' said Margaret. 'I can't wait to see her.'

'Who is Tommy Radford?' asked Victoria.

'Well, my dear, he's this older bachelor with a long illustrious career in the army, mainly overseas in the colonies. He lives the other side of Castle-west. Well, he went off to the Boer War in South Africa and has arrived back with, I believe, a bride!'

'But he must be in his sixties!' said Charles.

'If he's a day! Took us all by surprise, I can tell you,' said Margaret.

'Quick! Stand to attention at the doors!' Fennell ordered the footmen as he opened the doors to let the first of the guests in.

It didn't take long for the downstairs of the house to be filled, as champagne and wine was circulated by the staff to the elegantly dressed guests.

'Lady Armstrong, Happy New Year!' said Tommy Radford, appearing at her side.

'Colonel Radford, I'm so glad you could come. Did you bring your wife?' asked Margaret, looking anxiously at the array of women close by.

'Yes, indeed. Marianne!' he called and a very pretty blonde woman who looked not yet thirty stepped forward.

'I'm pleased to meet you all!' said Marianne in her South African accent as she smiled pleasantly at the whole gathering of the Armstrong family.

'And you, my dear!' said Margaret, shocked at her youth.

'I've heard so much about your family, I feel as if I know you already,' said Marianne.

'Well, the Colonel is one of our oldest–' Margaret stopped as she became conscious of the thirty-year age-gap between the two, '–I mean, *dearest* friends.'

'I have to say, as much as I love being here, the weather is frightful! We don't get this back in the Transvaal!' said Marianne.

'I'm sure you don't get many things we have here in the Transvaal, isn't that right, Colonel?' smirked Charles.

After dinner was served the dancing started in the ballroom.

Arabella looked on as Victoria charmed the room, effortlessly mingling and interacting with the other guests. She watched a group of women surround Charles as he entertained them with some story.

Marianne came up to Arabella. 'I have to say you're a most fortunate woman, Lady Armstrong,' she said, her South African accent cutting above the music.

'Am I?' asked Arabella.

'Married to such a charming, handsome, fascinating man.'

'Hmmm, I have to remind myself of that every day.' Arabella took a drink of her wine.

Marianne was watching Charles carefully. 'I'm sure you have to fight off the women hanging around him?'

'No, they usually run away themselves once they get to know him.'

'You're so funny! Not at all the dour woman they paint you as!' laughed Marianne.

'Thank you!' Arabella gave her a sarcastic look.

'Lord Charles has offered to take me and the Colonel out in his motor car for a ride.'

'I bet he has! I would be very careful if I was you.'

'Why?' Marianne looked alarmed.

'Well, the first time he drove a motor car he nearly killed himself and his two passengers along with him.'

'Oh dear! Not to worry – I believe in living dangerously.'

Later, as Charles was dancing with Victoria, both of them laughing happily, Harrison found himself standing beside Arabella. 'Would you like to–?' he gestured to the dance floor.

'Oh, yes, all right,' she said and the two of them joined the dancing couples.

They danced awkwardly, keeping a distance between them.

'Charles knows how to put on a good show,' said Harrison.

'Charles always knows how to put on a good show,' said Arabella. 'Are you settling into the new house all right?'

'Oh, yes, we love it. Victoria especially. Charles was very good to find it for us.'

She looked at him and arched her eyebrow.

They danced for another while without saying anything.

'We haven't had much time to speak since I arrived back,' he said.

She smiled and nodded.

'Yes...' he said. 'The first time you came to Armstrong House was for a ball, remember?'

She looked at him. 'How could I forget? Gwyneth's debutante ball.'

And what an unexpected outcome that had,

they both added mentally.

'You haven't changed a bit,' he said.

'Oh come on, Harrison! Two children and twelve years later, and a marriage to Charles! I've changed.'

She fell into silence again as they continued to dance.

'So what do you think of Victoria?' he asked.

'She's spectacular, Harrison, in every way; everyone says it continuously. Congratulations.'

'I hope you and she can be friends,' he added.

'Do you really think we can?'

'Why wouldn't you?'

'Come on, Harrison. Everyone else might be able to play happy families, but I was never good at charades. What happened years ago – with you, me and Charles – it hangs over us like a thick fog.'

'Well, Charles seems intent on letting the past be the past.'

'And what about you, Harrison? Can you let bygones be bygones?'

'Yes, I can. And if I can do so, then you certainly can too.'

'You put on a good act, Harrison, but you forget I know you. You could never hide anything, and when I look at you I see the contempt you still have for me in your eyes.'

Harrison became annoyed. 'You don't know me any more, Arabella. I'm not that person who was engaged to you all those years ago. You don't see contempt for you in my eyes, you see change. Because I have changed. After you deserted me for Charles I was heartbroken for years. I was a recluse in New York, I never went out. I went to work and went back home and never talked to anybody. And then I met Victoria and she saved me from myself. You're flattering yourself if you think you see contempt in my eyes for you. Because you see nothing for you. You're not important to me any more – you haven't been for a long time. Victoria is the only thing important to me now. Now the rest of us are trying to get on and become a proper family again – are you going to come with us?'

She found his words strangely wounding, his hope slightly irritating, his love for Victoria somehow upsetting.

'Of course I'll be friends with you and Victoria. As you say, if you can forget the past then who am I, who did the injuring, to hold on to it. But a word of warning, Harrison, you might have changed, but Charles hasn't.'

The music came to a stop and Harrison let her go and smiled at her. 'Thank you for the dance, Arabella.'

And then he walked off and joined Victoria.

A blanket of snow was on the ground and it was still snowing lightly. Arabella had escaped the party and walked across the forecourt and stood at the top of the steps looking out at the hundreds of stars scattered in the night sky over the lake.

'I thought it was you,' said a voice behind her.

She turned and saw Victoria there wrapped up warmly in a fur coat. Arabella pulled her shawl closer around her.

'Oh – you smoke!' said Victoria, surprised at seeing Arabella with a cigarette.

'Not really, I just steal the odd one from Charles. He doesn't know, nobody does.'

'Your secret is safe with me,' smiled Victoria, standing beside her and the two women looked out at the still lake in the darkness.

Victoria glanced at her watch. 'Fifteen minutes to midnight. We'll soon be in a new century.'

'Yes, Charles has ordered in crates of champagne to be opened when the hour strikes.'

'I look forward to it,' smiled Victoria. 'It's so good that Charles and Harrison are getting on better, don't you think? They used to be so close growing up. If anything good came out of Lawrence passing away, it's that.'

Arabella glanced at Victoria. 'I suppose...You're very lucky with Harrison – he's a wonderful man.'

'Yes, I am, aren't I?'

'You'll always know where you are with Harrison. He'll never let you down or deceive you or do things behind your back.'

'I know,' said Victoria, studying Arabella as the snow continued to land on her soft dark hair. 'I think Charles is wonderful too.'

'Charles is all things to all people. Expect the unexpected with Charles.'

'That can be exciting too! He's a lot of fun, I think.'

'Too much fun sometimes.'

'Why are you saying that?'

'I'm just saying you and Harrison have been spending a lot of time with Charles and you shouldn't really rely on him, for your own sakes, because he does let people down.'

Victoria adopted a cautious tone. 'Arabella … it's not my place, but I think you should give Charles a bit of a break.'

'I'm sorry?'

'It's just, having stayed at Armstrong House this past while, I can't help but notice that you do seem to argue a lot.'

'I beg your pardon?'

'I just wonder if you relaxed a little bit, perhaps you'd get on a bit better.'

'You don't know anything about it, Victoria!'

'I'm not saying I do! But I do understand people. Charles is, from what I can see, spontaneous and adventurous. That can be exciting, but I'm sure as well for you it's caused stress in the past. But if you accept him for how he is, well, your marriage might improve a little.'

'And we could all live happily ever after like yourself and Harrison in wedded bliss.' Arabella's voice dripped sarcasm.

'I'm not saying that. But you two obviously loved each other hugely to do what you did all those years back. I'm just saying a love like that never dies.'

'Oh, a love like that never does die, Victoria. I am still madly in love with Charles, for your information. It's just living with him that causes me the problems.'

'Well, if it's that difficult, why don't you just leave?' Victoria was becoming exasperated.

'Oh, you really don't know anything, Victoria. Not all of us have millions in our bank account and the carefree attitude that you have. I will never leave Charles. Firstly, I love him too much.

433

Secondly, I've sacrificed far too much for that love. Thirdly, people don't leave their spouses in our circle. People get ruined when they do that and their lives, particularly those of the wives, are destroyed.'

'I wasn't suggesting in reality you do it! I was just pointing out that everyone always has options in life–'

'Victoria, my marriage might not look like love's young dream from where you're standing. But it's my marriage, and it's the most important thing in my life. So why don't you continue fixing Charles and Harrison's relationship, and leave my marriage alone?' Arabella threw her cigarette on the ground and stamped on it, before turning and walking back into the house.

'Three, two, one – Happy New Century!' shouted Charles in the ballroom and the room erupted in cheers as paper confetti and streamers shot around the room.

Victoria had just arrived back into the ballroom and she went straight over to Harrison.

'Happy New Year, darling,' she said as she kissed him. Across the ballroom she saw Arabella standing beside Charles. Charles was happily celebrating but Arabella looked lost in thought.

CHAPTER 56

Emily was driving home, alone in a hansom cab through the streets of London in the early hours of the century. Other carriages and cabs passed hers by with groups of jovial passengers inside.

She pulled her coat closer around her and shivered. She had been at a New Year's party with Hugh at the house of one of his friends. The party had been a spectacular display of extravagance which Hugh had much enjoyed, as ever thrilled to be amongst high society.

He had paraded her around the party proudly, saying to everyone, 'Have you met my wife, Lady Emily Armstrong? She's the sister of the Duchess of Battington – yes, *the* Duchess of Battington.'

She had cringed with each introduction, although she should be used to it by now. And as the night wore on and Hugh got more and more drunk and loud, she had cringed with more and more embarrassment.

She had overheard two people talking.

'Is she really a member of the Armstrong family, and Gwyneth Battington's sister?'

'Believe it or not, yes.'

'But what's she doing with *him?*'

'I know! It's very peculiar. I don't think the family approved.'

'Approved! I'm not surprised – he's grotesque!'

'I think she must have been a little disturbed in

the head to marry him.'

She had moved quickly away from the over-heard conversation, frightened of what else she might hear.

'Ah, there's my wife!' Hugh said, coming sway-ing over to her. 'Come on, Emily, let's dance!'

'No, Hugh! I really don't want to!' she objected.

'It doesn't matter what you want. It's what I want that matters – after all, I pay the bills.' He grabbed her and pulled her out on to the dance floor and pushed people out of the way as he took centre stage. Then he danced her around in a drunken clumsy way.

'Hugh, I really need to sit down!' she objected.

But her words only made him hold her tighter.

'Hugh, you're hurting me!'

Suddenly he fell to the floor, pulling her down with him and the two of them lay sprawled on the dance floor with everyone gasping and staring at them.

Hugh roared with laughter as tears of embar-rassment stung Emily's eyes. She went to try and stand up but he grabbed her to try and pull him-self up and only ended up sprawling on the floor again. Finally two men dashed over to her and helped her up as a third man helped Hugh to his feet.

'Well, he's certainly dragged her down – in every sense of the word! Her father would be so ashamed,' Emily overheard a matronly woman say as the men helped her to a chair.

Emily sat there, trying not to burst into tears, as she watched Hugh stumble around the dance floor, unconcerned at what had just happened.

She stood up and went to the footman of the house and asked for her cloak.

The footman called her a hansom cab and she got in, instructing the driver to take her to Hanover Terrace. This was nothing new for her. Most occasions that Hugh insisted they went to ended up with him making a fool of her and him, and her leaving early, alone, nursing her wounded pride.

She looked out and saw some revellers in the street and they shouted jovial greetings to her.

She turned her head, ignoring them.

'Why look so sad?' one shouted after her. 'It's 1900!'

All she could think of was another year of this imprisonment.

She let herself into the house at Hanover Terrace and, exhausted, climbed up the stairs to her bedroom. Locking the door after her, she fell into a disturbed sleep.

She was woken a couple of hours later by a crashing sound downstairs. She sat up in bed. There was another smashing sound. She knew Hugh had arrived home senselessly drunk like he often did and was just falling into furniture and breaking it.

She heard the footsteps come up the stairs and then there was silence. Then there was a knock on the door.

'Emily? Lady Emily?' Hugh called from the other side of the door.

Emily huddled on the bed as Hugh then tried the door handle. Finding the door was locked, he started incessantly turning the doorknob.

'Emily, it's your husband, let me in,' demanded Hugh.

Emily sat shivering and not moving.

'Emily!' he started shouting as he banged at the door.

She wiped away tears as the banging echoed through her head. 'I won't leave till you let me in!' he shouted.

The banging suddenly stopped and there was a loud thud outside the door. Emily realised he had passed out. She finally lay down on her bed again and tried to get to sleep, but sleep would not come.

CHAPTER 57

Margaret moved out to Hunter's Farm without any fuss. In a way Arabella was relieved she was not there any more. She did tire of Margaret's constant criticisms and put-downs. Having said that, Margaret came and went from Armstrong House as she pleased as it was only down the road, often arriving for dinner or lunch.

Arabella realised she should be delighted at being Lady Armstrong and this beautiful house was now hers fully and freely. But she never realised the work entailed in running such a large country house. Margaret had done it like everything she did, so effortlessly. Arabella was constantly being asked for a decision, a choice, an opinion.

As predicted, Fennell the butler had married the assistant cook from the kitchen, and the new Mrs Fennell had been elevated to chief cook when the old one retired. Now, sitting in the drawing room with Arabella, Mrs Fennell had her notebook and pen and was going through the coming week's set of menus.

'What about lunch on Thursday, my lady?'

'Em, chicken,' said Arabella.

'But I thought we had agreed on chicken for Tuesday?'

'Oh, yes – turkey then.'

'Sure you won't get a turkey this time of year, my lady. They'll all be gone so soon after Christmas.'

'Well, roast beef then,' said Arabella.

'Roast beef for lunch?' Mrs Fennell raised a sceptical eyebrow. 'Only on a Sunday, surely, my lady?'

Arabella raised her eyes to heaven. 'Well, what do you suggest then?'

'Oh, it's not my place to be suggesting anything, my lady.'

'Why not? You're the cook.'

'Well, I can't take responsibility if it displeases his lordship or his guests. I mean, I think rabbit is lovely and could put it on the menu, but it's not to everyone's taste, so I can't take that responsibility. I remember we served rabbit once at one of Lord Lawrence's dinner parties, may he rest with the angels, and next thing one of the guests, a lady from Tipperary, threw up all over the place. It took two weeks to get the stains out of the carpet!'

'Our French chef in London used to prepare all the menus and all I or His Lordship had to do was approve them.'

'Well, this isn't London and I'm not a French chef, I'm glad to say.'

Arabella sighed. 'Let's leave the lunches for now and concentrate on dinners,' she suggested. 'Trout for dinner, Monday night, is that all right?'

'Perfect, my lady. And Tuesday?'

'Steak.'

Mrs Fennell gave her a concerned look. 'But I thought the Seymours were coming to dinner on Tuesday night.'

'Are they?' Arabella couldn't remember.

'Yes, and Mr Seymour doesn't like steak – remember, ever since he got that food poisoning...'

Arabella rubbed her temples. 'Mrs Fennell! I've a headache coming on – we're going to have to go through all this later.'

'But I need to discuss with you what produce you want from the gardens for the week, and the staff meals for the week, the stable boys' food requirements and what you want the children to have during the week. Lady Prudence has taken a dislike to porridge. Which guests are coming each day? Are Mr Harrison and his wife, the American, attending? Will Lady Margaret be here? And what food is to be ordered from the shops. Not to mention the liquor – we're very down on gin,' Mrs Fennell gave her an accusing look.

'Mrs Fennell!' asserted Arabella. 'My headache has to take precedence! Please come and see me tomorrow about all this, and we'll just have to make do today.'

'Make do!' Mrs Fennell was aghast.

'Yes – make do!' confirmed Arabella.

'Very well, my lady,' said Mrs Fennell, closing her notebook and standing up. As Mrs Fennell left the room she met the housekeeper waiting to go in.

'Good luck with that one!' Mrs Fennell tutted.

'Good day, my lady,' said the housekeeper on entering the room. 'I have a full agenda to talk to you about today. Will we begin with the linen in the servants' quarters?'

Arabella sighed heavily as the housekeeper began her litany of things needing to be done. She had already put the housekeeper off from the previous week, so she knew she couldn't use a headache as an excuse again.

At that moment there was a knock on the door and three workmen from the estate walked in, holding hammers and chisels. 'Can I help you?' asked Arabella.

'No, my lady, we'll try to make as little noise and mess as possible,' said the foreman as they walked past her to the gable wall and started taking the curtains down from the window there and measuring up around it.

'What are you doing?' asked Arabella.

The foreman turned, surprised. 'His lordship wants a French window put in here.'

'A French window?'

'Yes, and a balustrade terrace outside.'

'Whatever for?'

'He says so his guests can enjoy their cocktails out on the terrace on a summer's evening,' said the foreman as they started hammering the stone-

441

work around the window.

Arabella got up quickly and left the room as the hammering sound rattled around her head.

'What about the cleaning order?' called the housekeeper after her.

CHAPTER 58

Marianne Radford dominated the dinner table with her clipped South African accent and her theatrical gestures.

'I so love your house. Of course back in South Africa my family had a beautiful ranch house and thousands of acres of farmland. That, of course, was before the Boer War started. One minute we were having tea on the veranda and the next thing we were being fired on! If I hadn't got out in time I would have been rounded up and put in one of the concentration camps along with the rest of the women and children,' said Marianne, not looking at all upset at the thought.

'How awful! I believe what's going on there is horrendous,' said Arabella.

'We Boers are being treated atrociously... But then I met Tommy and he came to my rescue like a knight in shining armour,' she said, leaning forward and tickling Tommy under the chin.

'That was lucky,' said Charles.

'It certainly was! He organised me and my family to be evacuated from South Africa on the first liner we could get on from Cape Town. Didn't you, dinkidums?' She tickled him under the chin again.

'Eight people in all. I had to pull a lot of strings,' said Tommy.

'And did you then get married when you got here?' Arabella asked.

'No, before we left South Africa,' said Marianne.

'He made sure the deal was done before he got her out of the country,' Charles whispered to Victoria, causing her to stifle a laugh.

'And so here we are back living in your delightful colony,' said Marianne, smiling.

'It's not a colony, sweetheart,' said Tommy. 'It's a country, part of the United Kingdom.'

'But for how long?' said Arabella. 'It may be independent soon by the sound of things.'

'There will be a war first if they try to get independence,' said Charles.

'Oh, please, not another colonial war! I couldn't bear it,' said Marianne.

'I shouldn't worry – we Irish are great at talking about these things, but they never come to pass,' said Arabella.

'Yes, the Irish do like to talk,' confirmed Marianne. 'Our neighbour back in South Africa was married to an Irishwoman. We used to call her Irish Kitty. Of course the poor woman became a raving alcoholic and then she just became known as Whiskey Kitty!'

Charles was going through the rent books in the library while James sat opposite him sullenly.

'This is unbelievable,' complained Charles. 'There are more rents in arrears this year than last when Father was alive and running the show!'

'I know,' said James.

'Well, they can't blame bad harvests this year. It's good weather this year.'

James shrugged. 'In the overall scheme of things, the majority of farmers are up to date with their payments and only a small number are in arrears,' he said.

Charles closed the rent books angrily. 'They're making fools of us! I'm sick and tired of them!'

'If you don't mind me saying so, I think some of the farmers are sick and tired of you!'

'With me? But I never go near them or interfere with them – why would they be annoyed with me?'

'Exactly! You show no interest in them or their lives.'

Charles sat back arrogantly in his chair. 'So what am I to do? Visit their hovels and pretend to enjoy their horrendous cooking while their brats paw me with dirty hands?'

'Yes, if that's what it takes to build up a rapport with them,' urged James.

'I have no interest in building a rapport with them or indulging them.'

'Also giving the poachers to the police that time, well, it put you in a very bad light.'

'I really don't know what's wrong with this country! When a man can't protect his own fishing rights and expect a normal business arrangement and have payments on time with his tenants without having to listen to their maudlin stories and tales of woe!'

James sighed heavily. 'Yes, they resent paying

over the rents because they see it as their land that we stole from them in the first place.'

'Our ancestors were given the land by the Crown – we didn't steal anything from the fools! Besides, I can't run my business based on healing imagined historic woes that happened long before I was born and have nothing to do with me. I need the estate to run on a profit–'

'To fund your extravagant parties and lifestyle?' James mocked.

'To fund anything I want with, as it's my money!' retorted Charles. 'No – no, I'm not going to let it continue. I think the tenants are taking advantage of Father not being here any more.' He picked up one of the rent books. 'This family, Mulrooney, they are six months in arrears. We'll tell them they have to settle up immediately. I'm running a business not a charity.'

Charles drove the motor car through the estate quickly with James sitting beside him holding on for dear life.

Charles turned into the gateway and down a long dirt track before pulling up abruptly outside the cottage sending hens and geese flying in all directions.

A woman and a man came out of the front door as Charles hopped out of the motor car, followed by James.

'Ah, is it yourself, Lord Armstrong?' said Jack Mulrooney.

'Yes, who else would it be?' said Charles. He found what he saw as the farmer's insincerity irritating.

'We're very honoured having a visit from you – I'm Maureen Mulrooney,' said the woman with a small curtsy.

'Have you come to see the sick calves?' Jack's face was creased with tension.

'No, I'm afraid I don't have any time to see sick calves. What I'm here for is to discuss the arrears on your rent,' said Charles.

'Sure we can't sleep at night worried about it,' said Maureen. 'Won't ye come in for some tea and scones to talk about it?'

'I really don't have time, thank you all the same. James! How much is in arrears?' snapped Charles.

'Five pounds and four shillings,' said James uncomfortably.

'Five pounds and four shillings. We'll give you three months to pay the arrears, I think that's reasonable enough,' said Charles.

Maureen and Jack looked at each other in profound worry. 'But sure we'll never have that paid in that time. Not now the calves are sick and we can't bring them to market.'

Charles looked around. 'You have chickens and geese and sheep. Sell what you can and raise the money.'

'But, your lordship, that will never raise that much money!'

'Look, I feel sorry for your predicament, I really do. But it's really nothing to do with me. I rent you land and this house and that's where my interest stops,' said Charles.

Jack turned to James who remained speechless and appealed to him. 'Master James!'

'Master James doesn't have a say. He's not Lord Armstrong, I am. Good day to you.' Charles turned and jumped into his car. 'James – are you coming with me or do you want to walk back?'

James reluctantly turned around and sat into the car, tight-lipped.

'That's how you do it, no nonsense. They'll respect us all the more for it,' said Charles as he avoided a hole in the road.

That night James sat on the couch before a roaring fire in his farmhouse on the estate. It was well after eleven o'clock and he was getting worried. Suddenly there was a knock on the door and he went and opened it. Dolly Cassidy walked in and they embraced and kissed.

'What took you so long? I thought you said you were finishing early,' he said as he led her over to the couch.

'We had a bit of trouble in the bar I needed to sort out.'

Dolly Cassidy had grown up in that pub and there was no situation she couldn't handle in it. He never had to worry about her. 'Are you hungry?' he asked.

'No, I had some stew earlier on.' She took off her shawl and he put his arms around her. 'I'll have a drop of wine though.'

The ticking clock struck midnight as James and Dolly lay out on the couch in each other's arms and the fire began to die.

'What's wrong, love? You've been quiet all night,' she said.

'It's just Charles.'

'What's the bastard done now?' she asked, her face turning sour at the mention of his name.

'He's told Jack Mulrooney and his wife they've three months to pay their arrears,' said James.

Dolly sat up quickly and stared at him. 'What? But sure they'll never get them arrears paid in that time.'

'I know. I don't know what they'll do.'

Dolly smiled. 'The bastard wouldn't dare evict them. He wouldn't dare!'

'You don't know Charles – he does whatever he wants and he doesn't care what people think.'

'But – he wouldn't risk what could develop from an eviction... And can you not have a word with him?'

'I'm the last person he'll listen to. He expects me to follow his commands without question. They're having a garden party next month and he's ordered me to go.'

'You – at a garden party!' She stifled giggles.

'I know. He wants to control me like he controls everyone else,' James said angrily, staring into the fire.

She cuddled up to him. 'Well, don't worry about it, love. I'm sure it'll be all right.'

CHAPTER 59

Charles parked the car outside the Radfords' house and Marianne and the Colonel came out.

'I'm so excited! I've bought a new hat for the occasion – I'm so looking forward to this drive!' said Marianne as she sat up in the front of the car beside Charles.

'Sit in the back, Tommy,' she instructed.

Tommy looked sceptically at the motor car. 'Actually, I think I'll give it a miss. It looks a little bit unstable to me.'

'Quite stable, rest assured, Tommy!' said Charles, smiling at Marianne.

'No, I'm not going,' said the Colonel.

'But I've bought a new hat for it!' Marianne was devastated.

'You youngsters go off. I'll stay behind.'

'Are you sure?' asked Marianne.

'Yes, you head off.'

'Oh, thank you, dinkidums, we won't be long. Come along, Lord Armstrong, giddy-up!'

'Oh stop, stop!' begged Marianne as the motor car jumped along an uneven road.

Charles pulled over. 'What's wrong?'

'I'm afraid I'm feeling a little seasick!'

'But we're not on water.'

'Well, road-sick then! Oh, that's better,' she said, loosening the collar on her blouse and undoing the first button. 'It's so warm today,' she said, fanning herself with her hat.

'Isn't it?' He sat back and smiled at her.

'You drive the motor car most masterfully. I imagine you do everything masterfully.'

'I try to!'

'I was telling your wife how lucky she was in having you.'

'Did she agree with you?' he smirked at her.

'I don't know. She talks in riddles.'

'She must have been drunk. She likes to drink.'

'You poor man. I know with Tommy what it's like to live with a drinker.' She patted her face.

'Yes, I remember we used to call him Gin and Tommy!' Charles laughed.

'Oh, don't get me wrong, I adore him! He rescued me from certain imprisonment in a concentration camp back home. I'll always be grateful to him... But he's so old!'

'Didn't you realise how old he was when you married him?'

'I suppose I was carried away by the heat, dust and drama of the Boer War when I married him. He was a safe haven in very choppy seas.'

'We've all been there!' said Charles.

'Of course I could never have an affair,' she declared.

'No?'

'It would break his heart if he found out.'

Charles leaned forward and began to further unbutton her blouse. 'Who said anything about him finding out?'

'My sentiments exactly,' said Marianne as she lunged towards Charles and kissed him.

Charles was walking down the busy main street in Castlewest, holding Prudence and Pierce by the hands. People smiled and nodded to them as they passed.

'Good afternoon, Lord Armstrong,' said some.

Charles never had an affinity with the locals. He always viewed them as so foreign to him. But since Lawrence had revealed that his true grandfather had been a local, Charles' feelings towards them had intensified to utter disdain. He remembered his grandmother Lady Anna so well growing up. She had been such a graceful and dignified lady and he wondered over and over again what had driven her into the arms of a peasant. Whatever had possessed her to even contemplate such a thing? The knowledge of what she'd done gnawed away at him.

'Papa,' said Prudence, 'may we please not have to go back to the house this afternoon for classes and stay with you instead?'

'You've already missed the morning classes, Prudence, so no,' said Charles.

'But the new governess is so stupid! She didn't even know who the Tsar of Russia was yesterday.'

'Did you enlighten her?' He smiled down at his precocious daughter.

'Of course I did.'

'Good girl.' He patted her head.

'I wish Mama could order a right governess,' said Pierce.

'You mother does seem incapable of ordering anything correctly … except gin,' said Charles.

'Please, Papa, we don't want to go back to the

451

schoolroom today,' said Pierce.

Charles had planned a rendezvous with Mari-anne Radford later in the afternoon so it was impossible to meet their request.

'Sorry, children, not today. Anyway, it won't be long until Pierce is finished with governesses. He'll be off to school in England in a couple of years.'

'Why can't he go to the school here in Castle-west?' said Prudence. 'In that way he won't have to leave us, and he can come home every evening like the local children do.'

'Now, listen to me carefully, children – you must never forget as you go through life that we are not the same as the locals in any way. They have their world and we have ours.'

'Yes, Papa,' they both said together as they reached the motor car and climbed in the front with him.

'I'll tell you what,' said Charles, ruffling Pierce's brown hair. 'Sneak out tomorrow after breakfast, and you can spend the day with me then. We'll go fishing and shooting.'

'Oh, thank you, Papa!' they both said together happily. They adored being in Charles' company. He had no restrictions or rules and let them do whatever they wanted.

Charles suddenly spotted Victoria walking down the street and shouted, 'Victoria!'

'Hello there!' said Victoria, crossing over the street to them.

'Out doing some shopping?' asked Charles, spotting her full basket.

'Yes, just getting some supplies. Hello, Prudence

– hello, Pierce!'

The two children stared back at her without saying anything.

'Where's Harrison?' asked Charles, looking around.

'He's coming in to collect me later. But I finished earlier than I expected.'

'We'll give you a lift home, in that case,' offered Charles.

'Are you sure?' asked Victoria.

'Of course – children, get in the back seat and let your aunt sit up front.' Prudence reluctantly got into the back, glaring at Victoria as she sat up beside Charles and the motor car took off.

Arabella went into Prudence's room to say goodnight.

'Mama, do we *have* to like Aunt Victoria?' asked Prudence as Arabella kissed her.

'No, you don't have to like anybody you don't want to. Why?'

'It's just that Papa says we have to like Aunt Victoria.'

'Did he indeed? Well, you don't. Besides, she's not even your proper aunt, only by marriage.'

Prudence smiled happily. 'Good, then I think I'll choose not to like her.'

'Any particular reason?'

'I don't like the way she takes all Papa's attention from us.'

'Does she?'

'Yes, like today, we met her in town and she forced me and Pierce to sit in the back of the motor car so she could sit beside Papa.'

'And where were you bringing her?' Arabella sat down on the bed.

'We were giving her a lift home. And then she invited Papa in to look at some painting she had bought and me and Pierce were stuck in the car for ages waiting for Papa to return. I think she's selfish.'

'And ... and was your uncle Harrison at home in the house at the time?'

'No, he'd gone shooting, she said.'

Arabella quickly smiled at her and bent to kiss her. 'Go straight to sleep, there's a good girl.'

CHAPTER 60

Fennell walked around the tables that were arranged along the first terraced garden for the garden party, and covered with white linen table-cloths that fell to the ground. On each a silver tea service glistened in the sun.

Arabella came down the steps dressed in white and holding a white lace parasol.

'It's a lovely day for the garden party, your ladyship,' Fennell said.

She agreed it was as she stood looking out at the glistening blue lake stretched out before them.

Charles came down the steps, dressed in white flannel trousers and a striped blazer.

'We're all set, Fennell?' he asked.

'I think we can safely say we are, sir,' said the butler.

'What lovely weather! It reminds me so of South Africa,' said Marianne, kissing Charles on the cheek. 'Now, remember, Charles, you promised to partner me in tennis today. You don't mind, Lady Armstrong, if I steal him?'

'Be my guest, I never play tennis anyway,' said Arabella.

'Yes, so I heard.' Marianne gave her a dismissive look as she linked Charles' arm and led him over to the tennis courts. Victoria and Harrison arrived shortly after.

'Sorry we're late,' said Victoria, kissing Arabella's cheek. 'Our motor car had a puncture.'

'That's not a worry you'd ever have if you stuck with horses,' said Arabella.

'Carriages get punctures too, Arabella,' Victoria pointed out, tired of the fact that Arabella always had an answer for everything.

'Victoria, you're looking lovely today, as ever,' greeted Charles, hurrying over and welcoming them warmly. Putting his arms around both Harrison and Victoria, he led them away from Arabella. 'I need your advice on something. What do you think about investing in stock of an automobile manufacturer? I think, given another ten years everyone will be driving motor cars in Ireland.'

James walked around uncomfortably at the garden party, smiling and nodding to people. He took a cup of tea and walked off to the next flight of steps and went down to the next terraced garden which was quieter. He stood drinking his tea while looking out to the lake.

Victoria spotted him and, taking her own cup of tea, went down the steps to join him. She passed Prudence, Pierce and the other children playing a game.

'It's unusual to find you at one of Charles' do's,' she commented to James, smiling.

He looked at her and grimaced. 'I'm under orders. Charles insisted I came.'

'You don't usually obey Charles' orders, do you?' she asked.

'I used not, but now he's Lord Armstrong he's our lord and master, don't you know?'

She smiled sympathetically at him. 'Are we really so bad to spend a few hours with?'

'Oh, not you, Victoria!' He shook his head. He'd had many conversations with her since she arrived and found her nice to a fault. 'Just the rest of them are a pain in the behind.'

'You're very different from Charles – he lives for these parties and events.'

'That's because he loves everyone saying what a great man and host he is,' said James.

'I'm surprised one of these young women haven't whisked you off down the aisle yet,' she commented.

He jerked his head towards the party. 'One of this lot? You must be joking. I wouldn't be able to stick them and they wouldn't be able to stick me!'

They put down their teacups and walked along the pathways into the gardens.

'Everyone says how hard you work on the estate all the time, but you don't want life to pass you by as you're busy sorting out tenants' squabbles,' she said.

'I love my work on the estate,' he said.

'Well, as long as you're happy, that's the main thing I always think.'

'Oh,' he smiled, 'I am, most of the time.' He looked at his watch. 'I wonder, if I crept away would anyone miss me?'

'Have you something urgent on?' She noticed something in the expression on his face. 'My gosh, James, you have someone, don't you? Who is she?'

He went red with embarrassment. 'Nobody – you don't know her.'

She found herself getting excited. 'Oh, go on, tell me, James. I won't tell anyone.'

He sat down on the side of a fountain. 'It's nothing that serious. We've known each other for a long time though.'

'So, why can't we all meet her?'

'She's not one of us. She's from the town.'

'Oh!' Victoria nodded.

'She runs Cassidy's bar in the town ... her family are the Cassidys ... I've known her since we were kids. There's nothing permanent in it. Neither of us expect something permanent or want it from each other. But we get on really well, do you know what I mean?'

'I do, yes.' She sat down beside him and put her arm around him.

'And none of your families know?'

'No. I think Charles suspects something, but he doesn't know who she is,' said James.

'And what are you going to do about this situation?'

He started laughing. 'Nothing, Victoria. Sure there's nothing to be done. We'll just enjoy being with each other until she gets married or I get married.'

'And then say goodbye to each other?' Victoria was aghast. 'Oh, James, you can't let that happen. I mean if you've found somebody who truly makes you happy, then you should do something about it.'

'Victoria, are you out of your mind? Dolly Cassidy, much as I like her, is a publican in town; I'm an Armstrong. It would never be accepted, and to be honest, I'm glad. Things are the way they are for a reason. Look what happened to Emily! Dolly would never be accepted by this world, and in the meantime her own world would turn on her. I mean, Dolly isn't even from one of these Catholic professional doctor or solicitor families that are taking over the country. She's a local girl, through and through.'

Victoria frowned in confusion. 'So why don't you just leave each other then and find somebody else?'

He smiled at her lamely. 'Because neither of us wants to, or are sure if we're able to – for now.'

Arabella sat drinking tea and chatting amicably to the guests. But Marianne Radford, who was playing mixed doubles and partnering Charles, kept distracting her by constantly screaming and grunting as she played tennis.

'One for the Boers!' Marianne would scream every time she smashed a victory ball to the other side of the court.

Arabella observed her husband playing with Marianne and spotted something. She wasn't sure what, but there was a camaraderie that stretched beyond partners in tennis as they went up to each other and whispered something occasionally.

The Colonel had fallen asleep in his chair under the sun and suddenly Marianne was nowhere to be seen. Arabella scanned the crowd but was unable to spot her. She saw Charles hoof it up the steps from the garden and go into the house.

Arabella chatted away for another half an hour to the guests, but there was no sign of Charles reappearing. Concerned, she excused herself and walked up the steps and into the house. Fennell was rushing through the hallway with another full teapot.

'Fennell, did you see Lord Armstrong?'

'I'm afraid not, your ladyship,' he said, continuing on outside.

She checked the rooms downstairs and there was no sign of him and then she went upstairs. Going into the bedroom, she saw he wasn't there either and neither was he in the bathroom or dressing room of the bedroom. As she left the bedroom, she heard a woman's giggle down the corridor. She went down the hallway to where she could hear whispers and giggles coming from the Blue Room. She went and stood outside the door and listened. Then she bent down and looked through the keyhole. She saw Charles and Marianne cavorting naked on the bed. She stood up quickly, her heart beating fast. She leaned against the wall as tears sprang to her eyes. And then as she felt anger she reached forward for the door handle and then stopped herself. She thought for a while as the groans continued to come from inside the room. Then she hurried down the corridor and down the stairs.

'Fennell – can you bring me the spare key for the Blue Room,' she ordered.

'Right away, my lady,' he said.

She paused before going outside and wiped away the tears stinging her eyes. She walked smiling across the forecourt and down to the garden party.

Fennell arrived a minute later. 'The key, my lady,' he said, handing her the key. Taking the key she went and sat in the vacant chair beside Tommy Radford and gently nudged his snoring frame awake.

'What – what – oh I must have fallen asleep, Lady Armstrong,' said Tommy, waking up.

She smiled at him and then bent forward and started to whisper in his ear. His face started to turn red with fury. She then handed him the key which he snatched from her and stormed off up to the house. Arabella sat back and drank from her cup of tea, watching the house.

Finally Tommy Radford came storming out of the house and over to his carriage, followed by Marianne calling, 'Dinkidums! Dinkidums!'

Arabella watched as Marianne jumped into the carriage beside him and Tommy whipped the horse and they sped off down the driveway.

Twenty minutes later Charles came sauntering out of the house and down to the garden party.

'Charles!' shrieked Victoria. 'Whatever happened to you?'

Charles was sporting a swelling eye that was coming up in a black-and-blue bruise.

'Nothing, I just walked into a door,' he said, quickly sitting down and taking a cup of tea.

Arabella looked at him with disdain and satisfaction.

'One for the Irish!' she said to herself under her breath.

That night Arabella lay out on their bed sobbing. Their marriage was often a war of words, but this affair he had been having wounded her so much it hurt. She had never regretted marrying Charles in spite of everything, but as she thought of Harrison happily married she did feel regretful of other destinies that had passed her by or that she had willingly thrown away. And this affair he had been having with that Boer bitch Marianne Radford demonstrated exactly what he thought of her and their marriage. And yet she would not let Charles know how much he had hurt her. She would not even let him know she knew about his affair. She remembered her mother's advice on her wedding night. To keep one step ahead of Charles, never trust him, never take her marriage for granted. Those words had saved her marriage thus far and they would continue to save it.

Prudence and Pierce came rushing into the room.

'Mama, what's wrong?' asked Prudence as she and Pierce climbed up on the bed and started cuddling her.

She couldn't stop crying and their comforting

461

words only seemed to make her sobbing worse. Eventually she sat up and held them close.

'I want you both to promise me something. Whatever you do in life, never fall in love. Never give your hearts to anyone, as it'll only cause you pain. Do you promise me?'

'We promise, Mama,' they both said together as they hugged her back tightly.

CHAPTER 61

Present Day

The dining room had been refurnished with authentic antiques to replicate the era for the filming taking place there. Kate stood on the sidelines beside the director looking at the actors and actresses who sat around the table in Edwardian clothes.

Kate whispered to Brian. 'I think Arabella wouldn't be so exuberant. Studying her photos she seemed much more cool and aloof.'

Brian ignored her.

Kate whispered again. 'And Charles would be much more charming. He never looked stern in his photos. That's the whole point of Charles – he acted charming and cordial, but was ruthless beneath.'

'Kate!' snapped Brian.

'What?'

'Who's directing this film?'

'You are but–'

'Then let me direct!'

Kate held up her hands and backed away from him.

Kate shut herself away in the library at Armstrong House as she continued to work through the stack of records there. She needed to find out who that car at the crime scene belonged to. She came across photos of what looked like an Edwardian garden party at the house. She studied the elegantly dressed people in the terraced garden, Armstrong House standing proudly in the background, and spotted Charles and Arabella amongst the people there. There were horse and carriages parked in the forecourt above the terraces belonging to the guests and parked off to the side she spotted a motor car. She took the magnifying glass she had been using on the photos and held the photo up to the light. Comparing it to the car in the crime-scene photo, she realised they could be the same.

As she looked at all the elegantly dressed Edwardians she said out loud, 'One of you owns that car. One of you guests was somehow involved that night and led Charles to his assassin.'

She wondered how she could track down the owner of the car. Using the magnifying glass she couldn't make out the vehicle's registration number. As she researched the history of cars she realised registrations had started that very year – 1903. She decided to make contact with the Royal Irish Motor Automobile Club in Dublin and visit their archives.

'It was quite an exciting year for motor cars in Ireland in 1903,' said the guide. 'The Gordon Bennet Race was held in Ireland that year. It had to be held in the United Kingdom as the UK had won it the previous year. Trouble was motor racing wasn't legal in the UK, so the government passed a special act making it legal in Ireland only to honour the UK's commitment, and the race was staged here.'

'I believe there was huge public concern over motor cars at the time,' said Kate.

'Oh yes, they were seen as dangerous playthings for the rich,' said the guide. 'You're researching for a film documentary?'

'That's right, I'm trying to find out who owned a particular car that year and wondered if I could get any clue here,' said Kate.

'There were so few people owning cars, you might be able to find something. Most owners were members of the Royal Irish Automobile Club and it was a very exclusive club,' he said as he led Kate to the archives.

The guide looked at his watch.

'You've been very kind, thank you,' said Kate. 'I don't want to take up any more of your time.'

'Right, I'll leave you to get on and hopefully find what you're looking for,' smiled the guide as he headed off to his next appointment.

Kate spent the afternoon looking through Motoring Annuals and Yearbooks from the early 1900s. She was delighted when she found the Motoring Annual for 1903. She carefully looked through it and came to the list of members. As she scanned down the list of names she tried to see if any name jumped out at her that she might recognise as connected to the Armstrongs or with addresses near Armstrong House.

'Victoria Van Hoevan,' she said out loud as she recognised the surname.

She had known Nico was very distantly related to the famously rich American Van Hoevan family. As she continued to look through the Yearbook there were many photographs from the Gordon Bennett race that year. She stopped at one and stared at it. It was a photo of a man and a woman smiling happily, their arms around each other, leaning against a car at the race. Underneath, the caption read: *Harrison Armstrong and his wife Victoria Van Hoevan Armstrong at the race, July 1903.*

So Charles' brother Harrison, who had given a statement in the police file and who had said he brought Charles to the hospital the night he was shot, was the relative married to the Van Hoevan who was the registered owner of a car.

She quickly opened her briefcase, took out the crime-scene photograph and compared it to the photo in the Yearbook.

'It's the same car,' she said as she looked at the photos and saw the car registration plates were the same.

The man from the association approached her. 'Any luck?' he asked.

'Yes, yes, I've found something very interesting, thank you. Could I get a photocopy of this item?'

The man went off to photocopy the photo from the races and Kate went to a computer he had

465

given her permission to use. She went on to the 1901 census online and put in Harrison and Victoria's name and found they were registered as living at Ocean's End in Mayo.

'They were living only a few miles from Armstrong House and owned the car Charles was shot in,' said Kate aloud.

BOOK FOUR

1901–1903

CHAPTER 62

Emily entered the house at Hanover Terrace and the butler closed the door behind her.

'Did you have a good day shopping, my lady?' he asked as she placed her parcels on the sideboard.

'Yes, thank you. Is Mr Fitzroy in?' she asked, taking off her coat and hat and handing them to him.

The butler looked uncomfortable. 'He's in the drawing room, my lady.'

She nodded and went to the stairs. As she walked up the stairs she steadied herself and then crossed the landing and went into the drawing room. She was immediately hit by a cloud of smoke. Hugh was stretched out on the couch smoking an opium pipe, the evening sky darkening outside the windows behind him.

'Oh, you're back, are you?' he drawled, his head in a daze from the opium.

She stared at him in disgust. She turned quickly and left the room.

Arabella was deeply hurt by Charles' betrayal with Marianne Radford, although she never confronted him on it or even mentioned her name again. Marianne and her unfortunate husband suddenly disappeared from their circle.

But Charles had crossed a line. Now she knew

he'd had an affair and it illustrated what he thought of their marriage and of her. From now on every woman became a threat to Arabella. Charles had always flirted and enjoyed women's attention and Arabella had never paid much heed to it. But now she suspected Charles' flirting was not as innocent as she had thought. As Armstrong House continued to host a swirl of social occasions, Arabella found herself becoming suspicious of every woman Charles engaged with. No matter how tired she was she made sure not to go to bed until the last woman had left the house.

As Arabella scrutinised Charles' behaviour from across crowded rooms, she saw that no woman got as much attention from him as Victoria. He swarmed around her like a bee around honey. Joking with her, laughing with her, having deep meaningful conversations with her. What's more she seemed to get on marvellously with him. But then Victoria seemed to get on marvellously with everyone.

Charles came into the bedroom after waving the last of his guests off and found Arabella at her dressing table combing her hair.

He sat down on the bed and then lay out flat. 'I have to say Harrison and Victoria were in great form tonight.'

'Aren't they always? Wouldn't we all if we had millions of dollars and not a care in the world?' she said.

He sat up and, leaning on one elbow, looked at her scornfully. 'And what care in the world do *you* have?'

Mainly you, she thought bitterly but answered, 'I'm a mother, I've this house to run–'

'Ha!' He burst out laughing. 'Well, if you do, you make a very bad job of it.'

She turned to him furiously. 'I beg your pardon! I'm constantly meeting the heads of staff here.'

'Meeting them, yes, and doing nothing with them.'

'You're talking absolute nonsense, Charles!'

'Am I? Even poor little Prudence has started to take over your duties and directs the staff what to do, and she manages to do a better job of it than you!'

'Don't I attend all your do's and entertain your guests?' she defended herself.

'Oh yes, you attend all right, but you're not exactly the life and soul of the party any more, are you? You don't walk into a room and make heads turn like they used to when I met you first.'

'If they don't turn it's because years of marriage to you has changed me!'

'Everything seems to irritate you or annoy you. You take everything so seriously, except your duties as lady of this house. Why can't you be more like Victoria?'

His words were like a slap across her face.

'I mean, Victoria takes everything in her stride. She runs her house like clockwork, and she's not even from Ireland. She knows about business, runs her trust fund. She's so educated and socially comfortable with herself–'

'Yes, Harrison deserves the best because he is a

much better man than you!' Arabella retorted angrily.

Upstairs in the attic bedrooms Mrs Fennell was sitting at her desk, in her dressing gown, writing her diary.

'Come to bed, it's nearly one in the morning,' said Mr Fennell, waking up and seeing her by the oil lamp. 'Good gracious, what is that noise?'

'What do you think it is?' said Mrs Fennell. 'Only them two rowing again and nearly lifting the roof off the house. They've got even worse since Lady Margaret left.'

Victoria and Harrison were walking down the main street of Castlewest. It was ten o'clock at night and they were dressed up in their finery.

'Remind me again why we are doing this?' asked Harrison, sighing.

'We're doing it for your brother James. He has confided in me that he has some kind of a sweetheart that he feels none of us would accept. We're going to go into this bar that she owns and be perfectly nice to her and him – hopefully he'll be there – and let them know we don't see anything wrong in their relationship,' confirmed Victoria confidently.

'But we do see something wrong in the relationship! We've already seen Emily make a disastrous match, and we don't want James to go down the same road! It would kill poor Mother,' warned Harrison.

'Don't worry – both James and Dolly–'

'Dolly!' Harrison exclaimed in horror.

'–and *Dolly* are far too level-headed to contemplate marriage – that's what I got from the situation.'

As they reached Cassidy's Bar, Harrison shook his head. 'You know, I think Charles might be right for once – Father was too lenient on James. He did let him run too free. He doted on him a little too much.'

As they stepped into the bar, it was full of people drinking and being merry. Music was being played loudly and a fire blazed in the hearth.

'I can't see him, perhaps he's not here,' said Victoria, trying to see over the heads of the people.

'Oh he's here all right,' sighed Harrison, spotting his brother in the corner and pointing over at him.

'Oh, so he is!' Victoria was delighted as she began to cut through the crowd, smiling. 'Excuse me ... thank you ... excuse me, please...'

People stared at the bejewelled American and her well-tailored husband until they finally got to a wooden booth in the corner where James was sitting with a pretty woman of around thirty with big blue eyes and blonde shoulder-length hair.

'Harrison! Victoria! What are you doing here?' James was shocked at seeing them.

'We thought we'd come and join you – do you mind if we sit?' Victoria asked, smiling at the girl.

'Em, be my guests.' He was completely unnerved at seeing them.

'James,' nodded Harrison, sitting down, and then he nodded to the young woman politely.

The young woman had her arm around James's neck and was looking at Harrison and Victoria in

473

a bemused but unfriendly manner.

'And you must be Dolly?' said Victoria, stretching her hand across the table. 'I've been hearing all about you.'

'Have you?' She looked sceptically at James and then cautiously shook Victoria's hand before doing the same with Harrison.

'I'm–' began Harrison.

'I know who you are, I know who both of you are.' Dolly had a way of looking at people in a slightly mocking, slightly bemused way. 'What do you want to drink?'

'A red wine, please,' said Victoria.

'Seán!' screeched Dolly over the music to the barman. 'Bring over a red wine and a Guinness.'

'Right up, Dolly,' Seán shouted back.

'So what brings you in here?' asked James.

'We wanted to see where you spend time and meet your friends.' Victoria smiled at Dolly warmly.

'Well, you've seen it and you've met them,' said Dolly as Seán placed the stout and wine in front of them.

'How much is that?' asked Harrison, reaching for his wallet.

'It's on the house,' said Dolly.

'Thank you!' said Victoria. 'I believe you own the bar here.'

'Well, my parents do – I run it for them.'

'We've a lot in common,' smiled Victoria. 'I helped run my father's business as well.'

Dolly nodded to the diamonds and furs on Victoria. 'Your father's business obviously has better turnover than my father's.'

Victoria started laughing. 'Maybe, but your business looks like much more fun.'

'Your husband doesn't look as if he shares your opinion,' Dolly said, smiling at Harrison's uncomfortable facial expression.

Victoria kicked him under the table. 'He just loves it! You know, I've heard so much about these quaint Irish pubs and been dying to come into one.'

'So we're a circus now for Yanks, are we?' asked Dolly. 'To be stared at by you for your own amusement?'

Victoria nodded to a group of men who were staring at her and laughing amongst themselves. 'I think if anyone is the circus being stared at, it's me!'

Dolly leaned across James and shouted at them. 'What are ye staring at?'

The men quickly turned away.

'Sorry about that?' apologised Dolly. She looked down and saw Victoria's glass was nearly finished already.

'Seán!' she shouted. 'Another round of drinks!'

As the night wore on the drink flowed and everyone loosened up. Even Harrison looked as if he was enjoying himself, although he never let his guard down.

Victoria leaned across to Dolly. 'I'm really glad I met you.'

'You're not so bad yourself,' said Dolly, surprised that she had warmed to the millionairess wife of the local landlord's brother.

'It's been a pleasure meeting you,' said Victoria as they got up to go. 'I'd love if you and James joined us for dinner some evening, at our home.'

Dolly looked at Victoria, surprised, before looking at James and saying, 'We'll look forward to that.'

Harrison put his arm around Victoria as they walked down to the motor car.

'What exactly are you hoping to achieve by this?' asked Harrison curiously. 'James has always been different but I really don't know what he could see in a woman like that.'

'Harrison!' chided Victoria. 'You're as bad as your mother! I thought Dolly was delightful. Spirited.'

'But, having her to the house for dinner? Really! As much as I love you, Victoria, sometimes I think you'll never understand our ways.'

'Oh, I understand them all right, Harrison. I just choose not to lead my life by them.'

CHAPTER 63

Charles had summoned the family solicitor Mr Brompton to Armstrong House from Castlewest and they sat in the library talking with James.

'The situation is quite clear, Mr Brompton. I gave a number of tenant farmers an adequate amount of time to pay their arrears and they have not done it.'

'Can't do it! There's a difference!' snapped James.

'So what are you suggesting is to be done?'

476

asked Mr Brompton, who was a man in his sixties with round spectacles.

'I've given this considerable thought ... and I want them gone,' said Charles definitely.

'Gone?' asked Mr Brompton.

'Evicted, off the land, out of their houses – gone!' stated Charles.

'I see!' Mr Brompton looked surprised. 'The first thing then is to formally request they leave ... if they then refuse to go–'

'Which they will!' said James.

'–the next step is to get a court order and evict them forcibly, which as James says, is the most probable result.'

Charles nodded. 'Whatever course of action has to be taken.'

'Have you ever witnessed an eviction, Lord Armstrong?' asked Mr Brompton.

'Can't say as I have.'

'I have. It's a most pitiful sight. There's usually some degree of force used by the constabulary. The tenant farmers usually fight back, resulting in violence.'

'I'm aware of all this.'

'I'm just trying to point out to you the severity of the course of action you appear to be taking. The law is of course on your side, and you'll be working within the confines of that law. But the human cost of such an action is so great.'

'I've considered all that,' reaffirmed Charles.

'And you could be setting up a chain of events that who knows where it would lead to,' advised Mr Brompton.

'Hopefully it will lead to tenants paying on time

in the future!' said Charles.

'Even if you get those farmers evicted, you won't be able to re-let the land to someone else,' pointed out James. 'No other farmer will go and take land that another farmer was evicted from. There's huge solidarity there.'

'I don't need another farmer to take the land. I'm going to knock down the hedges between the farms and create huge new fields, like the American prairies, and we're going to go much more into cattle-rearing ourselves.'

'Most industrious!' said Mr Brompton, concerned by the whole proposal.

'This is the list of five farmers most in arrears who I want gone,' said Charles, handing over a sheet of paper to the solicitor.

'Very well. You appear to have made up your mind,' said Mr Brompton, tidying his paperwork into his case and standing up. 'I will do the letters for the farmers informing them their tenancies are terminated and to vacate their houses and land immediately. Good day, Lord Armstrong and James.'

Mr Brompton nodded to them and left.

James shook his head in dismay. 'I'm begging you not to go through with this, Charles. Father would never forgive you.'

'You heard what Brompton said, the law is behind me,' said Charles confidently.

'And who is going to hand these letters of tenancy termination to the farmers?' asked James.

'You are, of course!' said Charles.

James rode his horse into the Mulrooney farm.

The door of the house was open.

'Hello?' shouted James, jumping down from his horse.

A few seconds later Jack and Maureen Mulrooney came out of the house.

'Ah, Master James, how are you today?' asked Jack warmly.

'Not the best, Jack,' said James.

'I'm sorry to hear that, what's wrong?' asked Maureen.

James sighed loudly. 'Have you managed to raise the arrears on the rent?'

'No, I'm sorry. I'm sure if we're given just another few months we'll get them calves better and we'll be able to get the money then.'

'I'm afraid it's too late for that, Jack,' said James, handing over the termination notice.

'What's this?' said Maureen as Jack opened the envelope and read.

'You're kicking us out?' Jack looked up abruptly, shocked.

'I'm afraid so. I'm sorry, Jack,' said James.

'You're sorry!' exclaimed Jack.

'This must be a joke. There's never been an eviction on Armstrong land,' said Maureen.

'You're not the only ones. There are another four families being asked to leave.'

'But – but where will we go – what will we do?' said Maureen.

Jack suddenly tore the notice in half and shouted, 'I'll tell you where we'll be going – nowhere!'

Jack threw the torn notice back at James.

'Now, Jack–' appealed James.

'No! If that jumped-up fool thinks he can remove us from our home and our land, he's got another think coming,' shouted Jack. 'The Mulrooneys have paid for the value of this land over and over again with our rents this past century, and if you can't help us out a little in hard times – well, fuck you!'

'So you won't go peacefully?' asked James.

'We won't go at all!' shouted Jack.

James nodded and, sighing, got back on his horse and rode away.

Later James handed all the five notices back to Charles in the library, all torn in half by the respective tenants.

Pierce was playing with a train set beside Charles' desk.

'They're furious, Charles. They absolutely refuse to go.'

'As expected,' said Charles. 'Well, we have no option now but to go the legal route. I'll inform Brompton.'

'Charles!' shouted James, giving Pierce a start. 'Don't do this! Please!'

'You know your problem, James? You don't know where your priorities and your loyalties lie. Those people are nothing to us. They are merely peasants who are bad tenants.'

James turned and stormed out.

Pierce left his train set and came and sat on his father's knee.

'Why's Uncle James so mad, Papa?'

'Uncle James is a weak man, Pierce. One day you will be Lord Armstrong. Remember – never compromise. Never show weakness. Never show anyone weakness. In this life, you have to fight to the very end.'

'Yes, Papa.'

CHAPTER 64

Arabella sat in the drawing room one evening, discreetly observing Victoria and Charles interact. Harrison, Victoria and Margaret were also present. As ever Charles was focusing on Victoria and they chatted and joked amicably.

'Charles, is this true what James tells me? That you're evicting some tenants?' asked Harrison.

'I wish James wouldn't go around blabbing about estate business,' said Charles.

'Well, he's very concerned,' said Harrison. 'Is it true?'

'Yes, it is,' said Charles. 'I have to – they won't leave on their own accord.'

'But those families–' started Harrison.

'I know! I know! Have been here since Noah's ark! That's the problem with this country, it lives in the past!'

'But you're not going to forcibly remove them?' asked Harrison, shocked.

'I am, yes. I have to, the estate needs to run on a profit,' Charles defended himself.

'Charles, you can't do it! You can't put families out of their homes,' said Harrison.

'Why not? If they aren't paying for them any more?'

'But–' began Harrison.

'As I understand it, and as James explained it to me,' said Victoria, 'these people owe you money, Charles, and they can't keep up their payments?'

'Exactly,' said Charles.

'I'm sorry, Harrison, but I'm with Charles on this,' said Victoria.

'*What?*' Harrison was shocked.

'I mean, my father owns office blocks all around New York–'

'Don't we know!' said Arabella.

'And if the people who rent those offices can't pay their rent, then of course they must go! You don't stay in a place that you can't afford and expect the landlord to subsidise you!'

'Thank you, Victoria!' said Charles, smiling appreciatively at her.

'It's basic common sense and good business,' added Victoria.

'Victoria, there's a huge difference between the corporations your father rents to and these poor unfortunate families that are trying to get by,' said Harrison angrily.

'I don't see it that way,' said Victoria. 'Business is business, and everyone has to turn a profit.'

'Spoken like a true American!' said Arabella as she sipped her wine.

Victoria glanced at Arabella before continuing. 'Charles is making a very tough but obviously from his financial viewpoint *necessary* decision.'

'The Armstrong estate is not an American corporation, Victoria!' snapped Harrison angrily.

Victoria looked at Harrison evenly and spoke coolly. 'I'm aware of that, Harrison. Please don't speak to me as if I were a fool.'

'Trouble in paradise!' said Arabella under her breath.

'You know, Victoria, you're a very informed woman, but as has become painfully clear since we moved here, you're completely ignorant of the way things are done here in Ireland,' said Harrison.

'Oh, I'm aware how they're done all right! I just don't like the way they are done sometimes, that's all I'm saying,' said Victoria.

'Well, nobody is forcing you to stay!' said Arabella.

'And I *am* entitled to my opinion,' said Victoria.

Harrison turned to Margaret. 'Mother, have you nothing to say about all this?'

Margaret shrugged. 'Charles is Lord Armstrong, and he must run things here as he sees fit. That's the way it's always been, and I'll not undermine my son in his position in life, whatever my personal thoughts on the subject are.'

Harrison became even more angry. 'You know, Mother, you're always so by-the-book with doing things the right way. You always put family and tradition first. And you're deciding to sit on the fence with this because you think that, as Lord Armstrong, Charles cannot be undermined. But, ask yourself, is that the moral way? Would Father approve of what's going on?'

'Your father is no longer Lord Armstrong, Harrison, your brother is. We've no right to intervene or interfere.'

'Charles! Who'd ever have thought? You've nearly got a full room of approval for once in your life!' said Arabella.

Harrison turned to Arabella. 'And as Lady Armstrong, have you not an opinion on what your husband is doing?'

'Oh, I've plenty of opinions about it, Harrison, but I won't waste my breath expressing them – because it will do no good!'

Harrison looked around at them all. 'You know something – you all make me sick!'

He stood up and stormed out.

'Harrison! Harrison!' Victoria called after him, getting up quickly.

'Oh let him go, Victoria!' urged Charles. 'Harrison always likes to take the moral high ground with everything. Can be so boring actually!'

'I don't know what's wrong with him,' said Victoria. 'He doesn't have any right to dictate to you how you run your business, Charles, in the same way as you have no right to dictate to him.'

'And Charles does so love to dictate!' said Arabella.

'Arabella! If you've nothing constructive to say why don't you keep your mouth shut for once?' snapped Victoria. 'All you do is sit on your pedestal dishing out derogatory remarks all the time.'

'Excuse me, Victoria! But I will not be spoken to like that in my house!' said Arabella.

'Why not? Somebody needs to knock some sense into you!' said Victoria.

Arabella saw red. 'You sit there and–'

'Arabella!' snapped Charles. 'Victoria is our guest, please remember that, and we will be courteous to her at all times.'

Arabella stared at him. 'Oh, damn you, Charles!'

Arabella stood up and marched out of the room.

'Well, we're doing well tonight!' said Margaret. 'Two people storming out before I've even finished my pudding wine and we haven't even evicted a tenant yet!'

'I'm so sorry, Charles,' said Victoria. 'I shouldn't have spoken to Arabella like that. I was just upset over arguing with Harrison and took it out on her. I'll apologise tomorrow to her.'

'I shouldn't bother, dear,' said Margaret looking at the empty bottle of wine by Arabella's now empty chair. 'I don't think she'll remember it anyway.' She stood up. 'Well, after that eventful evening, I'll be off home to Hunter's Farm.' She bent forward and kissed Victoria. 'Goodnight, my dear.'

'Goodnight, Margaret,' smiled Victoria.

'Goodnight, Charles,' Margaret bent forward and kissed him and then looked at him sternly. 'I do hope you know what you're doing, Charles.'

'Of course I do, Mother,' confirmed Charles.

Margaret nodded and left the room.

Fennell came in with tea.

'Fennell, where's Harrison?' asked Victoria.

'He left already in your motor car.'

'Oh dear! He must be really furious! I've a lot of grovelling to do!'

'He'll be fine in the morning. If you want you can stay the night here?' offered Charles.

'No, I'd better get home at some stage tonight and try to build bridges with him,' she smiled and pulled a face.

'I'll give you a lift home later,' Charles offered.
'Thanks, Charles,' she said.

Arabella was up in their bedroom that night when she heard laughter outside. She went to the window and saw Charles and Victoria walk across the forecourt. Victoria sat into Charles' motor car. She listened, concerned, to Charles and Victoria dissolving in laughter over some shared joke as he started the motor car. She watched in dismay as they drove off together out of the forecourt and down the driveway.

Harrison came into the breakfast room at Ocean's End, looking sheepish. He sat down and the maid poured him coffee and left the room.

'Victoria looked at him curiously and coolly. 'You left in an awful hurry last night.'

'I know. I was very angry.'

'Obviously, to leave me abandoned like that. Very ungallant of you!'

'Come on, Victoria. You hate if you're not treated as independent all the time.'

'I know, but you took the bloody motor car with you! You didn't leave me with much independence without transport!'

'I knew one of the stable boys would drive you back,' said Harrison.

'Charles was kind enough to drive me actually.'

'I'm sorry! But if I didn't leave at that moment I would have said something I would regret.'

'To me?'

'Yes, and to Charles. What's he doing, evicting tenants? It's terrible!'

'I don't want to go into all that again, Harrison. You made yourself perfectly clear how you felt last night.'

'As did you!'

Victoria was bemused. 'I'm sorry, Harrison, but I'm not going to be one of these little wives who sits there nodding approvingly when her husband speaks, just because he's her husband! You knew that when you married me. And I'm really annoyed you spoke to me like that in front of your family.'

'You're annoyed! Imagine how I feel? Being contradicted so openly by you in front of them, in front of Charles!'

'Oh, I see!' Victoria sat back, nodding. 'And now we get to the bottom of the matter. It's because I sided with Charles you were so angry!'

'It really upset me, Victoria. You know what's gone on between me and Charles in the past—'

'But I thought that was in the past! You two have been getting on so much better now.'

'We are ... but last night it just all came flooding back. The way he can be. That ruthless streak where he doesn't care about anybody else but himself and what he wants.' Harrison looked disgusted.

'Well, I'm sorry, Harrison, but I like Charles, and I'm not going to side against him just because you're feeling insecure. And you really did have no right to challenge him about something that has nothing to do with you.'

Harrison sighed. 'I don't want us to fight over this. I don't want it to be an issue between us.'

She got up and walked over to him and put her

arms around him. 'Then don't make it one.'

He nodded, his face still troubled.

Charles parked his motor car outside Ocean's End. He took the jewellery box on the seat beside him and went up the steps and rang the doorbell. A minute later the butler opened the door.

'Is Mrs Armstrong home?' he asked.

'Yes, your lordship. I'll see if she's available.'

'Is that Charles?' Victoria called from the parlour. 'Come in, Charles!'

Charles walked into the parlour.

'Hello, my dear,' he said, bending down and kissing her.

'Tea?' she asked.

He nodded and sat down beside her as she took the teapot and poured him a cup.

She made a face at him as she handed over the teacup. 'How's everything at Armstrong House after the dinner party? Did things calm down between you and Arabella?'

'Things never calm down between me and Arabella. I was going to ask you how's everything between you and Harrison?'

'Oh, we ironed it all out. We both overreacted. We row so seldom it took us by surprise.'

'Unlike me and Arabella – our arguments never take us by surprise,' he lamented.

Victoria smiled with sympathy as she stirred her tea with a silver spoon.

'I've just felt so bad since that night,' he said, looking concerned. 'I'd hate to think I caused trouble between you and Harrison.'

'Oh Charles, don't be silly! You didn't come

between me and Harrison. We just had a difference of opinion. If we differed over anything it was politics and our view of the world. Nothing to do with you.'

'Still, I was feeling guilty. And I'd like to thank you for sticking up for me when it seemed everyone was against me.'

'Oh, I always stick up for the underdog,' she smiled.

'I got you this just as a token of gratitude,' he said, reaching into his pocket and taking out the jewellery box.

'What's this?' she asked, taking the box and opening it. She looked at the necklace inside. 'Charles! This is completely unnecessary!'

'Do you like it?'

'I love it!' She took out the necklace and marvelled at it. There was a note in the jewellery box and she opened it. It read: *All my love, Charles.* 'That's so sweet!' she said and leaned forward and kissed his cheek. 'There was really no need.'

'There's every need. You have brought happiness back into this family. You've given me my brother back. I never thought Harrison and I would ever meet again, let alone rebuild our friendship.'

'I did nothing really, but if I did bring some peace I did it for Harrison as much as anyone. He's much more at peace now.'

CHAPTER 65

Mr Brompton was very busy over the next couple of months arranging eviction orders through the courts for the five farmers at the Armstrong estate. Once the eviction orders were secured Charles gave permission for them to be enacted.

News of the pending evictions had spread through the estate, Castlewest and the county. People could not believe it and at first there was disbelief as opposed to anger.

The day was fixed for the evictions. The task of being present at them was imposed on James.

'You'll be hated after this,' stated James.

'Just as well I never lived my life worried about being popular with them like you and Father did.'

James rode his horse into the yard of the Mulrooney farm. He was accompanied by four men from the estate and a number of policemen from Castlewest. Maureen Mulrooney was out in the yard feeding chickens when she saw them.

'Jack! Jack!' she started shouting.

Jack came to the door of the cottage.

'Quick, Maureen! Get into the house!'

Maureen rushed into the house and they slammed the door and bolted it.

James got down from his horse and exchanged a worried look with the policemen.

He went up to the door, knocked loudly and shouted, 'Come on, Jack, don't make this any harder than it already is.'

'Fuck off! Get off my farm!'

'Jack, I appeal to you. Don't let this happen in front of your children.'

'It's you that's letting it happen in front of them!' shouted Jack as he turned and viewed Maureen who was sitting on the bed beside the fireplace holding their four children.

Outside a policeman stepped forward to the door. 'Come on now, Mulrooney, I've a notice of eviction here. Let's not have any trouble.'

'Fuck off!'

News of the police travelling through the estate to the Mulrooney farm had spread quickly and a large number of neighbouring farmers and their womenfolk came rushing down the laneway and gathered around the house.

'Get on home!' shouted the policeman. 'This has nothing to do with you.'

'It's everything to do with us! You can't throw them out!' shouted a man and the crowd started shouting angrily.

The policeman went up to James. 'Let's get this done as quickly as possible. The longer it goes on, the more chance there is of trouble.'

James nodded.

The policeman went and talked to his men. The men got to work and hoisted three poles into a pyramid in front of the front door. They then hung a battering ram from the apex of the pyramid by rope. This allowed them to swing the battering ram right back and let it go with its full force to slam into the wooden front door.

'Don't let them do it, James!' screamed a woman and the whole crowd started shouting and whistling loudly.

'On the count of three,' said the policeman as his men pulled the battering ram as far back as they could.

'One, two and *three!*' shouted the policeman.

The battering ram was let go and it slammed into the door of the cottage.

'*And again!*' shouted the policeman and his men swung the ram back into the door. They kept doing it until the door burst open. The policemen stormed into the cottage. James walked in after them.

James had tears in his eyes as the policemen confronted Jack.

'You've two minutes to leave this house,' said the policeman.

'I'll not leave!' he responded.

The policeman grabbed the man and started marching him to the door.

Mulrooney fought back and suddenly a fight started.

'Jack!' screamed Maureen as she rushed to her husband's assistance and started attacking a policeman.

The children started screaming and crying as both their parents were overpowered and dragged from their home.

As Jack and Maureen were pulled out into the yard the crowd erupted in screaming and shouting and piercing whistles. The Mulrooney children came rushing out after their parents.

Jack Mulrooney made a valiant attempt to re-enter the property but was quickly overpowered.

'Bastards!' shouted a woman from the crowd.

The policemen quickly went into the house and started removing all the furniture and loading it up on the Mulrooneys' cart outside. Maureen sat on the ground outside crying loudly as she was comforted by her neighbours. Once the cottage was emptied, the police used the battering ram to knock down the gables of the cottage, and the thatched roof fell in.

In the distance, Charles sat on his horse looking at the spectacle. He saw the angry crowd and the cottage being destroyed. He watched as the Mulrooney family were then led away from the property with their horse and cart which contained everything they possessed in the world to the edge of the estate and were left there on the side of the road. Charles turned and set off back to Armstrong House, not waiting to see the episode repeated at the other four farms being evicted that day.

CHAPTER 66

Arabella sat at the table having breakfast, looking at the front page of the county newspaper which had a headline *'Five Families Evicted from the Armstrong Estate Last Week'*.

She looked at the black-and-white photograph accompanying the article of the Mulrooney cottage after it had been destroyed and policemen standing around it.

As she read the article she was alarmed. She had never paid any attention to what happened on the estate. She could barely keep on top of the running of the house, let alone what happened outside its walls. Being from Dublin, she never really understood a country estate's running. But as she looked at the photograph and read the article she became anxious.

Charles came into the dining room in cheery form.

'I see you've made the front page,' she said, tossing the paper over to him.

He took the paper as he sat down and quickly scanned it before folding it over and starting his breakfast.

'What is going on, Charles?' she demanded.

'You know what's going on. We evicted some tenants in serious arrears.'

'But I didn't realise it would be like this!'

He looked at her in a bored fashion.

'Charles! Only you could be responsible for kicking off the next phase of the Land War!'

'Well, something has to be run around here efficiently, Arabella.

Let's face it, if it wasn't for Fennell and his wife, this house would be in chaos by now left to you.'

'Charles, that has nothing to do with these evictions!'

'It's everything to do with them, Arabella. Because you could never understand the workings of an estate like this – you're hopelessly inadequate to do so. You're hopelessly inadequate for the role of

Lady Armstrong, full stop. Because of a twist of fate, you ended up as Lady Armstrong, a role that you're not able or suitable for.'

'And by a twist of fate being born the first son you ended up being Lord Armstrong! A role that everyone says *you're* not suited to!' she retaliated.

'Well then! What a compatible couple we make! Now can I have breakfast in peace, please?'

A meeting was called at the McGrath farm in the aftermath of the evictions. The house was packed with tenant farmers from the estate. There were so many there the whole yard and field outside was jammed with people as they strained to hear what Joe McGrath said.

'As you all bitterly know, five farmers and their families were evicted from this estate,' he shouted. 'Five farmers who we knew as friends and neighbours ... most of us were related in some way to one or more of those families.'

There was a chorus of disapproval from the crowd.

'Five farmers and their families who had the misfortune to fall behind on their rents, as many of us have over the decades due to circumstances outside our control,' continued Joe McGrath. 'In the past we always made up for back rent once we could. We understood that as being the way here. But there's a new lord up at the Armstrong House. A new lord who doesn't care about the good working relationship that was always here. And now he just shoved those famers off the land and threw them on the side of the road like rubbish. Things have changed on this estate and we have to act to protect ourselves!'

The crowd erupted with shouts of approval.

'Because, today it's the Mulrooneys and the others being evicted – but tomorrow it will be you!'

There were screams of protests from the crowd.

'Lord Charles puts children out on the streets while he and his snobby wife hold posh cocktail and dinner parties up in their mansion. A mansion that you pay for with the sweat of your work!'

'Fuck them!' screamed a woman from the crowd.

'I call for a rent strike immediately. I call on all tenants on this farm to stop paying rent from today until those farmers are given back their homes and land!'

The people erupted in screams and shouts of approval.

Arabella was in the drawing room writing a letter when Fennell came in.

'Pardon me, my lady, one of the footmen wishes to see you.'

Arabella looked up from her notepaper. 'Oh, Fennell, can't you deal with him? I really have too much on today to deal with staff problems.'

And every day, thought Fennell.

'No, my lady, I'm afraid it's of a serious nature.'

Arabella sighed. 'Very well, show him in. Will you remain while he's here?'

'Of course, my lady,' said Fennell as he opened the door and showed the young man in.

'Sorry to bother you, my lady, but I have to leave your service today,' said the footman whose name was Anthony.

'That's very short notice, Anthony. Why can't you give a month's notice as expected?'

Anthony looked uncomfortably at Fennell. 'Because my daddy said I'm not to stay here any longer on account of those evictions, and I'm to return home to Castlewest without delay.'

'Oh, I see,' said Arabella, taken aback. 'And do you always do what your daddy tells you?'

'Yes, my lady,' said Anthony.

'I see. In that case, we'll be sorry to lose you,' said Arabella.

Anthony nodded and left the room quickly with Fennell.

As Arabella looked out the window she muttered 'Oh, Charles, what have you started?'

Charles was looking through the rent books in the library and he looked up abruptly at James.

'What's going on? All these rent books are blank for this month!'

'Charles, they've called a rent strike. They refuse to pay any more rents until you meet with them and you agree to their demands,' said James.

Charles sat back in horror. 'But they can't do that! It's blackmail!'

'There's not one farmer on the estate willing to break the strike.'

'But – it's against the law!'

'They're holding together as a union. They won't pay,' said James.

Charles got up and started pacing angrily. 'Who do they think they are?'

'Meet with them, Charles, negotiate with them,'

urged James.

'I most certainly will not! They'll regret the day they took this course of action. They might have been able to bully and intimidate every other landlord in this country, but they won't do it with me! Tell Brompton to come to me immediately. I'm going to serve evictions on another five farmers straight away. And I'll keep evicting five farmers every month until order is brought back on to this estate. They want a Land War? I'll give them a bloody Land War!'

The second set of evictions took place the following month as Charles intended. The following morning one of the gamekeepers reported an incident in the western part of the estate and Charles and James made their way there. There were fields of wheat in that part of the estate and when they arrived there they found the crops had been destroyed. The wheat had been trampled on and it looked like somebody had trampled horses through all the fields.

Charles stood there staring at the annihilated crops.

'Who did this?' he demanded, consumed with anger.

'Don't know, sir. One of my men spotted it this morning and reported it,' said the gamekeeper.

'It's obviously in retaliation for the evictions,' said James.

'Get me the police!' demanded Charles.

'I've made extensive enquiries, and I'm afraid nobody saw anything,' said the policeman to Charles later in the library.

'You can't do that kind of damage without people noticing who did it!' objected Charles.

'Well, if anyone saw anything, they aren't telling me, your lordship,' said the policeman.

'I see!' said Charles, furious. 'They think I'll back off over a few fields of crops destroyed, do they?'

'I do think they are trying to give you a clear message, Lord Armstrong,' the policeman pointed out.

'It's unbelievable that people can get away with this kind of behaviour.' Charles' anger was not subsiding.

'Without any evidence or co-operation from the people living nearby, there's nothing I can do,' said the policeman.

'It was probably the people who lived nearby who caused the damage!' shouted Charles.

'It's not wise to speculate in these circumstances, sir. All you'll do is inflame further anger,' said the policeman.

'Inflame! How much more inflammatory can the situation get? I've got hundreds of rents outstanding, I've got crops wantonly destroyed!'

'Regarding the next set of evictions, would you like to postpone them?'

'Certainly not! I want them done even more now,' confirmed Charles.

'Very well, your lordship. Good day to you,' said the policeman as he left.

CHAPTER 67

Charles was having a cocktail party in the drawing room. Harrison and Victoria were there along with the Foxes and other close friends.

'Fields and fields of crops destroyed, for no reason, other than spite,' said Charles as everyone sat around listening.

'And they're not paying their rents either?' checked Harrison.

'Not one of them!'

'So what are you going to do, Charles? Evict every last one of them?' asked Arabella pointedly.

'If I have to – yes!' said Charles.

Mrs Foxe leaned over, concerned. 'You have to be very careful, Charles. I mean, we had our own troubles with our tenants a few years ago. You can't underestimate them. They are very intelligent, and they know how to organise themselves.'

'Very intelligent! Pooh!' dismissed Charles.

'They are, Charles,' said Harrison. 'Just because they didn't go to our schools or universities doesn't make them unintelligent.'

'Well, I think the whole thing is disgusting,' said Victoria. 'The idea that they would engage in this kind of criminal activity. I mean it's bad enough they are on this rent strike – we know all about unions and strikes in America, I can assure you. But to destroy property like that! I think it's awful.'

Arabella raised her eyes to heaven as she drank her cocktail. 'Oh, shut up, Victoria! This isn't a moral debating club in Newport, or wherever you come from – this is the west of Ireland!'

The drawing room hushed as everyone felt embarrassed by Arabella's outburst.

Victoria turned to Harrison. 'Maybe we should be going. I think somebody has had too much to drink, and I really don't want an argument with a drunk, thank you very much.'

'I am not drunk! You condescending little know-it-all!'

'Enough everybody!' demanded Charles. 'Please! This is supposed to be a night of enjoyment. I don't want the agitation on the estate finding its way into my drawing room, if you please!'

Arabella sat back, glaring angrily at Victoria.

'Fennell, fill everyone's glasses, please – except Lady Armstrong's,' said Charles, and Fennell went around filling the glasses.

Arabella's angry glare switched from Victoria to Charles.

'Did you hear about that new play at the Gaiety?' asked Mrs Foxe and everyone started chatting about that topic.

'Fennell, put some more turf on the fire,' said Charles.

Fennell went over to the brass turf box and scooped turf and wood onto the fire until it started blazing. Suddenly thick black smoke started to pour out of the fireplace.

'What the...?' demanded Charles as he saw the thick smoke billow around the room.

'Quickly, open the windows!' said Victoria as the room became engulfed in smoke.

'It's too late for that,' said Charles, almost choking. 'Everyone out!'

Everyone raced to the door and opened it, only to find there was thick black smoke billowing from the fireplace in the hall as well.

Charles quickly ran back into the room and to the French windows which he opened. 'Everyone out!'

Everyone ran out the French windows onto the patio and started gasping and choking in the night air.

'It would seem that your turf was covered in some kind of chemical,' said the policeman the next day, 'causing this smoke reaction.'

'How did they do it?' demanded Charles.

'I imagine they just walked into your stables where you keep your turf and wood and they poured the chemicals all over it. I take it you don't keep those stables locked?'

'No. What a despicable thing to do!'

'I strongly advise you to destroy all your wood and turf supply – it's probably all contaminated with this chemical.'

'And there's nothing you can do again?' snapped Charles.

'I've spoken to your staff and they said they saw nobody unusual around the back stables. They probably came at night and did the interfering when everyone was asleep.'

Arabella walked down the corridor upstairs. It was

after ten in the evening and she was calling in to the children to say goodnight. She stopped as she heard a curious howling coming from outside. The howling was relentless and sounded like wolves. She had never heard a sound like it in all her time at Armstrong House and it unnerved her.

She walked into Pierce's bedroom.

'Mama, why are the wolves howling?' asked Pierce, sitting up in bed.

'They're not wolves, silly,' said Prudence, walking into the bedroom in her dressing gown from her own room next door. 'There haven't been wolves in Ireland since the great forests were cut down centuries ago.'

'Well, what are they then?' asked Pierce anxiously.

'They're the tenant farmers, of course, making those noises to scare us,' said Prudence who didn't seem too concerned by her own revelation.

'Prudence!' warned Arabella.

'I'm just saying!' Prudence defended herself.

'That's nonsense, Prudence, and you shouldn't say such things,' admonished Arabella.

'It's the truth, I tell you! I heard Mrs Fennell say it to the terrified kitchen staff,' stated Prudence.

'Prudence, I've told you before to stay out of the kitchens!'

'Why? Somebody has to check they are doing their work properly,' Prudence said in a matter-of-fact way.

Arabella felt a pang of shame at her daughter's comment, even though Prudence wasn't being intentionally nasty in commenting on Arabella's shortcomings as Lady Armstrong.

'Anyway, whatever is making the sounds, you're quite safe here. Nothing or nobody can get into the house,' Arabella assured Pierce as she kissed him goodnight.

Arabella was getting ready one morning in their bedroom when she heard a scream from downstairs. Panicked she hurried from the bedroom, along the corridor and down the staircase.

'What is it?' she demanded of the parlour maid who was standing at the open front door, looking terrified.

'Look!' cried the girl, pointing to a dead crow on the doorstep outside.

Fennell and Prudence arrived together.

'For pity's sake, girl! It's only a dead bird!' Arabella said angrily. 'It flew into the door.'

'A crow might fly into a window, but never a door, my lady! It's been left there as a warning.' The girl seemed terrified.

'Don't be so ridiculous!' snapped Arabella.

Prudence bent down and inspected the bird. 'No, she's probably right, Mama. Its neck has been broken.'

'Prudence!'

'I'm just saying!' Prudence said.

'Fennell, get rid of the revolting thing,' ordered Arabella before turning to the maid. 'And you return to your duties at once, without any further unnecessary silliness.'

The girl rushed off.

'The staff are a bit unnerved with everything that's been going on, Lady Armstrong,' said Fennell.

504

'I will not have the house disrupted by such hysterics, Fennell,' ordered Arabella.

'Very good, my lady. I'll have the crow removed at once.'

Prudence held Arabella's hand as they walked back upstairs.

'She's quite right, of course, Mama. The crow probably was left there as a warning to us.'

'Don't *you* start! And do not tell Pierce about it. I don't want him any more upset than he already is,' said Arabella as she reached the top of the stairs.

'Yes, Mama,' agreed Prudence.

Leaving her daughter in the corridor, Arabella went to her room. Once she got there she sat down on the bed and started to shake.

The incidents continued as did the evictions. One of the footmen was beaten up in Castlewest one night when he was leaving a pub. A carriage had one of its wheels tampered with, resulting in it coming off while travelling through the estate, injuring the groomsman driving it. Arabella was walking through the gardens one day and she saw the prized flowerbeds had been uprooted and destroyed. Charles went on as if nothing was happening. He continued organising social occasions at the house. But Arabella noticed whereas before their invitations were eagerly sought after, people were now politely declining, frightened of becoming embroiled in the conflict at Armstrong House.

Arabella was walking quickly through the hall

with Fennell. She tried the front door and found it unlocked.

'Fennell! Why is this door unlocked?' she demanded.

'We never lock the front door at Armstrong House, my lady, only at night.'

'Well, we will in future! I want this door locked and all the doors kept locked throughout the house.'

They went into the small parlour.

'Fennell!' she nearly shouted when she saw a window open. 'What's that window doing open?'

'I presume a maid left it open to air the room.'

Arabella walked across the room and slammed the window shut.

'Not in future! I want all the downstairs windows closed and secured at all times, am I making myself clear?'

'As you wish, my lady,' nodded Fennell and he backed out of the room.

Arabella waited till he was gone and then raced to the drinks cabinet and poured herself a strong gin.

Emily sat at one end of the table in the dining room at Hanover Terrace while Hugh sat at the other. They ate in silence.

She suddenly put down her fork and glared at him.

'What's your problem?' he asked.

'Your table manners are disgusting!' she declared with a look of revulsion on her face.

He glared at her before throwing his own fork down on his plate with a clatter, giving her a start.

'Oh, are they?' he said, his voice thick with anger and sarcasm. 'Are my table manners really disgusting?'

'Yes, they are. You manage to eat properly when we are with your friends, and I expect the same level of respect.'

'Respect? What do you know about respect? You sit there, like the queen of England, thinking you're better than me.'

'Well, if the cap fits!'

'I'm sorry if I don't eat like the fine people you were brought up with in Armstrong House.'

'You can try to eat like a civilised person!'

'If I'm so uncivilised why did you marry me?'

'I've asked myself that many, many times. I can only put it down to a moment of madness.'

Hugh picked up his food and continued to slobber over it.

'If you can't eat properly I refuse to eat with you.' She stood up and walked towards the door.

Hugh stood up and walked after her.

'Who do you think you are?' he demanded.

'I know who I am! I'm Lady Emily Armstrong. It's you who are pretending you're something you're not all the time. Throwing your money around, thinking it will make you accepted when everyone laughs at you and calls you names!'

'Shut your fucking mouth!'

'I will not be spoken to like that!'

'I'll speak to you any way I want, because you're my wife. A fact you seem to have forgotten lately.'

'Oh, I haven't forgotten it! How could I possibly forget it, when I'm stuck here under the same roof as you and your disgusting habits and manners.'

'What did you say?' He eyes bored into her angrily.

'Disgusting! You disgust me!' she shouted at him.

Suddenly his arm rose into the air and he hit her with the full force of the back of his hand. The force of the blow sent her flying across the room and laid her out on the floor.

She managed to sit up and held her hand to where he had struck her. He stood there, glaring angrily at her.

She struggled to her feet and stared at him. Then she raced across the dining room and out the door. She headed towards the stairs and she didn't stop running until she was in the safety of her room and had locked the door behind her.

CHAPTER 68

In the House of Commons an MP was giving a speech on the new Wyndham Act that had just been passed.

'With this Act, which applies only to Ireland and not the rest of the United Kingdom, the British government is making available funds that will be loaned to Irish tenant farmers in order for them to buy their holdings from their landlords if both parties so wish. It will provide landlords who are agreeable to sell with the price they demand and provide the farmers with the finance to buy and secure the land they work. The agrarian strife that has blighted Ireland has been a huge concern to the governments of this country for many decades. While we may think that the worst of this Land War ended in the last decade, I have heard only recently of the turmoil on the Armstrong estate in the west of Ireland which demonstrates the situation remains volatile and ready to erupt at any time. It is sincerely hoped that this Act will at last provide the mechanism to allow peace throughout the countryside of Ireland.'

The MP sat down as members of the house cheered in support.

'Charles,' demanded Arabella after reading an article on the evictions on the estate in the local paper, 'this cannot continue! What are you going to do to stop this disaster you have unleashed?'

'I'm not going to do anything! I will continue with the course of action I have started. I assure you they'll give in.'

'You can assure me? You can't assure me of anything! You've never been able to assure me of anything since the day I met you! You stumble from disaster to disaster, never thinking of the consequences, always thinking you know best.'

'And what do you do? You sit here in this house, looking out at the world scared!'

'If I'm scared of the world, it's because it has become a scary place because of you!'

'You've never been a good wife to me. Never! You've never supported me or my actions.'

'You never tell me what you're up to or what

actions you take until it's too late!'

'That's because I'd never get anything done if I told you anything. All you'd ever say is "No, don't do it!"'

'Yes, because everything you touch turns to poison! The children are scared–'

'Prudence isn't scared,' he said proudly.

'But Pierce is,' she said.

'If he is scared it's because you have made him so, with your fragile nerves! Besides, Pierce is now thirteen. He's going to be going away to boarding school soon.'

Arabella knew Pierce was due for school, but she dreaded the thought of losing him and only having him home during the holidays.

'So, you will do nothing to try and get a resolution with the tenants?' she asked.

'I will not be broken!' he confirmed. 'Even if you are.'

'And how you wish you were married to somebody like Victoria!' she said. 'Go on, say it, you're thinking it!'

'Yes, I wish I was married to somebody like her!' he shouted at her.

'And I wish I was married to somebody like Harrison! The difference is Victoria would never even have looked at you, but Harrison was in love with me, and I threw it away because of you!'

CHAPTER 69

Emily stepped out of the carriage, looked up at Armstrong House and felt an enormous feeling of relief to be back. She walked up the steps and went to try the door but it was locked. Unusual, she thought, as she knocked at the door.

'Ah, Lady Emily – welcome home,' said Fennell.

Emily had written the previous week saying she would be back.

'It is good to be home, Fennell,' she said as she entered the comfort of her home.

She saw Charles walking down the stairs.

'If it isn't my favourite sister!' said Charles on seeing her.

Emily raced to him and collapsed in his arms. 'Oh Charles!' she said as she suddenly started to cry.

A family summit was called in the drawing room at Armstrong House that evening with Margaret, Harrison and Victoria joining Charles and Arabella.

Emily sat on a couch, pale and thin. 'I'm not going back!' she declared. 'I'm never going back to him.'

'And what do you propose to do?' questioned Margaret, her face a mask of concern.

'I don't know. Divorce him, I suppose.'

'Divorce!' exclaimed Margaret, dismayed. 'On

what grounds?'

'Extreme mental and physical cruelty – do you want the details?' Emily challenged her mother.

'No – no, I'd rather not hear them,' said Margaret. 'This family has never had the scandal of a divorce and you can't drag us through the divorce courts.'

'All that can be decided later,' said Victoria. 'The main thing is that Emily knows she's safe and we support her.'

Margaret sighed loudly. 'Well, I suppose we were all preparing for this day eventually. It was a disaster waiting to explode with a man like that. Everyone warned you what you were marrying.'

'Everyone except Charles,' said Arabella, giving him a cynical stare.

'Does he know you've left him?' asked Charles.

'I just left a letter for him. I couldn't take it any more,' said Emily.

'You did the right thing,' said Victoria. 'And what are your immediate plans?'

'I don't know. My immediate plans were just to get away from him.'

'Well, you must stay here at Armstrong House for as long as you want,' offered Charles.

Emily smiled gratefully at him.

'If you can put up with everything that has been going on here,' said Arabella.

'Yes, I'm hearing awful stories about the estate,' said Emily.

Victoria said, 'Why don't you come and stay with me and Harrison? It'll be much quieter–'

'And safer!' interrupted Arabella.

'–than Armstrong House,' concluded Victoria.

'Victoria to the rescue again!' said Arabella.

'You're all very kind,' said Emily, looking at them appreciatively. 'But what I really just want now is my mother.' Emily looked over imploringly at Margaret.

Margaret smiled at her. 'Of course you must come and be with me at Hunter's Farm. I know what's best for you, I always have.'

Margaret held out her arms and Emily rushed across the room and enveloped her mother in a hug.

CHAPTER 70

Charles was walking down the beach with Victoria as the waves lapped against the sand. He had been explaining how some of the animals had been maimed on the estate in a new upscale of the Land War.

'Oh what a brutal thing to do! I can scarcely believe it!' Victoria was shocked.

'It was an awful sight to witness.'

'I can only imagine. How did Arabella take it?'

'How does Arabella take anything? Collapsed in a bundle of nerves and hit the gin bottle,' said Charles.

'Oh dear!'

'I hope you don't mind me coming over and unloading all this on you all the time?'

'Of course not!'

'It's just that sometimes I feel you're the only

person I can talk to, Victoria.'

'I know from my father dealing with unions how these things become so intense.'

'I feel trapped! I can't give in and yet I can't see how to solve it either.'

'Maybe if you talk to the farmers – reason with them.'

He looked so worried, she reached forward and hugged him tightly. He held her close.

Harrison walked into Ocean's End after returning from Dublin on business. He picked up the post and quickly looked through it.

'Did you have a good journey, sir?' asked the butler, coming and taking his suitcase.

'Yes, fine thanks. Where's my wife?'

'Mrs Armstrong went for a walk with Lord Charles, sir. They've been gone a while.'

'I see,' said Harrison and he walked into the parlour and left the post on a sideboard. He walked to the back of the room and looked out.

Victoria and Charles were coming up the steps from the beach, laughing. Harrison watched as Charles held out his hand and assisted her up the last steps. They walked through the garden, stopping occasionally to examine a plant or a tree and then made their way to the French window.

Harrison quickly made his way to the other side of the room. Victoria opened the French window as she was speaking to Charles.

'So the next thing the parlour maid said was,' Victoria suddenly adopted an Irish accent, *"'Ah, begorrah, sure you'll never roast them spuds and them still sitting in the larder!'"*

Charles and she laughed loudly as he closed the door behind them.

'Harrison!' said Victoria, seeing him. 'You're back early!' She went to him and kissed him.

'Yes, I caught an earlier train.'

'Good. Will you be joining us for dinner, Charles?'

'I'm afraid not, but thank you for the invitation. I have to attend to estate business,' said Charles.

He kissed Victoria on the cheek and clapped Harrison on the back.

'See you soon!' he said as he left.

'Attend to estate business? Destroy the estate's business, I think he means,' said Harrison, sitting down after pouring himself a drink.

'Oh, give the man a break, Harrison,' pleaded Victoria. 'He feels the whole world *is* against him.'

'That's because the whole world is against him after his ridiculous antics.'

'I don't care what anyone says. There's no excuse for the treatment he and his family have been meted. Maiming animals, violating property!'

'Oh, wake up and see what's going on, Victoria!' Harrison became angry. 'He's destroyed centuries of hard work and goodwill in a matter of months.'

'He knows he should have handled things differently, he told me so. The trouble is, what does he do about it now?'

'You've become quite the confidante to him, haven't you?' Harrison looked at her cynically.

'I'd like to think I've won the trust of all your family.'

Harrison looked pensive.

515

'What's the matter?' she asked, going and sitting beside him.

'Victoria, I've been thinking lately... I think we should go back to the States.'

'Back to the States!' Victoria was astonished. 'But why? We love living here.'

'We never planned to live here permanently. It was only ever temporary. We've been here far longer than I ever envisaged, Victoria.'

'But we can't run out on your family in their time of need, Harrison. They need our support with all this trouble going on.'

'It's exactly because of this trouble I think we should go back to America. I don't like living here any more with all this going on. We are Armstrongs too and because of Charles' actions we are being tarred with the same brush.'

'But you have been getting on so much better with him,' she said.

'Yes, our bridges are mended, and that is a wonderful thing. But his actions over the past months have made me realise that he has never changed. He is still the greedy self-centred man he always was, who will ruthlessly railroad over anybody to get what he wants.'

'I see,' said Victoria. 'I didn't realise how strongly you felt.'

'I do! And I fear if I stay here and continue to witness his behaviour, I will end up hating him again.'

'Well, that would be a disaster. But what about the rest of your family – James and your mother? And Emily, now that she's back. Don't they need us too?'

'They are all adults capable of looking after themselves, without the need for us to hold their hands. Besides, Mother has always been incredibly pragmatic. She wouldn't want to stop us from getting on with our lives.'

'Well, this has all taken me by surprise,' she said, looking despondent.

'And, don't you think it's time we started our own family?'

'We're both still young. I thought we decided there was no rush and we could just enjoy married life for a while?'

'I know, but not such a long while! I think it's time we started a family. And I don't want to bring up our children here, not with all this festering resentment towards the Armstrongs.'

'I'd certainly miss everyone and everything here. I do love it so,' she said, looking sad. She looked at his face. Harrison would only say something like that if he had given it considerable thought and decided what he really wanted. 'But if that's what you want, then we'll go back to the States.'

He reached forward and held her tightly.

CHAPTER 71

Pierce was to start school and there was great preparation readying him for going.

Arabella had thought he would be reluctant to go away to boarding school in England, but he seemed to be looking forward to it. She imagined all the agitation on the estate had made going away seem more attractive to him.

Arabella was making the journey over to England with him and the morning they were setting off was a flurry of activity.

'Are you sure you don't want to come with us, Prudence?' asked Arabella.

'No, I'll stay here and mind Papa,' said Prudence happily.

Charles bent down and hugged Pierce in the forecourt. 'Always remember everything I taught you,' said Charles.

'And remember everything *I've* taught you!' said Arabella, concerned that her son would ever use Charles as his model in life.

Pierce got into the back of the carriage and Arabella kissed Prudence.

'I'll see you in a week,' she said before turning to Charles.

They looked at each other.

'Look after yourself,' said Arabella, leaning forward and kissing him quickly before getting into the carriage.

Prudence and Charles waved as the carriage set off down the driveway, then walked back into the house with their arms around each other.

'I suppose I will be lonely now he's gone,' said Prudence. 'But I still have you and Mama, and grandmother and everyone else.'

'There's a good girl. Now you run along, I've some important work to do,' said Charles as he headed into the library.

He did have important work to do. He was expecting a visit from Edgar Joyce, their bank manager from Dublin. Mr Joyce had been wanting to meet Charles for some considerable time. Charles had been putting it off but now, with Arabella out of the way, it was an ideal opportunity.

Edgar Joyce was shown into the library by Fennell.

'How is the situation down here on your estate, Lord Armstrong?' asked Joyce, sitting down opposite him across the desk.

'We have everything under control,' Charles assured him.

'That's not what I've been hearing, unfortunately. Lord Armstrong, I've been sent down here to meet with you by the board of trustees at the bank due to the concern over your ever-deteriorating finances.'

'I see.'

'I don't know if you are aware just how bad your situation has become. The estate has been literally months and months without any payments from your tenants, resulting in no cash flow and large overdrafts.'

Charles felt himself become annoyed.

'I think, Mr Joyce, the fact that the Armstrong estate stretches to eight thousand acres means I am not on my uppers, just yet!'

'No, but if this Land War you're involved in continues much longer you will be! Quite simply, you are dependent on your tenants' rents and to begin this – war – with them was a huge act of folly on your part.'

'I didn't start it! They did by not paying their rents on time!' snapped Charles.

'Whoever started it, the problem now, Lord Armstrong, is nobody seems to be in a position to end it, tensions are running so high.'

'The problem is, Mr Joyce, that neither you nor the board of trustees have any idea of the magnitude of running an estate like this,' Charles defended himself.

'I quite agree! I don't, they don't, but unfortunately the situation appears to be that you don't either! You are aware of the new Wyndham Land Act passed by parliament?'

'I am, of course.'

'Many of our gentry clients around the country are choosing to avail of it. They are selling their estates for the amount they want to their tenants by the funds being made available by the government. It's a very good deal for landlords, better than anyone ever expected. Quite simply they are sick and tired of all this agrarian trouble and dealing with the locals, and opting to take the money and run. We consider you an ideal candidate for this opportunity.'

'Sell my estate! Have you any idea how long this land has been in my family?' Charles was aghast.

Joyce looked bored. 'I can hazard a guess, because I've lamentably heard the history of many estates around the country from clients who I have urged to sell!'

'And deprive my wonderful son of what one day will rightly be his?' Charles was furious.

'Put quite simply, Lord Armstrong, if you continue the way you are, all you'll be leaving your – wonderful – son is a title and a mountain of debt!

520

You obviously should keep the house here and a couple of hundred acres around the house to secure your prestige, past heritage and a small but secure future income. Although I would advise you to curtail your lifestyle considerably. This Land War you've engaged in has severely weakened your family's finances, and your own spending habits since you became Lord Armstrong would make a Bourbon king blush.'

'Excuse me?'

'You are not a Vanderbilt or a Van Hoevan – you are a member of a class that I believe has its best days behind it. And this government Land Act has thrown you a lifejacket that you should cling on to. In a few months your finances will be so bad that even the Land Act won't rescue you – my lord!'

Charles glared angrily at Joyce. 'Is there anything else?'

'No.'

'Then I wish you a safe journey back to Dublin,' said Charles.

Joyce stood up and nodded at him. 'Good day, Lord Armstrong.'

Charles was shaken after the visit from the bank manager. He had never been good at looking at the finer details of finances, which his experiences in London had testified to. But when he came into the Armstrong estate, he had believed all his money worries would be over. Only now to be told that his finances were in a dire situation. He summoned James to the library.

'The situation can't continue, James – we are

being starved of funds with those bastards not paying their bloody rents,' he raged.

'What do you expect me to do about it?' James had nearly given up hope on the situation at this stage.

'I expect you to solve it, as the estate manager!' insisted Charles.

'Oh, I'm the estate manager now, am I? You'd never bothered telling me that before, or ever listened to my advice to indicate I had that position,' James said jeeringly.

'I think they're near to breaking – I think the tenants will give in soon,' said Charles.

'They have no intention of giving in. Sure they aren't losing anything. They are still farming away and just not handing you their rents because of the strike.'

'They're trying to force me to sell them my land with this new Act by making things as difficult as possible for me,' said Charles.

James shrugged.

'The only thing we have over them is the fear of evictions. So we'll have to increase that fear.' Charles reached for the estate journals. 'We'll pick the first twenty families in this journal and evict them. Get Brompton on the case.'

'Twenty families all at once! You can't do that!' declared James.

'Why not? Since no tenant has paid a penny to me in nearly a year, they are all liable for eviction. And if I have to evict every last one – then I will!'

CHAPTER 72

Present Day

Kate hadn't rung Nico since she left for Dublin to do her next leg of research at the Irish Automobile Club. He wandered into the library. He raised his eyes to heaven as he saw all his architectural work had been unceremoniously shifted to a corner of the room. Kate had the whole room taken over with the documents and boxes from the attic. He wandered over to the pile of boxes with a big note saying *'To Do'* in Kate's handwriting attached to them. He started looking through the boxes. A lot of them were financial records stretching back to the nineteenth century. He imagined Kate had never even looked through them previously as she hated anything to do with finances. He sat down and started going through the boxes.

Returning from Dublin that night, Kate braced herself as she let herself into Armstrong House. She wanted to rush in and share what she had found out in the Royal Irish Automobile Club with Nico but decided it was best not to. It was obvious from their argument he didn't support her in this quest she was on.

'I tried ringing you earlier,' he said as she came into the room.

'I had my phone off,' she said.

'Find anything interesting in Dublin?' he asked.

She nodded in a noncommittal way and was surprised to notice Nico had a pile of documents out on the coffee table.

'What's all this?' she asked.

'I thought, with you being up in Dublin and us under time pressure for the filming, I'd give you a hand – so I went through some of the boxes in your *"To Do"* side of the library,' he said, half smiling at her.

She smiled gratefully at him as she sat beside him. 'Ah, thanks, Nico.'

'I ignored all the papers in the years before 1903. From what I can see Charles was in severe financial difficulty by then. Looking at the rent books, the tenants had stopped paying any rents the previous year. He had big overdrafts and there's a lot of letters from the bank to him warning him of his dire situation.'

'Very interesting,' she said as she started to take up the papers and look at them.

'There's also a letter from his solicitor the week he was shot saying that as per Charles' instructions he would start the ball rolling for the estate to be sold to the tenants under the Wyndham Act which would provide him with much-needed finances.'

'But we already know the vast majority of the estate was sold off after Charles was shot under that government act.'

'Yes – but we thought the estate was being sold as a result of Charles' being shot. This shows he had intended to sell it before that.'

'Very true,' said Kate, not wanting to come

across as unappreciative of Nico's work.

'But what was most interesting was these two,' he said, reaching forward and taking two papers and handing one to her. 'One is a copy of a bank statement depositing £20,000 into his account from a Hugh Fitzroy that week ... and this is a letter from same said Hugh Fitzroy.'

'And who is Hugh Fitzroy?' wondered Kate out loud.

'I checked on the peerage website of Great Britain and Ireland. He was married to Charles' sister Lady Emily, who we know gave a statement to the police when Charles was shot saying she was staying with her mother, Lady Margaret, that night.'

Kate's eyes widened at Nico's good work. 'I'm impressed!'

'You should be! Now read the letter and you'll be even, more impressed. It's on paper from the Castlewest Arms Hotel where he was obviously staying and dated the 6th of December 1903, two days before the shooting.' Nico sat back smugly.

Kate read the letter.

Castlewest Arms Hotel
Main Street
Castlewest
Co. Mayo
December 6th 1903

Dear Armstrong,
The £20,000 has now been deposited to your account as we agreed and find enclosed the copy of the bank transaction. I want to return to London without

any delay. Talk to Emily at once to make her see sense and return to London with me this week.

Fitzroy

Kate resumed her work in the library. What Nico had found concerning the payment and the note from Hugh Fitzroy had opened her eyes to another avenue. She checked the 1901 census records online and saw that Emily was living with her husband Fitzroy at Hanover Terrace in London. She then checked the 1911 census and discovered that only Hugh was living at the address with servants. Emily was no longer living there. Kate reasoned Emily had left her husband and that's why she was staying with Lady Margaret in Hunter's Farm, which explained why she had been in Ireland in December 1903. The 1911 census made Kate think it was a permanent separation unless something had happened to Emily in the meantime.

Checking the peerage website she saw Emily had lived until 1954 and so she hadn't died in the meantime. Emily never returned to her husband. Kate sat back, thinking, at her desk. The note to Charles indicated that Fitzroy had entered into some kind of a financial agreement with Charles to make Emily *'see sense'* and return to her marriage and London with him. Kate decided she needed to find out all she could about this character Hugh Fitzroy.

Kate came into the drawing room with print-outs from the internet.

Nico looked apprehensively at her papers and

526

her excited face. 'What have you got there?'

'I've been trawling through the online archives of the newspapers at the time to see if I could come up with anything about Hugh Fitzroy,' she said.

'How did you manage to do that? There must be millions of archives,' he said.

'There are! But I was able to narrow down the search by using the information I got from the census records of the time.'

'Clever old you!'

She smiled sarcastically back at him. 'What I did discover was that this Hugh Fitzroy was a very unsavoury man. He cropped up a lot in the social columns, attending this do and that do, and he appeared to be very wealthy.'

'Hence how he afforded to pay Charles' £20,000,' said Nico.

'Exactly, in what I believe was bribe money paid to Charles to get Emily to return to him, which I imagine she wasn't aware of. In this article from *The Times* in 1904,' she handed him an article, 'it says that Hugh Fitzroy was charged with attempted murder for trying to shoot a man who owed him a fortune in gambling debts in London.'

Nico quickly read through the article. 'But it says the charges were dropped because of insufficient evidence.'

'Yes, but look at this article from the *Daily Mirror* in 1905. The newspaper had just opened in 1903 and the article is quite salacious.' As Nico read through the article Kate continued to speak. 'Hugh Fitzroy was brought to court for brutally assaulting a Mademoiselle Claudine Farger, a daughter of a French Count, at Fitzroy's home in Hanover Terrace where the article says she had been staying with him. Claudine Farger had been courting Fitzroy at the time of the attack. She gave evidence that the man was a brute, often prone to violent attacks, with a vengeful and malicious personality. He was given a suspended sentence and ordered to pay Claudine Farger £5,000 or risk imprisonment.'

Nico nodded. 'And this man who we now know was violent with a temper was in Castlewest the week Charles was shot.'

'And, as we know Emily was here the *night* Charles was shot and hadn't returned to London with her husband, it's safe to say Fitzroy was still in the vicinity that actual night. And since Fitzroy had this Frenchwoman living with him in 1905 and lived alone in the 1911 census, it's safe to say Emily never did return to him.'

'Which means Charles got £20,000 from a violent and vengeful man and didn't deliver on his agreement to make Emily "see sense",' said Nico, piecing it all together.

'Could Fitzroy have been waiting for him at the gates to exact his revenge?' mused Kate. 'And the family covered it up as they couldn't have Emily involved in the scandal?'

'Or I'm sure if Emily discovered what Charles had agreed to, it would drive anyone to a murderous rage. Her brother selling her! Maybe the fox fur and shoe were hers? Also why the family went to such lengths to protect her,' offered Nico.

Since Brian had practically banned Kate from the

set for interference, she took the opportunity to return to the library where she had nearly finished going through everything there. She decided to take a look through the cook's diaries at the time. Mrs Fennell had continued working at the house until it was evacuated years later during the War of Independence, and like the rest of the occupants at the time had left many things behind in her hurry to escape. When she had gone through Mrs Fennell's diaries before she had found it laborious work. Mrs Fennell seemed capable of writing pages and pages of diaries filled with the mundane details of her kitchen being run. She used large-sized ledgers – no doubt provided by Armstrong House for official purposes – and they were filled with recipes, shopping lists and accounts. Previously Kate had gleaned just enough for the docudrama. She hadn't wanted this film to be distracted by the workings of downstairs – she wanted it to concentrate on the family.

She started looking through the diaries again, taking time to actually read them.

Kate soon discovered that Mrs Fennell also included passages and references to the Armstrongs, particularly Arabella who she was scheduled to meet regularly to take orders.

For the page of January 20th 1903 Mrs Fennell, after a full page writing notes on how she prepared a lunch of Shepherd's Pie, had written: *Meeting with Lady Armstrong 12 o'clock – cancelled – again!*

Her interest piqued, Kate continued reading the pages, making notes of the crucial parts that were nestled in amongst the domestic minutiae.

14th February – Valentine's Day – Not much ro-

mance between his lordship and her ladyship! Rowing till one in the morning.

8th March – Managed to get a meeting with her ladyship. Explained to her the difficulty we were having in the kitchen as some of the shops won't deliver to the house due to this blasted Land War and another kitchen maid walked out on me.

All her ladyship said was – we must manage as best we can!

30th March – Lady Prudence saw off another governess today. A kindly woman from Dublin, left in tears! Lady A said she had other things to worry about than substandard governesses!

12th April – a big dinner at the house tonight. Mr Harrison and his wife the American coming along with Lady Margaret up from Hunter's Farm. All hands on deck.

30th April – Order more gin! Lady A has drunk it all dry!

15th May – The two of them nearly lifted the roof off with their shouting and screaming last night! Lady A didn't emerge from their bedroom till two this afternoon! When I asked her about lunch, she asked – is it not dinner time yet?!

18th June – Terrible antics on the estate with the Land War. I don't know where she's hiding all the gin bottles, but they're disappearing at an alarming rate from the drinks store.

19th July – That brat Prudence has taken it on herself to start coming down to my kitchens and giving orders. As the mother seems incapable of running this house, her daughter seems to think it's her place to take over. We had some set to!

28th August – Young Master Pierce has been packed

off to school.

As Kate read on she found an alarming picture emerging of a house falling into disarray. And the more disarray emerged, the more Mrs Fennell started talking about the politics of the house rather than the domestic side of it. Mrs Fennell painted an alarming image of Arabella and Charles' marriage being conducted in almost a war-like situation. Arabella seemed incapable and disinterested in the running of the house and Charles' time was taken up with conducting the Land War. Kate became disturbed as she could almost sense the tense and destructive atmosphere that was there at the time. And as the diary continued closer to the date that Charles was shot in December the house seemed to be reaching a fever pitch, a boiling point of tension and rows.

Kate turned hesitantly to the first weeks in December, waiting to see what Mrs Fennell had written about the fateful night Charles was shot. At the bottom of a page she had written: *December 7th – Terrible news, Master James is leaving his post as estate manager! He's devastated and I've never seen such anger in him towards Charles.*

She looked at the next page and stared in disbelief – the page for the 8th of December had been torn out. Also there were no further entries in the diary for the rest of the year. Kate turned the blank pages in disappointment.

Nico had been in Dublin on business that evening. On his return he found Kate sitting up in bed with Mrs Fennell's diary, looking very dissatisfied.

531

'I can't believe it,' she said. 'Mrs Fennell ripped the page out and we'll never know what she had written for December eighth and ninth. And she had become gloriously indiscreet by then.'

'Which was probably why she ripped it out!' Nico pointed out.

'But what had she written? What had she seen and written that she felt she had better destroy it afterwards?'

Nico put his arm around Kate. 'Don't worry, maybe some things are best left not found out.'

'She names somebody else with a grudge against Charles – his brother James,' mused Kate.

Kate parked the Range Rover outside the house and, getting out, walked in a daze up to the front door and let herself in. She walked into the drawing room and sat down, staring into space.

She saw the box of cigarettes lying on the coffee table and reached out for them. She picked up the packet and was about to take one when she quickly dropped it back down on the table. She heard a car pull up outside and a minute later the front door opened and closed.

'Kate?' called Nico.

She didn't answer and a few seconds later Nico came in.

'Kate, we need to get the Renault to a garage, it's playing up again,' he said, coming in. He looked at her transfixed on the couch. 'Kate?' he asked, seeing her expression and coming and sitting beside her.

She slowly turned to him. 'I was at the doctor's this morning.'

'Is everything all right?' he asked, concerned.

'I'm pregnant.'

Nico's mouth opened and his eyes widened in shock. They stared at each other.

She wasn't sure if she was more worried or relieved that he looked as shocked as her.

Looking at his terrified expression, she suddenly burst out laughing.

'Kate?' he asked, even more concerned.

'Oh, Nico, you should see yourself!' she said between her laughter.

He started giggling too and then they both fell back laughing.

Ever since Kate had come to live at Armstrong House, ever since she had met Nico, she had always had an obsession with it and the Armstrongs who had lived there. But even after she had married Nico she never felt part of it. She always felt like an observer, an intruder standing at the doorstep of their history. But suddenly, since she knew she was pregnant, that had changed. The child she was carrying was a direct descendent from all those people who had lived in the house before them. The child would be part of them, carry the same genes and maybe the same outlook and characteristics of all those who had come before him or her. And she suddenly became aware of her own part in the history of the house.

'What has you looking so happy? Other than the fact you're to be a father again?' she asked as she kissed Nico. It was evening time and he had just returned home from a business trip to Dublin.

'I've been doing some work for your film,' he said.

'Oh?' She was curious.

He led her to the couch, opened his briefcase and produced Mrs Fennell's diary.

'I took it to a friend of mine, who I was at university with, to take a look at it. He's a scientist, working in forensic labs.'

'What could he do with Mrs Fennell's diary?' she asked, confused.

'I wondered was there anything he could do about the page that's missing,' he said.

'What can he do about a page that's been destroyed over a hundred years ago?'

'Quite a lot as it happens. As Mrs Fennell didn't write any more entries for the rest of the year after the fateful night, the page after was blank.'

'And?'

'And he managed to bring up the imprint of what she had written using something called electrostatic detection.'

'What the fuck is that?'

'It's a scientific device used mostly in criminal cases when they are trying to read any indentations on ransom or extortion notes.'

'I don't understand.'

'When a person is writing on a sheet of paper that is in a notebook or a diary such as this, the writing's impression or identification transfers to the paper underneath. This impression on the underneath paper isn't visible to the naked eye but electrostatic detection can pick up its imprint.'

'I see,' said Kate. 'So police use it in the case of kidnappers if they receive a ransom note to try to pick up any accidental evidence from who wrote the note. They'd want to be fairly shoddy kidnappers!'

'You'd be surprised how effective this is. It can pick up imprints through several layers of paper.'

'And did it work for us?' She sat up excitedly.

He reached into his briefcase again and handed her a sheet of paper. 'It's a bit sketchy in parts. But the print on the page came up and it's readable. It was a stroke of luck for us that Mrs Fennell used those large ledgers, as her entry for the 8th was a long one but fitted on one page.'

'Oh Nico!' she said, grabbing him and kissing him.

She could hardly concentrate she had become so excited. 'What does it say?'

'I haven't read it yet – I thought you should be the first,' said Nico, smiling at her.

She placed the paper on the coffee table and concentrated as she read.

8th, December 1903

What a racket went on tonight. I was sitting starting to write the business of the day in my diary when Lord and Lady Armstrong began a screaming match downstairs. The ferocity of their fighting made it impossible for me to write tomorrow's shopping list. Mr Fennell had gone to bed and as I sat at the desk here in our bedroom their screaming and shouting echoed through the whole house. Then I heard an engine outside and I went to our attic window and looked out and saw Mr Harrison's wife, the American Victoria, arrive up in her motor car on her own, even though it was very late. Mr Fennell quickly got dressed and rushed out and down the stairs to let her in. I went down with him and as we came to the top of the stairs we heard her ladyship unlocking the door herself and greeting Mrs Armstrong with the words 'Well, if it isn't the whore herself!' Myself and Mr Fennell remained hidden in the corridor upstairs as we saw the two ladies go into the drawing room where Lord Charles was.

It was hard to hear what they were rowing about from where we were upstairs. But at the end I heard Lady A warn that if he left her she would kill herself. We heard Lord A and Mr Harrison's wife leave the drawing room and he said he needed to get something from the library before they left. Afraid of being spotted, we went back to our room in the attic. We sat there fretting and I was looking out the window. A little while later Lord A and Mrs Victoria came out and rushed to her motor car. He took the keys from her and sat behind the steering wheel and they drove off at high speed. Worried about Her Ladyship, we went downstairs to check on her. We've checked everywhere, including her room, but she is missing.

Kate read and re-read the entry.

'So was Charles eloping with Victoria that night, or at least trying to before he was shot?' she wondered. 'And the Fennells say Arabella was not in the house when the shooting took place, contrary to what she told the police.'

'And she didn't seem in a good state of mind at all,' said Nico.

'But if Victoria was leaving with Charles,' said Kate, 'and Harrison discovered that, he might have got there first. After all, we know from the police report he was present that night as he took Charles to the hospital.'

'As was Emily, who was at Hunter's Farm,' said Kate. 'Not to mention Fitzroy in town.'

'The family went to great lengths to maintain that Victoria was in no way connected to this. There is no mention of her in the statements to the police or inquiry, and as we now know she was in the thick of it.'

BOOK FIVE

DECEMBER 1903

CHAPTER 73

Fennell came into the library and handed Charles an envelope.

'What's this?' asked Charles, worried it might be a resignation letter from the Fennells, as half of the house staff had left by now.

'It was delivered by a bellboy from the Castlewest Arms Hotel, your lordship,' explained Fennell.

'Oh?' said Charles, quickly opening the envelope as Fennell left. Charles read the letter it contained and sat back in his chair thinking.

Charles parked his motor car outside the Castlewest Arms and walked in.

He went up to the reception and pressed the bell. A few seconds later a young woman came out.

'Could you tell Mr Hugh Fitzroy that I'm here to see him,' said Charles.

The woman looked at him disdainfully. Like everyone else in the town she was fully aware of who he was and the many stories about his cruel behaviour up at his estate.

'Mr Fitzroy said you were to go on up to his room when you arrived. Room 25, third floor,' she said in a disrespectful tone.

Charles nodded and walked to the staircase and to the top floor where he found the room and knocked.

'Come in!' said the familiar voice of Hugh Fitzroy.

Charles opened the door and went in and found Fitzroy seated on a couch in the room, drinking whiskey.

Charles closed the door behind him.

'You've a cheek to show your face around here,' said Charles, walking into the room.

'Believe me it's the last place on earth I want to be,' said Hugh. 'Drink?'

'No,' Charles declined and sat down on a chair opposite him. 'What are you doing here, Fitzroy?'

'I've come to get my wife, of course.'

'Well, you won't find her in the Castlewest Arms.'

'I didn't want to go up to the house unannounced.'

'Wise.'

'How is she?'

'Not very happy at all, Fitzroy.'

'She just upped and left London without even saying goodbye.'

'Emily was always spontaneous, mostly to her own disadvantage.'

Hugh sat forward. 'I want her back, Charles.'

'Well, there's very little chance of that, from what I hear.'

'She won't leave me. She wouldn't dare put herself or your family through the scandal.'

'She's already bandying the word *divorce* around so much that it's lost its shock value around Armstrong House.'

'What does your mother think of that?'

'Lady Margaret appears to be not in the least opposed to you being out of her daughter's life for good ... in fact, there's a new-found mother-daughter bond between them that is touching to witness.'

'I can't lose her, Charles.'

'Yes, it's annoying when one of our toys goes missing, isn't it?'

Hugh stared at him. 'You've got to help me get her back.'

'I?' Charles said and roared with the laughter. 'My dear man, I've no intention of helping you get anything ever again.'

'But she'll listen to you, she always has. You can convince her to come back to me.'

'I've no doubt I could, but I won't.'

'If you get her to come back to me, I'll pay you twenty thousand pounds,' said Hugh.

Charles stared at him. 'You think I'd sell my sister?'

'Why not? You did it before!'

'Yes, on a deal that you reneged on.'

'I cancelled your gambling debt.'

'Yes, but you didn't pay off the mortgage on the house in London as you promised, the same house you now reside in!'

Hugh said nothing as he looked at the floor. 'I can understand how you mightn't trust me.'

'Trust you? You were nothing when I found you. A gangster from the East End. I established you, gave you connections, respectability and finally acceptance by allowing you to marry Emily. When you didn't pay that mortgage debt off, I was disgraced in front of my family and my wife. You did irreparable damage. Anyway, I've no time for any of this. I suggest you get on the next train back to Dublin, because she won't meet you, let alone go back to you.'

'Nevertheless, I will pay you £20,000 if you get Emily to agree to come back with me.'

Charles stared at him. 'Why do you think I'd ever agree to anything of the sort with you?'

'Because I know you.'

They sat in silence for a long while.

'I want no tricks this time like last time,' said Charles. 'The £20,000 has to be put in my account before I even approach the subject with Emily.'

'Give me your bank account details and I'll have the money wired into your account.'

Arabella had been lonesome when she returned after leaving Pierce at the school in England. The house seemed so much emptier without him.

Emily often came up to visit from Hunter's Farm. Arabella found the girl changed utterly. Gone was that rebellious stubborn young woman who defied everybody and did her own thing. Now Emily was more subdued, no longer doing the opposite of everything that was expected of her.

Arabella was lying in bed one night, Charles sleeping beside her. She was lying on her back staring at the ceiling, thinking of everything that had happened over the years and wondering where the present situation Charles had led them into would end. Suddenly there was a crash through the window and she sat up with a scream.

'What the fuck was that?' shouted Charles, jumping out of bed and racing across the room to turn on the gaslight.

As the room lit up, Arabella saw a window had been broken and a rock was lying on the carpeted floor.

Charles raced to the window and there was a sudden gush of light from a fire.

'Fennell! Fennell!' Charles screamed as he threw on his dressing gown and went racing out of the room. Arabella got out of bed and went carefully over to the window, avoiding the broken glass on the floor. Looking out she saw Charles' motor car was engulfed in flames. She started shivering with nerves as she left the room and quickly headed along the corridor and towards the stairs.

'Mama – what's happening?' asked Prudence, standing in the corridor in her nightdress.

'Get back to bed!' ordered Arabella as she ran down the stairs and to the front door which was now open. She stood at the door in her dressing gown as she watched Charles and the men-servants run to get buckets of water.

'The bastards! They've burned my motor car!' shouted Charles.

Arabella went storming down the steps and across the forecourt to her husband.

'Is that all you can say? Is that all you can say?' she shrieked at him. 'Your bloody motor car! When you've brought all this terror on our family, you bastard!'

Suddenly her hands started flailing and she was pounding his chest. He grabbed her arms and restrained her as the motor car continued to burn. Suddenly Arabella burst out crying. Charles looked at her as she fell to her knees sobbing. He had never seen her cry or break down before. Arabella desperately tried to stop the tears as she remembered the promise she'd made herself that Charles must never see that he had upset her. But try as she might, the tears kept flowing.

That night Arabella and Charles slept in separate bedrooms.

With his usual efficiency Fennell had the broken window pane in their bedroom replaced the next day and Arabella moved back into their bedroom. But Charles didn't and remained in the Blue Room. He steadfastly avoided her, not coming into the dining room for breakfast or lunch. In the evenings she would sit at the giant dining table eating on her own. She knew she had broken her number one rule, never to let Charles see he had broken her, the advice her mother had given to her on her wedding day forgotten in the drama of that night. They might have argued and shouted and screamed at each other over the years, but she had never broken down in front of him before and now she felt terribly exposed, her position weakened.

'Where's Lady Armstrong?' asked Charles, coming through the front door.

'She went out for a walk, my lord,' said Fennell.

Charles nodded and walked into the drawing room, knowing it was safe from her. He didn't want to see her. He didn't want to be in her company. The rock through the window and the car set alight had shaken him. But nearly worse was seeing his wife collapse into a sobbing mess in front of him and the servants.

He heard a noise and, looking out the window, he saw Victoria drive up and park.

He smiled at seeing her and couldn't wait to be alone with her. The room had an aroma of cigar and turf smoke. Damned Arabella, refusing to allow the windows downstairs to be left open to air the rooms, he thought. He quickly walked over to the French windows and opened them to allow some fresh air in before Victoria came.

Fennell showed her into the drawing room.

'Charles!' she said, coming over and giving him a kiss. 'What an awful shock for you! I was just down at Hunter's Farm and Lady Margaret told me all about the motor car. And the rock through the window! It's amazing nobody was hurt.'

'They don't care if anybody was hurt, Victoria.'

'And the police have no idea who's responsible?'

'No – do they ever? These culprits appear to glide through the night, unleash their terrible acts, and then disappear back into the night without anyone seeing them. But Fennell said he saw that thug McGrath loitering around the house earlier that day. He was one of the peasants I had evicted and he has no right to be on the estate. Fennell told him to clear off. McGrath's a violent man, you know. I reported what Fennel saw to the police, of course, and they said they will question McGrath about the matter.'

'So what are you going to do, Charles? You have to do something before somebody gets hurt.'

Charles sat pensively. 'Are you aware of this new Wyndham Land Act the government brought in?'

'Of course.'

'I've been advised to avail of it and sell the estate.'

'I see!' said Victoria, shocked but realising the logic in it.

'The tenants get to buy their land with money from the government and they get rid of me at the same time.'

Victoria was concerned. 'But you'd never sell the Armstrong estate, would you?'

'I'm beginning to think why not? We haven't had an income in months, we've run into severe financial difficulty. If I sold the land all my problems would be gone and I wouldn't have to deal with these bastards any more.'

'You have to think very carefully about what you're contemplating, Charles. The Armstrong estate has been in your family for centuries. And what about Prudence and Pierce?'

'I'd keep the house obviously and the land around it, spend more time in London.'

'What does Arabella think of all this?'

'I haven't discussed it with her. The only person I've said it to is you.'

'Charles – don't you think you should? It's her decision too.'

'I don't think it is, Victoria, not any more.'

'I don't understand?'

'I think Arabella and I are finished.'

'Charles!'

'I don't think either of us can stand the other any more.'

'Has she any idea?'

'No. I've said nothing. But we're in separate bedrooms and hardly communicate recently.'

'I knew you had been having problems, but many married couples do.'

'Except you and Harrison?' he looked at her quizzically.

'I wouldn't say that! We have many differences of opinions.'

'Really?' he said, interested.

'Of course. We've had one huge difference of opinion recently and I've had to give in to him, because I know it's what he really wants. We're moving back to America, Charles.'

Her words knocked him for six.

'When?'

'Quite soon. Harrison is already making the arrangements. It's strange, you'd think I would be the one wanting to move back home, but it's Harrison. I sometimes think he's more of an American than I am.' She smiled lightly.

'Victoria, you can't go!' he blurted out suddenly.

'I'm afraid we are going, back to Newport.'

'But – but what'll I do if you go?' he said, looking panicked.

She managed to smile at him. 'I'm sure you'll manage perfectly fine.'

'But you don't understand!'

Arabella was walking back from the gardens when she spotted the French windows to the drawing room open. She cursed the staff. How many times had she insisted that no downstairs doors or windows were to be left open? She quickly made her way across the lawns to the patio and climbed up the steps at the back of them and through the stone balustrade surrounds. She walked to the open windows and was about to slam them shut when she heard voices. She stopped and listened and recognised the voices as Charles and Victoria's. She leaned against the wall beside the open glass doors and listened.

'Victoria, I'm in love with you!' Charles said with a sense of urgency.

Victoria sat silent, unable to speak.

Charles reached over and grabbed her hand. 'Victoria, I love you. I've always loved you.'

'Charles!'

'You're the only thing I care for any more. The estate, Arabella, even this house they all mean nothing to me. It's only you I love.'

A sudden breeze came through the French windows, scattering the writing paper there across the room.

Startled, Victoria and Charles looked at the papers. Charles got up and walked over to the French windows and closed them shut before locking them.

Arabella was left standing outside beside the windows, leaning against the wall. She edged her way closer to the closed doors and strained to hear but she could no longer hear anything. Turning she quickly walked down the steps from the terrace and aimlessly walked back towards the gardens in a trance.

Charles came and sat down beside Victoria again.

'I've taken you by surprise,' he said, seeing the expression on her face.

'You've completely shocked me!'

'I had to say it. I can't just let you walk out of my life,' he said.

He reached over for her hand and she quickly pulled it away.

'How dare you! How dare you, Charles!' she said angrily.

'I only speak the truth.'

'Truth! You don't know the meaning of the word. Truth is just a word to you with nothing behind it. I am your brother's wife – does that mean nothing to you?'

'Of course it does! It shows how much I care for you, the fact that I'm saying this to you and making my feelings known. Knowing that this could destroy my relationship with my brother.'

'Your relationship with your brother! It clearly means nothing to you! You demonstrated that fifteen years ago when you robbed him of his fiancée. And now you're willing to do it again and rob him of his wife!' Victoria was astounded.

Charles reached out for her hand again.

'Don't even touch me!' she snapped, standing up. She began to pace up and down. 'To think that I convinced Harrison to give you a second chance. I forced him to befriend you again against his better judgement.'

'I know what I am, I don't deny it. But my feelings for you are real. Nothing has ever been more real to me in my life.'

'You've used our friendship as a trick to try and get me into bed!'

'I'm not talking about an affair, Victoria. I'm talking about you and me being together permanently. I've told you, I'll leave Arabella. I've also come into a windfall. With that and the money I'll get when I sell the estate, we can go and live anywhere. You can be Lady Armstrong, the Lady Armstrong that should always have been.'

'I don't want to be Lady Armstrong, or be anywhere near you ever again.'

'But we could have the world at our feet!'

'And leave a family in chaos and destruction in your wake? Are you mad?'

'But our friendship, our intimacy–'

'Our intimacy! Charles, I'm not more intimate with you than I am with James, or Emily – or your mother! Get this straight – it's Harrison I love, with all my heart and soul. I would do anything for him. I have no feelings towards you other than friendship – a friendship you have now destroyed for good.'

She walked quickly to the door.

'Victoria!'

She turned and looked at him as she opened the door. 'Go and sort out your life, Charles – it's a complete mess.' She walked out and slammed the door after her.

He got up and walked to the window and watched her hurry across the forecourt to her motor car. Getting in, she started it up and took off as quickly as she could.

CHAPTER 74

'And how are things on the estate today?' asked Charles as James walked into the room.

'Quiet. There doesn't seem to be much agitation luckily.'

'For once,' said Charles. 'I've been meaning to talk to you about a few changes I've decided to make.'

'Really?' James became worried.

'Yes. I've been giving things a lot of thought... I've decided if the bastards want the land so much, they can have it. I'm selling the estate, the greatest part of it anyway.'

'You can't be serious.'

'I'm tired of the whole thing, and now with the government providing money for a buyout – well, I'd be mad not to take it.'

James shook his head in dismay. 'And three hundred years of history will be wiped out?'

'Oh, come on, James, all the gentry families are doing it. It's more bother than it's worth. And with the money I get – well, I should be secure for life.'

'And what about the rest of us?'

'The rest of who? The family? Everyone has moved on, James, except for you. None of the family is interested in this estate any more. Mother is no longer Lady Armstrong and so it doesn't affect her. I don't intend to sell the house here or Hunter's Farm, so she'll remain living there.'

'And what about *me?*'

'Well, I can't be responsible for you any more, James.'

'But – but my whole life has been this estate!'

'You'll have to find a new life for yourself.'

'You've used me. You used me to run things when it suited you. To talk to the farmers because you couldn't talk to them and to carry out your dirty work, and now you're getting rid of me in the same ruthless way you got rid of those farmers and their families that you evicted.'

'In a few years there won't be any great estates left in Ireland. This country isn't conducive to them, as we have painfully witnessed recently.'

James looked fiercely at him. 'Father always said you weren't cut out to be a Lord Armstrong. He said you wouldn't be able for the job and he was right!'

Charles became angry. 'Father wasn't everything you thought he was either, you know.'

'He was wonderful, and he was so ashamed of you!'

'Was he indeed? As I said, Father was not everything you thought he was – he was not that great man you put on a pedestal.'

'You don't even deserve to talk about him. You've thrown away his legacy.'

'His legacy! He came to his legacy by chance! That day he collapsed, the day you said you heard us having the screaming match...'

'What about it?'

'He told me that day ... he told me that he was a result of an affair his mother, our grandmother, Lady Anna, had with a peasant. Lord Edward

Armstrong was not his father, some random peasant was!'

'How dare you try to taint his name!' James erupted in anger.

'It's the truth! I accused him of lying, but he wasn't.'

James sat up in his chair. 'I don't believe you, Charles. Why would he never tell anyone? He would have told me – we were so close – if it were the truth!'

'He didn't tell you because he was ashamed, and he knew the consequences of revealing the truth. He never told anybody, only me – that day, in a fit of anger.'

James's eyes filled with realisation. He felt shocked, but the feelings were quickly replaced with feeling sorry for the father he adored who carried that shame all his life. 'I'd never have turned on him over something like that.'

Charles looked at him coldly. 'Every time I look at you, I see him, that peasant who slept with Lady Anna. I don't see it in any of the rest of us. Maybe that blood was thinned out by Lady Anna's genes, and our mother's... But with you, it is there. The way you mix with them, talk with them, enjoy their company ... sleep with them even! With your tart from the town. You're one of them – you're not one of us. Whoever our real grandfather was, that's your legacy. And like him you'll be landless and penniless. Because now there's no role for you here any more and that's all you'll end up being.'

James stood up and turned and walked quickly from the room.

CHAPTER 75

Arabella was in complete shock over the next couple of days. It wasn't as though Charles' feelings for Victoria were a shock to her. She had always had her strong suspicions. But that Victoria had reciprocated them stunned her – that they were having an affair behind her and Harrison's backs. She had never liked Victoria, a fact she had never tried to even hide. But one thing she had thought was that Victoria was virtuous. That Victoria, with all her self-righteousness and confidence, was really no better than a woman like Marianne Radford astounded her. But then Arabella realised she shouldn't be at all surprised when it came to Charles. Hadn't she succumbed to his charms herself all those years ago?

She thought hard about how to deal with the situation. There was no point in confronting Charles – she knew that would never work, or had never worked in the past. She thought about how she had dealt with him when she had become pregnant with Prudence, involving both their parents. She thought how she had seen off Marianne Radford by involving her husband, the colonel. The way to deal with Charles was always through a third party.

Arabella knew Victoria went into Castlewest most afternoons to do some shopping or chat to the locals. Arabella instructed Fennell to have the carriage brought to the front of the house for her.

Charles was at his desk in the library, staring out the window, going over the encounter with Victoria. He remembered her anger and her re-action so vividly, the embarrassment and the shame he had felt. How had he got it so wrong? How had he let his emotions carry him away? Now he had lost Victoria's affection forever. They would move back to the States and he would probably never see her again. As he sat there he thought about his life. Everything that should have gone right for him had gone wrong. And Harrison had ended up with everything he wanted. He looked at the letter on his desk from Hugh Fitzroy with a copy of the transaction pay-ing the £20,000 into his account. He looked at the accompanying note from Hugh on Castlewest Arms Hotel headed notepaper telling him he expected Charles now to make Emily see sense and return to him without delay. Charles got up and went to where he kept his bank details and locked the papers in the filing drawer.

At least his money troubles were over for now.

Emily walked into the room. 'Hello there, Charles. I just wondered if you wanted to go out for a ride? It might take your mind off everything going on?'

'No, Emily, I don't feel like it... Sit down a minute, I want to talk to you.'

She sat down on the couch and he came and joined her.

'I've got some news for you.'

'Oh?'

557

'Hugh Fitzroy is here.'

'Here?' She got a fright and looked around anxiously.

'He's staying in the Castlewest Arms.'

'How do you know?'

'He contacted me and I went to meet him,' said Charles.

Emily stiffened. 'Well – what does he want?'

'You, basically. He's come to fetch you.'

Emily shook her head in disbelief. 'I'm never going back to that man or that marriage.'

Charles nodded. 'That's what I told him... I told him to clear off and never to bother you again.'

Emily visibly relaxed. 'Thank you, Charles.'

'I told him he was never to make contact with you or me again.'

'Thank you!' Emily leaned over and hugged him tightly.

The carriage pulled up outside Ocean's End and Arabella saw that Victoria's motor car wasn't there.

'Wait here for me, I won't be long,' Arabella said to the driver as she got out and walked up to the front door of the house. She knocked loudly.

A minute later Harrison opened the door.

'Arabella! This is unexpected,' said Harrison.

'Can I come in?'

'Of course.' He showed her in and closed the front door. 'Victoria isn't here, if you're looking for her,' he said as he led her into the parlour.

'It's you I've come to see,' said Arabella as she looked around the room.

Harrison nodded, suddenly feeling nervous. He

hadn't been alone with Arabella since they came to live in Ireland, and he wondered what on earth she could want.

'A drink? Or tea?' he asked.

'No, I won't be staying long,' she said, sitting down on one of the striped cream and red couches.

'All right,' he said, sitting down opposite her. There was an awkward silence.

'How can I help you, Arabella?'

'I've come to talk to you about my husband and your wife.'

'What about them?'

'There's no easy way to say this ... they are having an affair.'

Harrison stared at her in bewilderment. 'And your evidence for this is?'

'I found them together – expressing undying love.'

Harrison eyes were cold and glaring. 'You found them together? Where?'

'They were in the drawing room at Armstrong House. The French windows were open and I heard everything.'

Harrison sat in silence for a long time. 'I'd like you to leave my house, Arabella.'

She was astounded. 'Did you not just hear what I said?'

'I heard and I don't believe it. Now, please leave my house.'

'Your house? You mean the house Charles found for you and Victoria as he wheedled his way back into your affections, particularly hers! He's been playing you for a fool, Harrison, they both have.'

'Victoria would never be unfaithful to me.'

'Oh really? Do you really believe that? And tell me, Harrison, when I was having an affair behind your back with Charles for months, and it *was* months, Harrison, I expect you never believed it of me either?'

Harrison became angry. 'You were nothing like Victoria!'

'I think you'll find we're much more alike than you think! We seem to share the same unfortunate taste in men!'

'Whatever problems you and Charles are having in that minefield of a marriage of yours, do not try and drag me and Victoria into it.'

'Drag her into it? From what I heard she went running into it – running into his bed.' She became angry. 'The same way I did all those years ago!'

'You're a bitch, Arabella. You always were. I don't know what's going on in that twisted mind of yours – jealousy, I guess. Jealousy that Victoria and I are so happy and you and Charles are so miserable.'

'I can assure you Charles is not unhappy – he's very happy fornicating with your wife!'

Harrison stood up abruptly. 'Get out! Get out of this house, Arabella.'

Arabella stood up. 'I don't know why I expected you to have a different reaction from the one you're having. I've just told you your wife is sleeping with your brother and you react in the same weak way you did all those years ago with me. You're not going to do anything about this affair?'

'I told you to get out.'

'You've been a fool for Charles all your life, Harrison, and you always will be. He's done it to you again! After all these years ... and he did it the same way with Victoria as he did with me. Pretending to be your friend while he seduces your women.'

'I won't tell you again!'

Arabella walked to the door and then turned and looked at him. 'Maybe you should ask yourself what is it about you that drives your women to Charles? From what I see here today it's because you're weak. Maybe if there was some strength in you, some excitement, some fight, we wouldn't have left you.'

Arabella turned and walked out, slamming the door after her.

CHAPTER 76

Emily closed the front door of Hunter's Farm behind her.

'Darling, is that you?' asked Margaret from the parlour.

'Yes, Mother,' answered Emily walking down the short hallway and into the parlour.

Margaret was sitting on a couch, reading. 'Did you go for a ride with Charles?'

'No, he didn't feel like it.'

Margaret shook her head. 'I can imagine he had more things on his mind.' She sighed loudly. 'Your father would not believe what's been going on. He fought all his life to avoid this kind of trouble. Maybe I should have said something earlier to Charles. Tried to divert it from escalating.'

'You certainly never held back in telling me what to do!'

'That was different. I couldn't undermine Charles in his position in life. Where will it all end? I even keep a revolver in that bureau drawer now after the attack on Armstrong House last week. It's the children I'm concerned about – Prudence and Pierce.'

Emily came over and kissed her. 'Don't worry about it, Mama. I'm sure everything will be all right.'

Smiling at her mother, she left the room. She went upstairs to her bedroom, thinking about her conversation with Charles. It unnerved her greatly to think Hugh was only a few miles down the road. She knew Hugh and he would not just go back to London after a few harsh words from Charles, as he seemed to think. He would stay there trying to get her back. It had to be made clear to Hugh that she would never return to him.

Emily steadied herself as she walked down the corridor on the top floor of the Castlewest Arms Hotel that evening, having got Hugh's room number from reception. She paused and then knocked on the door.

A few seconds later Hugh opened the door and, not looking surprised to see her, said, 'Come in.'

She walked in and closed the door.

'You spoke to Charles?' he asked eventually.

'Yes, he told me you were here,' she said.

'You look well. We can get the next train out of here.'

Her eyes widened. 'I'm not going back with you, Hugh. Not now, not ever!'

'But – what are you doing here in that case?'

'I've come to tell you just that! I knew you would never take Charles' word for it, so I've come to tell you in person. Go home to London and leave me in peace and alone.'

'But you're my wife! You belong to me!'

'I belong to nobody but myself. I thought marrying you would give me freedom, but all it did was give me a horrible and cruel prison. Do you honestly think I'd go back with you – back to your sordid life and awful ways?'

'Yes, you have to!'

'I've seen things with you I never even dreamed existed! You don't even really want me back. You just want your Armstrong wife back so you can parade her around, thinking it will make you acceptable to society.'

'And what does Charles say about this?'

'Charles has nothing to do with it, but he completely supports me.'

Emily got frightened as rage erupted across Hugh's face.

'Did he not tell you that you should go back with me? That you had to come back with me?'

'Of course he didn't! He hates you as much as I do.'

'But I've just paid him £20,000 to get you back!' shouted Hugh.

'What are you talking about?'

'I paid him £20,000 so that he would convince you to return with me,' raged Hugh.

'What nonsense are you talking?'

Hugh ran over to a drawer, opened it and took out a copy of the bank transaction. 'See! I paid him £20,000 on the agreement that you would come back to me.'

Emily read the bank transaction and fought to hide her shock. 'Well, if you did pay him then you were a fool! He tricked you, because he certainly did not try to get me to go back to you – he encouraged me to stay away from you.'

Hugh was in a blind rage. 'It's not the first time he took money off me for you! He owed me thousands in gambling fees in London, and we reached an agreement that I would cancel them if you married me.'

'Charles would never do such a thing! Besides, he had no say on who I married.'

'Well, he did! He convinced you to marry me when everyone said not to, and in exchange I cancelled his debt. He sold you to me, Emily!'

Emily found herself feeling nauseous. Here in her hand was the evidence of a bank transaction for £20,000 paid that week to Charles. She remembered all the encouragement from Charles to marry Hugh.

'And he knew all about me, before we got married,' said Hugh. 'I'd brought him down to the East End where I was from. I showed him the warehouses of opium I owned. I brought him to the opium dens I owned and visited. I showed him the real me.'

'I'm going home, Hugh. I suggest you do the

same and I never want to see you again.' She turned and walked quickly to the door.

'You're not going anywhere. I've just paid £20,000 for you!' He crossed quickly to the door and blocked her. He started to move towards her.

'Keep away from me!' she warned as he kept coming towards her. She desperately looked around the room and saw his coat thrown over the couch. She raced over to it and grabbed it, her hands flying into the inside pocket, hoping the revolver he usually carried would be there. It was. She grabbed it and pointed it at him. He stopped in his tracks.

'Step out of my way, or I swear I'll kill you.'

Hugh stayed stationary as she moved slowly past him, pointing the gun at him all the time. She opened the door and edged out. She quickly placed the gun on the dressing table beside the door. Then she slammed the door shut and, panting, raced along the corridor and down the stairs.

CHAPTER 77

Victoria was in the grocer's shop, inspecting fruit and placing it into her basket. She looked at the time. It was nearly six in the evening. She had bumped into Mrs Foxe earlier and gone for something to eat with her in the new hotel opened in the town, which had delayed her.

'Victoria,' said a voice beside her and she turned to see Dolly standing there.

'Good evening, Dolly! How are you?' Victoria greeted her warmly.

'Shhh!' urged Dolly as she looked around the grocer's.

It was empty of customers and the shopkeeper was distracted by a child crying.

'I have to speak to you urgently,' whispered Dolly.

'I'll come by your bar when I'm finished here.'

'Do not! Do you know Connery's Castle, the ruin outside town?'

'I do.' Victoria was confused.

'I'll meet you there in an hour.'

'Can this wait until tomorrow? I'm already late getting home?' said Victoria.

'It cannot! I have to see you this evening! Don't tell anybody you were speaking to me!'

Then Dolly turned and walked away quickly.

Victoria drove out to Connery's Castle. She parked beside the ruin and waited. She wondered what on earth Dolly wanted and hoped it wouldn't take too long as Harrison would be worried about her. Seven o'clock came and went and there was no sign of Dolly. Another forty minutes went by and, annoyed, Victoria started the car and began to drive away. She was in no mood for practical jokes from Dolly Cassidy after her terrible encounter with Charles.

At that moment she saw Dolly heading towards her on a bicycle and she stopped the motor car.

'Sorry, I couldn't get away,' gasped Dolly. 'There were too many people still in the town and I couldn't make them suspicious by being spotted coming out here.' Getting off her bicycle, she left it resting against the ruined wall of the castle.

'What is all this about, Dolly?' snapped Victoria.

Dolly got into the passenger seat beside her.

'Well?' demanded Victoria.

'Tell nobody we met this evening,' Dolly said urgently. 'I've heard something and I have to tell you so you can act ... Lord Charles is going to be killed tonight.'

'*What?* By who?'

'I can't say! It's one of the tenants he evicted. I get to hear everything in my line of work and there's a conspiracy to kill him tonight.'

'We must go to the police at once if this is true,' said Victoria

'No! If you go to the police, they'll realise somebody informed, and my life won't be worth living, if I'll be left alive at all.'

'But why tell me? Why not tell James?'

'I haven't spoken to James in months. I can't be seen anywhere near him or any Armstrong with all this going on. I used to see you walk by the bar often in the afternoons and so I was watching out for you to catch you. Now, I have to be going before anyone suspects.'

'But what can *I* do?' Victoria was panic-stricken.

'Just get him away from Armstrong House tonight before it's too late. They plan to kill him there tonight.'

'And what about the others? Arabella, their daughter?'

'They won't touch anybody else or go near them. They have no gripe with anyone else. They'll wait for their chance and kill Charles tonight. Now

I have to go!' Dolly said, jumping out of the car.

'Why are you doing this?' asked Victoria.

'I could never live with myself in this life or the afterlife with the knowledge of a murder I could have stopped. Get him away from Armstrong House as quick as you can, before it's too late,' Dolly said and she raced over to her bicycle and nervously cycled away as fast as she could.

Harrison looked at the clock on the wall. It was half past eight. After Arabella had left he had sat numb for a long time. Her words repeated over and over in his mind. And then memories came rushing in. Charles and Victoria's close friendship. How she always defended Charles even to him, especially to him. How she was always calling up to Armstrong House. How he called over to Ocean's End, even when Harrison wasn't there. He remembered she said Charles had given her a necklace. He went racing upstairs and went and pulled open her jewellery drawer. He anxiously opened jewellery box after jewellery box until he found a necklace he didn't recognise. There was a note in with it. He read it: *All my love, Charles.*

Numbness seemed to take over him as he stumbled back downstairs with the jewellery box. And then he collapsed in tears as he understood what Arabella had said was true. That his lovely, beautiful Victoria had betrayed him in the most terrible way.

The clock ticked and the hours of the evening went by and there was still no sign of Victoria. Was she with Charles now? Where else would she be? Arabella's filthy accusations grew louder – 'fornicating'.

He wiped away his tears as he heard Victoria rush through the front door calling, 'Harrison? Harrison!'

She raced into the parlour.

'Harrison, I've heard the most terrible thing.'

'Where were you till now, Victoria?' he questioned coolly.

'Harrison, be quiet, I need to tell you something urgently.'

'*Where were you?*' he screamed at her, giving her a fright.

She saw his tearstained face. 'Harrison, what's wrong with you?'

'Answer my question – who were you with all evening?'

'I can't say.'

'You *can't* say!'

'I swore I wouldn't say. But Harrison, you must listen to me, we have to–'

'You were with him, weren't you? Charles.'

'Charles? Of course I wasn't!'

'Don't treat me as a fool any longer,' he said, throwing the jewellery box on the table in front of her. He waved the note that had been in it in front of her. *'All my love, Charles!'*

'I *told* you he gave me a necklace.'

'You didn't tell me about the note! The love note!'

'Harrison, you're being ridiculous, and we have no time for this tonight.'

'How long has it been going on? Your affair with him?'

'My affair!' Victoria was dumbfounded.

'I'm so blind. It took Arabella to point it out to me – though she is an expert on deception herself.'

'I have not been having an affair with Charles!'

'I don't believe you.'

Victoria's heart felt like breaking at his accusations. 'I admit Charles told me he is in love with me. But I was horrified and disgusted and told him so.'

Harrison started shaking with rage. 'And you never thought to tell me this?'

'I didn't want to upset you.'

'*Upset me!* You've destroyed me!'

'But nothing happened, I swear to you.'

'And I don't believe you!' Harrison sank down on the couch, cradling his head in his hands. 'I can't believe this has happened to me. *Not again – not again!*'

Victoria looked at her husband, a raging mess on the couch. 'Harrison, I've been told that somebody is going to try and kill Charles tonight. We have to go over to Armstrong House immediately and warn him and get him away from there.'

Harrison bolted up and he glared at her with bloodshot eyes. 'What rubbish are you spewing now?'

'Charles is going to be killed by one of the tenants. I can't say how I know, but it is the truth.'

'You must think I'm the biggest fool in the world! Trying to distract from your sordid affair with this story.'

'I'm not!'

'You expect me to go over and meet your lover

now!' Harrison was incensed.

'Look, Harrison, all this misunderstanding can be sorted out tomorrow. But tonight we have a priority and that priority is to save a man's life.'

'You're putting him before me?'

'Harrison, we don't have time for all this. Please, let's go to Armstrong House and get to Charles before it's too late,' she implored him.

'I never want to see him again, ever. And I don't care what happens to him.'

'So you'll let your brother be murdered?'

'If anyone wants to kill him, good luck to them. If they don't get him, then I will!'

She looked at him, horrified. 'If you don't come with me, I'll go on my own.'

'If you walk out that door and go to him now, we're over forever, and I'll not be responsible for what I do,' he warned.

She glared at him and then she turned and walked quickly out of the room. A few seconds later he heard the front door slam and the motor car start up.

By the time Emily got back to Hunter's Farm, Margaret had gone to bed. She wandered into the parlour and sat down. Her encounter with Hugh had been awful, but she always expected it would be. His revelation about Charles she could hardly believe. And yet she had seen the bank transaction for their latest deal. It all suddenly made sense to her. How Charles had manipulated her into marrying Hugh. How he had encouraged her all along the way. Her brother had sold her, as Hugh had said. And in doing so sent her into a disastrous marriage and ruined her life. Charles who she had always adored and admired. The one person she had always trusted and spoke openly with. And he had no regard for her and used that trust to betray her, fully aware of the kind of man he was letting loose on her. She got up and started pacing up and down. She had never been so angry in her life.

Arabella walked into Prudence's bedroom and found her writing at her desk.

'It's after ten, Prudence, it's time you were in bed.'

'But I'm writing a letter to Pierce, telling him everything that's been going on.'

'Try to leave out the more gory details, will you? You can finish it in the morning,' said Arabella, going over and kissing her.

'Yes, Mama. Goodnight.'

Arabella closed the bedroom door behind her and walked down the corridor. She decided the silence between herself and Charles had gone on long enough and she walked down the stairs to find him. She went into the drawing room and found him there, staring pensively into the fire.

'I think we need to talk, don't you?' she said, sitting down near him.

'Yes, we probably do,' he agreed.

'We can't go on ignoring each other, in separate bedrooms,' she said.

'No, you're right. We gave it our best shot, but I think we have to admit failure.'

'I'm sorry?'

'Our marriage isn't working any more. I'm not

sure it ever did work, to be honest. We were thrown together in such drastic circumstances.'

'I wouldn't say that. I think we loved – and love – each other very much, but I never know what's coming next with you.'

'Well, you won't have to worry about that any more.'

She shook her head, confused.

'Our marriage is over, Arabella. I'm leaving you.'

Arabella felt as if she had been struck.

'Oh no, Charles, you are not leaving me, that is one thing I can assure you of,' she said sternly, but with tears in her eyes.

'Come on, Arabella, there's no point in continuing with this farce of a marriage any more.'

'You wouldn't dare leave me!'

He looked at her and smirked. 'Do you really believe that? Do you honestly think there is anything in this world I would not dare do?'

'You wouldn't bring the scandal on the family. Your mother would never permit it!'

'I'm afraid with Emily's separation from Fitzroy, Mother is going to have to get used to her perfect family not being as perfect as she would like to portray. Besides, I'm not talking about the scandal of doing anything in court – we can just live completely separate lives and never see each other.'

'You have the whole thing thought out!'

'Yes, I'm selling the estate and will probably move back to London. I'll keep the house here for the hunt season and visit periodically as many gentry do with their country houses.'

'And what about our children?' she demanded.

'Pierce is in boarding school now, and I think it's wise that Prudence be sent to boarding school as well.'

'No!'

'You don't really have a choice in the matter. And I'm doing what's best for them. We'll share custody of them during the holidays.'

'And what do you suggest will happen to me?' she demanded.

'Do what you want, Arabella. You can stay here at Armstrong house if you want, as long as you keep out of my way on my returns.'

'You'd leave me alone in this house that I can barely tolerate, with all this resentment you created with the locals, without my children, while you go off and live the good life in London?'

'As I said, what you do is up to you,' he said.

After the shock subsided she felt herself become angry. 'I know what this is all about, Charles. I know why you're really leaving me. I know all about you and Victoria!'

'Have you been on the gin again? There is no me and Victoria.'

'I know you've been having an affair with her.'

'I thought you were going mad recently, but now you've just proved it!'

'Oh, and I suppose there was no you and Marianne Radford either, was there?' she said, a bitter satisfied look crossing her face as his eyes widened and mouth fell open.

'You see, you think you're so clever. But I've been two steps ahead of you all these years. I knew all about you and Marianne. In fact it was me who told her husband about it and sent him up to find the two of you in the Blue Room!'

'Why didn't you say something at the time?' he whispered.

'Because I didn't have to! So don't try and pull the wool over my eyes now about Victoria!'

'There is no me and Victoria!'

'I heard you together. I know; don't deny it. I've told Harrison all about it. I told him how you and she were carrying on behind his back, making a fool of him!'

'I can't believe you!' he roared, jumping to his feet.

She smiled at him. 'Oh yes, he was devastated, although he tried to cover it up.'

'What have you done?' he screamed.

There was a sound of a motor car driving into the forecourt.

They both looked out the window and saw Victoria get out of her motor car and hurry across the forecourt.

'And here she is! Your lover!' declared Arabella.

Charles crossed the room to the door.

'Oh no!' said Arabella, quickly blocking him and pushing him aside. 'I'll greet your mistress!'

Arabella walked out of the room and through the hall to the front door. Unlocking it she saw Victoria coming up the steps towards her.

'If it isn't the whore herself!' said Arabella gleefully.

'Where's Charles?' demanded Victoria as she pushed past her into the hall.

'I have to admire your nerve, Victoria. To come into my house to demand to see my husband!'

'Oh shut up, Arabella!' shouted Victoria as she

went into the drawing room, quickly followed by Arabella.

'What are you doing here, Victoria?' asked Charles.

'That's what I want to know!' jeered Arabella.

'Charles, you have to leave Armstrong House at once. You're in terrible danger if you stay here any longer,' said Victoria.

'I don't understand,' said Charles.

'I have learned that an evicted tenant is going to try and kill you tonight,' informed Victoria.

'Learned from whom?' demanded Arabella.

'I can't name my source,' said Victoria.

Arabella raised her eyes to heaven. 'More like Harrison has thrown you out after I told him about your affair. He's finally seen you for the tramp you are and now you've come over here to claim Charles.'

Victoria ignored her. 'Charles, we don't have any time. We have to go now. I'll drive you to the station in Castlewest and you can get the night mail train to Dublin until all this settles down.'

'So you *both* can get the night train, you mean. Running off like thieves in the night!' said Arabella.

'Charles!' said Victoria. 'Please! I'm telling the truth. You have to leave now. They're only after you – everyone else will be safe here.'

Charles looked at the panic on her face. 'All right, I need to get some things from the library.' He headed towards the door.

'Oh no, you don't!' shouted Arabella, standing in front of him. 'You are not leaving me, Charles. I will not let you go. After everything you've put me through during the years, I will not allow you to just run out on me with her.'

'Arabella, see sense!' demanded Victoria. 'Look what happened last week with the car set on fire and the rock through the window. That was a final warning, and tonight they're going to kill him!'

'If you leave here tonight with her,' said Arabella, 'then I will kill myself.'

'Don't talk stupidly, Arabella!' said Charles.

'You don't think I would?' she said. 'It wouldn't be the first time you nearly drove me to suicide. When I was pregnant all those years ago with Prudence and you refused to marry me, I was going to kill myself then.' Arabella saw Victoria looking shocked. 'Oh, yes, Victoria. I was pregnant with Prudence before I married Charles. His parents and mine had to force him into a marriage with me. It's our best-kept secret.'

'Arabella, I'm very sorry about all this, but Charles has to leave now, or else he will be killed,' said Victoria. 'You can sort all this out another day.'

'There won't be another day to sort it out because I will kill myself if you leave with her!' Arabella threatened again. 'Do not doubt me!'

'Charles, you'll miss the night train if we don't go,' said Victoria.

Charles looked at his wife and said 'You're so full of shit, Arabella,' before pushing past her.

Victoria ran out of the room after him.

Arabella stood in the room, transfixed, for a long time. Then she slowly turned and walked to the gun cabinet. Unlocking it, she reached in and took out a revolver and checked it was loaded. She turned and opened the French windows. Walking out onto the terrace, she crossed the forecourt and walked down the steps. And then she stumbled quickly through the gardens and down through the parklands. She didn't want Prudence to find her body.

In the hallway Victoria saw Charles rush across to the library instead of the front door.

'Where are you going?' she demanded as she followed him into the library. 'Charles! We don't have time for all this!'

Charles started to push a sideboard away from a wall. A safe was revealed. He sank to his knees and started to deal with the combination on the lock.

'Charles!' she shouted.

'Shhh!' he said. His nerves were getting the better of him and he kept missing the combination. At last it worked.

He rushed to his desk and grabbed a case then started filling it with the money and papers in the safe.

'Right, come on,' he said, fastening the case, and hurried out into the hall.

They went out the front door and Charles locked it securely behind him.

They then hurried across the forecourt.

'I'll drive,' insisted Charles.

Victoria handed him the key before getting into the front passenger seat. He started the engine and the car drove out of the forecourt and down the driveway through the parklands.

The countryside was lit with a full moon and just an occasional cloud passing under the stars, as Charles and Victoria passed under the bare branches of the overhead trees.

It was cold weather and Victoria pulled her fur coat tightly around her.

'We don't have much time to get the train,' she said, anxiously scanning the parklands. 'You can't come to our house because Harrison has lost control after Arabella told him those things about us,' she explained.

He nodded. 'Safer to just get out of the country for a while till all this calms down. Who'd ever thought it would come to this?'

She glanced at him, bewildered.

The motor car approached the entrance gates to the road. And as the headlights lit it up, they saw the gates were closed.

'Somebody's closed the damned gates!' said Victoria.

'Probably one of the gamekeepers,' said Charles as he slowed down the motor car and brought it to a halt.

Victoria anxiously looked around.

Charles went to get out of the motor car.

'No, it's quicker and safer if I go, in case it's a trap,' she insisted.

Victoria opened her car door and ran out. In the glare of the headlights she unbolted the gates and opened the left gate first and then the right one.

'Quickly!' she hissed.

He began to drive the motor car through the

gates. He stopped the car and she raced back and sat into the passenger seat.

She suddenly saw something move behind her.

Turning around, she saw Prudence emerge from under a blanket. 'Charles!' she screeched.

Charles turned around and saw Prudence sitting in the back seat of the motor car.

'Prudence!' he shouted.

'What's she doing here?' Victoria demanded.

'I can't it let it happen, Papa,' she said, her eyes fixed on Victoria. 'I heard everything! I heard what you said to Mama, I was outside listening. I won't let you leave us. I won't let *her* take you away from us!'

Suddenly she pulled a revolver out from under the blanket. She aimed the gun at Victoria and pulled the trigger. The bullet shot past Victoria through the passenger side of the windscreen. Victoria screamed as the bullet whizzed by her.

'Prudence! Give me that gun!' shouted Charles as he turned around fully to her and leaned forward to grab the gun off her. Suddenly the gun went off and a bullet fired into Charles' chest.

'Papa!' screamed Prudence as he slumped across the front seats, blood pouring out from the wound.

Victoria froze in horror as she heard a strange gurgling noise from Charles.

'Papa! Papa!' cried Prudence.

'Charles? Charles, can you hear me?' Victoria cried as Charles slumped down and she cradled his head.

'I didn't mean to do it! I didn't mean to hurt Papa!' Prudence was crying.

Victoria saw the lights of Hunter's Farm down the road. She turned and shouted, 'Run down to your grandmother's and get help as quickly as you can!'

'Papa!' cried Prudence.

'Will you go!'

Prudence got out of the car and began to run down the road to Hunter's Farm.

Victoria took off her fur coat and put it over Charles.

'There's help coming, Charles, there's help coming!' she whispered repeatedly to him.

CHAPTER 78

Arabella was in the woods leaning against the tree, holding the revolver. She stood there looking up at the stars in the sky above. She was thinking about Prudence and Pierce. She couldn't go through with it. She could never kill herself, she now knew. She started walking back through the trees.

A gunshot echoed through the night giving her a fright. Then another shot. She quickly made her way back to Armstrong House and let herself in through the French windows. She poured herself a strong drink.

Prudence hammered on the front door of Hunter's Farm. 'Grandmama! Grandmama!'

'What is all that terrible racket?' demanded

Margaret as she came down the stairs.

Emily was at the door, unbolting it. 'It sounds like Prudence!' The door opened and Prudence rushed in crying and raced into Margaret's arms.

'Papa's been shot! Papa's been shot!'

Margaret looked at Emily. 'What are you talking about, Prudence?'

'He's shot. He's at the gateway to the estate. Victoria said to get help here.'

'You stay here with Emily,' ordered Margaret as she quickly put on her cloak.

She rushed out into the night and hurried the short distance up to the gateway.

As she arrived on the scene she found Charles unconscious in the motor car, being cradled by Victoria with blood everywhere.

'My son!' she said, crawling into the motor car. 'What happened to him?'

'Prudence did it! She was hiding in the back and had a gun. She was trying to shoot me! But shot him by accident.'

Margaret drew back and looked at Victoria as if she were mad.

There was a sound of a horse and carriage coming towards them down the road.

The carriage pulled to a halt at the gateway. It was Harrison. He took in the scene before him and then jumped out of the carriage and raced over.

'Victoria!' He was frantic, seeing the blood over her dress.

'It's Charles. Prudence shot him.'

'Will you stop saying that!' Margaret shouted at her and quickly climbed out of the motor car.

'Quick, Harrison, you have to get him to hospital.'

He moved towards the motor car and recoiled at all the blood inside.

'Not in that contraption – it's covered in blood and there's broken glass – take him in the carriage,' ordered Margaret.

Harrison climbed into the front seat and he and Victoria gently moved Charles out and managed to carry him over to the carriage. He was slipping in and out of consciousness, and groaning as he did so.

'Get him to the hospital, Harrison. As quickly as you can,' urged Margaret. 'And do not speak to anyone as to how it happened.'

Harrison whipped the horse and they took off down the road.

Margaret spotted the revolver lying on the back seat of the motor car. She saw the case and placed the revolver in it. Clutching the case, she led the shaking Victoria back to Hunter's Farm.

Emily was trying to calm an hysterical Prudence in the drawing room as Margaret came in. Victoria remained cowering in the hallway.

'Grandmama, where's Papa?' asked Prudence as she rushed to her arms.

'He's been taken to hospital,' said Margaret as she tried to calm her granddaughter, Victoria's words ringing in her ears: *Prudence did it! She was trying to shoot me! But shot him by accident.*

She turned to her daughter. 'Emily, take Victoria upstairs and get her changed out of those clothes.'

Upstairs Emily silently ran a bath for Victoria

and laid out some clothes for her.

Victoria sat on a chair in the bathroom, staring into space. She noticed then that she had only one shoe on – she had lost the other in the pandemonium.

Emily brought some towels in. 'I'll leave these here for you,' she said placing them on the vanity table.

As Emily left the room, Victoria said, 'She wanted to kill me, Emily – the girl wanted to kill me!'

Emily nodded and closed the door behind her.

Margaret spent a long while trying to calm Prudence down. She then left her with Emily and came into the hallway. Seeing Charles' case containing the revolver, she hid it in a cupboard and locked it in. She continued upstairs and found Victoria changed into a dress Emily had left for her and sitting on the bed in Emily's room.

'Now, you are going to tell me exactly what happened,' said Margaret.

Margaret was coming down the stairs.

'How is she?' asked Emily.

'Not good.'

'I think she's in shock. Shall I fetch a doctor?'

'No! Do nothing,' instructed Margaret as they walked back into the parlour. 'I'm taking Prudence back up to the house – you follow up when Victoria is able.'

'But–' began Emily.

'Just do it!' snapped Margaret, reaching for her spare key to the back door of Armstrong House on the key rack.

Margaret walked up the road from Hunter's Farm, her arm around her granddaughter who continued sniffling. They walked to the main gates and past the car, the headlights still shining.

'Grandmama!' cried Prudence as she saw the dried blood.

'Don't look!' ordered Margaret as she led her past the car and up the long driveway to the house. She felt relieved when she saw the light still on in the drawing room. She led Prudence up the steps to the terrace and looking in saw Arabella alone, her face in her hands.

Arabella heard a knock on the French windows and got a fright. She got up and walked carefully to the windows and was astonished to see Margaret and Prudence there.

'What's happened?' asked Arabella loudly as she unlocked the French windows.

'Mama!' cried Prudence, rushing to her.

'What on earth had been going on?' demanded Arabella, seeing her daughter collapse in tears. *'Prudence?'* she panicked as she saw the blood splattered on her dress.

Between her sobs Prudence managed to speak. 'I didn't mean to shoot him, Mama. I heard you and him row and I came down to ask you to stop. And then I saw Victoria arrive and I listened outside as you all rowed. I heard Papa was going to leave us for her. I couldn't let her take him from us. I went to the library and took the key and opened the drawer where Papa keeps his gun. And then I went out the front and hid in the back of the motor car. But I didn't want to hurt Papa! They've taken him to the hospital!'

Arabella began to shake as she hugged her daughter, looking down at her blood-splattered dress. She looked at Margaret who just nodded grimly.

Arabella herself went into a strange shock when she heard what had happened.

If Margaret hadn't been there issuing orders, she would have fallen apart. Margaret gave Prudence one of her sleeping tablets and ordered Arabella to take her upstairs to her bed. As she waited upstairs, Margaret thought hard.

A long while later Arabella came back down.

'She's passed out,' said Arabella as she went to the drinks cabinet and just managed to pour herself a gin, her hands were shaking so much.

'I don't want to go back into that house,' said Victoria as she and Emily approached up the driveway.

'Mother says we have to,' answered Emily.

They saw a light on in the drawing room and Margaret standing at the French windows, anxiously looking out.

When Margaret saw them she opened the French windows and beckoned them to enter that way.

Arabella looked up as Margaret gestured them into the room and locked the French windows behind them.

'What's *she* doing here?' demanded Arabella, standing up.

'I told them to come up,' said Margaret.

'Look what you've caused!' shouted Arabella at Victoria.

'I didn't cause anything, I was trying to save Charles,' Victoria defended herself.

'You were running away with him!' accused Arabella.

'I was not, you stupid woman!' shouted Victoria.

'Enough!' shouted Margaret. 'I don't want to hear another word!'

'What are we going to do?' asked Emily.

'Nothing!' ordered Margaret. 'We will do nothing until Harrison arrives back and tells us how Charles is.'

The day was dawning and Margaret could hear the first of the servants stirring. The clock on the wall had ticked every minute during the night as the four women waited anxiously for news.

When they heard a carriage arrive up, Margaret jumped up and raced to the window.

'It's Harrison,' she said as she quickly ran out to the front door.

'He's still alive, Mother,' he said.

'Thank God!'

She saw his fragile and exhausted expression and led him into the drawing room where he was met with the frightened and apprehensive women.

Victoria rushed to Harrison and he hugged her. 'Forgive me, my love, for doubting you,' he said. 'Thank God I came looking for you!'

'Charles?' said Arabella.

'They operated on him and removed the bullet. He very nearly died. He's critical but stable,' said

Harrison, sinking down on the couch.

Arabella's whole body relaxed on hearing this.

Margaret nodded, relieved. 'Now, we don't have much time to act. We've very little time to save that girl upstairs from having her life ruined and all of us along with her. The police will have to be called very shortly.'

'The police!' said Arabella, panicking about Prudence. She hadn't even thought about that side of it. She sat in the Queen Anne chair shaking, a full glass of undiluted gin in her hand.

Margaret locked the door into the room.

Victoria sat down on a couch beside Harrison, his arm around her. Emily went and stood beside Arabella.

Margaret surveyed them all.

'This is what we're going to tell everyone. Victoria never came here last night. Charles left the house in his carriage to come and discuss estate matters with me. He left the house in a carriage, on his own, and as he was leaving the main gates, he was ambushed by a peasant farmer and shot. Harrison was visiting me at Hunter's Farm at the time. When I heard the shot, I opened my door and saw a peasant rushing by on the road with a shotgun. I called Harrison and he went down to the road and saw the carriage stopped up at the main gates, so we drove up in the motor car and found Charles unconscious in his carriage.'

All eyes widened as they stared at Margaret.

'But why are you saying such a thing?' demanded Victoria.

'Because it's the only way to avoid Prudence's life being ruined. If what happened comes out she will be finished.'

'Ohhh!' cried Arabella as she started to shake madly.

'I don't think I can go along with this lie,' said Victoria.

'You will go along with it! Otherwise it won't just be Prudence ruined, we all will be. Prudence says you were eloping with Charles. Is that correct?'

'Of course I wasn't!' shouted Victoria. 'I came to warn him I'd heard his life was in danger from a threat from an evicted farmer.'

'And you led him to his demise by doing so,' Margaret accused.

Victoria sank her hands into her face.

'But how can we get away with that?' asked Arabella, suddenly hopeful.

'Only we know what actually happened. Who will disbelieve us for a second? We are Armstrongs – they will not doubt us,' announced Margaret. 'Why would they doubt us? Charles was much hated and his life under known threat. They just blew up his motor car and threw a rock through his bedroom window last week.'

'It's a cover-up!' objected Victoria.

'What's the alternative? Prudence will be destroyed and so will we all be if the truth ever comes out. It'll be in all the newspapers, here, England, America. An earl shot by his daughter as he tried to run off with his sister-in-law, a Van Hoevan! And regardless of that not being the truth, that is what will be said, Victoria.'

'I don't want Prudence connected with this shooting,' Arabella said with determination as she shook.

'Emily?' Margaret asked.

'I'll say nothing,' Emily agreed.

'Harrison?'

Harrison turned to Victoria. 'It's our only way out of this. Mother's right, Victoria, the scandal will overwhelm us.'

'Victoria?' asked Margaret, staring coldly at her.

Victoria looked at Harrison and then finally nodded.

'Good. Now we've very little time to get the story watertight,' said Margaret.

There was a knock on the front door. Emily rushed to the window and looked out.

'It's a policeman!'

Margaret stood up with confidence. 'I'll take care of this.'

She walked out into the hall where she found Fennell coming up from the stairs behind the main staircase.

'I'll take care of this, Fennell. Return to the servants' quarters immediately. You and the servants are to remain there until I say so,' said Margaret.

'Very good, my lady,' nodded Fennell, looking bemused, as he quickly retreated back to the kitchens.

Margaret unlocked the door and found a young policeman standing there.

'Good morning, my lady. The hospital has reported an incident here. Lord Armstrong was admitted there last night after being shot. There's a motor car down at the gate that looks–'

'I need you to return to Castlewest with immediacy and inform your superior, Sergeant Cunningham, to come here,' ordered Margaret.

The young policeman looked at her, surprised. 'Could I just ask exactly what happened?'

'Young man, Lord Charles Armstrong has been shot by a criminal is what has happened. Now get me Kevin Cunningham!'

The young policeman nodded and rushed to his bicycle and cycled off.

Margaret came quickly back into the room and then watched as the policeman cycled quickly off down the drive.

'We need to get that motor car away as quickly as possible. Harrison, take Victoria away from here back to Ocean's End in the motor car and hide it. Wash it and have that windscreen removed.'

'But that policeman will have seen the motor car at the gates,' said Emily.

'Yes, we'll say Harrison abandoned it there last night as he took Charles to hospital in the carriage.'

'But he'll have seen the glass and blood in the car!' said Victoria.

'Never mind that,' said Margaret.

'But–' began Victoria.

'Oh shut up, Victoria and do as I say! I've known Sergeant Kevin Cunningham since he was a boy. He will believe me and never dare to question me, over what some silly young policeman thought he saw. Now go!' Margaret pushed them out the French windows.

CHAPTER 79

An hour later Sergeant Kevin Cunningham was shown in by Fennell.

'Lady Armstrong, this is appalling news. You wished to see me?'

'Yes, Kevin, come in,' said Margaret.

Kevin went into the parlour and interviewed them all separately. Margaret was interviewed first.

'I was at home in Hunter's Farm with my son Harrison who was visiting me. My daughter Emily had gone to bed. I heard a gunshot, Kevin. I was expecting my son Charles for a visit–'

'Why so late?'

'He had been busy with the estate all day and it was the only time he could see me. When I heard the gunshot I rushed to my front door and opened it.'

'Were you not frightened to open the door?'

She smiled at him. 'It would take more than that to frighten me, Kevin.'

Kevin nodded appreciatively.

'Then I saw a peasant man rushing by Hunter's Farm with a shotgun. I thought he might be a poacher or something. I called Harrison and he walked out to the main road and saw the carriage up at the main gates, where the man was running from. I was concerned over Charles as I had been expecting him, so we went up in the motor car to

see what was going on. We found Charles...'
Margaret broke off and dabbed her eyes with a handkerchief.

'Terrible for you... And?'

'And Harrison got him to the hospital as quickly as possible. We came up to Armstrong House and informed Arabella.'

'Why didn't you call the police straight away?' asked Kevin.

'I presumed Harrison had told you, and he presumed we were telling you.'

'Where's Harrison now?'

'He's at his home with his wife at Ocean's End. He was at the hospital all night and came straight here this morning to tell us how Charles was and collect his motor car. She must have been frantic with worry, wondering where he was.'

Arabella sat opposite Kevin, shaking.

'I'm sorry, I know how upsetting this is for you,' sympathised Kevin.

Arabella nodded.

'Tell me what happened, Lady Armstrong, in your own time.'

Arabella's voice kept breaking as she spoke. 'I was sitting here reading after Charles had gone down to visit his mother. Next thing my mother-in-law and Emily arrived up to tell me my husband had been shot and taken to the hospital.'

'You didn't think to go to the hospital?'

'And leave my daughter asleep upstairs at a time like this? No. Besides, after what happened to Charles we were too scared to go out and leave the house in case the gunman was still there waiting for us.'

'Very wise. Did you hear anything suspicious?'

'Not a thing.'

'What about the servants?'

'Nothing. They go to bed early.'

Emily came into the parlour and sat down.

'I really saw or heard nothing,' said Emily. 'I was at Hunter's Farm when Mother came and said Charles had been shot. We both came up to Armstrong House to tell Arabella.'

Harrison opened the door at Ocean's End.

'Hello, Kevin,' he said, leading him into the parlour.

'This is a very unfortunate business,' said Kevin, sitting down. 'I just left Armstrong House and everyone is devastated. I just want to ask a few questions so we catch the person who did this to your brother.'

Harrison nodded, sitting down.

'Can you just tell me what happened?'

'When we found him shot, I took him to the hospital straight away.'

'Sorry – there's one thing that I have to ask. Why not take him in your motor car? I believe you travelled to Hunter's Farm in that to see your mother?'

'The motor car is my wife's, and I find it un-reliable – it keeps breaking down, and I didn't want to risk it.'

Kevin nodded. 'They are unpredictable, they'll never catch on.'

'And that's it really. They operated on him when

594

I got him to the hospital.'

'You didn't see anyone suspicious as your mother did?'

'No, I didn't go to the front door of Hunter's Farm with her.'

'You wife wasn't with you?'

'No – Victoria was at home.'

'I won't take up any more of your time, you look exhausted. We're about to start interviews with everyone on the estate and in the town. I'm aware that one of Lord Armstrong's evicted tenants had made threats he would kill him a couple of weeks ago. A Joe McGrath. He's been in a lot of bother with the police before. We're trying to find him, but he doesn't have any family so we don't know where he is.'

Victoria sat in her bedroom in the same trance she had been in since the shooting.

Harrison came in and looked at her. 'The police have left.'

'Did they believe what you said?' she asked.

'Of course,' he said.

She nodded and stared out the window at the sea.

CHAPTER 80

Later on in the week Sergeant Kevin Cunningham was at his desk in the police station in Castlewest with the file on Charles' shooting opened in front of him. They had conducted extensive interviews on the estate and in the town. It was obvious Charles Armstrong was much hated and it was only a matter of time before something like this would happen. They were trying to locate an evicted tenant called Joe McGrath who had openly boasted he would shoot Charles. McGrath seemed to have escaped to America before they could arrest him.

A young policeman, Tadhg Murnahan, knocked and entered.

'I have those photographs developed from the morning after Lord Armstrong's shooting,' he said, handing them over.

Kevin inspected the photographs and saw the motor car with the bullet-hole through the windscreen.

'Did any of the Armstrongs know you took these photographs?' he asked, looking up.

'No, I took them just before I called to their house. It's as I told you, sir, there was a bullet-hole in the windscreen and blood all over the inside of the motor car,' said Tadgh anxiously.

Kevin nodded to him. 'Right. That'll be all.'

Tadgh made for the door.

'Murnahan!'

'Sir?'

Kevin hesitated then leant forward and said, 'I expect you to be absolutely discreet about this whole matter. Don't talk to anyone whatsoever about it – not even our colleagues. Do you understand?'

'Not a word, Sergeant. You can rely on me.'

'I know I can. Good work, by the way, Murnahan. With your grasp of modern police methods, I can see you'll go far.'

'Thank you, sir.'

After the young man had left, Kevin studied the photos intently. Then he reread Lady Margaret's and the others' statements. He sat back in his chair thinking.

It wasn't adding up. He thought about the Armstrongs. They were still very powerful. He remembered growing up on the estate and the food and clothes Lord Lawrence sent down to his family during hard times. He remembered Lady Margaret coming to his mother's sick bed in their cottage and holding her hand while she died.

And later on, Margaret had encouraged him to join the police force and had used her influence in Dublin to get him promoted to sergeant. He owed them a lot. And their influence could make or break a policeman's career. He knew this family. They had been the most powerful and respected family in those parts for years. What they said could not be doubted. Kevin took the photographs and buried them at the bottom of the file.

CHAPTER 81

Victoria stood at the back of the garden at Ocean's End looking at the waves lap against the beach. Soon she and Harrison would be the other side of that ocean starting their new life. She heard the motor car start up and turned and saw it being driven away from the house by the garage owner in Dublin it was sold to, its windscreen long since replaced, ready to start its own new life with a new owner.

She had relived that night over and over again in her mind. The gun firing first and only just missing her. The gun firing a second time and striking Charles. Victoria hadn't returned to Armstrong House again or met with any of the Armstrongs.

Their agreed deceit was a bond that she feared would break if she met them and spoke to them. Harrison had been in constant contact with them. She knew all that was happening through him. Charles drifting back and forth from critical status. Arabella a bundle of nerves. It wasn't clear what was pushing her over the edge – what had happened to Charles or what Prudence had done, or fear of the truth coming out. Margaret had reigned over all proceedings, her iron will and her surefootedness stoic and unbreakable. As for Prudence, Harrison never mentioned her and Victoria never asked. All Victoria knew was that her own belief in her capabilities, her own strength, had very nearly cost her her life. Harrison always said she thought she could fix anything and anybody. Now she was fully aware of how limited she was.

'Everything's been packed up,' said Harrison as he walked down the garden to her. 'The removal men will be here in an hour.'

She nodded and reached out for his hand which he took.

'We need to get going, or we'll miss the train,' he said.

His words brought back her own words that night to Charles and she got a shiver.

She nodded and smiled and they turned and walked back through the garden hand in hand.

CHAPTER 82

Summer 1904

Arabella stood at her bedroom window looking out at the sunny day. She could see two of the footmen carrying Charles across the forecourt with Prudence directing them. Charles was mostly in his room since he returned from hospital, but Prudence had insisted he get some fresh air that day. Arabella felt herself tremble as she replayed in her mind the last few months. Charles hovering near death for months. When he finally came home he could barely walk and rarely talked and needed a nurse at all times. If he could remember what happened that fateful night he never said, and went along with the conspiracy Lady Margaret had insisted on. It saved Prudence from ruin, and that was Arabella's main concern.

Then the government had called an inquiry and they all had to testify at that as well. Arabella remembered herself shaking with nerves as she testified. As for Prudence, the girl seemed unaffected. She had just been her normal self and Arabella often wondered if she had a mental block causing a memory loss of what she did that night. Arabella certainly never broached the subject – in fact, nobody ever mentioned it, as an unwritten rule.

'Mama! Mama!' shouted Prudence from the gardens, waving up at her. Arabella waved back and knew she must go down to them. She took a quick swig of gin and went downstairs. She walked down the steps into the terraced garden where Prudence had organised a table set up with afternoon tea. Charles was sitting in a wheelchair, staring out across the lake.

'Isn't it a beautiful day, Mama? I was just telling Papa he needs to get out every day and enjoy the weather and he'll be feeling better in no time,' said Prudence happily.

'Yes, if nurse agrees,' said Arabella, sitting down in the chair left for her at the table.

'I'm sure she will. She's much better than the last nurse I sent on her way last week,' said Prudence.

Arabella reached out for the silver teapot and started to lift it to pour herself tea. Suddenly her hands started shaking and the tea spilling. Prudence jumped up from her seat and grabbed the teapot.

'Let me do it for you, Mama,' she said, pouring the tea. She picked up Charles' cup and brought it to him. 'Do you want a sip yet?'

'No,' he said, his gaze never leaving the hills in the distance at the other side of the lake.

'No bother!' said Prudence, putting down the cup and sitting down. 'Just think, Pierce will be home from school soon, and we'll have the whole summer to be together! We can do all the things we used to do.'

EPILOGUE

Present Day

Kate and Nico were considering the information that had been revealed by the re-emergence of Mrs Fennell's last page of her diary.

As Kate looked around the drawing room she tried to imagine the scene that had played out there in 1903 between Arabella, Charles and Victoria which seemed to have led to him being shot that night.

'So since Victoria was in the passenger side of the car and that's where the bullet was aimed at, it seems she was the intended target in the car all along, and Charles somehow got hit in a cross-fire,' said Kate.

'We'll never know what happened that night – only the people there knew and they are long

601

gone. But you have uncovered enough to show what was really going on at Armstrong House during that period and how there was an elaborate cover-up,' he said, as he got up. 'I'll go put the dinner on.'

Brian was sitting at the island in the kitchen with Kate as Nico served them dinner.

'Well – go on,' urged Brian. 'What have you managed to find out for the film?'

'It's all led to a bit of a dead end, I'm afraid, Brian,' said Kate.

Nico and Brian looked at Kate with surprise.

'But you said you'd uncovered lots of explosive evidence,' said Brian.

'I don't think any of it is relevant to the film. I think we should stick to the official inquiry. Apart from revealing that the evicted tenant Joe McGrath was not responsible as he was about to dock in Ellis Island. I think he deserves to have his name cleared after all these years.'

Nico said nothing as he began to eat.

'So we continue to use the footage of Charles in the carriage?'

'Yes. As you suggested, Brian, we'll just use a silent prop gun and dub it later,' said Kate.

Later Kate showed Brian to the front door.

'Thanks for a lovely evening and congratulations on the baby news again,' he said, kissing her cheek.

'Thanks, Brian,' she said and she waited at the door to wave him off. She closed the door and went into the drawing room where Nico was waiting for her.

'What was all that about?' questioned Nico. 'Why didn't you tell him everything we've learned?'

She joined him on the couch and nestled up to him. 'You know, maybe there's something in that expression "Let sleeping dogs lie". Lady Margaret and the family obviously thought they had very good reasons to cover up that night. The trouble is although we can have a good guess, only they ever knew what did happen. And by producing all our evidence we're fingering a lot of people with the blame, when really only one person did shoot Charles.'

'I see.' Nico was very surprised at his wife's change of heart.

'And you know this child of ours is Charles and Arabella's great-great-grandchild. And in a hundred years' time maybe our ancestors will live here and maybe we wouldn't like them exposing *our* lives.'

'I thought you wouldn't mind that in the least,' he said.

'Well, I suppose I wouldn't. But I know you wouldn't like it, and maybe our child would hate it,' said Kate. 'I guess we have to think of the family name.'

He grinned at her. 'Spoken like a true Armstrong.'

'Maybe I am one, at last,' she said.

Nico walked into the drawing room and found Kate on the laptop at the bureau there.

'I'm looking forward to when the filming is over and we get our house back and our normal lives,' he said.

'Only a few weeks left now before they're gone. But I don't think our lives will ever be back to what we considered normal, not with the baby on the way,' she said happily.

'True. What were you up to?' he asked as she turned off the computer and came and joined him on the couch.

'I was just trying to find out what happened to everyone whose names came up with the shooting. Looking up censuses and old newspaper articles again.'

'And what did you find?' he asked.

'The Lord Chief Justice of Ireland called for an inquiry into the shooting. The government was desperate to finally stop the rural agitation in Ireland. Lady Margaret and the rest all testified at that inquiry which is what we worked from for the documentary. That Armstrong inquiry recommended even further action by the government to settle the Irish land problem for good. The government introduced another and final Land Act in 1909, which ensured the compulsory selling of estates in Ireland to their tenants. This final act saw the ending of the last of the great estates in Ireland. The great Armstrong estate was no more – all that was left was the house here and some land.'

'And what of the family?' asked Nico.

'Charles' brother James moved to England and lived on his brother-in-law the Duke of Battington's estate, which he managed for him. I saw on the peerage website he eventually married a cousin of the Duke.'

'And Harrison and Victoria?' said Nico.

'They moved back to America where they were a society couple. They had two daughters, one born in 1906 and another in 1908. Strangely, they called their first daughter Arabella.'

'Go on,' he urged.

'Emily lived at Hunter's Farm for a number of years with her mother Margaret who died in 1909. Emily's husband Hugh Fitzroy was killed in suspicious circumstances in 1912. The bulk of his money was left to his estranged wife Emily. She joined the Suffragette movement and became a leading voice in it. She then nursed at the front in the First World War and became a well-known travel writer after the war.'

'Anything further on Charles and Arabella?'

'Only what we knew. He never recovered from the shooting and died three years later.'

Nico picked up a photo of Charles and Arabella with their children. 'And Arabella lasted only a few years after him.'

Kate took the photograph and looked at the family in happier times.

'And that just leaves Prudence and Pierce,' Nico said.

'Yes,' Kate smiled. 'But that's another story.'

The publishers hope that this book has given you enjoyable reading. Large Print Books are especially designed to be as easy to see and hold as possible. If you wish a complete list of our books please ask at your local library or write directly to:

Magna Large Print Books
Magna House, Long Preston,
Skipton, North Yorkshire.
BD23 4ND

This Large Print Book for the partially sighted, who cannot read normal print, is published under the auspices of

THE ULVERSCROFT FOUNDATION